the galactic zookeeper's guide to heists and husbandry

a.c. huntley

This is a work of fiction. The story and all characters, places and incidents therein are fictitious. Any resemblance to actual persons, locales, or events is coincidental.

Published in the United States by Bena House LLC, Miami.

ISBN 979-8-9874506-1-1

Ebook ISBN 979-8-9874506-4-2

Library of Congress Control Number 2022923317

Printed in the United States of America

Cover design by Debby Aqua

First Paperback Edition

For J, my favorite child
(don't tell the others I said that)

Remember that no matter how dark the hour,
there is always opportunity for redemption.
It's a choice that begins and ends with you.

<u>Venture Into the Wild!</u>
Dare yourself to take a ride on the wild side at Hialeah, the zoo planet! Located in the quiet delta quadrant, Hialeah contains a curated collection of animals from all over the galaxy. Enjoy the comforts of our top-of-the-line hovercars while you observe the chandragan monkeys in their 30-acre sulfurous biodome, the venomous trabodian pigs on the grassy plains, and the fierce gorgons in a terrain carefully engineered to mimic their rocky mountainous home planet…

chapter one

I slam the hatch shut on the faded yellow hover-tram full of animal dung and give the metal a forceful bang with the palm of my hand. My shovel clangs on the ground as I wipe my dirty hands on my work-issued denim coveralls. Done for the day.

My boss's angry lecture from this morning flashes through my mind, some big to do about always leaving the shit-shovel in the guyerra enclosure. It's already dusk, but I can still make out the shovel on the crumbly desert dirt of the guyerras' habitat. I hate this object more than I've hated anything in my life, the symbolic end of all my dreams to care for galactic animals. It's the only thing they let me do out here.

Let me tell you something. The guyerras don't even notice dirty shovels. Those cunning predators will ignore anything that's not food. Griffith gets pissy when any of the animal enclosures are left messy for the tourists. I'm one hundred percent certain my boss cares more about the idiot tourists than the animals.

The ancient hover-tram lifts into the air silently, following its pre-programmed route to the farming fields and greenhouses where all the planet's food is grown. How is it that Hialeah –a broken-down, forgotten step-child of galactic civilization – owns a robotic hover-tram that can pasteurize carloads of crap and gently distribute it along acres of fields out in the valley, but they need an actual, breathing human to collect the shit?

Maybe it's because this broke ass zoo doesn't have any technology created after I was born, a whopping thirty-years ago. Maybe it's because they don't give a shit about their employees. Or… too many shits.

You know what? I'm leaving the shovel. Screw this place.

I need a drink.

I head back to the enclosure gate, a swinging panel in a fence made of plastic poles wired together with a rusty metal thinner than floss. It hasn't been repaired in a couple centuries, of course, so there are several guyerra-size holes along the bottom.

I spy motion off to one side, but when I turn my head, everything appears perfectly still. Which is alarmingly suspicious.

I scan the fence line. Some scraggly desert bushes dot the periphery. There's one bush that's especially close to a large fence hole. I focus my attention on that one and squint at the bare, lower branches covered in dusty earth. There's nothing hiding out down there. The bush leans against a boulder with a little tuft of… Wait. Is that red guyerra fur poking over the top?

I cast a sorry glance at the gate and heave a sigh. It'll be another five minutes.

I stride over to the bush, and the tuft of fur remains unmoved, only ruffled by the passing breeze. "I'm doing this for you, you know," I say aloud to the hiding guyerra. I pick a long, spiny-looking branch, and twist and pull until the dry bark cracks. At the sound of the snap, a set of pointy ears and intelligent eyes pop up to peer over the rock. The guyerra considers me. I'm way too big for him to consider me as prey. I'm not worth the fight. I am, however, a threat to his bid for freedom. His beady eyes focus on my movement as I walk over to the guyerra-sized hole in the fence. "I get it, you want to leave. Me too, bud. But if you get out, the lazy-ass jagoffs who run the zoo will have you butchered. Too much work to shepherd you back." I shake my head. "Bloody criminals, is what they are."

I weave the branch through the metal wire in several spots. It doesn't cover the hole completely, but it'll keep the guyerra in. I stand up and analyze my work. It'll do. For now.

I was naïve when I first got here. I told management all about the things that could cause problems around the zoo, like enormous fence holes. But they don't give a crap. General rule: if you point out system flaws to people who hate animals, you end up with every shit-related job on the planet. Forever.

I pause by the employee exit gate. The disappointed guyerra is watching me from a new vantage on top of the boulder, all eight furry legs bent snugly against his foxlike body. I point a finger at him. "Don't do anything stupid, now." I swipe my badge at the gate and hop on the empty car of the employee-only inter-region rail system.

Outside the employee after-hours bar, a daytime tourist tiki hut with snack and drink offerings, I hold my hand under the steri-station and watch as a wave of electric blue light travels over the length of my body. Shit-bacteria begone.

So, here I am. One of only three women working on this planet. I used to think I was good looking, too, but after living here, I wish that wasn't true. The chuff that passes for animal-caretakers around here stare at me so hard you'd have thought that, considering the numbers, at least one of 'em would have evolved x-ray vision by now. But does that make a difference? Oh, no. They're still happy to pin me with the most denigrating and demoralizing jobs every single shit-soaked day. And I've been stuck on this backwater planet for eight soul-sucking years. At this point, I've made such good use of the bar that I've blacked out more nights than I'd like to admit. Don't judge me.

I order three shots from Lionel, the fresh-faced grad and hobbyist bartender who thinks he can make money at this when grizzly ol' Nikolai couldn't. Fucking optimism, huh? I glance around the quiet tiki hut lit by swaying Christmas lights while I wait for my drink. The sound of an elephelk trumpeting in the distance overpowers the tinny sound of music playing from a cheap speaker behind the bar. Above, there are cutesy animal pictures and daytime drink offerings for off-world patrons who need a mid-tour break.

When my drinks arrive, I knock back the first two in rapid succession. Those don't count, I need them just to sterilize my insides. I stare at my third glass of methē, a good-enough alcohol supposedly laced with hallucinogenic venom from Trabodian cobras, and watch the twinkling reflections of the hut's red and green string lights as I swirl the amber liquid. Then, with a nod of acknowledgement to Bob Schwinn in the corner, the only gentleman in this void-forsaken place, I knock the whole thing back. Bob doesn't say a word.

"Saffron Savage," booms a raspy voice that can only belong to one person. A person I wish I'd never met.

Weasel, aka Tim Wiesel, is the 'contractor' who makes quick supply runs for our zoo. He's not an official employee, but he may as well be based off how much we rely on his services. You need more peat? He'll find a way to pick some up for you fast. Urgently need a brick of peli-pellets? He'll get us some within the day. Commercial quantities of LSD? Weasel will get it for us, no questions. Quick, too. For a price.

He's also got the drool-worthy body of a man who knows the gym more intimately than his quanta-com. But he's a mean cut of meat who only has eyes for the money. Turns out, he had eyes for my money too, and was using our steamy rendezvous to skim from my already overdrawn bank account. Once I stopped boning his nugget, I was small peanuts to him. Nowadays, he barely looks at me, and he straight out won't talk to me when he's sober.

"Eat a maggot, Weasel," I retort.

From the corner of my eye, I catch the dark swirls tatted along his sculpted arms and the edge of his ribbed tank top when he sits on the barstool next to me. I won't reward his stalker behavior by turning to face him. Weasel exhales his cigarette smoke into the silence. You'd think with all the synth he's dealing, he'd be addicted to something fancier than old fashioned cigarettes. He musta had several lung replacements by now, just to keep up with the addiction. But, honest to Bob, I'm in no position to judge.

"I was wondering if I'd still find you here," Weasel says at last, surprisingly steady and sober. "Good to know you're still drinking to deal with life, Ronnie. Dependable."

Classy gentleman, he is. He's also the only person in the universe who's managed to turn the name Saffron into something worse. I can't help it; I take the bait. "Why are you here, Weasel?"

"I've been trying to reach you all day. Where the voids have you been?"

Uh, I've been stuck here shoveling shit for the last eight years, dumbass. Except now I've been ignoring your comms to improve my quality of life.

I down my last shot instead of responding. The smell of Weasel permeates my senses. Cigarette smoke and cologne. It stirs some heart-thumping memories, as much as I wish it didn't. I'm about to be nice when he cuts me off.

"Actually, I don't care. I gotta talk to you about something. I got a proposition for you." He lowers his voice. "You'll end up with everything you've ever wanted."

Ugh, please. A proposition? I flip Weasel the bird. I don't have the energy for this brand of asshole at this hour of methē. I scoot my butt on the rattan barstool away from the smug scumbag, but even as petite as I am, there's only so far I can go. I angle my body to face good old Bob, even if he won't actually talk to me and is only an image on a tacky, orange messianic poster.

Bob Schwinn, Hialeah's founder, is depicted on his atrocious poster with, I kid you not, a glowing halo and palms pressed together in prayer over what looks like a ferret. Precisely which animal that is has been the subject of many passionate bar fights between us regulars, with varying levels of sobriety and varying levels of injuries as a result. We all work at a zoo, okay? Anyway, you'd think Bob was an actual saint based on the picture, instead of a grunt accountant from Terra who cashed out at the height of the AI boom three hundred years ago. The poster may be ridiculous, but it's still better company than my ex. That's for freaking sure.

"It's Lionel, right?" Weasel waves to the new guy behind the bar. "I need a drink here."

"Me too," I add. "Several."

"Ah, Saffron," Lionel replies hesitantly in his soft, fuck-me French accent. His cheeks have gone all red, but at least he can say my name properly. "You must pay for ze last three first."

"Come on, Ronnie. Honey." Weasel opens his hands. "Let me pay Lionel for a few drinks. It'll be just like old times."

"Augh." I give him the finger again. As if I would ever want to go back to that. It has been a crap-filled day, and now I have to deal with Weasel on top of it? I desperately need another drink. The elephelk sounds off again in the distance, and I get a brilliant idea. I push off the bar to my feet. "Be right back with some cash, Lionel," I announce, surprised by the soft slur in my words; those first shots finally catching up to me.

"Hey! Ronnie! Where are you going?" When Weasel doesn't get an answer, he gets up and follows me.

I lurch my way down the tourist's trail. It's paved and wide enough for our golf-carts, so walking this path should be a piece of cake. Of course, the first thing I do on the trail is trip over something brown and furry.

Knees stinging, I get up and brush off my palms as a drove of wild, snaggle-toothed bunniculas thunders past. It takes a full five minutes for the herd to clear the walk. Apparently, I frightened *them*. Those cotton-tailed bloodsuckers have lived freely on Hialeah for ages, ever since the first five escaped their enclosure centuries ago. At this point, the bunnies outnumber humans on the small planet, not just in population but in mass as well. If that's not downright terrifying, I don't know what is.

Weasel is at my side and is trying to cup my elbow with his hand, or some weird shenanigan like that. I jerk my arm away from him and totter towards my goal, one hand trailing along the fencing of the elephelk enclosure to brace myself. "Saffron! Slow down a sec. I've got to talk to you about something," Weasel says, keeping up with ease.

"You can bite my ass. I don't want to hear it." I stumble on toward the elephelk viewing station ahead.

I dated the guy for seven months, and it was the biggest mistake of my void-forsaken life. And I'm stuck on bloody Hialeah, so that's saying something. I used to believe Weasel was full of hope; that he and his ship were my freedom. For a small blip of time in my life on Hialeah, life here was bearable.

All the way up until I discovered the leech *was stealing money from my account*, every time we were bumping uglies, putting me into even more debt. And for what? To play at the guys' poker night. He's not even a gambler; he just wanted a bit of entertainment. When I caught him, he had the gall to ask, "Don't you want me to be happy, baby?"

In the elephelk viewing booth, I pause. I have enough presence of mind to glance above the poster demonstrating the structure of the elk-like horns on what's otherwise a pony-size version of an elephant. The camera is still up there, over the poster's top left corner. I calculate the best way to put Weasel to use.

"Listen," Weasel repeats, once he sees I've paused. The self-centered bastard assumes I'm waiting breathlessly to hear whatever it is he's dying to tell me.

I grab him by the shoulders and move him over to where he'll block the camera view. The other camera is to my back; it won't be able to record my hands. I fumble with my keychain until I've got the screwdriver out of my multi-tool. It takes me a few tries to connect to the hinges of the locked tip box, but it's only a matter of time. Eventually I've got all four screws removed, and the hinges no longer hold the top to the box. I lift the lid in the direction it was never meant to go, still held fast by the e-reader lock, and fish out a wad of cash from inside.

Weasel raises his eyebrows at me. "Classy, Ronnie, real classy."

"Says the pot who fucked the kettle over," I retort, still slurring.

He blinks, then with a casual shrug, pulls a few bills from the box as well. I glare at the bills still in his fingers, which he hastens to tuck into a pocket. "Such a pig wanker." My anger fuels enough sobriety to get the screws back in.

"Listen, Ronnie. Saffron," he amends, catching up easily to my side as I make my shambling return to the tiki hut. "I had an interesting offer today. From an interesting buyer."

I roll my eyes. I have less than zero interest in Weasel's 'interesting' deals. But he grabs my hand and pulls me back. We've almost returned to the golden glow of the tiki hut and Lionel's promise of drinks. I look at his restraining hand with a scowl.

"Just listen," he practically growls, his voice low and serious. He stops for a paranoid glance around us, then leans in closer. "I've got a buyer for the umemeh."

Instant resentment wells up at the mention of the zoo's newest animal. It's only been here for a few months, but I've already had my pay docked because of him. What kind of stupid, lowbrow idea is… Wait. I see his point.

The umemeh is an endangered species from Brin-177 which basically looks like a two-headed llama. A compound found in the umemeh's neck arteries is the main ingredient in a 'miracle' impotency drug, and Brin-177 sells the *only* legal version (which they distill from the arteries of umemeh who've died of natural causes). As you can imagine, the price of the drug is insanely high, but it pays for an advanced military to surround the entire planet and protect the beasts from poachers.

Our own umemeh is far less protected. He's a loaner from the bigger Gopika Zoo-Planet out in the Ursa Major sector. We had to beef up our own zoo security here on Hialeah to build an enclosure deemed 'safe enough' for the umemeh. It was a major expense, but we've seen a crapload of new visitors.

Understanding percolates through the alcohol. This could actually be a lucrative plan. I cock my head at him.

"Here's the deal. You help me get the umemeh out, and I give you a thirty-percent cut." Weasel leans back and nods to the zoo grounds at large, the red ember of his cigarette bouncing with his movement. "It's enough to get you out of this shit-hole."

Getting off Hialeah. Now that is something to think about. But what would happen to that stupid, crap-hiding umemeh?

Well, I wouldn't be actually killing it. Who knows what Weasel's buyer has in mind for it. Maybe they plan to build their own petting zoo. All I have to do is hand over one idiotic, useless animal, and that one act of sharing means getting out of my mountain of debt. The real selling feature, though, is having enough money to live somewhere other than this shithole zoo planet.

"Go on," I say to Weasel. "I'm listening."

chapter two

The lights are on low in the hallway at the dormitories where Weasel has insisted we continue this conversation. I swipe my wrist in front of the lock reader on my door, but it blinks red at me. "Nits," I grumble, and swipe again. This time it blinks green, and I'm greeted by a blast of hot, stuffy air as the door swings open. I prop some pillows up against the wall and sit on the bed. Cool air flutters against my face momentarily when my fan completes a sweeping arc of the room. It's eighty-five hull-breaching degrees in here. Our dorms weren't equipped with A/C like the tourist gift shops. Or like Weasel's ship, the *Cricket*.

Weasel stands in the center of my room, cigarette drooping from his mouth. He nods at the open window. "Uh. Should we close the window for this conversation?"

"Close that window, and I will kill you," I reply.

I pull out the cork of my newly acquired bottle of moonshine, thanks to the elephelks. I have alarming ideas percolating through the swirling maelstrom that is my inebriated brain-thing. Ideas for how to get back at Weasel after all this time. Ideas involving this umemeh job. But I need facts first.

Weasel gives one of his little shrugs and sits next to me on the bed, way too close for comfort. Him being in my room again irritates me like sand in the eyeball.

"Over there." I wave him further down.

Weasel stands up and examines the end of the bed, which is occupied by a pile of worn-but-not-terribly-dirty laundry. In an alarming twist, Weasel doesn't make a snarky comment about it. He gingerly picks up my soft plastic snow globe from the pile and sits on the edge of the clothing-mountain below. He lifts my palm-sized child's ball and sniffs it with a frown.

Once upon a fairytale-time, that plastic snow globe smelled like sugary cupcakes. A gift from my parents on my sixth birthday. See, I once had this unhinged childhood dream of caring for galactic animals – and the most impractical, broke ass hippie parents who fawned over such dreams. Now that I think about it, their judgement should have been in question from the moment they pinned me with a name like Saffron for having bright orange-red hair. What, was someone not going to notice it on first glance? It all went downhill from there. I took out mistake-sized loans to pay for xeno-zoology school. And then, because there is no market for zookeepers, I was stuck taking the only job offer that came my way. Even though it was on the devil's butthole, Hialeah.

That was eight years ago, and the snow globe smells only like dirty laundry now. It's still full of gel and the artificial sparkly snow (not to mention a plastic elephelk figurine, Arnold) but its soft, squishy plastic exterior has turned grimy and grey over the years. That's childhood dreams for you.

Weasel makes a face at the ball and tosses it down the bed at me. I scoop him up and huff on Arnold's behalf. "He can't smell worse than that death-stick you're inhaling," I snap at him. "Tell me what this is about, Weasel."

Weasel lifts thick fingers to his cigarette and raises it to eye-level and frowns at it. Small wisps of inquisitive smoke curl out of his nostrils before he lets out an exhale of release. He frowns and puts it back in his mouth.

"It's like this – you've got clearance for entering the umemeh enclosure, right?" I fold my arms. Obviously, I have the clearance. The umemeh shit doesn't collect itself. And sometimes, when he's buried it below a pile of loose leaves, I don't collect it, either. The stinging dung gnat infestation wasn't my fault, even if my boss doesn't agree. "All I need you to do is open the enclosure. I'll transport the umemeh to the buyer." Weasel turns his intense gaze towards me. "Ronnie, all you've gotta do is let me in."

"First of all, smoke-for-brains, my name is Saffron," I say, trying not to sound distracted.

It's not the nickname that's set my mind buzzing like a batted beehive. Whenever Weasel uses that phrase, "all you've gotta do," there's *always* a hidden catch. Always. That one little phrase has raised all the flashing red flags I've got.

"Saffron, come on. This is good for both of us."

Wheels are churning through the murky depths of my mind. I want money, but I don't want it that badly. Or maybe I'm being paranoid.

Aloud, all I say is, "I'll get fired."

"Like I said, Ronnie, uhm, Saffron. You'll have enough money to get out of this shit hole and live comfortably for a while. Ready for this?" Weasel pauses dramatically. "Five hundred joulos."

I hear my own gasp before I even realize my mouth is open. That's an insane amount of cash, and it would definitely get me off-planet and set me up for a few years. Normally I would jump at that faster than a cricket on steroids. The only thing is, I can't help the horrible, wiggling feeling lurking around my gut. He's going to frame me, isn't he?

"Could I hitch a ride out with you?" I ask, as a test. I already know the basics of the *Cricket*. The guy never took me anywhere on purpose, but look, we were fuck buddies for seven months. There were plenty of times when we were smacking the salmon and had to drop it for some "emergency" shady business run. I've seen the *Cricket* fly. The flight controls are so simplified on that old bus, a sleeping chimpanzee could fly it. I could help. If not with the flight controls, with the umemeh. There's no reason to say no.

"No. Can't do it," Weasel says, folding his arms. "Too risky. Get another ride through The Horse's Ass," he nods at my quanta-com. The Horse's Ass is the trading post just outside this star-system, with for-hire cabbies available on the quanta-market. "You'll have enough cash to pay your way across the galaxy."

There's no question anymore. The bastard is going to screw me over again, and he'll get off Hialeah and sleep like a baby in thousand-joulo bedsheets while I rot in jail. Not today, Weasel.

Well, I can think of one easy way to avoid being framed. It's probably a shit idea. No, it's definitely a shit idea. But drinking moonshine while making plans turns shit ideas turn into fully-fledged, elephelk crap-monsters. Just to screw him over, it would be worth it.

Why let Weasel have all the fun?

I could steal the umemeh. And I could steal Weasel's ship too. I could do this whole job myself. How hard could it be to figure out the rest of Weasel's plan?

I nod at him. "Who's the buyer?"

Weasel shakes his head, and ash flies into the air from his lit cigarette. "Need-to-know only basis."

"Bullshit," I reply. No, it's bigger than that. "Elephelk shit." I'm not actually pissed, but I have to ask. I'll get that detail from his quanta-com later. "When are you gonna to pull this?" I take another casual swig of moonshine, and Weasel looks hesitant, like he's about to tell me it's on a need-to-know basis again. "Listen, I'm gonna need to know in advance so I can book my immediate departure. Don't screw me over, Weasel."

He takes a deep drag from his cigarette, and the ember flashes bright. "So. You're in?"

"I'm in," I reply and let out my loud, signature burp. In my limited experience, if you're going to lie to an asshole, it feels much better to do it as belligerently as possible.

Weasel gives no reaction other than a long drag on his cigarette.

"Take off is tomorrow night," he says at last. "Get the umemeh to the launch pad by ten p.m."

"Ten p.m.," I repeat, thoughts trailing. Tomorrow? He's cutting it close on this one. If I want to make a move, I've got to do it now. Like, tonight.

"If you're in, I gotta take care of a couple things," he says brusquely, pulling off his quanta-com. Weasel breaks out a multi tool from his pocket and cracks his quanta-com wide open.

"Um. What is happening right now?" I ask.

"I'm removing the GPS nav. Don't wanna get hacked and tracked," he replies, cigarette flopping from the corner of his mouth. It looks easy, the way he moves and fiddles with these intricate gears.

"You sure that's a good idea?" Every time the breeze from the room fan sweeps past him, I cringe. I can't help it. What if some little circuit board flips away, or worse, gets lodged through an important bit of quantum tunnelling well? Weasel's not exactly an engineer. "Will it still work?"

"I'll be pretty screwed if it doesn't." He wipes his hands on his pants, then begins reassembling his quanta-com. Engineer or not, his business is shady enough that this might not be his first time. Still, I'm shocked when it blinks back to life on his wrist.

If I'm going to steal the umemeh, I realize, I'll also need my quanta-com to be untraceable. But I can't afford it if he fucks mine up; new quanta-coms aren't cheap. After a moment of debate, I ask, "Will you do mine too?"

"How much you willing to pay?" he replies, not even looking at me.

"You kidding me? *You're* paying *me*, remember?"

He glances at me skeptically.

"They can hack my GPS just as well as they can yours, dipshit," I retort. "Are you absolutely sure I'm not going to squeal if they put pressure on me?"

Weasel rolls his eyes. "Fine. Hand it over." I'm so flooded with relief that I don't even bother to ask questions. Once it's reassembled, Weasel collects all the removed parts and tosses them out the open window.

I smile at him nice and pretty when he sits back down on the bed close to me. "Now, for a very different matter of business," I say. *Like finally paying you back for all the times you've screwed me over.* But I don't say that part out loud.

I smile to myself as I root through my bag, searching through my daily zoo supplies. From the twinkle in Weasel's eye, I know he thinks he's going to get laid. I don't know why he thinks I carry my vagina in my messenger bag, but he was never the brightest of boyfriends. Just pretty.

I stretch my arm around his shoulder, and, vengeful tigrorilla that I am, jab the newly uncapped emergency tranquilizer dart into the sweet spot at the base of his neck.

His eyes dilate wide as the realization sets in. "Fuuuuuck, Ronnnnnnniieeeeeeee," he slurs, the concoction working its effect immediately. He sinks onto my pile of dirty clothes, but his jacked-up shoulder muscles make it look like he's being held up by a floatation device. "Fuuuuuckkkk......yoooooou."

"For the last hull-breaching time," I say as I yank off Weasel's wristband quanta-com, "my name is Saffron." But the bastard doesn't even hear me. He's out.

I stare down at his quanta-com, thinking about the best way to use it. I consider stealing the device itself, along with his accompanying touch rings and lenses, too. But I give up on that just as quickly. Those parts of the quanta-com system are cheap and interchangeable anyway, and I don't need another set. Mostly, it would take an annoying amount of time to take off each silicone ring from his cigarette-stained, pickle fingers. Consider it my gift to him.

"Too bad you're not awake to meet my friend, Karma. She's a bitch," I say, already scrolling through Weasel's recent contacts. There it is. Several voice comms, right at the top of the list, made to an encrypted number whose name is represented by triple Xs. Very stealthy, Weasel, very stealthy.

I'm not nearly as loopy as when I first hatched this plan, which is good because I should probably be a little more sober when I speak to my new employer. I'm still buzzed enough to have some liquid courage. I tap the comm button on triple X on Weasel's quanta-com and patch it through to my own quanta-com.

"Jhelloh?" asks a heavily accented, brusque male voice.

"Plans have changed," I say into my quanta-com, trying my hardest to sound smart, and not a few drinks in. "Your operative is… indisposed." I poke at Weasel's limp body. "I'll be leading the umemeh job, and if you need to reach me, you can contact me at…" I rattle off my own quanta-com number, which according to some magical science, identifies a microscopic well within my wristband device as the destination for quantum-tunneling communications. Sounds like total crap salad, right? Anyway. "42, 31, 88, 2104."

"Jha, jha," rasps the man. Even his laugh has an accent. "And is our mutual friend…taken care of?"

I glance over at Weasel.

I hate the guy, but I sure as shit am not going to kill him. No payday could be enough for that job. But the emergency deer tranq should do a pretty good job at wiping his memory. Don't ask me how I know this.

"Yes," I reply. "All I need is the delivery destination. Everything else is in place."

The voice on the other end doesn't reply immediately.

I step in with bravado I don't feel to force his hand. "Annnnd the price has just gone up to double."

"You are very entrepreneurial little one, I see," says the man with heavy breathing. "But the price will remain five thousand joulos."

I stifle a gasp. Five thousand joulos? That liar Weasel tried to get me out of his way with ten percent!

"Oh-kay," he says jovially, as if 'taking care of' people is an every-day part of his business. "I send destination details to new quanta-com number you gave me. I also warn that if you try any funny business, I jhave no problems with my guys taking care of you." The deep voice pauses. "Do you know who I am, little entrepreneur?"

"N-no," I stammer. I have not drunk enough for this conversation.

"Ah, forgive me. My name is Greel Truyoza. Now, do we jhave understanding?"

Greel Truyoza? The most notorious, cut-throat mob boss in the galaxy?

"Uhh. Yes. Understood," I reply, finally getting ahold of myself.

"Good," he replies, and the line is cut.

I exhale through pursed lips. My quanta-com lights up again; I've received destination coordinates from an untraceable number. I blink absently at the quanta-com without processing for a full minute before I snap out of it. The rendezvous coords are so foreign to my own that, at first, I think they were sent in code, until realization dawns. They're that different because they're on *the other fucking side of the galaxy.*

And then I'm all alive again. Shakily, I sort through my plans for the next hour.

Weasel is still a problem. That tranq will only keep him out for another ten hours. I paw through my belongings to find the pill I need for this situation. Of course, it's at the very bottom of my bag in a corner full of lint and crumbs. I place the linty pill under Weasel's heavy tongue. Dirty or not, it'll keep me safe. It's basically LSD for riled-up animals who really need to chill out, but more importantly, it won't interfere with the tranq that's already in his system. Plus he'll show up as positive on his next drug test, which will invalidate any claims he might have against me.

This time, I'll be the one who screws him over. I send a quick text from Weasel's quanta-com to Triple X. "Cargo on its way. I gotta lay low for a bit. Send the $$$ straight to my acct." I nod. That should look pretty incriminating.

Then, remembering how Greel Truyoza told me to make sure Weasel was 'taken care of,' I hurry to send a text from my own quanta-com, just in case the notorious mob boss is the kind to get easily confused.

"That was from me. Don't send the bastard any $$$. Just trying to keep the authorities off my trail."

He sends me back a reply. It's a solitary emoji: a fucking smiley face wearing sunglasses.

I don't have time to think about mob bosses who use outdated emojis. I still need to clear Weasel's bank account before I leave. Waste not, want not. Right?

I lift Weasel's quanta-com and punch in the request to transfer five hundred joulos to my illegal, encrypted and unregistered digital wallet. Ironically, that wallet was something Weasel set up for me a few years back because loan sharks were seizing every payday that was deposited into my official bank account. My illegal slush account has only ever seen small change and payment for odd jobs around the planet, so this will be the most money the wallet has ever held. Well, Weasel may not have been paid the full five grand yet, but even the five hundred he promised me is a sweet first step. The screen blinks at me – it's too far away to connect to the biometrics in his quanta-com finger rings. I lean closer to Weasel's sleeping body and try again.

The dots swirl on the screen. A two-toned bong sounds, and the transaction is rejected. He didn't even have the five hundred joulo he promised me! "Motherfucker...." But I shouldn't be surprised. When has he ever been honest about money?

Gritting my teeth, I try to transfer a smaller amount, cutting it in half this time to two-fifty. This, at least, goes through with a welcome chime. What a miracle. I mutter while I try for another transfer, this time for one-hundred joulos. Another chime, and I feel another wash of relief. So that came through, at least. Three-fifty will have to do. I've got to hurry this shit up if I'm really doing this tonight.

I toss his quanta-com back on his sleeping body. Then I actually take the time to put it back on his wrist. It's upside-down, but good enough. I give Weasel's head a parting pat. Poor bastard.

No, I correct myself. This is the man who betrayed my trust. This is the man who stole from me when all I had was debt and hope. This is the justice he deserves.

I grab a grey scarf and tie it around my face, and pull on a black-hooded sweatshirt. Have I mentioned my hair is the color of a carrot jammed in an electrical socket? Very incognito.

No, a hood won't even matter. The key for the enclosure. It's coded to my name. I'll still be linked to the crime. Shit.

Oh, screw it all. I'm finally getting the voids out of here. That's what's most important. Five-thousand joulos can buy me a lawyer to fight any legal muscle they throw at me. Plus, that Gopika zoo was really shady about how they acquired the umemeh in the first place! That should take the legal system for a good loop. Wait, scrap that. Five-thousand joulos can buy me a new identity and Hialeah won't be able to find me ever again.

I cast a glance at the discarded elephelk-globe and at my already overstuffed bag.

"Arnold," I say, squatting down to the ball's height. "Wanna come along on a fun trip?" Arnold doesn't respond. I shove him in my bag anyway. He's come with me this far.

I manage not to topple over when I get up, shove a few more pairs of clean undies in the bag, and take several gulps of the moonshine. The stuff isn't as potent as I need it to be, but it's better than nothing.

Now all that's left to do is corral an animal that's dumber than rocks in a void. Piece of cake.

chapter three

Okay. Yep. That moonshine kicked in faster than expected.

I trip on every miniscule crack in the pavement and crash into walls that come out of nowhere, I swear. I'm not great at a straight-line sobriety test in the best of conditions. The underground personnel tunnels have trams and moving walkways that are all shut down at this void-forsaken hour. The lighting is at a bare minimum. I have fallen on my hands five times already and my wrist is smarting something fierce. By the time I get to the umemeh enclosure, which is unlit at night, I have had enough. I click the light on my quanta-com. I don't care if I'll be more visible on security camera; this plan will go to shit if I break a wrist in the very first hour.

I do pull my hood lower over my forehead, though. Call it moonshine logic. Even though I used my personal key badge to unlock the umemeh's enclosure, I'm hoping that with my hoodie and face covering, there'll be some deniability as to who actually performed this part. To be honest, I'm not thinking too clearly.

I think I need to keep it that way.

"Ohhhhh sweet, dumb, stinky animal, where the voids are you?" I call in a lighthearted, cooing voice. I creep slowly along the wall of the open roaming space. The umemeh enclosure is a two-hundred-fifty-acre grassy plain that mimics the animal's natural home territory, but in the wild, the animal likes to sleep up close and tight with its pack. There's no way he'll be out in the open.

I aim the weak quanta-com light at dark recesses and the plant-deserted cavities below tree branches. Basically, in every conceivable spot a beast that sleeps standing up might currently be hiding. The quanta-com's beam of light is only a pathetic thing in the encompassing blackness, so when something pint-sized darts on the path right at my feet, I stumble and fall.

I let out an involuntary yelp. I'm physically okay, though, and nothing hurts. But I slap the dirt in frustration anyway.

But one bunny is not alone. One bunny is never alone. When I hit the ground, I startled an entire horde of bunniculas. The earth-thumping and leaf-rustling seem deafening. Great job, secret agent.

I wait and try to calm my tingling nerves as the bunnies continue their mass exodus from one side of the path to the other. The noise can't be that bad, can it? Surely not enough to alert the guys asleep by the security cameras.

Then an entire flock of tropical birds erupts in cacophony, startled from sleep by the bunniculas.

"Fan-fucking-tastic," I mutter as I pick myself up amidst their frightened caws. Finally, once every last bird and bunnicula has gone and the enclosure is all silence again, I get myself off the ground and back onto the small footpath.

The farthest lamp on the fence turns on. Then the next. And the next in line.

"You've got to be kidding me," I mutter.

I drop back down to the floor and scoot under the shrubbery. My sweats are dirty from sleeve to ankle. My butt is covered in a veritable cornucopia of detritus and an invasive smell is beginning to making my nose hairs shrivel. I'm sitting right next to a pile of shit. Unbelievable. It's not my fault this animal hides his shits better than government secrets; even the stinging dung gnats haven't found this one yet. I should never have had my pay docked over this, and I certainly shouldn't have to sit right next to a fresh deposit. This animal is the worst.

My breathing has turned into a pant while I wait for someone to show up and investigate. An irritating sting at my ankle forces me to glance down so I can shove the offending branch out of the way. Only when I look, it's not a branch.

"Seriously?" I ask the bunnicula who's been innocently sipping at a midnight snack. "Shoo," I tell it, waving my hands at it. She pulls her head off my leg to get a better look at me. Her creamy tan and white fur is tinged with red around the mouth, her adorably snaggly teeth, smaller than those found on males of the same species, are awash in crimson.

"You got plenty of other snack options around here, okay, Barbie? For Bob's sake, it's a zoo." I wave another hand at her, and she takes an uncertain lop away. She stops after only a couple feet, waiting to see if I'll ignore her again. I sigh. She's not my biggest problem right now. I turn my attention back to the more pressing issue of the lit up umemeh enclosure.

All the floodlights in the enclosure have switched on. But nothing else is happening. No approaching footsteps, no sirens. The night guards, Soros and Ming, are usually busy with their spectator sports and too lazy to get off their asses. Even still, I'm surprised they paid enough attention to turn on the lights. What the crap, guys? Why tonight? I pray to an ingrained image of orange Bob Schwinn that those two douche-bros take a few more sips of beer and find a new winner to bet on in their sporting event.

It feels like a year before the lights turn dark again, with a powerful clang as each lamp shuts off one at a time. I take a shaky breath before I stand back up and wipe the dirt off my palms. The disappointed bunnicula hops away, disappearing into the underbrush.

"Come onnnn, you dumb umemeh, where are you?" I call out quietly, a lot more uncertainly. Why didn't it wake up from all those lights? "If I get arrested because of this, I'm not going to pet you." Because that's all the umemeh wants in the middle of the night. Don't judge me, I'm not sober.

Desperation is creeping in with a welling of bile in my throat. If I don't find this stupid, idiotic, fur-brained animal – an animal who literally couldn't figure out how to hide if he wanted to – I will be so screwed.

Then, something wonderful happens. A putrid smell accosts me. A smell so strong it makes me tear up. It's not a nervous system response, I'm actually happy. That stank is the telltale smell of an animal with two brains.

The umemeh is hidden behind a droopy tree branch. As I approach, I see the umemeh is leaning both sleeping heads up against a chain link fence. I take a wary glance at the gate for the security cameras that are supposed to be posted at regular intervals. There are none right at this spot, and for the first time ever, I'm thankful to Hialeah management for their shoddy zoo upkeep.

I place a hand gently at the base of the umemeh's left neck and pull it towards me. It exhales deeply but does not budge. I wrap both hands around the neck this time and tug more firmly. The head bobs downwards, and back up again. This idiot is still sleeping. What am I supposed to do, slap him?

…Which head?

Just as I'm debating it, my quanta-com lights up with an incoming call from Soros, the security guard. I let it ring a few times before deciding it would be suspicious if I didn't answer.

"Savage? Where are you right now?" Soros sounds bored. "We found some funny activity in a restricted area under your badge number."

Shit, shit, shit.

"I am *busy*," I reply. My heart is racing. I have to play it cool. How do I normally talk to him? I've disliked Soros ever since he passionately tried to 'teach me' that women were biologically designed to serve men, so I don't talk to him any longer than absolutely necessary.

"Savage, I don't give a shit. I just need to file a report. Where are you?"

My thoughts are running wild. He probably thinks my quanta-com has glitched. I need a plausible lie. "I'm with, um, I'm with Weasel. In my dorm. Ask Lionel. You're interrupting bang-time, shit-for-brains." I click the comm off and let out a stream of air through pursed lips. That didn't sound suspicious, right?

Now, something is pushing back the front of my hoodie and is rubbing against my hair. "What the..?" I reach up to feel a warm breath and a muzzle at my fingertips.

The umemeh's awake. Time to get off this planet.

I put a hand at the base of the umemeh's necks and try to lead the way when something wrenches my head up painfully and suddenly. The umemeh's not just nuzzling my hair; he's *eating* it. I guess I don't need to guide it with my hands, then.

Slowly, I inch forward one step at a time, umemeh in tow. The umemeh is content to allow its lower body to move along with me. Tears spring in mechanical reaction to the sharp pain. This animal has made me cry twice in the last ten minutes, and I'll be pissed if I get arrested after all that.

I pass the zookeepers' supply box on the way out and grab a handful of addicto-nip treats. Thank our Savior and Sponsor, Bob Schwinn, the umemeh prefers them to my hair.

As I yank the hoodie firmly back over my forehead, my fingers trail over my still-smarting scalp. I steel myself for the rest of this maddeningly slow journey. The spaceport is only a mile away. I can do this.

———

I CAN'T DO THIS. I'M GOING TO RUN OUT OF TREATS. I AM GOING TO die a drawn-out, painful, bald death. In jail. That thought's on repeat with every slow-as-molasses step.

"Stars be loved," I mutter when the empty space port finally comes into view. It's a huge lot the size of several football fields, all paved over with cracked concrete. It's dark out there, but there's enough starlight to know that it's mostly deserted. The usual.

Weasel's ship is the only ship clamped into an extendo-dock. The rest of the extendos jut out of the asphalt pad in the same rigid pose, but empty, which makes it look like someone herded together an army of oversized geese and buried them to their necks in an asphalt sea. Other than his ship, the strip is deserted. Well, except for the zoo's ancient hovercars, but those don't count. Any one of the hovercars might have just enough room for the umemeh in there next to me, but barely. But they all travel slower than a turtle's ass. Very safe for airsick tourists, not useful as escape vehicles.

I hold my breath as I approach the *Cricket*. Pretty much all of my plan to steal this ship hinged on Weasel being a lazy twaddle. He probably never got around to revoking my boarding and computer privileges.

I wave my quanta-com over the *Cricket's* docking lock, and it blinks red at me.

That's not good. That's really, really bad. Did that knob Weasel actually revoke my boarding privileges?

The umemeh bellows and spits in frustration. I haven't given him a treat in all of three seconds and he needs immediate satisfaction. "Not now!" I whisper angrily. The umemeh spits again, and this time hits the ship's boarding sensor. "Seriously?" I ask. I pull out a spare sock from my bag and rub the sensor clean. I hand the umemeh a treat. "This is not a reward for bad behavior, you hear me? This is bribe money. Stop being an impatient bastard. Please."

I take a deep breath, and hold my wrist-bound quanta-com aloft so that it hovers over the cleaned sensor. This time a green light blinks to life. Thank Bob.

A ramp descends from the butt of the black cylindrical vessel.

Of course, the two excited heads of the umemeh begin sniffing different portions of the door frame. In opposite directions.

"You'll rip yourself apart," I mutter. "I can see why those neck muscles are so special." I pull one of the umemeh's heads back to center, but he brays at me. The grasped head whips angrily in my face and I take a quick step back. Not fast enough to miss the wad of spit that gets lobbed in my face. Great. Just great.

Time to finish off those treats, now. We need to move. I pull out the last handful of treats and wave one in front of idiot head number one, then idiot head number two. No one's spitting now. But between you and me, idiot head number one will not be getting this treat. "Next time, you better rethink your anger strategy," I tell him.

At the top of the ramp, I take one last glance about the space port. Still dead as a concert hall in a pandemic. Same as it's been for the last decade.

I heave a sigh of relief once the ramp finally inches to a close, leaving us alone in a dark and cold metal cylinder. We've made it on board. But holy elephelk farts, I have so much more to do to actually get off the ground.

I allow the umemeh to roam freely inside the *Cricket*. My boots echo off the cavernous metal of the hold as I strut towards the cockpit at the other end. This whole place is full of sharp angles, and I'm gonna need to do something to cushion the umemeh for liftoff. He could die if his head knocks into something, and then where would I be? A broke-ass bitch with a dead umemeh.

I happen to know Weasel's got one item in his ship that's actually soft.

"Where is that flea-ridden mattress?"

Closer to the cockpit is the shit show that is Weasel's living quarters. There's a compact pull-down table covered in old take-out food containers and energy drinks. They're all overturned and strewn about beneath the zero-grav protective glass cover-box that's been left open on one side. It's no surprise containers are littered all over the floor there, too. There's a heavy dumbbell set, all clipped in, right next to a pull up bar and treadmill and harness contraption that've been bolted to the floor and walls. There's the smell in here I remember from last time, a mix of stale food, ashes, and sour sweat. It's disgusting in here.

Further searching reveals a very stained, unadorned mattress where it's tethered upright to the cargo boxes. About twenty loops of strapping have been used to hold it upright.

"Seriously, Weasel?" This is super overkill for a man who knows how to disassemble a quanta-com.

I pull at the straps, but quickly realize that'll take too long. We'll have to use it this way. I tug the umemeh forward, past anonymous boxes hooked and locked to walls. I have to expend way more of the treats than I'd expected to make the dumb beast move. "Just... let me tie you up!"

But the umemeh is too excited by the overturned empty food containers at the table. I work against my makeshift lead to pull him towards the upright bed, when I realize the smarter way. I grab an armful of those crusty, greasy containers, and throw them at the bed itself. Some old noodles cling to the mattress and form a constellation of new stains, but with the preexisting bouquet, it's hard to be certain.

I work on coaxing the umemeh to lean up right against the mattress. Umemeh almost never lie down; it's so hard to get both heads in agreement that they've forgotten how. Using the mattress straps as a tether point, I wind my rope around the umemeh's body in the way that'll most likely hold him down without breaking a leg, all while he nibbles on my hair, which is somehow more interesting than dangling noodles or sauce stains.

A bright light turns on from somewhere behind me with a clang. It's enough to make the umemeh jerk back. I turn around, arm covering my eyes with my elbow. It's coming from outside the ship.

The entire docking station has been illuminated with stadium floodlights, and all that asinine light is flooding through the line square windows in a row above the control panels.

"Shit."

We've got visitors. I run to the control panel and slam the locks and jam my palm over the engine-start biometric keypad. Time to find out if Weasel left me on the key-permissions list, or not.

The *Cricket* whines to life.

Outside, Mishel, the dock master, is running towards our ship, yelling at us. I can't make out what he's going on about, but I'm ninety percent sure all he cares about is an unscheduled departure. I have no idea if he knows about the umemeh yet, but if Soros and Ming aren't here yet, they will be. Really freaking soon.

The umemeh begins braying at me. "I know, I know. But listen. This is not a good time for complaining," I say. But when I glance at the umemeh, it does not look good. He may be tied up, but those two heads keep bobbing about. There's no way they'll survive the extra gravity of liftoff.

"Fuck, fuck, fuck," I mutter. I paw through my bag for some extra rope. I fumble quickly and fashion a makeshift double harness and tie the umemeh's two heads together. The umemeh spits at me, this time from head number two.

"No treats for you either, McSpitser!" I yell. "I'm trying to keep you alive!" I restrain his neck against the smoothest portion of the nearby crate I can find. The mattress is not long enough.

The umemeh is panicking at this point, pushing his legs against the constraints. He will hang himself if he manages to break his legs free. I root around in my bag again and come out with a tranquilizer dart. The case comes with a total of eight, and now I'm worried it won't be enough for this trip.

"Sorry, bud," I mutter, and jam the tranq into the nearest of the umemeh's tied up necks. The beast sags against his restraints.

I jump into the flight seat. I stare blankly at the controls. I thought I would have more time to figure this out. There's a blinking light on a disengage button, so I hit that. There's a shit-ton of switches, and I have no clue what they all do. On the main screen, though, is a beautiful thing. It's a message from auto pilot.

"Begin automatic takeoff sequence?"

"Fuck yes!" I jam my ringed fingers into the air space over the computer's spherical holo-sensitive space. Already the computer is blinking out a new question for me. We're low on fuel. And the computer wants to know: Where are we going?

Uh.

I tap in the first destination that comes to mind: The Horse's Ass. I pray while the ship does the fuel calculations. The Horse's Ass is as local as galactic neighborhoods get, and if she can make it that far, I'll be able to refill on fuel there.

The *Cricket* blinks verification at me.

I sink back into my crash couch with relief. Mishel is waving his hands outside, more frantically. I slam the takeoff holo-button.

My ears are overwhelmed by the roar of the engines. Within seconds, the *Cricket* takes off. Within minutes, we're out of Hialeah's atmosphere and shifting gear to interstellar travel. Hialeah's slow-ass shuttles have nothing on us.

It is then that it hits me: I'm free.

I'm finally, *finally* free of that zoo planet. Free of the feeble sunshine from its pathetic dwarf star, of its grime, of its misery-inducing debt. Free of its assholes. I close my eyes in relief.

I'm free.

chapter four

The four-hour journey in Weasel's cargo convoy proves to be chase-free. And also, gravity-free. When I unstrap, I propel myself over to the umemeh first. He's perfectly fine, sleeping like a two-headed baby. A baby with a bad spitting habit. I float on past the umemeh and start taking stock of the cargo shelving. A trip across the galaxy will take a couple days. I'll need to pick up some food at The Horse's Ass, too.

When I pass by Weasel's exercise corner, I pause. He only ever left that nook for business. Or for banging. It's easy to imagine him still there, doing those repeated motions of resistance pulls, cigarette flopping at a funny grav-free angle from the edge of his mouth with each exhale.

The ship computer pings with a new notification.

I kick off the wall and head back over to the controls. Do we have a tail? Already? I flit my hands over the sphere and hit display.

A time-stamped, recorded message fills the vid-screen. A scruffy looking police officer is half-whispering into the camera and glancing over his shoulder every two seconds.

"Ho! Weasel, you disable your quanta-com? The police are set on the trail after your girl – they got a warrant and all. They'll follow her GPS, so you should be safe, ho-bro. I made your warrant disappear, like we agreed." He glances back over his shoulder, and rubs his nose with the back of his hand.

My pulse is too loud in my ears. I cannot believe what he just said. There's a warrant out for my arrest? Already? I knew Weasel was going to frame me, but that was really bloody soon.

Wait. They can't track me anymore! Weasel took out my GPS. I'll be okay, for now.

The dirty officer looks back at the screen. "Oh, one more thing, ho-bro. They put out a galactic impound order on the *Cricket*. I'll see if I can slow down the impound order with a virus, but you'll have to abandon her at the next port. You better pay me that thousand joulos, ho. I'm going to a lot of trouble for you."

The video screen clicks off, and the hold is so quiet it's as loud as a scream.

Shit, shit, shit. This wasn't supposed to happen so soon. Police? Arrests? Where were they all these years on Hialeah? I don't know why I thought I could avoid all this, but I wasn't planning on any of that happening. I glance around the space, feeling trapped in his small cargo transporter. I feel the stinging in my eyes, but I won't let myself cave into misery. I'm too close to freedom to give it all up. I can do this.

I'll have to abandon the *Cricket* at the next port and hope that dirty cop's virus covers my ass long enough to get by without scrutiny. I don't have much faith in this guy, and I sure as shit ain't paying him. He can take it up with Weasel for all I care.

But now I have a new problem. If I can't travel on the *Cricket*, I'll have to find a different transport in The Horse's Ass. It is a space port, though, so this problem shouldn't be impossible to fix.

I leave the captain's controls to float over to the umemeh. His eyes are blinking in a dazed confusion, but he turns to sniff my hair once I'm in range. It doesn't take long before I feel the familiar tug as he nibbles in his semi-conscious state. Everyone wants a piece of me. But you know what? I prefer this company to anyone else's.

———

WHEN THE *CRICKET'S* AUTOPILOT PULLS INTO THE ORBITING TRAFFIC lane at The Horse's Ass, there's an automated computer exchange of information with the gate authorities. I pray on every last tranquilizer dart that the police-bro's magic worked. The *Cricket* is out of fuel and we can't go anywhere else. I've got no other options; this is it.

I hold my breath, waiting for the intercom to blink on with angry interrogators. But nothing happens. No voices start shouting at me from the console to stay put, or whatever. A landing number blinks on the screen, as well as a countdown to the anchorbot that's on its way to reel us in. I am highly suspicious of the radio silence.

Still, I go and make sure the umemeh's still securely strapped in so that he doesn't break something when we encounter the grav-generator of the station. He snorts into my hair sleepily, but otherwise looks fine.

When the *Cricket's* ramp finally opens at The Horse's Ass, I stick my head out just far enough to peer around the edge of the doorframe. There are people bustling to and from their ships, but there's no army of police officers waiting for me to deboard into the space station. I stick my head out further. No one coming down the gate looking angry. There's a bored customs officer at the checkpoint to enter the station, but the entire hallway of this gate is completely clear of angry police. I don't know how long that will last.

The umemeh bellows at me, straining at his straps.

"Yeah, yeah. I'm coming." I rush over and begin untying all the stupid knots, leaving one loop of rope along his necks, in case I need to tug him out of the action. As if it actually matters much, since he moves at the pace of frozen iguanas. I'm bracing myself to literally drag him through the station, but as soon as he's free, the umemeh's heads bob their way over to the open door, drawn by the freshly cycled port air.

I tug my black hoodie firmly over my forehead to cover my treacherous hair and tuck my scarf securely over my nose and mouth. I dig in my bag for my heavy-hangover sunglasses and use them to secure the scarf in place. It looks suspicious as space fungus but I'm not taking any chances with the station's facial recognition software.

I brace myself to exit next to the rare umemeh. *Look cool. What would Weasel do?* Well, he's a shit role model, anyway.

I have over three hundred joulos in my bank account. That's enough to pay for a hotel room or a place to hide in the station while I find someone to transport us over the next leg of our journey.

I head down the ramp, hemp leader rope held firmly like I'm the boss in this situation. The umemeh is not completely tranq-free, ambling along even slower than usual, which I didn't realize was possible. I start to notice the funny looks we're getting from other people loading and unloading their ships. Or rather, looks the umemeh gets. I should have expected that, since two-headed llamas are not exactly inconspicuous. Which I hadn't considered when I came up with this plan three shots of methē and a few good swigs of moonshine in. This is bad.

What if I throw a paper bag over one of the umemeh's heads? Then he would look just like a totally normal llama with a paper bag over an... unusually large deformity. No, no. The paper-bagged head would get pissed. Plus, he would spit his way out of it.

I hold my head up high and begin the walk of doom.

Like any spaceport that doesn't get a shit-ton of foot traffic, The Horse's Ass isn't well-maintained. Aside from the interior decoration that's a century out of date, the place is dotted with those outdated holo-cast commercial billboards, and every single time a holo-ad pops out at us, one of the umemeh's heads goes to investigate. And when I manage to pull one head free of the holo-graphic advertisement, the other gets interested in it. And because these holo-cast billboards line every wretched inch of the terminal, we are moving slower than a twice-dead snail. Shitfaced fucking sin, please, stab my eyeballs out with rusty nails.

Or better yet, the umemeh's eyeballs. All four of them.

He stops, again. This time, he won't be moved, enraptured by another crappy holo-ad.

"I swear to Bob, you're going to get us arrested," I whisper aggressively. "We need to *move*." I double back to physically pull the umemeh's head out of the projector range, and he brays at me. It may be a half-mile to exit through the terminal gate, but it will seriously take me two hours to get there.

Maybe I'll skip the hotel. That was optimistic. All I need to do is find one of those shady dudes who lurk around port gates offering cheap tours, one with a ship capable of traveling interstellar distances. For the right price, I'm sure one of them will let me hitch a ride to Greel Truyoza.

I'm really hoping those shady dudes exist in more than just movies.

My gaze flits to the end of the terminal, the current goal of this year-long trek. The middle-aged, overweight customs agent who presides there is now making repeated and pointed glances in my direction. *Shit. This is brilliant,* I think to myself, pulse racing. I try to calm myself. *She's not part of the interstellar police, so there's no way she's gotten notification for my arrest yet.* My panic rises, anyway. *I steal an umemeh only to be caught at the closest port. Great. Just great.*

I slide up and stand in line, like everyone else. It's starting to feel really hot in here. I yank my scarf down lower on my neck and inhale the cool port air, but it doesn't help my anxiety. I have the money I took from Weasel, but that's it. If I use a chunk of it on a bribe now, I won't have enough to pay for passage on another ship.

Maybe Greel Truyoza will wire me more once I've got the ship? I gulp. That doesn't sound likely, even to me. He wasn't exactly the most friendly of businessmen.

More people are looking my way and pointing. I begin to

sweat heavily. Does *everyone* have to stare at my bloody umemeh? Surely, that's all this can be. They can't possibly know there's a warrant for my arrest. Right?

That's when I glance back at Weasel's ship.

The *Cricket* is being swarmed by security officers. A squad of black-clad police march up the ramp with big black guns aimed and ready. Other black-clad authorities are milling about the base of the ship, talking into commies and looking really angry.

It's only a matter of minutes until they realize I'm standing right here.

chapter five

I wheel into action, a plan springing to mind that very instant. "Ah. You know," I say to the person behind me in line. "I think my llama needs to use the restroom. Excuse me."

I try to smile politely, but it turns out a little too much like a grimace. The woman eagerly scootches over to one side.

"Yoo-hoo," she calls. As if my talking to her were the only invitation needed to open the floodgates of her curiosity. "Isn't that a umemeh?"

She asked the question so loudly I believe the entire bloody station has heard it.

I force a chuckle. It's been a while since I've laughed casually, so it sounds demented. "No, lady. Of course not! *That* species is endangered. This right here is a llama with a genetic defect. Two heads. Poor thing was unwanted by his mother," the lady's face wears an expression of doubt, so I press my point home with forced lightness in my voice. "No umemeh's today. Sorry to disappoint."

I tug the umemeh along more forcefully towards the garbage bay, which is adjacent to the port entrance. I already smell terrible. Hiding out in literal garbage shouldn't be a problem, right? At least, until the heat is gone.

There's a security officer posted in front of the large rolling garage door that opens to the dump. Why the voids would they post a security guard by the garbage? Is there *that* much stolen crap flying through the Horse's Ass?

Well, actually. Yeah. That makes sense.

The security officer stares at my animal for a long time, chewing thoughtfully.

Please just let me through, I pray. *Please just let me through.*

"That an umemeh?" He finally asks.

"Ah. Nope! Just a llama." I wait, but the guy hasn't moved a muscle. "…A llama that needs to take a piss."

"How can you tell?"

"Well, he's been my seeing-guide-llama for the last eight years," I say, making it up as I go along. Between the sunglasses and hoodie and the grey scarf wrapped around my neck, my lie may actually be passable.

Except that if an umemeh were a guidance animal, their owner would have died a thousand times by now. Also, I'm pretty sure pretending to be blind is a new low for me. "I can always tell when he has to take a piss," I add lamely.

"Not that! I meant the llama part. Don't umemeh's have two heads?"

"Well, I had them engineer a second head onto this one to help with the seeing stuff," I retort.

I can't help but cast a glance at the police activity around the *Cricket.* One of the officers by the ship is staring directly at us, scratching his head. Shitshitshit.

I turn to the garbage-bay bouncer with fire in my veins. "Look, mister—"

"That's officer!" He interrupts with a kind-hearted smile. "My name's Officer Dan."

"Okay, look, *Officer Dan.*" I put my hands on my hips. "Llamas can hold their piss for three days. But when they've got to go, they've got to go. So, if you could just let me through?"

He still appears skeptical. And he should, because it's all total bullshit. I mean, umemeh's can hold their piss for three days, but llamas? They piss every three to six hours.

"Look," I add. "You can follow me in and keep asking about… *Fred* here. But if we stand out here any longer, one of us is going to be mopping llama urine off a half-mile of space terminal."

Officer Dan chews his tobacco again slowly, then nods. He slams the button for the garage door open, and I trail after the eager umemeh into the holding chamber. Here, in between sets of garbage bay doors, the floor is marked by the skids of thousands of dock-worker's dollies and accumulated grime. The stench of what lies beyond the next door is more evident, and both of "Fred's" heads are sniffing the air in different directions.

"Travel often?" asks Officer Dan as the door begins its ascent back to closed behind us. He presses a button to stop it from closing all the way completely.

"Ah, not that many places are so accommodating to someone with my… special needs." Burning asteroids, I really should have come up with a better lie. I am a sucky human being.

Officer Dan nods, and wrenches the wheel on the exterior of the next door. Once he's gotten it unlocked, he slams the next garage door button, and the inner door begins its slow opening descent from the ceiling. The quiet, high-pitched, chuckling sound emanating from inside the garbage compactor is really irritating, but the umemeh looks excited. Great.

"So how did you come by a seeing-guide llama?" The officer asks once the door completes its descent.

I pretend I can't hear him over the ambient sound. And anyway, I've got a new serious problem. The moment the inner hold-door to the enormous garbage cavern opens, the umemeh pronks down the ramp, and I have to pretend to trail along. I wonder if any umemeh over the course of history has ripped his body in half out of excitement, because we might be about to witness a first. His two heads are eagerly turning in every which direction, and his poor body is getting conflicting signals from both brain centers.

Look, I get it. If it was my first time seeing how space turkeys were farmed, I'd spaz out too. Except, I only have one head.

The cavernous garbage hold is filled not only with garbage, but with hundreds of thousands roaming space turkeys. And the umemeh is trying to play with them. All of them.

I lurch forward over unsteady, rotting ground and accidentally drop the rope lead. I have to scurry to catch up with the umemeh, who's managed to delve pretty far into the turkey-covered garbage fields. The fields stretch as far as the eye can see and cover the entire lower level of the station. Which means there's a good chance that if I don't keep up, I might actually lose him in here. I hurry to catch up to the umemeh, but it's not easy to wade through the turkey farm. With each step I take, a volley of gobbles erupt from the unsuspecting turkeys below, followed by the sound of feathered wings beating furiously to get out of the way. The commotion sends up loose feathers and garbage stench up towards my face.

"How are you able to find your llama when he goes out to pee? Does he know to come find you?" Officer Dan calls behind me.

I stop dead in my turkey-stomping tracks. Holy fur licking felines, I seriously need to come up with better lies. Officer Dan is too smart to fall for my spur-of-the-moment bursts of idiocy. This won't work for much longer. Which leaves me with one conclusion: I'm going to have to knock out a security officer.

"I have a…" I say, but there's no way he can hear me over the ambient turkey noise. I try again, but this time, I yell. "I have a special whistle," I say loudly, a new plan wheeling to place. "It's, uh, in my bag here! But I can't find it. Would you mind?"

I pause and take a deep breath, but the officer has not responded. I can't knock him out if he's not within reach. And if I turn around and head over to him, he'll know I can see. Well, kill me ten ways to port. I started this lie, and now I need to stick to it. "I'm not sure how to get back to where you are, Officer Dan? Would you mind coming over here?"

There is no way any sane human would tread through a garbage dump filled with space turkeys. What if the guy has figured me out? What if he slams me in here, and leaves me to get evacuated out into the vacuum of space with the rest of the garbage?

Okay, well. Technically, there *are* the turkey cages where the birds have been trained to migrate to when the warning lights flash, but I really don't want to have to cram into one of those with a shit ton of birds clawing at my face. Plus, there's no way the umemeh would fit in one. Officer Dan wouldn't evacuate harmless ol' Fred, would he?

The squealing trill of turkeys getting stepped on informs me that Officer Dan is actually on his way over. My pulse quickens. I can't believe this is going to work! But wait. How am I gonna knock him out?

I bend down and reach beyond the layers of turkey carpeting to grab the first hard object my fingers encounter. It's an unopened can of turkey soup. Fan-fucking-tastic. I keep it on the other side of my body, beyond the officer's line of sight.

"You know," says Officer Dan as he nears me. "I haven't seen your Fred over there relieve himself yet. You sure about him needing to go?"

He still believes me! Bless his heart.

"It might be too much excitement for him," I say. "If you could just help me," I add, holding my bag out to the man. "The whistle is supposed to be some bright red color? It should be right in there."

As the officer leans over my bag, I hit him in the head with the can of turkey soup.

"Ow! What the fuuuh—" He glances at me, caught in surprise, but anger is growing there.

Crap. Why did it have to be a can of soup?

Desperate, I grab the familiar-looking taser gun off his belt and fire it at him. Officer Dan collapses in a heap of spasms and is quickly lost below the carpeting of turkeys. Two thin wires trail from the nozzle of the gun below the line of sight and indicate where he's fallen. I stare at those wires for a long, frozen minute. This was just a nice dude trying to help a blind lady, and I'm a shit human. I groan when I realize it's even worse than that: He isn't just a nice dude. He's a security officer.

I've attacked a security officer.

Turkeys are trilling as they walk past my still-electrified wires, and it's making me nervous. Now, of course, I remember that the outer garage bay door was not shut all the way; if another officer comes in here to investigate, I'm toast.

Shitshitshitshitshitshit.

Okay. Breathe.

How do I turn this stupid thing off? I examine the outdated taser weapon. Well, it might be a good idea to take my finger off the trigger. Right. I drop the weapon on the ground near where the officer's fallen. My no longer boozed-up brain latches onto a memory. One of the officers by Weasel's ship watched me come in here. If they head this way and find me with an assaulted officer, I'm toast. Extra burnt, crispy toast. I need to sneak out of here and find a new hiding spot, pronto.

I head over to Fred. The fucker. Has he noticed any of this commotion? No, of course not. Both his heads are buried below mountains of turkeys, happily eating shit-soaked garbage. "Sorry to ruin the party," I tell the umemeh as I tug on his rope harness. Despite his lowing, I haul him, one forceful step at a time, up the dump exit ramp. Turkeys squawk their disappointment as I stomp over them. Even after I get the umemeh into the holding chamber between the two sets of doors, I feel a twinge of remorse over Officer Dan as I close the inner garage door.

I'm not incompetent. I still spin the wheel to lock the door; it would murder every living human on the entire port if they evacuated the garbage chamber with any of the hatches left open. I do feel bad, though. I pull a black mark-it-all out of my bag and, in big graffiti letters, scrawl, "OFFICER DAN IS IN HERE – SAVE HIM."

I squint at my letters. Oh, Bob. I fix the A's and the R's. And make extra-large dots over the I's, just in case. I sure as shit hope they can read that.

I hit the button for the second garage door to ascend, and try my best to casually glance about. No one's looking our way. Garbage doors open and shut about a million times a cycle in any space port terminal. Every ship that comes to port has something to dispose of, even if it's just the discarded wrapping from delivered cargo. No one's looking in my direction at the moment, not even the customs agent.

One of the umemeh's garbage-smelling snouts begins to nuzzle my hoodie, and I push him out of the way to get a better glance at the *Cricket*. I'm surprised to find that not only are officers still swarming around the ship, they've begun unloading boxes of unmarked cargo, too. Huh.

This is the only free shot I'll get. I don't know where to go from here, but this is the perfect moment to make a move. I eye the ventilation duct, which is way too small for me, not to mention the umemeh. Then all the people going and coming from various ships, but each ship is watched over by a posted guard, counting and ticking off the contents as they're loaded and unloaded. That's when I notice the one ship that doesn't have someone standing guard. And it has an open cargo door! We have a winner.

Through the massive spaceport windows, I see the sprawling name of the ship, "*Waterloo*," printed on a clean white exterior of a standard conical interstellar vessel, the kind that uses the forward thrust to generate gravity. Whether or not this is my golden ferry ticket will depend on the cooperation of the ship's captain. I can figure out that part later. What I do know is that it is the perfect place to hide with the umemeh. At least until I've got a better plan.

Casually, I walk the umemeh from the garbage bay over to the open cargo hatch. The closer I get, the more I'm noticing that the plyo-foam and carbon-plank boxes inside are huge. Massive.

Large enough to house my bedroom kind of massive. Which is odd, but perfect for my needs. If I find an empty one of these babies, the umemeh is as good as invisible. My heart is doing a butterfly dance as I step into the cargo space and take a quick check behind me at the dock to make sure we haven't sparked anyone's attention. It's business-as-usual out there as far as I can tell. Satisfied, I bang the door-shutting lever and seal us in. The cargo hold is blessedly dark, so I click on the light on my quanta-com.

The umemeh has begun chewing on my hair again.

"Not now, Fred." I swat him away. Then, remembering I'm low on treats, I pull back my hoodie all the way. I need to lure him further in towards the bigger cargo boxes somehow.

Traditionally, cargo holds are neither oxygenated nor pressurized in-flight. It's a dumb place to hide with a stolen animal for a flight, but as long as the ship's docked in port we'll be safe. I don't plan on staying in here long-term. Once those security officers lose interest in me, I'll be on my way to finding a cooperative ride. I just have to hang low for a few minutes.

The umemeh and I squeeze along past rows of oversized boxes hooked into the floor in such tidy lanes that it looks like a miniature city. One crate has been left open, plyo-foam padding strewn about the floor. A hasty check confirms that the carbon-plank box, which is the size of a small booth, is empty. I make quick work of stacking the plyo-foam into a corner and lead the umemeh inside. I have to get back out to lean the crate lid against the vertical opening. With a little see-saw wiggling from the inside, I manage to pull the lid almost completely shut against the open box edge. When there's only the faintest line of light visible from the resting lid, I heave a sigh of relief. It's done. We're safe, for now.

I lean against the crate wall. The smell of this animal in a confined space may be overpowering, but the umemeh and I are well hidden. Even if someone comes to take a peek through the cargo hold, they won't find us, unless they're being very thorough.

I sink to the ground.

What have I gotten myself into? It takes me a minute to wrap my head around the severity of this situation. There's a warrant for my arrest. I've stolen an endangered species, gotten involved with a mob boss, attacked a security officer, and tranquilized a scumbag of an ex-boyfriend. Well, the last part is the only part I don't feel bad about. That backstabber got some of my good LSD.

I can't believe that Weasel framed me.

Scratch that. I can definitely believe it.

The umemeh starts vocalizing grunt sounds, and he butts at my head with both of his.

"What do you want, boy?" I ask as nicely as I can muster. Tears sting at my eyes. He makes the grunting again, more insistently. "Do you want food? Water?" I think about the supplies I've carried along with me in my bag, and realize I haven't brought him anything to eat other than that crummy handful of treats. Some trafficker I'm turning out to be. And now I'm failing at animal care, too. I rub my arms as tears begin to roll down my cheeks.

The umemeh makes the noise again, and failing to get a response from me, does what he's been trying to tell me about all along: he pees.

Being an unusual animal, it is understandable that you may have never seen a umemeh urinate before. Let me tell you what umemeh pee is like: It smells like horse shit. It is hot. And there's a lot of it.

I wasn't completely lying to Officer Dan before. Umemeh bladders are constructed to hold urine in for a long time. When they finally do go, every three or four days, there's a high quantity of urine to expel. So when the umemeh in the crate with me begins to urinate, it is a full, ten-minute affair.

My feet are soaking wet, even though I hastily stood on the pile of plyo-foam once he'd begun his business.

Once he's finished, he begins nibbling on my hair affectionately.

"You've got to be kidding me," I say, mostly to myself. I've spent my fair time with animal feces, but this situation feels pretty bad. There's a pain growing behind my eyes. I am very, very sick of my life choices at this point. How did I end up here, standing in a dark cargo hold in two inches of piss?

Because this was my chance to be free of Hialeah, forever. If I can just make it through the umemeh piss and a few nosy security officers, there will be five-thousand joulos waiting for me at the end of all this.

I get a hold of myself.

Money. I'll need more to grease the right palms and book passage. More importantly, I need to see if my buyer has the connections to work some magic on the police warrant. That would help.

"I'm calling Greel Truyoza right now. We're getting the voids out of here."

chapter six

Greel is happy to hear from me. My voice comes out in a hot, angry whisper-yell as I'm forced to explain my current predicament and need for more money.

"But you jhave umemeh?" he asks.

"I do."

The line is quiet for a couple seconds. "I send you five hundred joulos now."

I begin to protest.

"If this is not enough, I send my people to pick up umemeh from you. And if I arrange transport, I pay no more."

"I – You –" I stammer.

"I pay this guy, Weasel, fifteen-hundred joulo already. I assume you took it. This is fair amount for removing umemeh off this zoo, Hialeah. If my guys do rest of pick up, I pay no more."

I bite back on a response. Of course, that wanker Weasel would have squandered money. I should have known. Weasel and his gambling debts. But this leaves me in a bigger shit-hole of a problem. If I want Greel Truyoza to do the pickup, all I'll have left is a measly hundred-fifty joulos. And after bribing my way through The Horse's Ass, I won't even have that much.

"No, no. That's fine," I decide. "I'm perfectly capable of

booking my own travel –" *and earning the entirety of the sum you promised.* "I just need an advance."

"Did I tell you umemeh must be alive at delivery?"

I roll my eyes. I mean, who wants a dead umemeh? Now is not the time to ask him what his plans are for the animal, but a new unsettling feeling begins to form in the pit of my stomach. What if he doesn't want the umemeh for his private petting zoo? Everyone knows what umemeh carotid arteries are used for, and that they have to be harvested within minutes of death. What if he plans on killing the animal the moment I deliver it?

"Yeah, yeah," I mutter.

"Good. If no, I pay you nothing. If it is dead, you owe me two-thousand joulos. Plus interest."

I nearly choke on my own saliva. Greel Truyoza doesn't wait for my response, and I'm left with my mouth gaping at a blank screen. I'm in no position to negotiate, anyway.

A chime sound moves me from my stupor, and I click through my quanta-com to confirm that my encrypted wallet has been cushioned with Greel's money. With the added five hundred, I've got seven-hundred-fifty joulos in total. I'll have to make that work or else I'm dead meat.

I need to get a copy of the manifesto of all ships currently docked in The Horse's Ass. Every dock engineer should have one. With a manifesto, I could reach out to the captains one by one, feeling them out to see who's bribable, and skip passing by the custom agent's desk entirely.

Wait, what am I thinking? I glare at the source of all my troubles. What am I going to do with him while I'm out bribing captains for passage?

"Ugh," I say to the umemeh. "Just... stay put."

It was a completely gratuitous mouth-fart of a sentence because the umemeh is fast asleep. Standing up, heads bobbing to different beats, he seems at peace. Which, come to think of it, is not a bad position to be in. He's in a box, not making noise. I could probably leave him here for a few hours. I glance over at the cargo box lid that I've managed to pull fast against the opening. I'll make sure the lid is attached nice and snug, and Fred won't be going anywhere.

But before I can make a move, the cargo bay around us fills with artificial light.

"Mind if we take a look around?" asks a female voice, seemingly apologetic.

Shit.

"I'm telling you, everything here is to code," insists a second voice, a man. "I watched over the unloading myself."

"I know, Sergeant Reyes, I know. It's only… Well, I shouldn't be telling you this. There's been a report going around of a trafficker with a stolen animal. I'm not saying you would ever knowingly shelter them!" the voice blubbers to the other's defense. "I just want to make sure they didn't sneak in here to hide. Without your knowing, of course."

Shit, shit, shit. I pull myself closer to the umemeh and try to make myself as small as possible. I sincerely hope this box doesn't look suspicious. And that none of this piss is dribbling out of the container. I huddle closer to the animal, the odor from his matted fur invading my nostrils. There comes the sound of boots walking through the space, but there is no way to tell how far or close they may be.

"A stolen animal?" asks the second voice. It must belong to that Sergeant Reyes. "This would be the galaxy's worst place for a trafficker to hide with an animal. Our hold is not kept pressurized or oxygenated! The poor animal wouldn't stand a chance after takeoff."

"The trafficker either," supplies the first voice.

"Garbage is sent to space-vacuums all the time. Sounds like a fitting end for a trafficker. My sympathies lie with the animal," Sergeant Reyes replies, voice cold as stone.

I wince. Clearly *this* ship captain is not of the bribable kind.

"Alright." A hand raps on the distant doorframe. "All looks good in here. Keep a sharp eye out, Sergeant, and let me know if you witness anything strange. Your help is very much appreciated. As always, sir."

"Thank you, Mel. I'll see you next time, yeah? Say hi to the girls for me."

"Will do, Sarge."

The rest of their pleasantries are lost over the sound of the mechanical doors thundering to a close, and we are once again immersed in darkness.

"Shit." How much time do I have to give them to leave before I can sneak out without being observed? I count to one hundred, and after one last glance at the sleeping umemeh, wedge the lid open, and sneak my way out of the box. I press my ear to the cargo bay door, but I can't hear anything over the hum of the ship's electrical systems. My hand hovers near the bay door buttons.

My heart is pounding. What if they're still outside making small talk? I'd better wait a few minutes. I check my quanta-com. Five minutes, then I'm out of here. We need to get to another hiding spot immediately.

I continue to stare at my quanta-com in the dark, watching the elapsed seconds go by. Five minutes takes a really, really long time. Once the count gets down to thirty seconds, however, I hear a roaring sound that fills me with dread.

The entire cargo hold is vibrating; the ship's engines are warming up for liftoff.

This means that any exit through the bay doors right now will most definitely be noticed, if not physically impossible. And that port agent, Mel, didn't sound too amenable to animal traffickers.

My mind quickly turns over my options for escaping this situation, but there aren't many choices. Here's my new plan: after liftoff, when the crew is no longer strapped in, I'll do something to get the attention of a cargo technician. I'll bribe him or her with all the joulos Greel has sent me, and they'll let me stay in their bedroom, out of sight, until the ship gets into the next dock. That isn't too much to ask, is it?

Okay, that's a shitty plan. But I don't see any other options.

I run a quick calculation in my head. This is an enormous cargo hold. It's a cavern of a cargo hold, that's what it is, and it is currently filled with oxygen. There should be enough to last me and the umemeh through a five-minute liftoff, right?

How much oxygen does an umemeh need, anyway? It may have two sets of snouts, but the umemeh only has one set of lungs. I hope that math checks out.

I have an even more immediate problem. We're about to lift off, and neither me nor the umemeh are restrained. I can't have that idiot of a mammal die in here, for fuck's sake.

A new, terrible prospect springs to mind: I *could* let the umemeh die here in a cargo hold. I could still get a rescue for myself, lie low with some cargo technician, and walk off this ship seven-hundred-fifty joulos richer. One day, that asshole sergeant will find a dead umemeh in his cargo hold and have no idea how he got there.

Okay, don't judge me. The thought would occur to you too, if you were facing potential death. I only entertained the idea for a fraction of a second before rushing back to that crate. And anyway, Greel Truyoza is no man to mess with. If I ran off with his seven-hundred-fifty joulos without delivering his package, he'd chase me down and have me slowly tortured. Before somehow transforming my flesh into two-thousand joulos, plus interest. I shudder. I'm pretty sure Greel Truyoza is much worse than anything this cargo hold could throw at me.

Hastily, I dig the rope from my bag and slip a makeshift harness over the sleeping umemeh's necks, praying he doesn't wake up. I can't be wasting tranquilizers for every takeoff, and we're going to have a few more of these in our future. The roaring of the engines gets louder, and I scramble at the walls and floors of the empty crate for a place to secure my rope.

"Fuck! Voids! Shit!" I curse. And curse. And curse.

Once the umemeh looks like he's tied in good enough, I finally give a thought about myself. "Shit!" I yell as I scramble out of the crate, letting out another pool of umemeh piss as the crate lid is opened again. I take a look back. "No, no, no!" The crate lid is loose. Leaving loose items laying around during takeoff is basically asking to get impaled. I jam the lid under the weight of a latched-in box, making sure it's wedged tightly in the gap. The sound of the engines is nearly deafening now.

My gaze darts around the room in a panic. I spy some unused cargo strapping attached to a far wall and secure myself into it. It'll at least hold me in if we turn upside down for liftoff, but it sure as shit won't protect me if that loose crate lid comes flying at me.

This is the shittiest plan I've ever had. I am going to die. I'm going to get hunted down and tortured. I'm going to suffocate. I'm going to get squashed to death.

"Fuck, fuck, fuck!" I yell as we begin our acceleration out of The Horse's Ass gravity well.

Then, there's a big explosion of noise from the cargo hold around me, and everything goes black.

chapter seven

Well. I'm not dead.

When I blink my eyes open, I have a monster of a headache jackhammering through my skull. I'm pretty sure that's a good indicator of oxygen deprivation, but Bob, it hurts my brain when I move any part of my body.

As fast as I can handle, which is basically a turtle's pace, I unstrap myself from the wall. Beyond my visual field, the umemeh is whining, and each moan makes my head shatter into a thousand jagged pieces. Apparently, I'm not going fast enough for him. "Fuck… you," I whisper, because that's about all I can manage.

Like molasses, I move to the umemeh's crate.

The genius has tried to get away from his restraints. One of his heads looks nearly strangled. This is bad.

I work on releasing the strangled neck from the rope first, then I free him completely. He stumbles as he tries to leave the box. The head on his half-strangled neck looks just as panicked as the other one, so I am comforted that at least he'll die in one undamaged piece. I take a step forward after him, only to fall over in blinding pain.

Shit. This is it. We're going to die in a cargo hold.

I'm going to die covered in piss.

There's a small enough tug of thrust-grav that both me and the umemeh are still sticking to the floor, so our ship must still be accelerating. I can't make my brain sort that through. Is that good for my chances? Or does that mean immanent death? My body feels light as I crawl over to the door. Or try to, anyway. The floor of the hold has cargo contents strewn all over, which makes for a mountainous obstacle course when I can barely move to begin with. Open boxes, colorful rubber-plex pipe connectors, cannisters. It looks like a full-on explosion took place in here.

I seem to remember this space looking like a tidy city when I first entered, and I have a niggling feeling that I am the cause of this mess in the Sergeant's cargo hold. Not that I give a rat's ass. I need to get out of here.

Thedoorthedoorthedoorthedoor…

I realize I've been crouching with my face pressed up to the cool metal of the door for some time now. I try to knock on the door, but I'm leaning against my hands. I give it a more concerted effort this time, but in my weakened state, I end up tapping it, rather than banging. It's something a dog – and even a bunnicula – would respond to, but terrible for getting another human to notice me.

Voids, I need to get up. My body is unresponsive, and my brain is asking me to stab myself through the eyes to rid myself of the pain. The umemeh is lowing at me, which makes me want to stab the animal's brains too. I do not have the energy for that kind of precision targeting.

This is not going well.

Slowly, on shaky legs, I get to a stand and press my face against the door's port-window. In fact, my entire body is pressed against the door, because I don't have enough energy left for standing. I try to bang on the door as I'd planned, but my arms are no longer responding.

Click. Click. Click.

Whir. Click.

Something's happening. Each noise brings a new wave of pain, and I cannot fathom what any of it means.

Rrrr. Rrrr. Rrrr.

The door slides out from under me, and I fall into the decompression chamber that's beyond the cargo door. I'm lying on the floor of the four-by-four chamber, and the umemeh squeezes in and stands over me, lowing and lowing. He almost sounds human, too. I must be really delirious.

Shut up, you whiny little hyena. We're both going to die, okay? Do you really want that to be the last thing we hear? But the asshole keeps whining and whining and I do feel a little bit bad that he's dying too.

The door behind me tries to shut, but gets caught on my legs. I can't move them, and my head is pounding with the absolute worst pain ever. The door tries to close us into the decompression chamber again, but again gets stuck on my fucking legs. If that door can't shut, no one can rescue us from inside the ship. We'll die in this un-oxygenated space, six inches from survival. But my legs won't move.

At this point, I'm okay with dying as long as it makes the pain go away. I'm done, so very done, with all this shit.

A black-clad person rushes past me, shuffles my legs past the cargo door, and it slides shut behind me. Someone other than me is cursing soundly. Remotely, I can hear the sound of running footsteps and sense my body being jostled about. But my mind is being smothered by intense, aching pain and really can't be bothered with details.

———

I come to my senses with a megalithic headache (though not one as brain-hemorrhaging as before) in a tidy medical bay. Next to me is a happy umemeh.

Unlike me, the umemeh seems totally recovered. One of his

heads is bobbing along merrily, and his other head is chewing on my hair again.

I groan.

My bright, orange-red curls are fully unfurled, uncovered and splayed all over the bed. What's left of my hair, anyway. No use in trying to be inconspicuous now. The rest of me is in a medical gown of some sorts. At least I'm not still in the piss-soaked, shit-stained coveralls from the zoo.

I take in a deep breath from the oxygen mask, and a white-clad medical officer with grey hair approaches me.

"She's coming to, Sergeant," the doctor says, double-tapping her quanta-com index ring with her thumb.

Sergeant? Did she notify Proper McRighteous Jerkface that I was here?

"Didja haveta…" I slur into my mask, mouth dry as kibble.

"I wouldn't attempt speech just yet," says the doctor, back still turned towards me.

I try to watch her from the periphery of my vision. What I see is instantly alarming. It looks like she's lifting my bag of treats and tranqs and tossing it into a cabinet. And now… Is she doing what I think she's doing? She is. She's locking the cabinet door with her quanta-com pad. I haven't landed in the middle of a quarantine, and there's no need to confiscate *shit*. I try to calm my breathing and tell myself it wasn't my bag; I didn't get a good view.

The doc turns to me, eyebrows raised. "You've been subject to extreme oxygen deprivation and may experience permanent brain damage. Luckily, the umemeh survived the ordeal completely unharmed."

"Of course he did," I mutter.

"Again, I recommend holding off on speech for now. Incidentally, anything you say may be used against you in a court of law." *Crap.* "I'm going to ask you a couple of health-related questions, and you can blink once for yes, and several times for no. Okay?"

"Mmmnph." I say, and raise a hand to slow down this inquisition. My tongue and cheeks feel gummy. "Wait," I add, and pull the mask off my face and alternately stretch my lips into a wide grimace and a kissy face. "Better. Mouth better. Head hurts. Lots."

The medical officer folds her arms and narrows her eyes at me. Clearly, she's not fast on the uptake.

"Do you…" I roll my jaw. "…have *anything* for this headache? There's an icepick cleaving its way directly through my skull."

She raises an eyebrow. "Your name?"

"Saffron-needs-a-painkiller-Savage. Who are you? Doctor Malpractice?"

She taps away at a screen. "Miss Savage, then. Are you currently experiencing any nausea or vomiting?"

"Seriously? You can see me. Do you see any vomit?" I try to push myself up to sit, but the headache crushes me back down. "Please. Do you really…? Can't you give me *anything* for a headache? Anything at all?"

She grabs my fingers with her own frigid hand. "Can you feel this?" she squeezes three times.

"Ice queen." I inhale sharply. I'm still slurring a little. "Yes."

She calmly proceeds to grab my other hand. "How about this?" This process repeats with toes as well.

She scrolls through a few screens on her pad, then gives me a disappointed stare. "It appears as though you've escaped with only an irritating personality disorder, which unfortunately may be permanent."

"I was an asshole before too," I reply automatically. My head hurts something fierce, and all the doctor does is fold her arms and purse her lips at this. "Ugh. Don't stand around being all judgy, okay? I'm having a really shitty day. It's not like I wanted to go through that."

"I would be curious to hear *what* exactly you thought would happen?" booms an angry deep male voice that my adrenaline gland recognizes. There's no mistaking that voice, the exact same timbre as the one I heard from inside the cargo hold. The one who described animal traffickers as garbage.

Sergeant Reyes strides up to my bed, and he looks very, very furious.

Shiiiiit. I was not prepared for the fact that he's drop-dead sexy. Clean cut, rugged, dark-haired, and handsome. His uniform is crisp and tidy with three golden stripes and a star on his shoulders. And he's so-very-cross. Oh, Bob. Why did he have to be hot, too?

"It's, uh, not what you think," I stammer.

"What I *think*," he replies, fire glinting in his eyes, "is that you're an animal trafficker who's endangered the life of a rare species, and then, the survival of *my entire ship*," his voice is rising and causing an explosion of pain in my head, but burning asteroids, I can't help that my vision lingers on how nicely his shoulders fill out that uniform, "by forcing one of my cargo workers to open the doors and lose a significant amount of our ship's air and pressure! So tell me," he says, glaring at me like a mac-daddy of alpha doms. "Tell me why I shouldn't turn this ship around right now and hand you over to the authorities. Tell me," he repeats, "how this could *possibly* be something other than what I think."

"I…" I falter. I close my eyes, and the pain recedes enough for me to *think*. A little.

I cannot use the seeing-guide-animal excuse again this time. … Right? No, no, by now they've seen me using my eyes to track their movements around the room. Why didn't I plan a better lie for this adventure? I peek at my interrogators. The doctor has her arms folded and is staring me down. The Sergeant is glowering at me, and only the umemeh appears relatively calm. Obviously, they all care way more about smelly, idiotic Fred here than me. That's when an idea strikes me.

"I uh, used to work at a zoo," I begin. "I did this all for him, for Fred."

I notice a beat of uncertainty flicker through the Sergeant's eyes. *Bingo.*

"Fred is an umemeh. But he was being mistreated at the zoo! He was alone in his enclosure, and…" I reach through my mind, back a decade to when I'd been to zoology school. When have I ever actually needed the knowledge I learned back then? Definitely not in Hialeah, if that's what you're wondering. The old info's still up there, if a bit rusty.

"Umemeh do better in the wild with a lot of roaming space. This umemeh was kept in a tiny enclosure. Also, by nature, umemeh live in packs" – because they're too dumb to survive in the wilds otherwise – "and this one has lived alone his entire life. I just had to do something. You can look me up. Saffron Savage. That backwater zoo-planet Hialeah should still have me listed as an employee." I start grabbing wildly for straws. The headache is not exactly helping with my creativity. "I was planning to refuel at The Horse's Ass and fly to the umemeh home planet. But the guy I hired to get me out of the zoo, this asshole, Weasel, reported me to the cops, and, well. I had to hide. And I obviously picked the wrong place." I close my eyes. The residual pounding in my brain skips a beat or two with my eyes closed, but it's still there. At least an image of the sexy Sarge leaves an afterburn on the backs of my eyelids. "Look, do you guys have anything for a headache? My head is really killing me right now."

"Doc?" the Sergeant asks, and I can hear her grumbling as she goes to a cabinet and begins rooting around noisily. He turns his burning gaze back to me, jaw twitching. "It's an underfunded zoo. I'm sure he wasn't the only animal living in sub-optimal living conditions. You can imagine my skepticism that you chose to 'rescue' this particular animal."

"Yes, okay? Yes, I stole a rare umemeh. But the zoo who owns him? Gopika? They acquired him from a shady dealer to begin with. I honestly think it was from black market umemeh trading." This part, at least, is true. "On the provenance document Gopika shared with us, the umemeh home world Brin-177 was highlighted as a spelling error, which I thought was weird. So I used my bosses' system privileges to look up the umemeh's tag number in Brin-177's directory. It was listed as 'deceased.'" If he has any brains at all, Sarge won't need me to explain that some forger has recycled an old tag number. Now – time to weave in the lie, plus a good twist of pity factor. "I wanted to bring Fred to his home world to give him a chance at the life he deserves. I… didn't count on being caught so soon. Or on getting stuck in a cargo hold."

To judge by his facial expression, the pitchforks and torches have been abandoned and he's only contemplating detainment. *Improvement.*

"Oh, come on!" the doctor exclaims shrilly, throwing her hands up in the air.

"My headddddd," I grumble. No one pays me any attention.

"So. Miss Savage," Hot Sarge says, and I open my eyes with enough time to see him finish reading over the doc's tablet. "What can you tell me about the umemeh home world?"

I squint at the Sergeant. Is he truly the most clueless hunka' meat in the universe? *Everyone* knows about Brin-177. And their money. Not to mention, their insane military. Then I catch the glint in his eye.

He's testing me.

Well, if he wants a performance, this is one of the only things I can actually do for him. Xeno-zoology degree to the rescue. Literally, the first time that's ever paid off.

I start spouting off facts.

"The umemeh natural home is the planet Brin-177, which is composed mostly of marshlands and a temperate climate. Their food source is the local vegetation, and their natural roaming territory is two-hundred kilometers squared. Umemeh are typically found ranging in packs of twenty to thirty, with the older dams caring for the young of the pack. They reproduce once in a lifetime, which keeps herd sizes small." I eye the Sergeant. He's frowning as he listens, and his eyes go unfocused and brooding as he considers this unexpected twist. It's time to sell my lie and seal this deal.

"It's illegal to take an adult umemeh off Brin-177 alive, but there's a high demand for them at zoos across the galaxy. So a few zoos with money convinced Brin-177 that they should be the ones to 'save' any infant umemeh that are unwanted by the herd. Every time a baby umemeh – a cria – is born, the dam introduces it to the herd, and then the herd helps with the parenting responsibilities. In the wild, a communal effort is needed to raise the young because of their" – *complete lack of intelligence* – "distractibility. Without that dam's introduction, the herd would shun the newborn cria as alien, and it wouldn't survive. So zoos line up to adopt newborns *if and when* a mother umemeh dies during the childbirth process. Then the zoos raise the orphaned cria all alone and with inferior living conditions. The poor orphans," I say nonchalantly. "It's something that anyone with a beating heart should care about." And stars be loved, my lie is sounding better and better. I hurry on to flush it out completely.

"That's true for the umemeh at most zoos. But the story is even worse for Fred. Listen. Fred was not an orphan. I'm ninety percent sure he was created in a test-tube in some seedy black-market laboratory. I've already told you that Gopika Zoo's provenance documents are fishy. Oh, Gopika paid for him, no question there. But what kind of universe do we live in? Bred in an underground lab, raised in captivity... Fred's never stepped foot in the wilds, where he belongs. He's never lived with a pack, never had another umemeh companion. I was going to bring him home. It's where he deserves to be."

Sergeant Reyes looks thoughtful. The doc is crossing her arms.

"Hey, can I get that painkiller?"

The doc presses her lips into a firm line, but hands me the pills and drink.

"Alright, you can stay," says Sergeant Reyes. The doc starts muttering and walks away. "Don't get me wrong. Stealing the umemeh was illegal," he frowns. "But it's the right thing and I have some leeway to look the other way. So, if you're truly returning this umemeh to the wild," he peers at me and I nod vigorously, "Then when you get off at the next port, you will book travel directly to Brin-177. And until then," he raises his eyebrows at me, "if I get any indication *whatsoever* that you plan on selling this umemeh for personal gain, I'm handing you over directly to the authorities."

"I can*not* believe you are allowing this," mutters the doc from the back wall.

"And I cannot believe you would insinuate that I, a graduate of Groebel's School of Xeno-Zoology and recipient of the… uh… nnoying-ay amma-lay humanitarian award, would ever *sell* an endangered animal for my own benefit!"

The doc blinks at me, incredulous. "Seriously?"

"I can barely believe it either." Reyes shakes his head. "As I said," Hotpants points a finger at me, "Any indication, at all, that something underhanded is going on, and I'll have you arrested. Understood?"

I gulp painfully and nod. "Of course," I say, and lean back into the clean linens. When was the last time I slept on clean sheets? It's probably been over a decade, truly. I close my eyes.

My quanta-com buzzes away on my wrist below the sheets, and I'm too afraid to check it in front of the doc. What if it's Greel Truyoza checking in? I am still bound to the deal I made with that devil, and he's going to kill me in ways Hotpants could never even think of. Arrest? A field day in comparison. I swallow painfully.

All I have to do is keep up this charade until we make it to the next port.

I can do this. I've already made it through a little oxygen deprivation. I've lived on Hialeah; I can survive anything. Hang it all.

I close my eyes again, and this time, I allow myself to fall into the darkness that rushes at me.

chapter eight

"There's no way," I say, huffing between words, "that this is normal." The trees around me are bare in the frigid fall season, and a distant bird caws in response. Even though the employee track in the Hialean Highlands slopes upward at a moderate incline, it doesn't usually pose a challenge for me. Nor is it typically so creepily desolate.

I pant for breath as I trek towards the yellow crap hover-tram that waits for me, only a mile climb ahead. A spotted four-eared lynx staggers past me, half-dragging itself down the mountain. Odd behavior for a feline that's usually quite agile.

My own walk soon becomes erratic, weaving back and forth along the lane. I put out an arm to prevent myself from walking into a bush off the track. Then the trees start blurring into the grey sky, and my stomach flip flops. Black spots bloom in my vision. "What... the... voids? I... didn't... even... drink," each word is a struggle to get out, "before... my shift."

I have the presence of mind to tap my rings to activate my quanta-com display.

"Oxygen deprivation alert." Painfully bright letters flash across my retinal lenses. "Warning: Hypoxia State sustained for 20 minutes."

My head is starting to ache. "I need..." I pant, "to get back." I stumble back down the path, wondering if the four-eared lynx ever made it out, or if any of those blurry patches on the ground are collapsed animals. But I can't even stop to investigate. My head is being cleaved apart by intense pain and each step is an extraordinary effort. "Get… back."

I collapse on the employee rail car at the foot of the Highlands and ride it for hours until I have the physical strength to move on my own again. My muscles are floppy rubber. When I trust myself to walk safely, I force my way into my boss's office.

Griffith's rounded body perks up from its signature slump behind his desk, and his grey eyebrows form deep, angry furrows. "You're telling me you didn't collect any of the manure in the Highlands? For the whole day?"

"That's not the point," I retort. "Griff. The O2 sprinklers are out in that region. All the animals – in the entire region – will have to relocate. What if… Oh, Bob. It's hibernating season. What if the dromidaire-bears go up there to hibernate like they do every year? They'll all die!"

"Stop being so dramatic. Any animal with two brain cells will do what it needs to survive, Savage. What else do you want? You want me not to dock your pay? Because I've got to tell you, it's not going to happen."

My shock dissolves into anger, like granules of sugar in boiling water. "I am not risking my *life* to collect *crap*," I reply, voice rising. "You're out of your mold-addled mind if you think it's legal to dock my pay!"

He slams his meaty hand against the metal desk. "No crap, no pay. You know the deal. What do you care, anyway? We all know your bank account's been seized. Your salary goes straight to the loan sharks."

I grind my jaw, but try to stuff it away in light of the bigger concerns at stake. To calm myself, I perform my mental ritual of adding this conversation to the many lawsuits and police reports I can only file in my imagination. In real life, my reports mysteriously disappear every time I submit them to the police system.

And I've tried, many times. The police never come out here to the edge of the known galaxy. The unspoken rule is that anyone who chooses to live this close to a void is on their own.

Fleetingly, I wish the familiar wish, that my parents weren't hippies. That they lived in a society where people used quanta-coms and galactic currency instead of their commune where all electronics are forbidden and a fair-trade system is used to exchange goods. For all they know, I'm out in the universe happily tending to animals. Living the dream. But there's no point in going down that path, and just as quickly as it came, the thought vanishes.

I ball my fists by my thighs. "Send someone to repair the O2 sprinklers, Griffith. There are *hundreds* of species who live in those Highlands."

"Oh, cry me a river." He waves a hand dismissively, then his eyes home in on me. "Wait. Is this a hormonal thing for you? Is that what's going on here?"

And there we have it: Asshole Griffith in a nutshell. If I want to help those animals, I'll have to do it a different way. He'll never change. "Fuck you, Griffith."

"Anytime, sweetheart. You know that. While we're on the topic, listen. I've got some advice for you. You want to do some good around here? Loosen up a little. You're too uptight. Show more cleavage. Do *something* to boost morale! You know what your problem is? You're not a team player; you need to share the goods. If Victor from accounting wants to cop a feel from time to time, *let him* without getting so whiny about it. If you want people to start taking you seriously, you need to start treating others better."

I am vibrating with anger. "My *body* is not a communal salsa dip!"

"See? This is exactly what I'm talking about." He gestures in my direction and grimaces. "You complain an awful lot, but where's the team spirit?"

"I'm not showing titty to save the animals, Griffith. Fuck you."

"Your choice, sweetheart."

I storm out of his office.

———

"Wake up," a prim female voice slices through my dreams. "Trafficker. I know you can hear me. Wake. Up."

I groan and screw my eyelids down tighter. Apparently, one side effect of oxygen deprivation is my subconscious forcing me to relive my previous experience with hypoxia, along with all the charms of Hialeah. I squint with one eye to see if my silence has succeeded in ridding me of that shrew of a doctor. It hasn't.

She gives my shoulder an insistent tap. "Trafficker. Get up."

"Oh, were you talking to me?" I feign innocence and stretch out dramatically. "You pronounced animal rights activist wrong."

"Please. We are both intelligent women; lies are unnecessary. You do need to remain awake, however. It is dinner time, and your presence has been specifically *requested*." The doctor manages to say that last word like it really means mandated. With a hint of a smile on her worm-like lips, she adds, "You are no longer welcome in my medical bay."

"Was I ever?" I say under my breath as I sit up. The doc either pretends or legit can't hear me, intent as she is on rubbing the umemeh's head and cooing when he muzzles her hand. She beams when his other head comes over to investigate. Honest to Bob, she's nicer to animals than her actual patients. But that's fine. I don't need her to like me; I just need her to not report me to the police, like that backstabber, Weasel.

"Ticktock," she hums, raising a brow at me. She continues to pet the umemeh, and apparently sees no contradiction here.

"Wow. I get it, okay. Can you at least tell me where I'm supposed to go?"

The med bay doors open, and a dirty man in coveralls shuffles in.

"Right on time!" Doc straightens her coat and puts her hands into the noiseless, electronic washie for sterilization. She continues speaking while her hands are under the special light. "Saffron Savage, meet Pete Lombardy. Due to pure coincidence, sheer idiocy, or both, Pete here was your cargo bay rescuer. He'll show you to the mess."

I scrutinize the newcomer. His face is noticeably dirty, from the mud smears to the patchy, scraggly beard-thing attached to his chin. A forest green floppy cap, or maybe a sadly deflated balloon, lounges on his oily hair. As far as male specimens go, he's about the average of what passes for normal on Hialeah. I probably don't look much better myself. Or smell any better, I frown as a whiff drifts up from currently exposed armpits.

"Welcome aboard the *Waterloo*," Pete grins a gap-toothed smile and takes off his cap to perform a sloppy bow.

"You saved my life, my man. Thank you." I wave my hand in a triple loop, which is the only fancy way to respond to a bow. Doc makes a huffing noise, but Pete grins. I begin to pull myself out of bed but stop when too much skin is exposed to the chilly air in the med bay. I'm still wearing the medical gown.

"Um. This may be the local fashion rage, but I'd hate to take it from you, Doc. Plus, I'm sure you'll need this paper-thin gown for something. Like, to use as a tissue. Or a pasta strainer. My old clothes will work fine for dinner."

"Those were chuted to the vacuum," the doc replies, looking up from her pad.

My mouth opens and shuts several times. "You can't just…!"

"Your clothing was flea-ridden and full of excrement. I can't comprehend how they allowed you to pass the full pathogen scan at The Horse's Ass." She waves a hand absently upwards. "A pair of coveralls have been issued to you and left in your new room. Normally I'd allow my patients to borrow a robe, but in this case," she raises her eyebrows at the umemeh, "I couldn't be sure you wouldn't sell it behind my back. And now, you may get your alcohol marinated skeleton out of my infirmary. It's high time to make room for patients who don't self-inflict their injuries."

"Hey! I didn't self-inflict anything!" I glare at her, my eyeballs practically blazing fire. The universe fucked me over royally with Hialeah, and even though I'm trying to claw my way free, it hasn't stopped throwing punches. How was this insensitive woman ever approved to treat patients? Like, who thought it would be a good idea for her to be in regular contact with other humans? Living ones, no less. Before I can gather a more coherent retort, Pete lugs me by the arm into the hallway and out of the impending war zone. The umemeh lops along behind us happily, attention focused on my hair. One of his heads nuzzles me by my ear before his other head butts me from behind. I swat him away and take in a deep breath. It's only then that my awareness of my surroundings manages to filter through the red. What I see surprises me. The white-and-grey hallways are immaculately clean. Nothing like the employee dorms on that shithole Hialeah.

"Alright, so *that* was the medical bay," Pete says, a hint of humor crossing his face.

"Oh? It wasn't golf at the Rivington?" I try to match Pete's careless tone and easy pace. "Coulda fooled me by the stick up Doc McIceberg's butt."

"Yeeeeeah." Pete spreads his hands apologetically. "Sorry about that. Doc Williams plays it pretty narrow. If you want to get her to start screeching over the loudspeaker, ask her if you can use her med bay to cook up a batch of cannabis moonshine." He cracks a smile.

I snort. "In her med bay? I may be oxygen deprived but I'm not that stupid." I stop as Pete gives a cough. "Wait. Somebody actually asked her that?"

"It was me. I asked her," he confesses with a sheepish grin. "And after she squawked into that mic *and* put me on probation with the Captain, she stared down at me through those glasses for a week."

"Who *is* the ship's Captain?" I've continued to shelter a small hope that I can work my way into the Captain's good graces, despite the Sergeant and Doctor's cold welcome.

"You've met him! Sergeant Reyes. Ex-military guy, really buff? Stickler for the rules."

My hopes deflate into a sad puddle. Right. "It's a miracle anyone on this ship is sane. Between Sarge and Doc on everyone's asses all the time, ya'll probably miserable working here!"

"Oh, I wouldn't say that. Not at all," he says, walking alongside me in the hallway. "Hey, did I hear you were from Hialeah?" I nod. "I think…" Pete squints up into the air and drifts off into a conversational lull. Suddenly he snaps his fingers. "Yeah! That's the place where they have squirrel cock-fighting, right?"

I squeeze my eyes shut, but the din of fifty dirty, stinking men shoved around a makeshift arena shouting and cheering fills the back of my mind. "Uh. Technically we're a zoo. Well, not we, anymore. But, yeah."

A sour pit has formed in my belly at the mention of that dark place. I place my arm around Fred's left neck, the side with the head that gets more easily distracted. This was all a way to escape that place, and now look at me. Half-naked and indebted to the most demented criminal alive in the galaxy.

I'm too engrossed in my dark thoughts that when a screeching and flapping sound fills the hallway, I duck too late to avoid an incoming projectile which zig-zags directly into my hair.

"What is it?!" I shriek at glass-breaking octaves, all while fearfully swatting at my hair. There's an animal of some kind trapped in my curls and desperately trying to escape the knotty, knotty nest that Fred's made of it. I start hopping around and swinging my head from side to side to dislodge it. "Pete!" I scream. "Peeeeeete!"

"I got it!" he yells in my face. "Keep still! I'll get 'im!"

"Easy for you to say!" I reply, but I force my legs to be stone when Pete reaches into my tangles. I can't help but jerk reflexively when the thing flutters against my head.

"Be still or you'll hurt him!" he says urgently, and his breath smells like dead dog.

"That wasn't even a concern!" I yelp. The umemeh snorts

repeatedly from both heads, but he's staring at me directly with his right head, where his jaw is rapidly working in a circular motion that is all too familiar. "Oh no. Oh no, no, no! Pete, do not freak out the umemeh. He'll spit."

"Just be *still*," he replies, working at my knots while each second frantic animal movements make more of them.

I whimper. The umemeh's left head snorts angrily, eyes now trained on my hair and wide in fear. When the right head brays, the left side chimes in, too. That's all the encouragement the right head needs to lob a spray of spit directly at my face, which catches in my eye. "Shitfaced fucking sin!" I yell and rub my stinging eye. With a surprised squeak, an object darts down the hall back towards the med bay. Or at least, tries to dart. He's zig-zagging as he goes, drunkenly flapping his stupid wings.

I take a minute to watch him fly away in silence.

"So, we have a small bat problem," Pete says in the conversational lull.

I wait for my heart to stop thudding so fast. "Why. In. Void's. Name. Do you have a *bat problem?*" I wipe the rest of my face dry, rubbing my hands against the flimsy medical gown. Pete belts out into an emphysema-laden laugh, the gaps from his missing teeth on prominent display. "Seriously," I reply, irately. "This is *not* a bat's natural habitat!"

"Well," Pete replies, straightening out. "Doc thought it might be a good idea for the ship's garden. You know, with all the guano."

"Are ya kidding?" I can't believe they decided to home bats for their crap. "Humans stopped using bat guano since their pre-space-age days. Ready-made, manufactured fertilizer is available everywhere. Dirt cheap, too."

"Hah. Well, Doc thought it would be more organic this way, and Sarge kinda has a thing for animals." He takes off his cap to scratch behind his ears and shrugs. "Hindsight is twenty-twenty I guess."

"And now you have a bat problem," I say darkly.

"Yeah. They mostly keep to the garden, and sometimes they roam about when the lights are low. They've been acting a little batty lately," he nudges me at his own joke. "They've been comin' out when the lights are full on. But generally, they keep the mosquitos under control. They're a good thing."

"A good thing?" I mutter a curse. "Unless you're selling bat meat, there is no void-forsaken reason you haven't called pest control… Hey." I stop in my tracks. "What *does* this ship do exactly? Other than rescuing animal rights activists and their idiot animal companions. *Are* you selling bat meat?"

"What! No way," Pete grins. "We sell shitters!"

My heart skips a beat. "No."

"Yeah!" Pete responds enthusiastically. "…And all their parts. We all gotta crap, but our shitters are the kind that'll keep 'em down, if you catch my drift. You know, with space and odd gravity or whatnot. Good business, good people."

No. No. No.

I did not leave my job shoveling shit to be involved in anything that remotely has to deal with shit, ever again. I rub my eyeballs through closed lids. "Pete, I'm going to need to know exactly what kind of intoxicants are available on board this ship."

"Oh! Well that's a bit of a good thing here," Pete replies, brightening up. "We have an ongoing ship-brewed cannabis moonshine that we all contribute to, even the doc."

I stop and blink through my surprise. "Wow."

"Yeeeeah. Turns out, as long as it's not in her med bay, she's okay with it. I did some research, since cannabis is pretty easy to grow in a hydroponics rack. Stir up a weed tincture with a mint syrup and, bam! You've got our ship's signature blend. I like to call it Mint-Trip. Guaranteed to fuck you up real good." He pauses and turns to me. "As it turns out, there are buyers at every port for that shit!" Pete practically beams. "Now I'm pretty much everybody's best friend!"

"I'll bet. Wow. I'd be happy to test it out for you. If you ever, uh, need an outside opinion."

"Oh, yeah, sure!" Pete replies. "This one's your room, here. Lucky number thirteen." Pete's already stopped at the end of the hallway, and he waves at the door in front of him. "Should have everything you need, including your own washie," he says, referring to the handheld hygiene device that Hialeah didn't even have the decency to give us. We had to use old-fashioned water, and pay for it out of our salaries. "The bathroom's the door at the end of the hall… oh, right. Right next door to you." He jerks his thumb at the door at the apex of the hall, ninety degrees to my own. "Looks like you got the lucky spot." He gives a rasping chuckle.

Festering ring-faced narwhal, will my life ever not be filled with poop? At this rate, I'll be buried in a porta-potty coffin.

"Oh, it's not so bad!" Pete says. "The bathroom ain't so loud as in other places. Unless Guppy's in there. Then the whole ship can hear him take a shit. I swear, that guy's farts should be weaponized!" Pete takes another long wheezing laugh.

"Charming," I say, taking a step past Pete to take a look at my new room. Any lingering hopes about my temporary reprieve come crashing down like an egg hitting pavement. The room is a long narrow box, wide enough for two twin beds and nothing else. One, or both beds can be folded up to make room for someone to actually move about in there. There, on the red fleece blanket of the open bed, is a folded-up pair of blue coveralls. Stars be loved.

I glance back and forth between the clothes and the animal behind me. I don't know how the umemeh is going to fit in that crayon-box of a room, let alone enter it willingly. How the voids do I do this?

This would be a lot freaking easier with addicto-nip. And/or LSD.

"Heya, Pete?" He's drumming out a tune on his leg while checking messages on his log a couple paces down the hall. "Pete," I repeat more insistently, and this time get his attention. "My bag. Did you find it on me by any chance when you rescued me? It's got treats and stuff for the umemeh."

Pete's face lights up with a grin when he sees me talking to him. Like a puppy. "Yeah, sure. I think. All of your shit should be together. We'll have to ask the doc for it."

So I wasn't being paranoid. The doc has locked away my bag, and there's no way she'll give it back. If she searches it, she'll find my tranquilizers. And my LSD. It may be commonplace to carry that around on Hialeah, but last time I traveled the galaxy, it wasn't legal elsewhere. "I need that bag back, Pete. For girl stuff." It's a lie, but one that usually heads off any questions. "Would you mind?"

Pete looks like he's about to object, but the umemeh's actually gone in to explore bedroom number thirteen of his own volition. I make the most of this Bob-blessed moment and hustle in after him. "Thanks *so* much, Pete! You're the best!" I shut the door on his face.

I hear Pete's footsteps receding as I lean against the closed door. I take in my new room. A glorified closet. The room is tidy, at least. And the corners have no grime. Like, zero. Maybe they have slaves or bots going around with toothbrushes and tooth-picks to get this place as sparkling as it is, but I sure as shit am not about to imitate their insane levels of sanitation myself.

I take a deep breath. It feels good; I'm not going to lie. To be off Hialeah, and somewhere clean, for once. To be free. Even if it's with an idiot umemeh on some terrible journey for Greel Truyoza. For the first time in years, I don't have to live with a bunch of testosterone-addled men who keep trying to demoralize me. I don't have to live with mountains of animal dung. I'm free, and I'm clean. My eyes are stinging slightly, and I blink rapidly.

The umemeh's started nibbling on the uniform that was laid out on my bed. "Oh, Fred," I say, and gently rub his neck to get him off my clothes. With a sigh, I yank off the medical gown and get into the comfortable, sturdy fabric of the ship's coveralls.

When Pete knocks on my door again, our clothes match perfectly. "No dice," he says with an apologetic shake of his head. "Doc said the bag's been confiscated."

"Oh, for the love of Bob," I say. "Did she have any suggestions for how I'm supposed to care for the umemeh? Because all my treats and tranqs are in that bag."

Pete scratches behind his ear. "Bob? I thought the umemeh's name was Fred."

I frown. I've lived on Hialeah for so long, I've forgotten that no one else has heard of Bob Schwinn, messiah of ferrets. "Bob's a Hialeah guy." I quickly wave to dismiss mention of our orange savior. "Pete, focus. How am I supposed to feed the umemeh?"

He shifts uncomfortably. "She said… She said Cap'n wants the umemeh to come to dinner."

You've got to be kidding me. "In the mess?"

"That's what she said."

"What the fuck." I fume. "The umemeh is an animal! A large, very smelly, non-intelligent animal. What are they thinking?"

I freeze as realization dawns. Hotpants Sarge hasn't stopped testing me. He wants to see if I play the role of the animal rights activist; he's probably expecting me to feed the umemeh out of my own hands. And if I can't pull it off successfully, it will be all the proof he needs that I'm selling Fred for my own personal gain. But I'll show him; I'd play any part to get free of Hialeah. I curse him anyway as I tug Fred along through the hallways.

"Oh, good news!" Pete calls back to me. "Cap'n gave the go-ahead for some Mint-Trip tonight! He said we're to give you a warm welcome."

"Really?" That's the first pleasant surprise I've had this whole journey. I could use a strong drink. "Thank the mother loving apes."

So, it's not all storm clouds and thunder after all.

chapter nine

The Captain, aka Sergeant Michael Reyes, is already in the mess when we arrive. I forgot how sweat-worthy he is. Maybe it's because I haven't seen a cleaned-up version of a man in just under a decade, but holy hotpants, someone please hold me back before I start drooling publicly.

On second thought, scratch that. The dude's got three women fawning all over him by the food line, so I'd have to fight a crowd to get there. Plus, he'd probably snarl at me or have me arrested or something. There goes that idea.

I nod over at the women. "Let me guess," I say to Pete. "Everyone wants to date the captain?"

"What? Nah. It's not like that. Well, except for Juliet." Pete brings his head closer to mine to look at the group at the same angle as me. "She's that young, pretty one there, with the lipstick."

That's how they talk about her? I shake my head, but I don't explain to him what it's like living on Hialeah. A 'pretty' woman would be targeted with sexual harassment from day one. She'd wash out in a month – if she had the funds to leave. If not, she'd try really hard to not be the 'pretty one' anymore. I pull out a strand of my half-chewed hair to examine while Fred is still busy at work on the rest of it. I haven't thought about looking 'pretty' since… well, since before Hialeah.

I'd forgotten that life in other places could be not-nightmares.

"So, over here'r the trays and shit," says Pete, gesturing to an obvious stack of blue plastic next to a buffet line. Behind the line, I can make out a multi-armed robot on wheels who is resupplying empty trays and stirring others.

"That's the cook back there. Say hi to Otis," Pete tells me.

I wave. "Hi to Otis."

The robot stops and turns his glass, multi-faceted disco-ball of a head towards me. An LED screen behind the glass lights up with a smile and eyes facing my direction. Which is at too odd of an angle against his shoulder to be remotely human-like, but on the other hand, his head is a fully-rotating disco ball. I'm just grateful he's not showering me with strobing lights.

"Otis, this is Saffron," Pete says. If he's bothering to introduce me, it must be an intelligent robot, then, only a short step below the most enhanced level of human intelligence. Intelligent robots are great for many things, but conversation's not one of them. It's the lack of emotions that cripples them. Unlike human-machine hybrids, or hybes, who have the intelligence of computers and the emotional finesse of humans. Of course, that varies with computer and human models, but at least they can hold down a nuanced conversation. "Heya, Saffron, you got any dietary restric'shins?"

I shake my head. "Edible food is a plus."

"I *only* prepare edible food," replies Otis, with a voice that emanates from somewhere in his chest region. "Every meal is prepared from a foundation of Gorga-star band nutrient packs and a blend of whichever raw ingredients we have available, most typically a mixture of green leafy or tuberous vegetables. They are added in ideal proportions for a delicious and nutritious meal. Certainly, an edible one."

So, sarcasm is out with this one, then.

Fred, who must have caught a whiff of the food, has abandoned my hair and is trying to cram one of his heads below the glass counter that's designed to keep the food sanitary.

"Fred!" I yell, before remembering that the animal doesn't actually have a name, nor will he respond to Fred. But my call was enough to attract the attention of the room. It's dead silent and thirty-odd eyeballs are aimed my way. Great. Now I have to go through with the whole act. "Hah. Um, Fred! Darling," I say, my mouth curling around the unfamiliar word. How the void do namby-pamby animal rights activists talk? "My love," I add, but my mouth feels like it's in a sneer. I try to work it into a smile. "Fred, sweetheart!" That's better. I think. My mouth is smiling. "Please get your head out of there. I'll give you some fresh vegetables, my sweet darling."

Wow. Wash my mouth out with soap.

"That looked like the most painful sentence you've ever said in your life," calls Sergeant Reyes from his table. He's grinning.

"Did she just..." Pete is obviously enjoying drawing out this moment. "Did you just call the umemeh *darling*?" He guffaws. "You may be savvy, Saffron Savage, but *sweet* sure ain't your thing!" He lets out his rasping laugh, and other chuckles emanate around the room. They're all laughing at me.

"Fuck all you motherfuckers, okay?"

Reyes' grin grows wider.

"He's an umemeh!" I protest, angrily throwing my hands in the air. "Why did you want him here?! How the voids am I supposed to keep him from sticking his head into a sanitary food space?"

"Wildlife is not permitted within the sanitary glass enclosure," says Otis in monotone.

"See?" I gesture to unhelpful Otis, then move to get Fred. "While we're on it, why the voids can't I have my own supply bag? This would be so much easier with the supplies I brought from the zoo!" I shove my hands on my hips.

"Everyone, meet our 'Savvy' Saffron Savage," Sergeant Reyes

says in a booming voice, walking over to join us at the line. The room erupts in grunts and hellos. "Savvy, this is everyone."

I'm thrown by the new nickname, but I'll take it. Honest to Bob, I actually like it. I manage a little wave. "Yeah, yeah. Thanks." Reyes is standing eight inches away from me and I think I could lick eighty percent of his chest muscles from here, but he's looking at me all smug, so now is not the time to appreciate the sizzle. I can be all business. And animal loving. "Hey, look," I say, sticking one hand on my hip and thrusting out a leg. "Reyes. Do you have any lettuce or cabbage of any other leafy greens I can feed Fred? I don't want him to keep bothering Otis."

"That's Captain or Sergeant to you," Reyes says with just enough caution in his voice that says he knows how to spank a woman and have her scream it. Before I can scoop up my dropped jaw, Reyes turns and fishes out an entire head of cabbage from behind the partition. "Will this do it?"

"Yeah," I say, blinking. *Business*, I remind myself, and snap to it. "Right. Absolutely!" I grab it out of his hands and, in one fell motion, rip the sphere in half, handing the sergeant one of the halves. "Do me a favor. Hold this in front of Fred's right head. The two don't communicate."

Captain Hotpants raises his eyebrows but does as he's been asked. Meanwhile I wave my half of the cabbage in front of the idiot's left head, which is currently trying to turn itself sideways to get into the slitted opening on the glass case that's meant for hands to grab plates. Fred's left head is diverted by the cabbage, and I swing him around front to where Sergeant Reyes is feeding the other head.

"Thanks, Sargie. I got it from here." I nod as I grab the cabbage half away from him, and feel a flood of satisfaction when I notice the look of aggravation on his face. Waving both cabbage halves in front of the umemeh, I lead the idiotic animal, both heads in agreement, over to a back corner, where I unceremoniously shred the two cabbage halves and leave them in a mound on a bench by the rear wall.

"Poor guy!" exclaims Pete. "You gonna let him eat off a bench?"

"Are you joking?" I stare at Pete incredulously, and realize that no, he wasn't trying to be funny. "You do know that Fred doesn't use a fork and knife when he's in the wild?"

"No, no. Pete's on to something here," says Reyes, a glint in his eye. "Fred's our guest. I think he should have a spot at the table. In fact, we should sit him right next to you. That way, you can know when he needs to get more food and catch him before he starts sniffing around in places he shouldn't. What do you say?"

I glare at Reyes. He must be insane! But the big oaf is smirking at me. He's testing me, again. I glance around the room, at faces with varying levels of comprehension of the subtext here.

"Sure, right, fine," I say cautiously. "Only, I wouldn't want to, uh, make everyone else uncomfortable. You know. The smell and all."

"Nonsense!" Sergeant Reyes says with a grand hand wave. "I'm *inviting* him to the table! If it really bothers anyone else, I'll be the one to sit on the other side of Fred. Besides, he's adorable!"

I stare at Reyes like he's lost his void-forsaken mind, but he's smiling dreamily at Fred. I had forgotten Pete's comment about the Captain and animals. "This is unbelievable," I mutter below hearing range as I scoop up the shredded cabbage confetti and bring them over to the table. The groupie girls clear away a spot, and I can hear them grumbling too.

"Guess we won't be having salad for the next few days," Lipstick Juliet remarks loudly to her friends with a sniffle. I may have been as naïve as her when I first moved to Hialeah, but I was never this entitled. I have no patience for that attitude when this is Fred's only available food choice.

"No salad?" I say aloud to Lipstick, placing a hand to my heart. "Oh no! We'll have to eat the other five hundred dishes Otis has prepared! And with that risky animal hanging around, we might even have to skip the gold cutlery and lace napkins! How ever will we survive?"

Juliet blinks several times, then aims a frown at me. "You're really quite rude."

I roll my eyes. "Yeah, well. Life ain't a song for all of us, Lipstick."

"All right, all right," says Sergeant Reyes, getting between us. "Our guest is obviously from a different planet where there are strikingly different manners. And food choices." He shoots me a warning glance as he steers me over to my seat at the table, right next to Fred. Once I'm seated, Reyes stands on a nearby chair to address the rest of the room. "Our feisty friend here is, in fact, an animal rights activist! And I'd like us to facilitate her rescue mission with a warm welcome. Everyone, I've asked Pete to break out the Mint-Trip tonight."

A rowdy cheer goes up through the group. Maybe he hopes that getting me all liquored up will loosen my tongue, but the joke's on him. I've had years of drinking practice on Hialeah.

"You all know your own tolerance levels," Reyes continues. "Don't drink so much you can't work next shift. Yes, I'm looking at you, Dimitry."

Guffaws sound all around the group, but the only one who actually looks unhappy is Juliet. Maybe the drink doesn't have enough lettuce content for her. Who knows.

A steaming mountain of goop is plopped on the table in front of me. "I got you a plate," Pete gestures to the pile of food he's set down. "Since I know you have your hands full with Fred. Personally, I hate that green stuff, but the brown glop is delicious. Even if it looks like bird shit. You should try it." Pete shrugs. Then, he does the unthinkable for any guy on Hialeah, all of whom were trying to get in my panties. Pete walks away.

I'm left speechless. No slime-ball winks, no mention of my titties. He just went to get his own freaking food.

"I think the words you're searching for are, 'Thank you,'" says Sergeant Reyes, sitting to the other side of Fred.

I open my mouth to say, "Fuck you," but shut it before I let anything fly. What is going on here?

"I haven't, um…" I try to explain. "People aren't exactly… nice on Hialeah. Not without a reason." I glance back over at Pete, who's now speaking to a frowning Juliet. I sit down by my food and blink rapidly. "And fuck you, anyway," I add quietly to my plate.

"You're welcome," Reyes replies, but I'm not sure if he heard me correctly beside Fred, who's noisily tearing his cabbage leaves between us.

I decide not to repeat it.

chapter ten

"Saffron," Sergeant Reyes says after I've gotten in a few bites. He gestures with his fork at the two women down the table from him. "I want you to meet Lucy and Gisella." The two women by his side smile at me.

"Gisella's our chief engineer." The one closer to him, Asian and freckled, gives me a small wave.

"Glad to have you aboard," Freckles says with a genuine grin.

"Hi," I reply, then push Fred's inquisitive head away from my dinner plate.

"Lucy in the pink there is my navigator," the pale woman at the end wearing a hot-pink fuzzy hat smiles serenely. "Brilliantly skillful," Hotpants adds.

I nod and gently steer another umemeh head away from my plate and back to his cabbage pile.

"Marc, over there," an older, grizzled man grunts, "also works engineering, along with Guppy and Dimitry." Two perfectly handsome, attractive specimens each wave in a very normal way. But this is way too many people for me to remember. I'm starting to get overwhelmed.

"You've met your rescuer, Pete, who works in cargo," Reyes continues. "He does our grunt work, along with Boris." A large mountain of a man nods at me through mouthfuls of food. I wave, and completely give up on keeping the umemeh away from my goop. If it's not one head, it's the other.

"Juliet here," he gestures to the frowning Lipstick, "is studying to be a navigator, and has been working with Lucy over our last voyage."

Reyes looks up at the ceiling. "The only one you haven't met is Rosemary, my second in command. She's on the bridge now. She and I take turns during dinner call, but otherwise, we prefer to have all hands present for family dinner."

"You've turned your ship into the Family Funhouse?"

Sergeant Reyes nods, but his attention is elsewhere. "Something like that. Speaking of everyone, where's Doc Williams?"

"Yeah, I really gotta speak to her," says a blonde dude down the table between bites. He was part of the clusterfuck of introductions Hotpants just rolled out. Dimitry, maybe? His eyebrows are furrowed, but his tight body is a hot nugget I wouldn't mind dipping. "S'not for me," he says swallowing down his mouthful. "Something's going on with Burt. I did what she told me but he's acting even sicker."

Burt. Burt. Burt.... I run through the list of names that were thrown at me like a carousel, but the name Burt doesn't ring a bell. I cast a glance around the table, but everyone is looking very concerned in Dimitry's direction. Maybe he has an alter-ego?

"Awww," says Freckles. "Poor little guy."

"What's going on now, Dimitry?" Hotpants asks.

"I mean, it's what you can see. He's just laying about and stuff. He's not eating or anything either. I'm worried about him."

I do a quick glance around the table, and they're all ooh-ing and aww-ing at Dimitry.

"What'd Doc Williams say?" Reyes presses him.

"She said it might be arthritis and to give him a micro dose of anti-inflammatories. But that made him worse. He won't even respond now. I'm really worried, Cap'n." He frowns down at his coveralls pocket and scratches a little orange fuzz-ball there.

Holy shit! That's not a fuzz-ball, I realize, it's a pygmy orangutan. A very, very still, pygmy orangutan.

"Is he dead?" I ask.

Twenty angry eyes rivet towards me. "He's not dead, you insensitive monster!" exclaims Juliet, tears in her eyes. This only confirms my suspicions about her ability to last on Hialeah.

"Hey there, paper skin!" I put my hands up in mock surrender. "I was just asking. We have these little dudes on Hialeah, too. They're a riot!" I walk over and lean in to inspect Burt. "Can I see him?" In response to the concerned looks, I add, "I'm a trained zoologist."

Gently, Dimitry lifts the limp fuzzball and places him in my palm. Still warm.

"He hasn't gotten into anything, has he?" I ask. A flicker of uncertainty goes around the table. "I only ask because this one time, on Hialeah, something like this happened to Jerry at parliament. He was a pygmy orangutan, too. Let me explain." I delicately hand Burt back to Dimitry. "On Hialeah, we have the pygmy orangutans put on these fluffy white wigs to hold a mock-parliament for the tourists. It's a sold-out house, every time. The Speaker of the House, Jerry, was a total ass." I snort, remembering that pint-sized ball of Trumpian posturing.

"No way!" Freckles exclaims. Gisella, I think her name was? Her jaw is literally hanging open.

"Yeah, seriously. Well, first of all, we paid them tic-tacs. You know, the harmless little sugar pills? Yeah. Those. Orangutans, even the small pygmy dudes, understand the concept of trade. And Jerry would get extra, for being Speaker of the House."

"Can we go back to the parliament part?" Freckles asks.

I raise my eyebrows at her. "A whole group of pigmy orang-utans is really freaking adorable. They're pretty solitary by nature, so when you get 'em to sit around a table they just screech at each other. Which is like, so true to the real-life dodos we've got running this galaxy. And, as a bonus, when the pygmy orang-utans get *really* mad they start throwing peanuts."

"Tic-tacs, Savage. Where were you going with this story?" asks Sarge. One look at him and you would think the guy had no sense of humor at all.

"Right. So this one day, it's Marook on duty when it comes time to hand out the daily tic-tacs. Only Jerry, the over-eager pygmy, jumps into Marook's pocket to take them on his own. Well. He *did* find a bunch of little white pills."

Juliet has her hands covering her mouth.

"Yeah, Marook is a complete moron. Who carries MDMA around in an open pocket *in a pygmy enclosure?* Anyway, Jerry the orangutan fishes it out and waves the bottle around. Little white pills shower the enclosure like it's confetti. The whole parliament goes wild, and luckily, most of 'em only get their hands on one pill a piece. The lot of 'em get completely stoned and looked a lot like your guy there, Burt. They all ended up fine, except for Jerry. Well, Jerry was one greedy, fat dude. He used that muscle to grab three or four of them, and –"

"Alright. That is *enough*," cuts in the captain, fierce and angry. "Dimitry, tell me that Burt hasn't had access to any consumables."

It should be a question, but he says it in such a deadly way that you know Dimitry will be turned into dust if the answer is yes.

"I... uh... don't think so?"

The captain whips his furnace gaze back at me. "What symptoms would a pigmy orangutan have if they consumed a human dose of MDMA?"

"Mostly the same as humans?" I shrug. Thank you, Hialeah, for providing a shit-ton of experience in this one area. "Dilated pupils, lower heart rate and breathing. Only, I wouldn't give 'em anything that kills their kidney at the same time. Like anti-inflammatories. Give him time for his system to flush it out, and he'll recover."

"Dimitry," Reyes says. "You need to meet me in the bridge after dinner."

"Yessir," Dimitry replies, swallowing down a bolus of fear.

My quanta-com chimes, and I tap my middle finger ring to bring up my messages on my contact lenses.

There's a new message from Weasel, under an old message from Greel Truyoza, labeled "Boss" in my quanta-com. Shit. Fuck. Shit. When did I miss a message from Greel Truyoza?

Weasel: You fucking bitch. You're going to pay for that.

Boss: What is the status of the umemeh?

I swallow. Keeping my hands under the table, I tap out my response to Weasel on the projected keyboard, visible only in my contact-lens view. Even if there's a table in the way, the quanta-com can still pick up my finger motions through those rings. "Up yours" takes all of two seconds to write. But as for Boss McKill-Face, I'm going to need a longer message. I glance around the table, and sure no one's watching me, tap out another message. "All well." I take another peek around the table, then add, "Will update you when out of risk of detection."

That will have to do for now.

"Hey, Savvy," says Freckles. Gisella, I correct myself. I won't win any favors by calling her the wrong name. "Can you also check on Prisha Shanti for us?"

I blink. She can't possibly mean the historical figure who negotiated a peace treaty to end the first inter-galactic war. That woman's been dead for centuries. "The *who*, now?"

Captain Reyes perks up at this. "That's not a bad idea," he presses his fingers to his lips, and glances in my direction. Other hopeful eyes turn toward me from around the table.

"Prisha Shanti hasn't had access to Dimitry's stash!" Juliet adds quickly, with a flash of anger in her eyes. "It'll be outside her area of expertise."

"I'm not sure about that," replies Gisella. "Savvy obviously knows a thing or two about animals."

"Literally the *only* thing you get with a xeno-zoology degree," I mutter.

"And if Prisha Shanti were acting, er, more normal," Gisella adds, "we wouldn't need the earplugs."

"Earplugs?" I ask, rising to the bait. I knew it was bait, but I can't help it.

"Prisha Shanti is our defense skunk," Captain Reyes cuts in, scowling. "As of now, she's refused to – well – skunk."

I stare at him from the other side of Fred, then I snort out the loudest guffaw. Bats, a pigmy orangutang, *and* a skunk? That endangered ancient Mondi animal is more rare and coveted than an umemeh. "You guys are kidding me, right?" I go full steam here, filled with glee. No one owns a defense skunk, not without millions of joulos in the bank. Even the zoo who loaned us Fred doesn't have a skunk!

"You don't run a shitter parts business," I exclaim. "There's no way! It's a cover for the GSPCA or some shit like that! Either that, or you're animal traffickers! Tell me I'm right. Am I right?" I glance around the table, still grinning. But I only meet faint, polite smiles in response.

"No... Why aren't you smiling?" After I've asked, the silence is oppressive. Freckles gives me a sympathy smile. "You really do sell shitters?" I blink at the quiet nods that answer me.

"Technically, Dimitry brought Burt along with him as a personal pet when he joined the crew, but we've all adopted him," Gisella says magnanimously. "The bats were meant to be a functional addition," she shrugs. "And Prisha Shanti was a rescue from one of our shadier clients." She gives a worried glance at Sarge.

I groan and bang my head a few times on the table.

"Are you feeling okay?" Gisella asks.

"I was hoping that my life *wasn't* mothballed in a cocoon of crap."

As if on cue, Doc Williams walks in, shooting glances in my direction. She marches directly over to Reyes, and whisper-shouts something in his ear. Based on the number of times she glances in my direction, I'm assuming it's about me.

Oh. It's probably about my bag. She's finally gone through the contents.

"No. It's okay, Doc. That's to be expected. Really," Reyes says in a firm voice. "Let's talk more about this later. Why don't you get some of the green slop from Otis before it's gone? Make yourself a cup of tea with milk?"

Doc stares, unbelieving, at Sergeant Reyes, before she huffs off to the food line.

"She's very protective, Doc Williams," Reyes explains to me through the umemeh heads. But my head is spinning from everything else.

"You have milk?!" I reply, disbelieving. The black-market milk supply on Hileah was one of the paltry benefits of living on a zoo planet, when most other places in the galaxy use synthetic colloids. "You have real milk here, too?"

Just then, Pete comes by with a glass bottle of Mint-Trip and pours me a cup. "Yeah, but only the crappy kind our tea-o-matic can fabricate. Do *not* try it. They say it's an exact replica, but it tastes like chalk. Doc's the only one who likes that stuff."

I open my mouth to respond that a tea-and-milk-vending machine is still a vehe-rrry expensive machine, even if it only cooks up crappy milk. Before I say a single word, Pete adds, "It is kind of nice seeing everyone once a day-cycle. The whole family dinner thing."

Well, I guess I can play Happy Families if I get to drink while doing it. I've drunk my way through much worse and lived. I knock back my ice-cold Mint-Trip and a familiar sting in my eyes and kick in my throat makes me feel all fuzzy and warm. "Don't go too far," I say, coughing at Pete, who's grinning ear-to-ear. "I'm gonna need a few refills."

"I *told* you she could drink!" Pete exclaims while he fills a cup for Sergeant Reyes.

"Hey, Cap'n," I say, holding out my glass for a refill from Pete. "Couldja ask Doc to bring over another cabbage on her way back?"

Sergeant Reyes snorts into his Mint-Trip.

"Hey, Pete!" calls Gisella from down the table. "Don't you finish that bottle! There better be some for me!"

"Come on!" exclaims one of the engineering guys—maybe Guppy? "Last time you drank more than half the bottle! I had to do *all* your work the next day!"

"That's because I was *off-duty*, you moron!" Gisella responds. "Guppy, stop complaining about everything. Pete, don't listen to him."

"Off-duty my ass," Guppy grumbles. The other engineers at the table begin ribbing Guppy, and everyone begins teasing each other. But they're all still smiling – no punches are being thrown, no low-down insults. Just honest to fucking Bob, good-natured teasing.

It's actually… nice. Who knew real people got to live like this? I blink, cup paused half-way to my mouth.

"Hey. Cabbage-head. You okay over there?"

I glance under the umemeh's snout to Reyes, who's apparently been watching me. I swallow thickly. "Cabbage-head?" I ask, trying to lay the skepticism on thick.

"Your hair. Umemeh food." He shrugs.

I nod. Fair.

"You all right, Savvy?" He's looking at me with real concern, and I can't take it. I pull my head back out of his visual range of sight.

Okay, I'm literally hiding behind an umemeh. But, voids.

Everyone gets days off on this ship. They're all smiling around the table, and they're all so freaking friendly. And not one of them knows what it's like to live a single day on Hialeah.

"Yep," I lie. "Totally fine." I knock back my second drink.

Fuck me if I don't enjoy my time while I'm here. I'm off Hialeah. I refuse to stay there in my mind.

chapter eleven

"Savage, get up!" warns a deep voice, stern and demanding. "Saffron Savage!"

I'm well aware of my own name – there's no need to be calling it out at unseemly hours. There's a sudden flood of blinding light in the room and I bury my head under pillows and bedding. I groan when the covers are tugged right off my head.

"Morning, Savvy!" Sergeant Reyes booms.

"Noooo," I croak, hoping this is some very bad dream. I squirm back under the safety of the fuzzy red blanket.

"You *sure* she's okay?" comes Gisella's hushed voice.

"Yeah, she's okay," replies Reyes. "Get up, Savvy."

"Mmmmmmm," I moan, tucking the covers over my pounding head. Exactly how much moonshine did I drink last night?

"Aren't you so cute?" Gisella says in an irritating falsetto. "Yes, you are! You're adorable!"

"She better be talking to the umemeh," I say, eyes glued shut.

"No, she was talking to the elephelk," Reyes replies. "Get out of bed, Savage. You're working today." I snort, still blissfully warm under my starched white sheets. There's no way that's happening. "Maybe I didn't make myself clear. *You're working today.*"

I peek out from under the blankets and squint at Reyes in the overly-bright light. One eyebrow is raised, and his lips are pulled into a firm line. He looks pissed.

"You destroyed our cargo hold. You are eating our food. So, yes, Savage. You are working while you're taking passage on board our ship. There are no free rides."

"I've a splitting headache," I moan, leaning back into my pillows. I'm hit with a flash of inspiration. "Sick day! That's what I'm taking. Today."

But the captain is having none of it. "Either quit drinking or learn to take painkillers. I didn't think you were the type to fall apart over a wee-bitty drink or two."

That gets me sitting straight up in bed. I aim a warning finger at him, and Righteous Reyes smiles primly in response. "*There* you are. I told you I could get her up, Gisella." He casts a quick eye over my naked chest, revealed by the fallen blanket. In that one second, my blood rushes to my head, hot and fast. I yank the blanket back up to my armpits. But all he says is, "Savage, get dressed and report to the cargo bay. You're working for Pete today."

"What!" Clearly my titties were not properly appreciated. Worse, he's making some truly alarming declarations. This is all a bit much. I glare at Sergeant Reyes. "Not cargo!"

He quirks one eyebrow. "Unless you've got any other skills we should know about?" My mouth goes dry.

"Personally, I would love another woman in engineering," Gisella comes to the conversational rescue, a hopeful twist in her voice. "Any chance you know how to work a motherboard?"

I gulp. "Animals. That's my specialty."

"That's right," replies Sergeant Reyes. "And what a noble sacrifice you're making on behalf of this umemeh. We all appreciate your specialty." His voice is so bone dry that it comes out like a barb. "But while you're here, you're going to have to pay your way. Report to Pete."

Reyes has turned away, and my mind starts scrabbling for any ideas. Voids, do I wish I had spent more time on excuses. The umemeh is butting at my head with one of his, and I grab at straws. "I think the umemeh might need to, um, take a nap? And he definitely needs me to watch over him. Here in the room. So he can... be comfortable?"

"It's funny you mention that," Reyes says, and by the way he peers at me, I can tell he's about to deliver a bad news bomb. I gulp. "I spent a long time reading about umemeh last night. It would be cruel to keep him confined to any one room." Reyes gestures vaguely around. His gaze cuts to me sharply. "Which, I'm sure you knew."

"Right." I wave my hand in a go-on gesture.

"Which is why you're rescuing him to begin with."

"Yup. Uh huh." I nod vigorously. "Right."

"So, moving forward, Fred is free to roam the ship. From what I've read, his instincts will prompt him to continue using the same fifteen-meter radius area for... the call of nature. We've already established where that will be, and who'll be cleaning that up." He glances meaningfully at me, and I shrink down under my covers. Did I mention I had a bad feeling about this?

"In fact, Fred won't be interested in any of our wires, or anything that isn't food. Unless it's hair."

I groan and rub a hand over my choppy, uneven head.

"Fred's free to roam about?" Gisella asks, amazed.

"Yup, welcome to our newest mascot!" Reyes beams.

"Temporary," I grumble, begrudging any cheer from this living sour cherry stick. "Temporary mascot."

"Right. Which brings me to my last point. We'll have to make an extra stop for you, since our next berth was supposed to be Latoya's Delicatessen and Corner Port, ten-thousand light years away and in the opposite direction from Brin-177. Not to mention, a thirty-day trip. But don't worry," he says, as I have started relaxing back into my pillow. "We'll drop you off first. Gisella here is researching our options."

"I wanted to ask you," she says brightly. "Do you have any

specific port you'd recommend? You must have done some research already. For us, the bigger the port, the better. That way, there'll be more of a chance to sell product and not take these days as a complete loss. I mean, financially."

I stare dumbly at Gisella's hope-filled face, while my thoughts cycle rapidly. I thought *everyone* knew about the direct shuttle to Brin-177 from Surf & Ceebu, which is only about a hundred lightyears from The Horse's Ass, but apparently not. Surf & Ceebu is a port that's literally bigger than Mondi's moon. It's an insane, multi-layered planet teeming with every variant of intelligent life possible; from human-machine hybrids, to humans with particular organ augmentations and exoskeletons, to us boring primitive schmucks who don't have the cash to change a void-forsaken thing. Oh, and every form of intelligent robotic life you can imagine, of course.

More notably, it's famous on Hialeah for being an outpost for the Brin-177 military, who offer a guard-escorted transport service for tourists wishing to visit Brin-177.

Well, for tourists *without* a questionable criminal background. A category that now excludes yours truly. There's no way I'll squeak by on Surf & Ceebu with a super conspicuous umemeh.

Worse, if they catch me on Surf & Ceebu, those brutes will take Fred from me, and Greel Truyoza will be pissed. No, he'll be more than pissed, he'll be in a spit-flecking, frenzied rage. And my soul-crushing blood-debt will be called in, and he'll drink my soul for tea while three manservants flay my flesh for evening dinner. My blood starts to pump a little faster.

I vigorously shake my head. "Nope. I don't know anything. Nothing. Not a thing!" *Shut up, shut up, shut up!* I bite down on my stupid lips.

Gisella frowns. "Well, there are a few choices that are in the four- to six-day range that won't delay us immensely from Latoya's Delicatessen and Corner Port."

Please don't let it be Surf & Ceebu. I repeat the silent prayer like a mantra. Maybe regular people –non-zoo people – have never heard about the whole Brin-177 military outpost on Surf & Ceebu?

My brain is already whirling to motion. If it's any other port, literally any other port, I'll be okay. Once I know where we're going to dock, I can notify Greel. I'm all kinds of screwed, but if I can just deliver this umemeh, the nightmare will be one step closer to over.

I glance back over at Reyes, whose face has turned stony again. "Can you tell me when you guys decide on a port?" His jaw is set. "Or even, like, the top five choices?"

"No," he replies, simply and firmly. "We wouldn't want any traffickers to catch wind of it, now would we? The fewer people who know our destination, the better." He glances at his watch. "You're almost late for duty, Savage." Reyes turns abruptly and heads out the door.

Gisella shoots me an apologetic glance before scooting out of the room, following the nicest ass you've ever seen. Physically, at least. In personality, he's just a plain ass, without the charm.

I lug myself out of bed, doing a half-assed job of hauling the blanket with me. "Hey! What about some painkillers?" I call after them.

"Dispensed solely by Doc Williams," Sergeant Reyes replies from down the cramped hall. "Head on over to the med bay and then report for duty."

Oh, no. That's a firm nope from me.

This is going to be a long day.

———

I meet Pete by cargo bay C, where the umemeh and I were first discovered.

"Heya Savvy." He rubs his cap several times. "All right, so it's like this. C-Bay's where we keep the full-kits: pre-fabbed, fully-built bathrooms. It's our money room," Pete explains with a gap-filled grin. He waves his hand in the direction down the hallway.

"A-Bay's got electronic hookup conversion kits. That's mostly used by Gisella and the engineering team if we gotta do an install with an older ship or something. And B-Bay's got smaller parts for repair. Toilet lids n' vacuum motors and whatnot. The locker room's here, by C-Bay." He walks over to an open doorway. "You ever need a dolly or a non-pressure tool, it's all here."

Pete walks in and bangs a blue locker door in the lineup. It squeals open, and Pete pulls out a bright yellow, pressure safety suit. It's this ill-fitting, floppy rubberized thing that looks like someone's repurposed an oversized latex glove. "These are what we wear if we gotta head into the cargo bays during flight. Ain't no oxygen in there, as you know."

Pete starts pulling on the horrid yellow suit over his clothing. I take a tentative step in from the hallway, and Fred pushes past me into the antechamber to sniff around at the lockers. They're all the same cobalt blue to me, but Fred's left head is insisting that one of them in the left corner is fascinating, while the right head is stubbornly interested in Pete's locker. At this rate, he'll rip himself in two and end this charade earlier than expected. Good old Fred, true to character.

"Tell the umemeh's not here to take a piss again?" asks a hefty, grizzled cargo hand emerging from C-bay. The guy slams his hand against the locker wall.

I start. The umemeh spits, and a wet gob smacks the locker wall and slides down slowly.

"Boris?" Pete says, a tone of urgency creeping into his voice. "Have a care. We are in the presence of *delicates*," he says waving a hand in Fred's and my direction.

"Who you calling delicate?" I growl.

Boris continues hanging up each item of his suit gingerly. "Yeah, well, I don't give a shit. That piss soaked straight through my suit! What is that stuff? Is it straight up acid?" he asks, peeling away wet layers of his sweater.

"Ah." I now understand the animosity. "Yeeeeah. Umemeh piss is pretty bad. Sorry."

"Couldn't potty train him, eh?"

Actually, Sergeant Reyes was right about one thing. Fred will only be making his tinkles in one place for the rest of this ride. But I don't feel compelled to explain that to locker-slamming Boris.

"He's a wild animal." I reply. "Also, he only pisses once every three days. Give him a break."

"Hey, whoa," says Pete, stepping into the conversation, half-suited up. "No one's attacking Fred here. But the piss has got to be cleaned out of cargo. Savvy, use the small suit in locker six. It should fit you. You're coming in with me."

"Oh, no," I wave my hands apologetically. "I don't know anything about cargo holds. I couldn't possibly."

Pete puts his hands on his hips and stares me down like I killed his grandmother right as she was baking cookies.

"Riiiight," I say. "But I do know a lot about umemeh piss, I guess? I'm coming."

Pete nods and returns to getting dressed. I open locker six.

"What in the far voids is this?" I pull out a wad of limp, hot-pink rubber. "No. Oh, *absolutely* not!" I back away and put my hands on my hips.

Pete turns to look at me again. "It's either that, or Boris's wet one."

I can still smell Boris's suit from here. I grind my teeth together. "Fine," I say at last. Years of harassment on Hialeah have bred a mortification at being caught in the color pink. I reach for the pink suit, then hesitate. There can be no evidence of me having ever touched this. "If you take a picture of me in this, you will die. Understood?"

Pete doesn't answer, but then again, he's already interfacing with his quanta-com, fingers fluttering in the air as he reads off his lenses. I'm pretty sure he's ignoring me. I stare at the neon pink monstrosity. What living creature would allow itself to be seen in the vicinity of that suit? It's like the color pink decided to scream and vomit at the same time, made even more cringeworthy by cartoonish, neon green and yellow flowers. Hideous doesn't begin to describe it.

I grumble as I pull the small suit off the locker wall and begin shoving my legs in.

"Good thing Juliet's spare suit fits her." Boris nods in my direction.

That explains it. Naïve, privileged Juliet. Would I have ever worn something this pink before I moved to Hialeah? I can't remember – it's been too long. What I do know is that Juliet and Hialeah are like oil and water.

Boris is clearly headed off duty, but he's stopped to chat with Pete on his way out. "What's she going to do with the umemeh?" Boris asks Pete. "We don't have a suit that'll fit it."

Pete frowns. "That is a good question. Why don't we ask her?" He turns to me, literally two feet away.

I bare my teeth at Boris in an approximation of a smile. Boris's eyes go wide, and that makes my twisted black heart happy. "Boris?" I ask innocently, and flutter my lashes. "Wanna give Fred a ship tour? You're going off duty, aren't you?"

Boris throws his palms out in self-defense. "Whoa. Whoa. Whoa. Hold it. You're not leaving him out here, are you?" I shrug, and Boris's mouth gapes open. He recovers enough to ask, "Shouldn't you, like, tie it down or something?"

"Nah. It would kill itself trying to rip free. Wild animal, remember? Also, it's dumb as rocks. No survival skills. Umemeh and rope does not make for a good combination," *as I've learned from experience.*

Boris scowls at the umemeh. "You can't let it roam around here and destroy things."

Well, actually, that would be lovely. I mean, it would make my work days come to an end if I had to babysit the moron all day long. Boris is still frowning. Maybe if I rally him to my cause....

"I can't help it if he destroys shit out here." I pretend to clean my nails. "I can't help it if he takes a crap by your locker," I add with a shrug, and sweep my gaze up in time to see a wild flash in his eyes. Never mind that Fred would never actually shit out in the open; umemeh habitually hide their shits. That's all beside the point. "Not my problem," I say nonchalantly. "Take it up with the Captain."

"Oh, you better believe I will," Boris replies.

"Don't worry about him," says Pete after Boris storms out of the room. "He'll warm up to the umemeh eventually."

It takes me a minute to realize Pete is concerned for me. As if Boris hurt my feelings or something. I'm supposed to be playing the animal rights activist here.

"It's just that poor Fred is so misunderstood," I say, trying to stand the way I imagine a crybaby with too much time on their hands would when whining. I put my hand to my forehead in a feigned melodramatic pose. "He's an animal with feelings like everyone else. I hope Boris didn't hurt Fred's feelings!"

I peek over at Pete, but he's busy fiddling with the zero-grav wet-vac. I have no idea if my performance has sold him or not.

"Well, fuck him. Time to clean umemeh piss." Pete's gaze flicks up from his quanta-com. "How in hull-breaches are you not suited-up yet? Animal rights activists can suit-up just like the rest of us clowns. Come on, Savvy. You're not getting out of this. Hurry that shit up."

I sigh and return to the task of suiting up. I still haven't had any painkillers. But I'm starting to like that he's calling me Savvy; he's the second person to do that today. It sure beats "Ronnie" – and the asshole who gave me that nickname.

I square up next to Pete once I'm all dressed. "You got any Mint-Trip on you?" I nod towards the cargo door. "To properly brace for the job ahead?"

"Not while *on duty,* you incompetent plate o' lox," Pete replies, rolling his eyes.

My mouth drops. Apparently, my only almost-friend on this ship has turned into yet another hard-ass boss. What's a girl gotta do to catch a break?

chapter twelve

I peel away the layers of wet suit. A lot of cargo needed to be wiped clean of piss, and apparently, I'm the brute force of that operation. The irony is that the cargo in question is brand-new, space-worthy, piss-receptacles. But for some unfathomable reason, the toilets have to be clean of piss *before* delivery, even if they'll be pissed on from now until they malfunction in five to ten years.

I've left a shit-shoveling job for a piss-scrubbing one and you can bet your ass I'm cranky about it.

"Laundry chute's over there. But it's only the fabric parts," Pete explains. "The rubber has got to stay here and stink up the place. At least till we get to a dry cleaner at the next port. It ain't gonna smell like a bed of roses in here."

"Well, It's not *my* fault the umemeh pissed up your cargo hold." Pete fixes me with a disbelieving stare. "Okay, fine." I fold my arms. Maybe it is. But he doesn't have to guilt-trip me about it. "It still smells better than shoveling shit on Hialeah," I add. "In case you were wondering what a degree in zoology might get you."

I return the hideous hot-pink suit where I've been instructed. I am kind of happy that I've made Juliet's suit smell like piss. Not just any piss, but umemeh piss, famed for its skunk-like potency. I smile at the thought of Juliet discovering it.

Two coverall-clad men enter the lockers area right as I slam the blue metal locker over the offensive suit.

"Hey! You're an animal rights activist, eh?" asks the younger of the two, sporting a mustache.

"Savvy," says Pete, "You remember Guppy and Marc from dinner last night?"

I glance back and forth between them. One man's got silver hair and glasses, and the restrained manner of a man who spends too much time in close contact with electronics. The other, mustache guy, is short and so young he must be a recent graduate. They're both complete strangers to me. "Uh huh," I reply.

"They really have a pygmy orangutan parliament back on Hialeah?" Mustache asks. If I had to guess between the names, I'd go with Marc.

"Guppy," says Pete. "She don't like to talk about Hialeah."

"No, it's okay." I crack a smile. Right. His name is Guppy. "Those little guys are a real trip!"

Just then, a screeching sound fills the room. I take a step back as a black and white streak zooms into the room. The furry creature scampers up to Mustache-Guppy's shoulder, where it stands, pointing a cute little finger at me while shrieking full-volume, right next to Guppy's ear-hole.

Guppy jerks violently to get the thing off his shoulder. It proceeds to scurry up the torso of the brooding Marc, who frantically tries to bat it away. Guppy and Pete both have their hands clamped over their ears, ducking and trying to back out of the room. The screeching is echoing off the lockers, creating a triplicate effect, but I can only stare.

Marc manages to toss the black and white animal off him and back away from the room. The creature is now aggressively taking a stand against me, raised to his full one-foot height. But I've most *definitely* been in this position before, and it has just occurred to me that no one else on this ship knows what in voids is going on.

"Prisha… Fucking… Shanti," I say, finally placing the curious reference made at dinner. I can barely hold back my grin of delight. "You are very definitely not a skunk, you clever genius, you!" Three men are peeking into the room around the corner, and based on the looks they're giving me, they're concerned that I've gone insane. "It's okay!" I call to them over the noise, and wave them over.

In light of Prisha Shanti's continued shrieking, they do not move.

I purse my lips together and emit five lilting whistles. Prisha pauses her shrieking to listen. I make her wait a minute, and when her hackles start raising back up, I repeat the trill. She's still staring at me, but her front legs are slowly lowering back to the ground. Good.

"You guys can come back in now," I say. Prisha eyes me suspiciously, and her paws begin to lift their way back to her aggressive stance. I whistle for her again, and she calms down enough to come give me a sniff. It's only then that the three grown-ass men cautiously re-enter the locker room.

"Did you ever find it strange," I ask them in a calm voice, my hand extended for Prisha Shanti's curious whiskers. "That Prisha Shanti has bright yellow eyes?" The three cargo workers glance back and forth between each other before giving me a collective shrug. "Or that she's got this fucking beard around her neck?"

"You, uh, think she's sick with something?" Guppy asks.

"*Varecia verigata variegata,*" I reply with a nod.

"Is it serious?" Marc asks.

"Can it be cured with medicine?" Pete asks. "Because I gotta say, we'd all be happier if that shrieking thing came to an end."

I shake my head. "It's terminal." The three men look stricken, and I take pity on them. "It's *also* her species name," I add.

The three grease monkeys are confused for a minute, before Pete shoots me an accusing glare. "She's not sick?" Pete asks.

I can't quite manage to hold back a smile.

"You had us going all worried and –"

"How could you *possibly* think Prisha Shanti was a skunk!?" I exclaim, interrupting him. "Do you even know what a skunk looks like?"

Pete scratches behind his green hat. "Uh. Black. And white. Like Prisha Shanti?"

"Black and white? That could describe a fucking zebra! That's all you had to go with?"

"If Prisha Shanti isn't a skunk," Guppy says, brows furrowed, "What in voids is she?"

"*Varecia verigata variegata*," I reply. The dudes all stare at me, not any happier. I sigh. "Otherwise known as a black and white ruffed lemur?"

It takes a moment for the words to sink in.

"So she's not a skunk?" Guppy asks.

"That would explain why she was such a bad defense skunk," Marc says slowly.

"No shit," I reply.

"What's a lemur do?" Pete asks. "I mean, like, for defense?"

I laugh. "You've seen it. Or," I correct myself, "I should say, heard it."

"Shiiiiiit," Pete says, letting out a whistle between clenched teeth.

"She is kind of useful with those little hands though," Guppy adds.

"What he means to say," Marc interjects, "is that Prisha Shanti is a pickpocket."

I raise my eyebrows. "I'm not surprised. The black and white ruffed lemurs from ancestral Mondi are clever little suckers. Back at Hialeah, they've opened their cage about sixteen times since I started working there." I hold up a finger. "Every single time, they used a stolen key card to do it."

Pete whistles through his teeth again.

"You sneaky little skunk, you," Marc says, cooing at Prisha Shanti.

"*Not* skunk," I mutter. But no one's listening to me. They're too busy sharing the news on their quanta-coms.

I have this distinct, unfamiliar feeling settle in my gut. I *think* I'm pleased. But I'm not sure. I haven't felt this in a long time.

———

WHILE MARC AND GUPPY BEGIN TO PULL ON THEIR RUBBERS FOR their shift, Prisha Shanti climbs Pete like he's a lamppost, and comes to a rest on his shoulder.

"You naughty creature, you," he says, stroking her fur. "Let's bring you back to the greenhouse." He glances up at me. "Hey, Savvy. What do you think that umemeh of yours got up to while you were working today?"

I examine the cargo bay antechamber. There's no new piss in here, at least. Not today, anyway. "Not one ass-licking clue."

"Ass-licking?" Pete repeats, then lets out a rasping chuckle. "Good one!"

"He's probably trying to cram his dumb heads under that glass case in the mess," I add. That animal has a proclivity for dangerous neck positions. "I'll go see if I can find him. That is, if I'm off-duty, boss?"

Pete grimaces. "Oh, no! Don't call me that." He shakes his head. "I'm just Pete. And yeah, you're off duty. Generally we – well, I mean, the cargo crew – we're usually off-duty during transit. But since we got the hold to clean up..." He trails off and understanding dawns on me.

Boris's animosity towards me makes so much more sense now. They all should hate me. They're working during their off-time because of me! Shit, I don't think anything would move me to work on my off-time back on Hialeah. I can't wrap my head around why Pete, or any of them, are being nice to me.

Pete shrugs. "It's happened before, when things weren't tied down properly. Last time, it was Boris's fault, by the way, so don't take any shit from him. Anyway. When we *do* have to work, the standard hours are five on, five off, five on. Then off ten. So yeah, you're off for a bit. Just be back here in five hours."

"Great. More fun with piss," I say with false cheer. "Wouldn't miss it for the universe."

I stalk the hallways of the ship in a half-hearted attempt to discover the umemeh. The farther I go, the more the black cloud lifts from my mood. The corridors are empty and clean, and I've circled this level three times without any sign of the umemeh. But I don't feel like going up to the mess, or the cockpit, or any of the places where I'll find people. Even if the umemeh's up there.

If he's been up to trouble for the last few hours, another fifteen minutes won't make a difference. The carpets here are maroon, the walls are fancy grey with virtual portholes, and there's an absence of funky odors. Compared to Hialieah, this is a Dreamliner. So I keep walking around the halls of cargo level to let off some steam.

If there's one thing to miss about Hialeah, it's all the walking. Back there, I walked about seventeen miles a day, broken up, to get from one enclosure to the next. I've been cooped up on this void-forsaken ship for less than a day and I really, desperately want off. For very, very many reasons.

"Sahhh-vvvvy!"

I stop short and turn to see Gisella striding down the hallway, her straight, jet-black hair streaming behind her. "Saffron!" she scurries to catch up with me. Up close, I see her freckles only span her nose and upper cheeks, like she's been dusted by a fairy's wings. Hers are also much smaller and cuter than my own freckles, which cover every inch of my pale skin like the splatter of raindrops on concrete. Or like piss splatter on the walls of a cargo crate.

"Hey!" she says amiably once we're finally side by side. "We decided on a port!" She furrows her eyebrows. "The captain ordered strict secrecy, but Saffron, I love it and I think you will too!"

I swallow back bile. *It's Surf & Ceebu, isn't it?* I want to ask. But voids, I can't even form my mouth into saying the right words. My spit has disappeared, and my heart is thunking hard enough to break free of my chest. Shit.

What am I going to do? I glance at one of the holographic port windows. I can't jump ship, I don't even own a jet pack. Or a portable supply of oxygen. Or three, for both of the umemeh's fucking heads. Greel Truyoza owns me so fully that if he pulls a leash on his end of the galaxy my ass will get whiplash. Then he'll send someone to make sure I get disemboweled and live to remember it. Shitshitshit, I am about to hyperventilate in the halls. Gisella chimes in.

"Oh my gosh. Were you lost?"

I get a grip on my anxiety and glance around at the empty hallways. Okay, right. I can see that it might look like that. Do I tell her I was trying to enjoy my only good habit from my last eight nightmarish years? And then started having a nervous breakdown over the looming prospect of getting arrested and-or pulverized into hamburger meat?

"I was searching for the umemeh," I whisper. Great way to sound like a psycho, but there is an awfully painful lump in my throat. I take a deep breath.

"Fred? Oh, he's up on the bridge." Gisella grins.

I blink several times. "I'm sorry. What?"

"Yeah, he was so cute! You *may* have noticed our captain has an affinity for animals, and Lucy said Fred doesn't bother her, so he's hanging out up there."

My jaw falls open. The umemeh is a stinky beast, even if he's cute. The bridge cannot possibly be large enough to make his presence tolerable. And isn't Juliet supposedly on the bridge shadowing Lucy?

"How is, um, Juliet enjoying Fred's presence?"

"Juliet? Oh, don't pay her any mind. She gets jealous when anything catches Michael's attention. She'll get over it."

"Michael?" I cycle through the names I've learned so far, but honest to Bob, I can't remember any Michaels.

"You know, the captain. Sergeant Reyes?"

Right. Captain Hotpants. He's more than just a body. I knew that. On one hand, I get why anyone would be jealous of Sergeant Reyes's attention. But how can Juliet be more jealous of the umemeh than she is of me? I glance down at my coveralls. Do I really pose so little risk of capturing the captain's attention? I frown. "Okay then. I'll go get Fred off the bridge. Make Juliet's day a little easier. Especially seeing as she's been deprived of her favorite food."

Gisella falls in line with me and steers my elbow towards the elevator that I did not know existed.

"She's a good kid. She really is. She's just young, that's all. I'm sure you remember what that's like."

"Are you calling me an old hag?"

Gisella frowns as she clicks the button for the bridge. "No. You know what I mean. Juliet's young and fresh out of school. Where were you when you first got out of school? Didn't you ever make any stupid decisions?"

I snort on the exhale. "Yeah, I made a shit-ton of stupid decisions. And I paid for them. For the last eight years."

"Girl, we've *all* said and done some stupid stuff. Cut her a little slack, is all I'm saying."

The elevator doors bing open to what was supposed to be the bridge, but instead we've landed in a large tea-room with fancy leather chairs and mahogany laden consoles. Smooth jazz music quietly emanates from speakers around the room. I glance behind me at the elevator, and the electronic display that announces our location. Bridge.

"Did we get off at a board meeting at billionaire row? Where in voids are we?" I keep searching for any visual hints of familiarity, and that's when I notice the people here.

Sergeant Hotpants Reyes glances back at me from a leather chair with a console, and gives me a nod. A fuzzy pink hat catches my eye, and pale, wan-faced Lucy nods to us from her long shiny black glass table (which I now see contains faintly illuminated blue holographic buttons). Juliet glowers at us from Lucy's side. The man with the pet pygmy orangutan – Dimitry – is by one of the consoles typing away and ignoring us all.

There is also a Black woman in a cowboy hat petting Fred, whose heads are bopping along to the nerve-grinding music. I'm pretty sure I haven't met her yet, because that cowboy hat is badass.

The annoying jazz music rolls on.

"How do you all not go insane from the shitty music?" I wave at the speakers. "If I had to work in here, I'd literally chop my ears off to jam the speakers."

At this statement, the umemeh notices my presence and lops over to me. True to nature, he begins nuzzling my hair.

"Yeah, it's Michael's thing," Gisella says, waving dismissively. "The music's better when Rosemary's in charge here."

"Only if you have no taste in music," Sergeant Reyes replies with a snort, and meets us by the elevator. "Rosie, you okay to take over?"

The cowboy-hat-wearing woman nods. "Sure thing, Sarge." Instead of taking his spot in the captain's chair, though, she walks over to us. "But I'll introduce myself first. You must be Saffron. I'm Rosemary Larson, and sometimes our captain *actually* remembers his manners." She ribs Captain Hotpants, and his cheeks darken. "It's nice to meet you." I respond with a handshake.

Hotpants clears his throat.

"Yes, Michael. I'm taking over. Computer, play Rosie's playlist."

The jazz music stops immediately and is replaced by rhythmic sounds of… is that pre-space-age country music mixed with rap?

Reyes spreads his hands. "Who's got poor taste in music, I ask you?" Reyes asks me, a hint of a smile lighting his eyes. "Rosie, these are clearly two genres that were never meant to be mashed together."

"That is where you are *wrong*, sir," replies Rosemary from the captain's chair. "Historically speaking, one in every four cowboys in the original Wild West was Black. Nothing goes together better than rap and country. It's like potatoes and green slime. Get with the times, old man."

Reyes shrugs and shares a conspiratorial wink with Gisella and me. "See what I have to deal with? Historical my ass."

A smile is tugging at the corners of my mouth.

"It's actually pretty good!" Gisella chimes in. "You should come by and visit sometime when Michael's off-duty and…"

"Alright, that's enough," says Sergeant Reyes, cutting Gisella off sharply mid-sentence. My smile fades fast. "I bet our animal rights activist hates the carbon emission footprint here in the bridge but is too polite to tell us." Captain Reyes smiles in a way that bares his teeth but doesn't reach his eyes. I am perfectly placed to see Rosemary, behind Angry Man, giving Gisella a knowing look. He doesn't see it, though, still staring intently at me. "Isn't that right, Savage?"

"Right. Of course." I try to pull my head away from the umemeh's attention.

"We won't force you to spend any extra time in the bridge than is necessary," he says, then considers Fred's work on my hair. At this rate, I'll be bald within the hour. "I think your umemeh's hungry."

"Genius observation," I reply.

He nods. "I'll show you the greenhouse, if you want. Then I've got to make a few personal coms. Gisella, can you join us?"

She frowns, her mind clearly occupied by some deep train of thought. But aloud all she says is, "Sure, I'm up for a greenhouse visit."

This time, we take the stairs up to a modular outcropping above the bridge. Sergeant Reyes insists that the umemeh is not to allowed to enter, so we leave him behind in the bridge, much to Juliet's disappointment.

"Shhh," Reyes says, waiting for me and Gisella at the top of the stairs, two steps ahead of me. "You don't want to wake up the bats." With that, he turns and enters the room behind him on the small landing.

I refrain from commenting on the idiocy of housing bats and follow him into the small, dark, glass-domed room. The scent of damp dirt invades my nostrils, as if the small, thirty-meter wide space is full of it. But the floor is a clean tile, filled with tidy rows of hydroponics shelves, each with their own light contraption. Green vines trail from one rack to the next, reaching out into human walking spaces. Above, along the framework of the glass dome, sleeps a colony of hanging bats. And someone has strung up a cheap, colorful array of fairy lights all around.

"You have a hundred thousand joulo ship..." I begin, staring in wonder. "But you didn't have enough money to light this place with regular lights?"

Sergeant Reyes chuckles. "I think that's the first time I've ever heard her come out of her cranky mood. Gisella?"

Gisella gives a tight smile. "Apparently, all we had to do was give her romantic lighting. Who'd have thought it?"

But I can't help but be wowed in here. The modular room is truly magical. We're in a dome made entirely of glass! All around us is the sky of stars, enhanced by strings and strings of romantic mood lighting artfully draped about the space. I can feel the body warmth of Sergeant Reyes standing next to me, and when I turn to smile at him I realize what a significant miscalculation I've made. I'm staring up into the eyes of a very fine man who is standing so very close to me. My heart rate kicks up a notch, and I can't help it, but my breath catches.

Only he's most definitely *not* interested in me. After a moment of me staring into his eyes like a fucking idiot, he breaks away.

"Over here is where we grow the cabbage," he says, clearing his throat.

Gisella steps into the void Sergeant Reyes had only recently occupied. She puts a hand on my arm, and I don't jerk back.

"This is it. It's all we've got." He waves at a short row of green stuff growing on a shelf, and his voice becomes laden with sarcasm. "I know you've got the kindest heart of everyone on board and would feed the umemeh everything you possibly could, but try to pace yourself." Sergeant Reyes glances at us two ladies standing together. His eyes have a hard glint to them, and his mouth is making that firm line again.

"Uh," I clear my throat. "I hear you've decided on a port?" I carefully avoid mentioning Surf & Ceebu. I cannot bring it up. I will not bring it up. But still… "Is there, uh, any chance you want to share some specifics?"

Reyes shoots an angry glance at Gisella, who shakes her head.

"You'll find out in about four day-cycles! We've all got to do our part to keep those animal traffickers in the dark, eh? And now, I've got a few coms to make. Gisella, can you stick around with our Savvy friend and make sure she doesn't uproot the whole garden for that umemeh of hers?" He offers a tight-lipped half smile to indicate he's joking, and Gisella rolls her eyes.

"Eff you," I say, but my heart's not in it. Or maybe my heart's there for the literal wish.

"Come on, Savvy," Gisella says once Sergeant Reyes departs. "They're over here."

What *in voids* is happening to me? Why am I feeling anything other than revulsion for this Righteous Sergeant? It must be the warrant. It's put me in a funk, or something. All sentimental now.

I blink rapidly as I pry through the dirt.

I need to get off this ship. I've got a fucking job to finish.

At the next port of call, I'm calling Greel Truyoza the very moment I get off this ship. Before any Brin-177 muscle gets a chance to collect the umemeh. Truyoza will know what to do. I'll have him arrange my transportation and get the fucking umemeh off my hands. All I have to do is make it to the next port of call. Even if it's Surf & Ceebu.

I glance up at the ceiling to look at the stars. The bats are in my way at this angle, and what the shit is on their noses? *Oh.* I think I can solve their bat problem.

I blink my stinging eyes and find Gisella in my field of vision. The only question is: Do I want to help them?

chapter thirteen

I've just thrown a cherry tomato down the hallway for Fred to chase when a series of loud clicks vibrate through the air, followed by a grinding noise.

"Prepare for docking procedures," comes Reyes's smooth voice over the intercom.

"What?!" I exclaim. It's been only two day-cycles, *way* shorter than the four-day journey Hotpants mentioned. I have no disguise ready if this stop proves to be Surf & Ceebu, and no plan. I'm hoping to hear more over the loudspeakers, but exactly one second later, both Fred and I jolt into the wall as the ship shudders. Hard.

"A little advance warning next time!" I yell at the ceiling. With a wobbling gait, I get closer to Fred. Close enough to see his necks are fine, anyway, and he wants to eat my hair again. So he's totally normal, then.

My mouth feels really dry as I glance around the empty hallway. Shitshitshit. Pete comes running down the corridor, heading past me towards the cargo bay C.

"Pete!" I call after him. "What port are we in?"

He turns to me, as he runs, for one step. "No port!" his eyes flash wildly to match his wide grin. "Black space delivery!" he yells back over his shoulder. And just like that, he's out of the hallway.

"Black... space delivery?" I ask the empty hallway. Or, I suppose, Fred. But Fred is now busy snuffling about for the lost tomato again. A black space delivery means we're not remotely close to any port, but docking directly with another ship. No one ever does that because without a port's AI, docking is stupid-levels of hard and you need to have a kick-ass navigator, or else you risk losing parts from your ship and possibly some of your oxygen and crew, and who the voids wants that? No toilet is worth *that* much money.

"Well, now I have to hear more," I say to Fred. "You wait here, okay?" But this time, I don't even glance back at the animal as I head towards the cargo bay.

Pete's already suited-up and in the hold when I get to the lockers. Holy crap, he's fast!

Guppy is also in the C-hold with Pete, while Dimitry waits in the locker room with a quanta-com pad and a mover-bot. In the distance, somewhere aboard the ship, I can hear Prisha Shanti shrieking.

Dimitry glances at me as I enter, a frown on his face.

"Got any advice for me here? Little guy is totally freaking out." Dimitry reaches down to pet the pygmy orangutan frantically climbing in and out of his pocket.

"Looks like he's moving okay." I reach out for the furball in his pocket, and he scurries along my arm. I chuckle. "Fully recovered, then?"

"Yeah. No problem there. But he always gets antsy anytime Prisha Shanti starts screaming." Dimitry frowns. "Me and him really shouldn't be a part of a black space delivery."

Prisha Shanti's shrieks have ceased for the moment, and Burt is back to his cheerful self. I gently return Burt to Dimitry's shoulder, and he happily scampers back into his pocket. "Who the voids is this black space buyer, anyway? To risk this?"

Dimitry quirks an eyebrow. "Ever hear of the Spiff?"

"Uhhh." I squint at the ceiling.

"Oh, come on!" Dimitry exclaims. Burt scampers in and out of his pocket in surprise. "You've got to have heard of him!"

"I've been stuck on a zoo planet for a decade. A zoo planet where new pants-closures were the hottest technology trend!"

"The mole?"

"Yeah, the mole. We only got those about five years ago."

Dimitry winces. "Well, uh, the Spiff is a notorious outlaw. Don't insult him by not knowing him to his face."

"Don't even be in proximity of his face, Savvy," adds Reyes as he strides in. "Dimitry – Gisella and Guppy are working this install, and Boris is on his way." He shoots me a glance. "It took more than a few insults to get him up."

"Thanks, boss. I wouldn't want the Spiff to catch sight of Burt."

"Dimitry, it would never come down to that, and you know it. You don't have to worry." Hotpants puts his hands up defensively. "All I asked you to do was prepare the dolly for when Pete and Guppy get out. I could just have easily asked Savvy."

I squawk.

"All I mean to say is – *neither* of you are client facing. Just hold on to the void-forsaken dolly for two more minutes."

Well, now I'm offended. Rude. He is just so freaking rude. "Why can't your clients see me? Is it the hair? Because I can cover it."

"No, Saffron, it is not the hair." Reyes runs a hand through his own dark hair, pushing back the locks that had been dangling over one eyebrow. "Look, what do you know about the Spiff?"

"I know that he's an incredibly notorious outlaw." I scowl at him.

Reyes nods. "Right. Steals from the rich to give to the poor. Space's very own Robin Hood. I don't suppose you have any idea how much a live umemeh could sell for?"

Is this another one of his tests? Shit. I blink innocently at him. "No clue. How much?"

"Two million joulos."

I choke on my own saliva. Two *million* joulos?!

"Now of course *you* would never be in the animal trafficking business, so I wouldn't expect you to know. But you can*not* let Fred come into the Spiff's sight. Got that? I don't want any questions from him, not even the slightest suspicion that something is different than the norm." Hotpants wags a finger at me. "Both you and Fred stay out of sight for the entire delivery and install. Got that?"

Did he just say two million joulos?

"Savage?" Reyes snaps his fingers a few times.

"Right. Right. Got it," I mumble.

"Now, I don't think the Spiff would even consider buying or selling Fred himself, because selling an umemeh is an incredibly stupid idea. Umemeh are not exactly inconspicuous, are they?" I swallow hard and nod. "But if he caught sight of Fred, the Spiff would most definitely peddle the information of Fred's unprotected existence to every mob boss around the galaxy. If he is spotted, we get attacked. By at least five different mob hit squads all at once."

"Oh." My mouth drops open. "Shit," I add after my brain has finally caught up. Forget Truyoza. I'll be dead.

"That's right, Savvy. Now look. We've already docked with the Spiff's ship, but we're not opening the doors till the cargo's all loaded up. So I have to ask you. Is Fred currently out of sight?"

"Wha?" I pretend I didn't hear him, while images of Fred snuffling the carpeting around the corner flash through my mind. I guess Reyes came to C-hold from the other direction.

"Is. Fred. Out. Of. Sight," Reyes repeats, teeth clenched.

"Oh. Right. Right. Yes, of course." I mean, he will be. Soon? I'll take care of it.

A chime alerts us that Pete and Guppy have opened the inner cargo hold door, and Reyes and Dimitry are momentarily distracted. I take the opportunity to scooch out the door.

"Oh, Freddypoo?" I call as I round the corner to the hallway where I'd left him. I can just lure him out with some hair-bait and get him tucked into a room in no time. Except I do have to find him, first.

I step on something that squishes audibly beneath my boot. When I check, I discover a very squashed cherry tomato.

Fred is nowhere in sight.

Gisella comes rounding the corner moments after. "The captain?" she asks breathlessly. Wordlessly, I point to the cargo area.

"Wait!" I yell before she rounds the corner. She turns to me, impatient. "Fred?" I ask, my voice coming across on a register that makes me sound somewhere between hopeful and clueless.

Gisella shakes her head. "Haven't seen him. Sorry!" And with that, she disappears.

I jog around the bend and check the training room. Marc is in there alone with the weights and equipment that remind me too much of Weasel. I jog on and peek through the glass doors into med bay. There's only a frowning, stationary Doc Williams, tapping away at a screen. I'm not poking a stick in *that* hornet's nest so I bound up the stairs to the next level to check the mess. It's the only place where he gets his food. It's also the same level as the docking doors that lead to Spiff's ship. But when I poke my head through the mess doors, the space is mockingly empty, save for Otis humming back in the kitchens. "Oh, Saffron, is that you?" Otis calls from around the corner. *Not now. I don't have time for this!* I think, and dodge back into the hallway.

Where the voids else would Fred go?

I race up another level to check my room. It would be a void-forsaken miracle if Fred independently decided to go take a nap at this moment. But a quick peek through the door confirms that I'm an idiot for even wondering it.

Up another level then, to the bridge. I speed up the stairs towards the sounds of Prisha Shanti's shrieks, and am amazed that I've come to know this place so well I can check all the likely spaces without thinking twice about the ship's layout.

Fucking tits, he better be on the bridge.

But when I burst into the bridge, there's only a startled Rosemary, Lucy, and Juliet to greet me.

"Fucking shit!" I exclaim.

"Whoa, whoa, slow down buttercup," says Rosemary. She pulls out a round red lollipop to speak to me. "Say hello like a normal person."

"I, uh." Shrieks resound from above. So, they've locked Prisha Shanti in the greenhouse, then. But there's no way they'd leave double-muncher Fred up there unsupervised. Right?

Rosie raises an eyebrow and puts the lollipop back in her mouth.

"Hi," I try again. "Was Fred here?"

"He was," Rosemary replies with a dip of her cowboy hat, calm as the ever-still sea of stars she travels.

"Well?" I say louder than I'd intended, rolling my hand in the universal onward motion. "Where in hull-breaches is he now?"

"Relax!" Rosemary rolls her eyes. "I had Juliet bring him back down to your room. Want a lollipop?"

I take a deep breath, calmed for half a second. Wait a shitting second. I just came from my room! My very empty room. Shitshitshit.

"Uh, actually?" Juliet chimes in from down the bridge. "I thought you told me to take him down the stairs."

Rosemary frowns. "I said take him downstairs to quarters. Remember? We can't let the Spiff see him." She pauses. "Juliet?"

Juliet doesn't answer. She bites her bottom lip.

"Juliet, what did you think I meant?"

"I thought…" Juliet stammers. "I thought you just meant… Down… the…. stairs."

Lucy glances up from her display, and our eyes all rivet towards that slight motion from her bright pink hat as her head turns to us. Lucy is her usual silent self, but she cocks her head at Juliet. Now *that* feels like a death sentence if I've ever seen one.

"I just thought you meant *down*," Juliet repeats, stammering.

"Yes, we all know the fucking direction. Thank you for that." I make a face at her.

"That was unkind!" Rosemary calls after me on my way back *down* the stairs.

"Remind me of that when I'm not dead!" I retort over my shoulder, taking the stairs two at a time towards the docking level.

Fred and his bopping heads have a penchant for ending up bopping in all the wrong places. It's just my luck, he's probably snuffling around the docking doors. No, with my luck, he'll bop right into the door-open button and walk straight onto the Spiff's ship.

I round the corner of the hallway that leads to the docking doors in time to see the *Waterloo's* job crew greeting some man who looks remarkably like an old timey pirate. There are just... so many other fashion choices available. For the love of stars, why would anyone voluntarily go out with striped red pants and a black pirate hat with a peacock feather? I mean. This person is clearly a monster.

Pete and Guppy are directing a mover-bot loaded up with a ten-foot box, along with several smaller boxes sliding above. Hotpants Reyes is shaking the pirate's hand warmly and laughing with him. My heart is hammering away in my chest, but I can see very clearly that Fred is not here.

I take a step backwards, trying to inconspicuously erase myself from view. Nothing to see here, fellas.

"Reyes! You old dog," yells Pirate dude. "You didn't tell me you've started hiring such attractive red-headed wenches! Much better looking than these two," he snorts at Pete and Guppy. "Why'int you give me your best crew, eh?"

Hotpants turns to me, his easy affect completely transformed into a stoniness.

"That? She's just a passenger, Spiff. One who is completely incompetent, too. You wouldn't want to share a table with her."

Harsh burn, Reyes. I take another step backwards. At least he hasn't seen the umemeh. If the worst thing that happens is him seeing me, we'll be okay. Reyes might die of an apoplectic fit later, but no one's going to come trying to kill us.

"She looks like a real fiery one, that one," Pirate Spiff adds.

I groan. Can every stranger not compare my personality to my flaming hair? How much further till I disappear back around the corner? I take another step back. Except this time, I back straight into something large and warm behind me.

And then, it nuzzles my hair.

Shitfaced fucking sin.

"Hey! Whoa, Reyes, I knew you had a hot business, but you selling an umemeh out here?" The Spiff takes an eager step forward.

Sergeant Reyes puts a hand to restrain Spiff. "Definitely not an umemeh, Spiff," he replies. "We're just in the toilet industry. Scout's honor."

"Yeah? Then what in the voids is that! Toilet business, my ass." He roars an obnoxious laugh. "My ass, get it!?!"

Time for me to step up. "Hey. Are you assholes discussing my narc-sniffing llama?" I ask innocently.

"Narc-sniffing llama?" asks Guppy, incredulous. Pete elbows Guppy hard. "Oh. Sorry. Right."

"Yup. We *were* talking about him," Pete cuts in.

"Yeah, he was a top of the line police beast until my folks hired him for me," I say with fake bravado, trying to make sense of this new idiotic lie. "He's supposed to steer me away from nut products. I'm deathly allergic. Yeah. The police trained him to, uh, sniff out anything that started with the letter N. Cover their bases, you know." Donkey's ass, do I need to shut up now.

"Huh. That's a narc-sniffing llama?" asks Spiff, shifting uncomfortably further away from Fred. He squints at us and scratches his beard-scruff. "Why's he got two heads then?"

"Don't be such an asshole. They're conjoined twins. That hurts their feelings, and then I have to feed 'em a pound of LSD to get 'em to stop moping around," I add lamely. Why in Bob's name have I not thought of a better lie by now?

"You do not feed your work animal LSD."

"I do when he's lying around all day anyway, ya insensitive pig. And unless you're supplying, you should apologize to Fred here."

Reyes, standing behind the Spiff, is waving at me frantically to cut the shit. Or that he wants to kill me? Could go either way. He places a firm hand on the Spiff's shoulder and tries to pull him towards the doorway. "Sorry about that, Spiff. I warned you she wasn't in her right mind, didn't I?"

Spiff turns to eye me suspiciously. I guess not everyone believes this steaming pile of garbage, apparently. Time to try plan B: run away.

"Oh, Freddy," I call sweetly. "I don't know why you were getting so upset about this hallway. I'm sure there aren't any narcotics down this way. You must have steered me wrong, my sweet two-snouted boy."

The Spiff shifts closer to the door of his ship. Thought so, motherfucker.

"He must have smelled this gyro-900," Reyes says, in an extremely lame save. "Newest, hottest flusher on the market. Works in Zero-G." He winks at the Spiff. "Special attachment for the ladies, too."

Spiff shrugs. "I don't really give a shit." He grins at his own joke, and Pete emits a raspy peal of laugher. Reyes only tightens his lips. "The old crapper was barely more than a glorified closet, and my entire crew has threatened to mutiny. Never mind it was them who broke the void-forsaken thing in the first place."

"No problem," replies Reyes, using a hand to guide Spiff back to his own ship. "I'm glad we could do business with you, out here in no-man's land. You're lucky we were flying this way!"

"And what way was it, exactly?" Spiff asks, turning back to me and Fred.

"A true businessman will never reveal the secrets of his

clients." Reyes raises an eyebrow, and gives a hint of a smile. Spawning bunniculas, he's good. "Don't forget - that's why you trust me!"

With enough of an unspoken threat hanging in the air, Spiff seems concerned enough for the time being to be led back to his own ship. Reyes shoots me a death glare before the door shuts between the two corridors.

I lean back into Fred.

"Well, that was clusterfuckingly horrendous."

Fred whines.

He doesn't usually do much in the way of vocalizations, so this takes me by surprise. Then, shit, I realize when I've heard him whine before.

He dutifully starts loping off to the stairs to the cargo bay. I take one look after him before I sprint into the mess hall. Maybe if I find a bag or container in time, I can catch some of the urine before he pisses all over the place.

I glance about the mess hall, desperate. Otis only shakes his head and throws platitudes at me in high volume before I just leave and dash back out empty handed and race to catch up with Fred.

I find him just arriving in the cargo locker rooms. I open my locker, hoping to find something that will work as a makeshift collections bag because I cannot spend the next two days mopping and washing out piss from the carpeting. I cannot. I will not.

I begin throwing things out of the locker. Behind me, I can hear Fred snuffling for the perfect spot to bless with a golden shower. That's when I decide: Fuck Juliet's suit. Just fuck those neon flowers. I grab the entirety of it and haul it over to Fred, who's now pawing a random spot of carpet. Piss will probably slide off the outside of this stupid rubberized thing all over the floor if I just put it down. What if I hold it open, like he's going to piss into a bag? I hold Juliet's suit open at the neckline directly under Fred's dangly bits and look away. I'm hoping the smell won't be so bad this way. But then a rude brush at my fingers alerts me that Fred is on the move again.

Still holding Juliet's suit open under the pour spigot, I try to keep up with darling Fred. But when his back leg steps on the bottom of Juliet's suit, I almost lose my shit. Both of Fred's heads have lifted in alarm, and now that I'm paying attention, I can hear Prisha Shanti's shrieks getting louder. But I don't have time to deal with her right now. My biggest problem is that Juliet's suit is trapped below two hundred pounds of umemeh and most definitely will not be available for catching any piss. I tug at the neck opening and try to draw it closer to the downspout, but no luck. I'm still about a foot away. If he tries to piss now, I'm totally fucked.

Fred snuffles the ground again. Then takes a step. Hallelujah! I can move the suit. I quickly tie the floppy legs of it over my shoulders, and resume the position, hoping the neck aperture right below his man-gly-bits. He snuffles again, and takes three more steps.

"For the love of Bob, Fred, just take the stinking piss!"

That seems to be all Fred was waiting for, because at the very moment I say "piss" a torrential stream starts cascading out.

You know what neon floral latex suits are good for? Containing a high volume of liquid. Humans *are* made up of mostly water, so that makes some sense.

You know what neon floral latex suits are terrible at? Preventing splashback.

———

After safely tucking Fred away in my room and scrubbing off every inch of my skin till it's raw, I find my way back up to the bridge.

"You look shiny," says Rosemary, rolling the lollipop around in her mouth.

"Don't even ask," I mutter.

"So was Fred actually in his room?" Juliet asks innocently, petting Prisha Shanti, who is basking in the attention.

"He is now," I retort. "After Spiff saw him."

Rosemary tenses up. "Spiff saw him?"

I nodded. "I said he was my narc-sniffing llama."

Lucy spins to me. She pushes her pink hat up her forehead and her white hair behind her back as she looks me up and down. "You… said…. what?!" I think – no, I am one-hundred percent certain those are the first words I've ever heard Lucy say out loud.

Rosemary folds her arms. "You said what?"

I chuckle. "You're not going to believe this."

"No. I'm not. And I wonder why Spiff did," cuts in Juliet.

"Says the person who left Fred in the direction of *down*."

"Ladies," warns Rosemary. Juliet folds her arms, and a dismayed Prisha Shanti climbs to her shoulders.

"Savvy, quit picking on Juliet." Rosemary points the lollipop at Juliet. "And Juliet, stop being such a negative nailhead. Assume, for the rest of our time together, that Savvy is actually a competent human."

Well, shit. I don't assume that about myself.

"Think you two can manage that?" Rosie asks.

I glance over at Juliet, who's furiously staring at a wall.

Rosemary clears her throat and raises her eyebrows. Somehow that alone is enough to scare the shit out of me. Musta done the same for Juliet, because she's staring at Rosemary with tearful eyes.

"Okay, listen up," Rosemary continues in her unhurried, even voice. "We are on a working ship, and we all have to see each other for the next two days and remain professional. And not kill each other. Savvy? You know, actually, you seem like the type who gets punched a lot."

No need to confirm that last bit. She made her point. "Fine," I say at last, and roll my eyes. "I'll be nice." I will not apologize for her suit, though.

"I'll be kinder, too," Juliet says.

Rosemary puts her hands on her hips, and stares at the two of us miserable specimens critically. "Fantastic. Now. Savvy, this is a full-kit install, and it's going to take a while. Sit down, relax." She glances over at Juliet. "You too, Juliet. Group bonding experience."

"But...!"

"That's an order."

Juliet plops down on the viewing couch as far away from me as possible. It's not like I bite. I cross my arms. Lucy remains stationary at her nav table, but Rosemary's heading away from us with purpose. Rosemary lands by the insta-tea-o-matic in the corner. After three steaming philo-cups appear on the tray, she pulls out a flask and pours generously into each. My eyebrows go up as she heads back our way with the tray, a Prisha Shanti running along by her heels.

When Prisha Shanti jumps up to the back of the couch to get a glimpse into my cup, I notice she's got a long, green peacock feather tucked under one armpit. When she presses her face too close to the tea in my hands, I shoo her away.

"You're not making Lucy join us?" I ask Rosemary, looking over to where Lucy remains at her fancy black glass desk. All I can see from here is her pink hat and white hair, and at my question, Lucy turns to smile apologetically at me.

"Someone's got to make sure we stay on course," replies Rosemary, unconcerned.

This sounds more and more like Rosemary's expecting me to get all cozy with Juliet, the last person in the universe I want to nuzzle. I tuck myself more tightly into the farthest corner of the couch. "Where's, uh, Gisella? Maybe we should have her join, too."

Rosemary's lips firm into a flat line. "She's the lead engineer working the install. Any other questions, or can you deal with this like a big girl?"

I look down at the spiked tea.

"Computer?" Rosemary snaps her fingers, and pre-space age

country rap fills the bridge. She snatches the flask from me, takes a swig, then hands it back. "So, Savvy. Fred's a narc-sniffing llama now?"

"Oh, for sure!" I grin and wipe my mouth clean. "A seeing-guide llama too."

"But he's got two heads!" Juliet exclaims. "Who would believe that?"

"Oh, *that*. I've had the second one sewn on. Double the noses, double the fun."

Rosemary snorts.

Lucy gets up from her desk and moves a leather armchair closer to us. Rosemary raises an eyebrow, but Lucy only shrugs at her.

"When did you use the seeing-guide llama excuse?" Lucy asks, with something like excitement glittering in her eyes. Well, I'll be hammered.

"Oh. Poor Officer Dan," I say with a smirk, because I know this is going to be a wild story.

REYES BLOWS THROUGH THE BRIDGE DOORS TWO HOURS LATER. Apparently, it takes a long time to get a zero-g toilet installed the right way. "Begin disengage, now!" he barks at Lucy. "Savage!" he exclaims when he catches sight of me. "What in voids' name was that?"

"From what I hear," replies Rosemary, "it was conjoined twins."

Reyes visibly startles and rounds on Rosemary. "What? You heard about that?"

"It was our fault, Sarge. We were the ones who let Fred loose. Savvy was the one who saved the day here. Cut her some slack."

Reyes casts another glance at me. He runs a hand through those long strands of hair that have somehow fallen back into his eyes again. "I need a shower," he announces to no one in particular.

"Tough install?" Rosie asks.

Reyes snorts. "It wasn't the install that was the problem. The whole place stank like the inside of a BuenoBean's bathroom," he explained, and is received by a collective groan. There isn't one of us who hasn't heard of the mega chain fast-food restaurant located in every port of the galaxy. Every item on the menu was made from a type of bean, and, well, their bathrooms smell worse than shit.

"What the breaches happened with Prisha Shanti?" he asks Rosemary.

Rosemary shakes her head. "She must have figured a way out. We're going to need a new lock up there."

"Yeah, well the Spiff was pissed." He glances over at Prisha Shanti, still perched on the couch and cleaning herself. "At least she got us something out of that exchange."

"Too bad she didn't bag any of those narcotics," I mutter.

"And you," he says turning to me. "You do understand that now, we'll have every mob ship in the vicinity on our tail."

Rosemary turns grim. "You think we have to worry about the umemeh?"

"All the way till it's on Brin-177," Reyes replies, rubbing his hands over tired eyes. "Rosemary, see if you can get our overly-chatty chef to manipulate the Spiff's outbound coms. If he can alter them, even by just a little bit, it might be enough to throw them off our trail. And Savage, I need to speak with you. Privately."

I've had a couple more swigs of Rosie's moonshine since I've been up here, and I don't particularly feel like having a new hole ripped out of me like this. "Aren't you going to shower first?"

His mouth firms into a line, and his nostrils flare. This is not a guy used to be disobeyed, I can see that. "Savage? Upstairs, now."

I groan, but dutifully follow him up the stairs to the dimly lit greenhouse. The smell of damp earth and plants assaults me all over again. Voids, I've missed being on planet.

"Savage," he repeats once the door shuts behind us. I'm swaying, kind of, and he puts an arm out to right me. "Have you been drinking?"

"Whaaat? Me? Noooo. Never," I reply.

His eyes already register disappointment.

"Do you know the best way to catch umemeh piss before it gets all over a cargo hold?" I ask, somewhat manic.

"No. What is it?" he replies, frowning.

I shrug. "Beats the crap out of me!"

"Savage?" he asks as I laugh. "Savage!" he repeats, louder. "Is there a new mess in the cargo hold that needs to be taken care of?"

"Sir, no sir!" I reply, adding in a very sloppy salute.

Reyes just sighs. "Savage, do you know why I asked you up here to talk to you?"

"To take advantage of my wily incompetence. My fiery feistiness? What was it he said?"

"No, Savvy," he replies firmly. "When I asked you earlier if Fred was out of sight, you told me he was. That was a lie."

"Hmmm." I've been using his arm to hold myself up steady, but now I full on lean against Reyes. "You were already so mad."

"Saffron, I get *angrier* when you lie to me. Always." He peels my head off his chest long enough to look me in the eye. "That will always make things worse. Always. Just be honest."

I duck my head back into the safety of his shoulder, out of line of those dark searing eyes. "Mmm," I reply. "I liked it better when we talked about how feisty I was."

"I never said those words," Reyes replies.

"But you thought it," I add, somewhat hopeful.

"No, the Spiff did. Would you like to rest your head on *his* shoulder?"

I groan. "You're no fun."

With a swift move, Reyes sweeps me up off the floor, carrying me in his arms. "Come on. Let's get you to your bed. I'm heading down to hit the head anyway."

"Take me with you?" I ask hopefully as he gently carries me down the stairs like some dewy-eyed bride.

"In your dreams, Savvy."

"Oh yeah," I reply. "In yours, too."

At that, he only raises an eyebrow, but I think I see the corner of his mouth twist up in a smile. And then, jouncing against his chest in an artificially lit stairwell, I fall asleep.

chapter fourteen

I blink into the dim cabin lighting. My quanta-com is buzzing away on my arm and my head is pounding something fierce.

"Mmph. Not yet," I mumble at my quanta-com, assuming it's someone trying to tell me I'm late for duty. I toss on my palette and get a faceful of Fred's shoulder. I move my nose free of his smelly fur and look up to find him asleep standing up beside me. His heads are swaying and I let my eyelids fall shut to the hypnotic rhythm. Rudely, my quanta-com ignores my sleepy-state and keeps buzzing. I throw back the covers.

"The cargo bay better be on fire," I harumph as I give in with a tap to my pinky ring. The contact-lens display bursts to life, way too bright in my eyeballs. A thousand messages from Greel Truyoza populate the air before me.

Boss: I need status update (*4 hrs*)
Boss: Why Spiff posting on dark-nets about two-headed llama? (*3 hrs*)

Shiiiiiiiiiiiiit. I take a deep inhale.

Boss: I not paying twice. You tell me where you are. And that Spiff post is coincidence. (*2 hrs*)
Boss: Location? (*2 hrs*)
Boss: If I have to pay Spiff to shut up, I will take it from your contract. (*1 hr*)
Boss: If there is no status update, I will terminate contract (*5 min*)

Fuck fuck fuckity fuck. I run my hand over my hair. This turned to shit real quick.

Boss: I need response within 24 hours (*3 min*)
Boss: If no response, I assume each party for himself. (*1 min*)

I scramble up to a sitting position and tap the air where my lenses project a brilliantly lit keyboard.

Me: I was asleep. Cargo is secure.
Boss: Location? Ship name?
Me: Why do you need to know? I'm on my way. I'll be there.
Boss: I need more than that. Give me ship name.

I gulp. Giving Greel Truyoza the name of the *Waterloo* could endanger the whole crew. I mean, I'm an ass but I'm not a pyscho.

Boss: I not paying Spiff for information. I already pay you. You will tell me.

For the love of stars, why did the Spiff have to post about Fred? I slam my hand on the bed as a new message from Truyoza buzzes on my arm.

Boss: I need info. Now. Or the clock starts ticking.

My blood starts pumping in hot.

Me: What the shit does that mean?
Boss: Rescue operation. We come look for you in 24 hours.
Pinging and swinging. Some collateral damage. Gets
messy. I can't leave loose ends flying around.
Me: What? I told you I have it under control.
Boss: What you tell me and what is true are not same thing.
Boss: Give me name of ship. Name of captain. And I will
extend deadline to full 72 hours for you to get to me. Before
I take it out of your hands.
Boss: This is guarantee.
Boss: Unless there is new problem.

Still, I hesitate. I may resent Sergeant Reyes for his attitude and for refusing to tell me their next port of call, but after being in Truyoza's claws myself, I can't bring myself to put anyone else there. On the other hand, I don't want Truyoza's 'rescue operation' to come out here and cause 'messy collateral damage.' That sounds like the worse of the two options.

Me: If I give you names, do you promise won't touch the
ship? Or the captain?
Boss: You have my word.

I stare up at the still dark ceiling of the room. Heavy Handed Mob Boss is getting impatient, who would have expected it. I don't even know if it's possible to get the umemeh to him in seventy-two hours, but if I fly straight to him from my next port, I might be able to make it. At least, if I get off this ship in the next day-cycle or so, then Reyes and his crew will be in the clear. I'll be on another ship, with some other captain for Truyoza to harass.

Unless Reyes does screw me over, in which case, he deserves everything he gets.

Whatever. I'll give Truyoza information. Everyone here will

ultimately remain safe, none the wiser. He'll keep his promise, right? Promises are like gold in the mob... right?

Boss: Details. Now.

I sigh.

Me: The cargo and I are aboard *the Waterloo*.
Boss: And the captain?

I gulp. This one comes harder. Truyoza could probably look up the ship's manifesto on the intranets, and ship captains are listed on every official berthing document. So I don't know why it's hard to tap out the actual letters, but somehow, this hurts more. I swallow again, and my mouth feels like sawdust.

Boss: ...

"All right! All right!" I wave my hand in the air, and Fred snorts awake in surprise. I give an exasperated sigh. "Fine."

Me: Captain Michael Reyes.
Boss: (pound fist emoji symbol)

It feels like I've knifed the captain in the back. Fuck me, I like this crew. If my life had turned out differently, I could have seen myself living with these people on this ship. Maybe that's why it feels so awful.

I lay back down on my bunk. It's not like I had much of a choice; I can't magically get out of this deal I made with Greel Truyoza. I knew he wasn't a great human when I started this plan, but I was desperate. I was stuck on a nightmare planet and up to my eyeballs in debt. No one could blame me for wanting to escape that life. But it's like the Universe has it out for me. First that asshole Weasel reports me to the police. Then I land a ship with a morally righteous captain, and now Truyoza wants to attack. Every single void-forsaken time I try to get myself from under one pile of shit, another collapses on my head. I'm just trying to survive, here.

The problem is that now I feel more shitty, not less.

I sigh and rub Fred's neck. One of his heads, the closer one, was woken by my outburst and is gently nibbling on my hair. The other head remains asleep.

"Fred, what am I going to do?" He snorts into my hair, and continues to gently munch away. I don't know what kind of response I was expecting from an idiot animal who would break both of his necks trying to eat two different shrubberies if left on his own for longer than twenty-four hours. I know that I had no other way to get out of Hialeah, but more and more, it feels like there's an elephelk sitting on my chest.

I sit up in bed. "Alright, enough. You're going to strip me bald at this rate. I'll get you more food, Fred." I pull my hair free and quickly dress in the standard blue crew coveralls.

Leaving my door open for Fred to roam about, I head over to the cafeteria on a hunch. Six heads of immature, sickly cabbage won't be enough for Fred for four days of travel. I've been rationing carefully, but I was told to leave some over for Juliet. Hence, my newest brilliant plan.

"Otissss!" I call through the salad bar in the cafeteria. "Hey, O.? You back there, buddy?" Honest-to-Bob, why would an intelligent robot hover around the cafeteria during off hours? I sure as voids wouldn't, if I worked there.

"Toodly-doo there to you, Miss Savage," comes the automated cheerful reply. The disco-ball head zooms towards me, along with the rest of his stupidly shiny body on smooth wheels. I bet those wheels of his have fancy shock absorbers that they'll never have to use on these polished floors. "I've been wanting to speak with you! But was there something I can help you with today?"

His voice is too cheerful, and comes with an accompanying chime each time he talks. He has no reason to be this happy.

Whoever programmed him to have this level of cheer should be taken out back and tortured for a few hours.

"It's actually for Fred." I reply. "You know, the umemeh."

"For Fred! Of course." He's as bubbly as ever. His voice is loud and booming, and a stupid staccato beat accompanies his responses, transforming everything he says into a funky musical sing-song chant.

"Do you mind if you – I mean, would you be able to – that is, switch off the –" I bite off the words *incredibly annoying*. I'm trying my hardest to remain calm and collected. "— the music? While we're talking?"

"Sure thing there, Missy," he replies with the same zip. Sans music, he still sucks. Well, I wanted to be polite, but this torture needs to end.

"Can you make the umemeh some peli-pellets?" I blurt out.

"Ehmmm. That sure is one interesting request because that happens to be a recipe I do *not* have on hand!" he exclaims. "Did you know that I have seventeen thousand, seven-hundred and thirty-five recipes currently stored in my memory banks?"

"Do any of them meet the umemeh's daily dietary needs?" I ask dryly through gritted teeth.

The disco ball head whirs around in a rapid circle, and his LED eyes remain in place. I'm sure his eye-sensors are elsewhere and this is just a projection of eyeballs, but the visual effect of having a rapidly pulsing light reprojected in a new location ever micro-second is giving me an impression of a silkless gumby spider, the kind who spin their black and white spotted carapace shield to hypnotize their prey right before spraying them with venom.

"Cut that out. That's really creepy." I'm not in the mood for any of this extra shit. "Who dialed up your personality to this level? This can't be normal. Who did this to you? I have to know. Was it Reyes?"

Otis's head slows to a stop, and his LED mouth reforms into a frown. "Aw. I can see I've upset you there. Sorry for that, neighbor! My previous boss, Five-Fingers, did tinker with my personality back when I was in his employ, and once I came to work here, Master Gisella did some tinkering as well. Now, just who is responsible for what is pretty darn tough to tell from where I stand!"

I blow out an impressed whistle. While I never heard of the Spiff, everyone in the galaxy has heard of Five-Fingers. Before I moved to Hialeah, he was most famous for stealing the first ever quanta-drive ship at its prototype unveiling in front of the government capital. He even managed to evade being pinned with charges for that, too. Last I heard, he was incarcerated on some puny charges – comparatively – for hacking uber-wealthy private bank accounts. How the hull breaches did the Waterloo get Five-Fingers' used equipment?

"You guys aren't really in the shitter business, are you?"

"Number one in the industry for reliable transport and install of sanitary equipment," Otis replies cheerily. "Our captain happens to have a soft spot for those he perceives to be broken in some way, though I can assure you, I am perfectly functional."

"That's questionable," I mutter. I clear my throat. "Another question for you. Are you able to manufacture antifungal medications? That is, if the doc doesn't have any in stock?" Otis's head starts spinning and I can tell I'm in for more of the ridiculous musical replies. "On second thought, forget it. Don't answer," I say hastily. "And please, if you don't want me to vomit, cut that out."

I shouldn't have asked. It's not my job to fix everything on this stupid ship. What I do need – all I need, actually – is for me and Fred to get off this floating toilet. Alive. And to do that, I need to feed the umemeh.

"You'll be pleased as punch to know that I *now* have seventeen thousand, nine hundred and thirteen recipes in my easy-access storage, plus an additional seven lined up –"

"Otis, the point," I hiss. "Cut the rest."

"Well. It was all to say that I uploaded a few new recipes for peli-pellets over the last two minutes, but you'll have to tell me if we are looking for a tundra diet, savanna, or steppes. I assume the weight class is for that of an adult umemeh –"

"Steppes," I say, and turn on my heel. I can't handle one more second of this conversation and be polite at the same time. Who cares if this guy was messed up by Five-Fingers? We've all been fucked over in our own special ways. Get me the voids out of here.

"Ohhh, Miss Savage!" he calls after me. "I was hoping to talk to you, friend!"

I keep walking.

"I wanted to recommend you shut off the GPS tagging on your quanta-com."

I stop dead in my tracks. I turn back to the robot, whose cheerful disco-head is still smiling at me from behind the bar.

"What did you just say?" I ask in a half-whisper.

"Well, as I'm sure you know, as an ANDI3500 model, I was built for systems connectivity. Of course, I wasn't always programmed for meal preparations. My inter-spatial operative board has been wired with two plar-dons, a soup-annihilator, in addition to a –"

"Otis!" I yell. "Stop spewing –" I clamp my mouth shut. When I finally trust myself to speak again, I manage to spit out the words, "Please? Get. To. The" — Fucking — " Point."

"Well, all this to say," he continues, not the slightest bit miffed. "I am able to read personal communications as well as the quanta-com channels accessed by everyone aboard the ship."

My mind races. Can he really read all personal communications? Like the ones I just exchanged with a certain mob boss?

Otis blathers on. "Of course, I do know a thing or two about privacy! Yes, I doodly do! Gisella taught me all about that very important factor after I inadvertently, most inadvertently, caused a fight to break out onboard. It most certainly is *not* appreciated if I tell Captain who is watching which pornographies, and who is stealing bandwidth from someone else's quanta-com bites. But, nevertheless, I do have access to all outgoing and inbound information. My standing orders are to tell Captain Reyes if there's ever anything critical for him to know, with parameters strictly defined as preventing harm to come others, and –"

"Otis?" I gulp. I really need him to get to the point. "The GPS."

"Right. Well, based on your communications with a-one entity you've labeled as 'Boss,' who, based on signal tracking is a particular Mr. Truyoza," he begins cheerily. I cough several times, choking on my own saliva. Otis plows on, "And the context of your personal messages with him, I am fully aware of your plans for the umemeh. Now, you'll want to know, that I did *not* report it to Captain Reyes because I was told only to report things that could directly cause or ship or crewmembers any harm. And based on my calculations, Miss Savage, your journey won't continue for much longer. In fact, you should be pleased that I have deemed there to be absolutely no risk whatsoever to the umemeh. Nor is there a risk to the crew or ship, despite your most recent interchange. When your mission fails, both Captain Reyes and the police will be able to take protective actions against Greel Truyoza, thanks to me, and the communications I've recorded. So there is no need to report this information at this juncture. Isn't that pleasing? You don't look pleased."

My blood is pounding in my ears. He's been recording my conversations with Greel Truyoza to submit it to the police when I fail. He's certain I *will* fail! I close my hanging open jaw several times before I can put together two thoughts in my head.

"Just so that we're on the same page. You have deemed my chances of success *to be zero percent*?" Because that is the least offensive thing I can think to say without warning him of his upcoming murder.

"Oh, yes indeed-a-roo! Absolutely. But there *could* be a point zero zero one chance of your success, if we're feeling optimistic. Which was why I wanted to warn you about the GPS. You're welcome." He concludes this statement with a little tri-beep flourish and a small roll backwards.

"What," I grind out slowly, "*about* the GPS?"

"Oh. I see where the confusion is! The letter acronym GPS stands for the Galactic Positioning System. It's accomplished via a chip installed in–"

"I know what a void-forsaken GPS is!" I holler. I cast a hurried glance about the empty cafeteria around me. "*What*, darling Otis," I say, my hushed whisper as aggressive as a Malanese Chimpoodle about to strike its prey, "*what* would you like to warn me about my motherfucking GPS?"

"Why! There is no reason to be so curse-prone, young missus! I am trying to assist you! You've been nothing but insulting for this entire conversation. I am bound to tell you that this has moved you firmly out of friend territory, and I am not obligated to help someone who is not a friend." The robot makes a *tsk*ing sound and starts rolling backwards.

"What? Wait, wait, wait." The backward retreat continues, but he keeps those LED eyes pointed towards me. Okay, he wants me to grovel, then.

"Otis. Please!" I'm not really sure what a robot needs in terms of groveling. I put my hands together in Bob Schwinn's famous poster pose, and Otis pauses. Maybe he's as out of touch with humans as I am. "Listen, I'm sorry. I'm under a lot of stress. Can you please" – not be a motherfucking asshole – "please, tell me your warning about my GPS?"

Otis makes a sniffling noise. Ironic for a robot without a nose. "I only would recommend that you remove the tracking chip. Your chances would be fractionally better."

Remove it? It's already been removed. Way back on Hialeah, before I ever got on the *Cricket*. By Weasel. ...Oh.

Asphyxiate in a burning asteroid storm, Weasel. I *cannot* believe he screwed me over.

Fuck. Yes, I can.

"At the speeds we're travelling, your GPS broadcast should be blurred to a five-lightyear radius. And *that* is readable at a distance of thirty-lightyears. So there's a high chance the police will find you at the next port. Zero risk for Fred, as I said."

I rip the quanta-com off my wrist. I'll throw it out an airlock! Yes, that's what I'll do.

But I'll need access to my encrypted wallet. And Bob help me if Greel Truyoza tries to reach me and gives me another timeline for a response…

Okay, I will *not* throw my quanta-com off the ship. I'll smash it to smithereens *after* I save the communications doo-dad and the banking chip. Or I'll disable the GPS thingie-mabobber on my own.

I glance at Otis. "Heh. Heh. Any chance you could, uh, make some modifications to my quanta-com device?"

"No siree," he replies in that all too-cheerful voice. "No can do! Since joining the Waterloo's crew, I've been strictly prohibited from making modifications to crewmember's electronic devices. Personally, I suspect this has something to do with the modifications I made to give someone access to the Risk cheat codes on game night, but I, hey! Heya, Miss Savage?! Where are you going?"

But his other calls after me are lost once the cafeteria doors close behind me, and the only sound that fills my ears is the satisfying loud clomp of my heavy-duty, shit-stomping boots. Otis can't help me, so it's time to do what I've always done. I'm going to protect my own kick-ass self.

chapter fifteen

"Hey, Gisella." I try to make my voice sound upbeat over the bedroom's intercom, but I don't think that function works on my voicebox anymore.

"Hey Savvy!" She, on the other hand, has no problems with genuine warmth. "Everything okay?"

I shoot another glance at the flickering image cast by the portable holo-projector in my small room. My quanta-com is on the narrow ledge of the folding shelf. Or what's left of it anyway. Screws and metallic parts litter every inch of available table space, which, let's be real, is expensive real estate in this matchbox of a bedroom. Another tinkling sound alerts me that I've dropped yet another miniature screw.

"Fuck," I mutter, bending down to find that bacterial sized pain in the ass.

"Savvy?" Gisella asks, her voice laced with concern.

"Sorry. I –" I bang my head on the bottom of the shelf in the process of righting myself. Tons more metallic objects shower the floor around me with a cacophony of clinking noises. "Mother. Fucking. Shit!"

"Savvy. Don't move," Gisella says urgently into her quanta-com. "I'm on my way to you."

"No! No, don't come," I yelp hastily.

Okay, burning asteroids, I *wish* she could come. If there was anyone on this ship who I wish could remove the GPS tracker for my quanta-com, it would be Gisella. But you can't just ask a straight up non-criminal to do a questionable activity for you. It would raise all kinds of alarms. And once the quanta-com is in her hands, and with her curiosity raised, I can't trust Gisella not to peek at my personal message history. It's one thing to luck out with Otis being a socially clueless moron, but I'm pretty sure it would be harder to slip this past Gisella.

"Don't come. Sorry. It's a bit of a mess in here." Which was true. I live with an umemeh, okay? And yes, he does still sleep standing up in this room next to me for some inexplicable reason.

"I wanted to ask you –" I get up and scan the holograph projector again. "I was just curious, I mean. Where would one find a, um, neo-synchronous-eyelash, if one were to look inside a quanta-com?"

I glare at the stupid device on my folding shelf. In the silence that follows, it feels impossible that this collection of odd-shaped miniature bolts could ever have functioned, or that it will ever function again. What were the chances I could do this right? I'm a zoologist, not a mechanic. Thank the mother-loving apes that I messaged Truyoza before I started this bloodbath of technical difficulties. I told him I'd be in touch in two days, when we got to the next port. I have definitely fucked this one up.

I clear my throat. "Never mind, you can forget I asked."

"Wait, wait. I'm pulling up the schematics," she answers quickly through the intercom. "What made you get curious about that piece of machinery?"

"Oh, I was just... wondering if I could do the engineering thing. You mentioned more female engineers, but it turns out a blind monkey would be better at this than I am."

"You said the neo-synchronous eyelash, right?" She wasn't even paying attention. "It's the one thing in there that looks like a cheap piece of duct tape. It has electrical wiring in it, so if you're going to try moving it, don't let it rip."

"Thanks, Gisella. Owe you one." I hang up on her and set to picking up all the miniscule pieces on the floor. I've now lost three hundred parts but learned what a piece of tape looks like. I hate this device.

I stare at the linoleum marbled floor tile again. What I really need is a magnet, I decide. That will make a floor sweep a snap. I do actually own a magnet, and I did actually take it with me out of Hialeah. It is most definitely in the bag still located in Doc Samuel's infirmary. I've done the best I can do with the inept hands I've got, so I get back to removing the stupid GPS.

I'm proud to report the neo-synchronous eyelash is now removed. And unripped.

I read through the next direction on the holo-projector.

"Seriously!?" I exclaim, and only narrowly miss banging my hand on the shelf. It lands on the wall, and while the parts all jump at the shock of it, they stay on the table. More or less. "What the voids is a mellifluous binary footer? Why the voids wouldn't they label these diagrams? Why does this have to be so void-forsaking difficult!"

I wait a minute for my rage to die down to the point I believe I can keep my voice at a normal level.

"Hey Saffron!" Gisella answers the intercom on the first ring. "Everything okay over there?"

"A mellifluous binary footer," I say. I was wrong about the whole keeping my voice steady. I sound demented. "What. The. Voids. Is a mellifluous binary footer?"

"The good ol' MBF," she says.

"The what now?"

"Oh, nothing. I was joking around. You know what, I can see my humor isn't going over very well. Do you see the square screw right below the eyelash?"

"Why in the name of all that is intelligent would someone manufacture a square screw?"

"Yeah, that was good ol' Baumann. He was the engineering architect behind all the old quanta-com models. Apparently square screws take up less room in a shipping container than round ones. Like, five joulos worth of more screws can be added per crate. So."

"Bees."

"So, you'll need to loosen it with a square screw snipper tool." She pauses. "I want to tell you that the device is colloquially termed the s-cube but you'll only think I'm joking."

"Believe me, Gisella, nothing about this could strike me as funny."

"Right. Use the s-cube to torque that thing past the quad-pilons on either side. It should pop right out."

"With an s-cube."

"A term that is short for square screw snipper. You do have one of those, right? Kind of looks like a mini fork-lift. They come in pretty much every multi-tool."

I groan. Like the multi tool in my confiscated bag? "Yep. Thanks, Gisella."

After hanging up, I stare at the disaster on my shelf. Maybe it isn't too late to toss it out an airlock. Before I can act on *that* insanely tempting impulse, banging on the door startles me.

"Open this door, Saffron," comes the thundering voice of Hotpants Reyes. I cast a glance back at the quanta-com. There's no direct proof I'm a criminal because I have a destroyed quanta-com, but boy, it looks ugly.

I open the door to find Reyes heavily leaning on the door-frame, sparks in his eyes. I know I should be scared by that look. I know I should step away, but I can't. Maybe it's because I'm feeling guilty of selling him out to Turyoza. Maybe it's because he's breathing hot and heavy this close to my bedroom. But I'm feeling soft.

"If I find out you've been destroying ship property," he begins, raising a finger at me.

I raise my eyebrows and pout. "Me? I'm the picture of innocence."

"A neo-synchronous eyelash?" he asks, exasperated. "I was

with Gisella when she got that comm. You're up to something. You may as well tell me now."

I blink several times, not sure why he cares so much about this. I twist my shoulders so he can see the carnage past me in the doorframe. "I was tinkering on my quanta-com." I can read him as the lines on his face relax and he realizes just how close to me he's standing. "A project that was halted because my multi-tool is still in Doc's custody." I sniffle and try to sound like I know what the voids I'm talking about. "Apparently, I need an s-cube."

"Get a spare one from Doc."

"Any chance you'll allow her to release my shit back into my own custody?" I bat my eyelashes at him and place one hand on the doorframe, millimeters from his shoulder. I give him a meaningful look, hoping to turn him into a compliant sleaze-ball like every other man on Hialeah. But then, like shutter gates slamming down, his eyes go stone cold.

"Any chance my cargo hold is cleared of piss yet?" I balk at this. "I thought not. Get a spare multi-tool from Doc. She's got plenty." And with that, Reyes stomps back down the hall. I can't help the small zing I get from watching his ass as he walks away.

Walking back up to those infirmary doors takes a surprising amount of willpower. It's like my brain has grown an aversion to it, like how I can't drink jinquilla anymore after that one time I had too much of it. I've definitely had way too much time in that tin room. It doesn't get any better with the frosty reception I get from Doc.

"Liver finally quit on you?" she asks by way of hello. "Because I can't imagine any other medical reason you'd need to be here."

I snap my mouth shut. I *had* meant to discuss what was plaguing those bats but fuck that. In the words of a very annoying robot, no siree-doodly-doo.

I think I may be getting hysterical.

She raises an eyebrow at me.

"My bag," I say. "I need it back. It's got my multi-tool. And treats for Fred."

"Confiscated," Doc replies, returning to the three-dimensional, globular shapes on the holo-projector in front of her. "Speak to the captain about it."

"What are you playing over there?" I ask, peering at her holo-screen. "Is that Tetris?"

"This," says the Doc, snapping her holo-projector off, "is not a game. I research how to apply aggressive cancer morphologies to inflatable wound patches. In case you were actually interested." She scans me from head to foot.

I can't help it. I'm a little bit impressed. "That was a mouthful." Doc lets out a long sigh. "Sargie said I could get a spare multi-tool from you?"

Her eyes dart to me, fierce and quick. "That is Sergeant Reyes to you," she snaps. "And the spare multi-tools are in the rustoreum." She gestures towards the counter. "Though I don't understand why he would consider loaning you one. Even one of those."

The rustoreum? Great. I'm sure it'll be swell at torquing a square screw. I open the case and the humming of the automatic cleaner pauses. A collection of crusty brown, oblong objects are inside.

"What, did you just put it in here? After discovering it at the bottom of a lake? For the last five centuries?"

Doc rolls her eyes. "Take it or leave it are your only options, Miss Savage."

Just as I'm staring at the ancient devices, wondering if any of them are capable of putting my quanta-com back together in the remaining day and a half aboard, I hear my name being paged over the loudspeakers.

"Yo, Saffron. Where the eff are you?" Pete's raspy voice rolls over the loudspeakers. "Get your ass over to crew duty."

Doc glances at the clock on the corner of her projector. She frowns. "Didn't shift start twenty minutes ago?"

Right. I wrap my fingers around the multi-tool and start sprinting down the hallways.

I have no idea how Pete will punish me for being late a second time, but last time I was late, he made me scrub the lockers.

I am not scrubbing lockers today. First of all, they are clean. Any residual odors are your own problem.

Second of all, I am not scrubbing lockers again. That's just not right.

chapter sixteen

I stare at the assorted miniscule metallic pieces in the baggie in the quiet privacy of my room.

"Fuck you," I say to the baggie. I don't know if I'm talking to Greel Truyoza or Captain Reyes at this point, but I'm blinking back tears.

No, I can't fucking put the quanta-com back together. Yes, I'll get in contact with the Control Freak of a Mob Boss once we land. And yes, that will be soon enough.

Two hours ago, the ship started the clockwise wind-down through traffic into the port. Not that uptight Reyes bothered to notify me about it, obviously. From the holo-windows, it looks like a micro-planet.

My stomach clenches at the thought of moving darling Fred through another port. He's about as inconspicuous as an animated blinking neon sign, lit on fire, and zapping lasers. I'm supremely screwed. Plus, there's also a good chance this port is actually Surf & Ceebu with the Brin-177 military outpost. Somehow it's come down to either a parading an umemeh past Brin-177 personnel or signing up for a protracted and painful death by mobsters. Thanks for this journey, impotent mob boss, thanks a lot.

We're docking in another fifteen minutes and my first task

will be to replace this bag of crap. My sight passes through the clear plastic baggie and to the clean flooring behind it. The floor makes me snort. It's no longer a charming mystery how Sergeant Reyes's hallways get so pristine. It's been a total of four soul-sucking days of cleaning dirt from lockers and hallway moldings and holy pill-loving pygmy chimps, I am so done with this cleaning thing. I sleep with a fucking umemeh! I've never been the kind to be bothered by a bit of dirt. *Life* is dirty. It was plain cruel to make me scrub baseboards with a toothbrush.

A groaning and clicking reverberates through the ship in that special coupling way that it does. I jump at the sound. My nerves feel all jangley with electricity. I've been locked in my room for the last two hours, scheming. All my brooding while Fred was completely MIA has amounted to one really absolutely brilliant grand plan: Wing it.

I haven't come up with anything more detailed. As soon as Reyes gets off my ass in that station, I'll find a quanta-com and contact Greel Truyoza.

"Savvy? Saffron Savage, please meet us up on the bridge," Rosemary's voice says politely over the ship's loudspeakers.

Shit. It's time. If there is a Brin-177 security detail patrolling the gates of Surf & Ceebu, I'm done for.

I straighten my crew coveralls. I push back my hair out of my face so at least I won't look deranged in my police pictures. When that doesn't work, I plait it into a quick side braid. If I'm marching to meet my captors, at least I'll look presentable.

"Savage." Captain Reyes snaps over the loudspeaker. He's way less polite than Rosemary. "Get up to the bridge. Now." I can hear Rosemary protesting in the background before the loudspeaker shut off. *At least not everyone here is an asshole*, I think as I head to the elevators.

"Why? Why can't he let me off the ship and into police custody without harassing me? Why does that asswipe gotta call me to the bridge, like a kid to the principal's office?" I ask the empty elevator. The words sound all hollow and sad. "He's just a big old… jerk! The biggest, stupidest jerk of 'em all."

The doors bing open, and Sergeant Michael Reyes is waiting for me, leaning against a mahogany wall like it's a magazine photoshoot. Fred's heads are bopping along to jazz music further back on the bridge.

"What do you want?" I ask, folding my arms.

"Hello to you too!" says Sergeant Reyes, grinning smugly. Too smugly. Apparently, his mood has completely flip-flopped in the last two minutes. Psycho. "We're about to unload some cargo at The Hobo's Towel."

I blink several times. The Hobo's Towel? "Not Surfff…" I shut my stupid mouth. I almost blurted out Surf & Ceebu. "Not Servant's Den?" I try to salvage my idiot self with a well-known port near my folks on Minerva, hundreds of lightyears away. "I mean, that's great. The Hobo's Towel is great."

"Do you know it?" Gisella chimes in from beyond. "We stop here all the time. They always need spare parts, and they've got good paying customers. We love this place!"

My gaze reverts back to Reyes' odd smile, and I quickly run through all the facts that I've ever heard about The Hobo's Towel. If I remember correctly about Weasel's supply runs for Hialeah, The Hobo's Towel is a small, man-made asteroid. A shitty place with even shittier security. I have no complaints. I close my open-mouthed jaw and take a deep breath. Okay, I'm not about to die. I'm not about to be arrested. I wonder if this is some sort of trick, because I can't believe *something* is going right for once.

Reyes is looking at me like the cat who broke into a zoo planet's illegal dairy farm. My mind races for reasons he might be this smug. Is he going to trap me on this ship forever? Or… is he going to escort me all the way to Brin-177?

"Look, Captain Reyes. I already worked your cargo. I did my time. You've gotta let me go. I'm not your slave."

"Not at all! We wouldn't dream of delaying your mission to Brin-177. Not in a million years!" He's smiling now, but the smile is so painfully fake, that I glance around the room to make sure no one's about to run me clean with an axe.

No one rushes to murder me, and I turn my attention back to Reyes. "Yeessss, that's correct. I am traveling to Brin-177," I reply slowly. Something is still not adding up. "*Why* did you call me up here?"

"I wanted to make your life easier for you!" Reyes opens his arms in a gesture of welcome. "Traveling with an umemeh is so difficult and requires so much self-sacrifice. We've all seen what a great big heart you've got. I thought I would do the nice thing and help you!"

My gaze flicks behind Sergeant Reyes, where a beaming Gisella is approaching. Her smile is genuine. Sergeant Reyes, on the other hand, not so much.

"What the hull-breaches have you done?"

"Only good things, I swear!" Reyes places a hand over his heart in a caricature of kindness. "I called up an old friend of mine from the military. Another animal rights activist, just like you." My hopes are sinking really fast at this moment. "His name is Lieutenant Crenshaw Bremerton," Reyes continues. "Old, old buddy of mine who's still well-connected with the military. And guess what? He volunteered to take you the rest of the way."

What? No. Nonononono. This cannot be happening.

"Yes! He'll fly you – *and Fred* – directly to Brin-177! He even offered the service free of charge. Isn't that fantastic? That way, you don't have to worry about booking your own passage. No worries about evading the police. As I said, he's *connected*. You're all set!"

I put my hands on my hips and stare at him.

"I am capable of booking my own passage," *fuck you very much.*

"Of course you are," he replies, drawing it out with so much cheesiness that Gisella looks at him funny. She rolls her eyes behind his back, gives me a meaningful glance, mouths "sorry," and walks away. Reyes continues, oblivious and gleeful. "Of course, you could do it on your own. I thought this would be a nice surprise. A gift. To be kind to you. Don't you want to thank me?"

"No," I reply firmly, cutting off the "fuck you" that I'd truly like to add. I blink rapidly. I have a seventy-two-hour window to get to Truyoza, and he will freak out if I get on a ship flying directly to Brin-177. This cannot happen. I try the classic non-committal lie. "I don't know what Bremerton's ship is like. It might not work out for the umemeh. I'll check it out and see what my other options are. I'm not promising anything."

"Well," Reyes replies with a dangerous gleam in his eye, leaning in. "I wouldn't want anyone to get the wrong idea that, you know, you might be an animal trafficker. And that's what would happen if you refused a free ride and started comming up a storm on The Hobo's Towel."

Reyes winks at me, and in this moment, I hate him. I truly fucking hate him. He's known, all along, exactly what I was doing. He pretended otherwise in order to get me to do free labor while I was on board his ship.

"You're a deranged psychopath," I say quietly, radiating anger. Gisella is too far away to catch it, but Reyes has heard me.

"Coming from you, that's a compliment," he replies, breath hot and venomous in the space between us. There is no more false sweetness left in his voice, no more fake smiles. The mask is off, and it is obvious how much disdain he has for me.

"You can't force me. I'm not doing it."

Reyes raises his eyebrows. "Oh yes, you *are*." He continues in a heated voice. "Let me tell you what will happen if you do *not* get on Lieutenant Crenshaw Bremerton's ship, which is docked right next door to us at the port, by the way." I hiss at this. "If you do not get on that ship, I'll have to assume you've been lying to us this whole time. Imagine that! And, if you've been lying to us, then I'll have to assume you really are an animal trafficker. So, if you do not get on Bremerton's ship, I will call the police and have you arrested. Immediately."

I glare at his raised eyebrows and folded arms. This man is evil incarnate. I was *this* close to ending my blood debt to Greel Truyoza.

"Okay. Fine. I'll get on to Bremerton's ship," I reply, angry as a burning asteroid storm. *You don't corner me, asshole. You picked the wrong woman to out-maneuver.* "But I can't promise you that you'll like it. Umemeh are just so unpredictable, you know?"

Reyes gives the most pained impression of a smile I've ever seen in my life.

"In that case," he says, "if you and Fred would just come with me. I'll walk you straight over."

It's not as if I have any other choice. I have never met Lieutenant Crenshaw Bremerton, but I can tell you one thing.

Righteous Fucking Reyes has made a big, fat mistake.

chapter seventeen

The cold, scrubbed air hits me as I lead Fred out into the harsh light of the port at The Hobo's Towel. It's the second time in a standard week that I've put my feet down on non-Hialean soil and even though I'm still mad as a batted hornets' nest, I feel a thrum of excitement to be off-world.

I glance around the terminal. It's got the same set up as The Horse's Ass, only this place is a lot swankier. The Hobo's Towel has those fancy virtual reality commercials along the walls where if you step through the holo-ad into the booth, you can spend your day buying things in completely fake – but super awesome – surroundings. I don't get the chance to check any of them out (nor does Fred for that matter), because Righteous Sergeant Reyes over here is shepherding me to the dock right next to ours.

As we head down the ramp from the ship that's been my porta-potty prison, I cast a sour glance at its open cargo bay doors. The place I scrubbed free of acidic umemeh-piss, in a suit, for two days. The place I thought would be a good shelter back at The Horse's Ass in a moment of idiocy. If only I hadn't seen this open cargo bay, this umemeh would already be delivered. Probably.

"Lieutenant Crenshaw Bremerton!" Sergeant Reyes calls to the man who's standing at the end of the ramp.

"Animal rights activist express!" the robed Bremerton exclaims jovially, with a cocky smile and a wave towards his ship.

If that's a Lieutenant, I'm a fucking playboy model. The guy is a crumbly thousand years old, but nevertheless, he's decked out in a red silk robe and quilted slippers. He's smoking a pipe – in a terminal! – and has a stupid pointy mustache under a greying, blonde mop of hair. One of his eyebrows is raised at me.

"Michael Reyes! You old dog. You never told me this lady friend of yours was such a ravishing beauty! I dare say, even with the strange matter of the unusual haircut," he tips his head, "your animal rights activist is startlingly gorgeous. Had I known the way of things I would have become an activist much earlier, I assure you."

"First of all, fuck off." I point a warning finger at him on behalf of all women of the entire universe. And half a million Blorts, who've often had their animal rights activism undermined because of their unconventional appearance. "Second of all, Reyes, we need to talk."

"As you can see," Reyes says to the bewildered Bremerton. "It's what's beneath that veneer that really matters."

"Oh dear, is it that time of month again?"

"Reyes? I'm going to murder him." I figure that warning is fair enough. I step forward, and Lieutenant Bremerton blinks mildly at me, as if he's never been assaulted before in his life. I shake my head. "You want me to share a flight with him?" I ask Reyes. "I couldn't share trillites with him. Not even if they were surging in my body and I was in danger of dying from a cytokine storm."

"There's more than enough room on the *Ev-REE-olly* for the two of you to keep your distance." Reyes chews his lip sourly, and I can't help it if my mouth physically wants to respond to that. I turn to evaluate Bremerton's ship just to change the view, and Holy Bob, Savior and Sponsor.

The *Ev-REE-olly* is one sleek motherfucker. It's what happens when a billionaire's toy has an orgy with a team of artists that took themselves too seriously. Shiny and black, decked out with upscale lights and leather. The ship's name is in sprawling iridescent letters across the side. I squint at it. Apparently, *Ev-REE-olly* is spelled *Euryale*. Only a privileged dipshit would spell a name full of nonsense letters. Below '*Euryale*,' the words "*The Lil Deuce Coup*" are stickered on in a marginally smaller font, equally bright.

"He spelled douche coop wrong," I announce.

I hear Reyes snort. "That's deuce, as in the number two," he replies, condescension dripping in his voice.

"Oh, no. No, no no. Is this another shit ship? I'm not traveling in a shit ship. No way, Reyes."

"Not two as in shit, Savage. Deuce as in two-seater. But yes, you will travel in that ship, no matter what cargo it carries, or you will be handed over to the police."

I give a skeptical glance over at the *Euryale*. Nothing about that screams two-person occupancy. If anything, it screams lavish redolent parties are held here, slathered in golden engine oil.

Crenshaw Bremerton stops tapping at his quanta-com and gestures at Fred behind me. "So, is this the umemeh, then?"

"No. It's an armadillo with a birth defect," I snap as I turn back to Sergeant Reyes. "Did you say this friend was an animal rights activist?" I ask him. "The leather finishings on his spaceship alone probably caused the extinction of a species!"

"He's been reformed," Reyes replies innocently. "More importantly, he'll take you exactly where you want to go. So." Sergeant Reyes shrugs in a way that implies I have no choice.

"What if he plans on selling Fred on the black market? I can't trust this guy! And I'm definitely not getting on a spaceship with this lunatic!"

"I can assure you," says Lieutenant Bremerton, "I have no need for the money."

"Shove off. We know you're loaded. And all that smoke is bad for the umemeh, too. I'm not getting on that ship."

"Well, it's like I said," Sergeant Reyes says, his mouth forming a firm line. "If you don't get on the good Lieutenant's ship, I will have to call the police. Just in case, of course."

I cannot get on this ship; Truyoza will make me and everyone around me very dead. There's no way this will work. I glare at Reyes, but he's not budging. I cast another glance back at Lieutenant Bremerton's ship. Fuck.

"I've got to pick up some supplies at the port. For Fred. And for me."

"Oh, no need, darling. I've already stocked up on everything the beastie could want. Cabbage, grasses, and even a potty room." Bremerton gestures magnanimously. "It was the best my guys could manage last minute."

"Okay." I blink several times in the wake of this statement. "Your wealth is obscenely offensive. Could you, like, tone it down a few billion when you condescend to talk to me?" I reassess the situation. I need to get alternate transport and comm Greel Truyoza. Immediately. Billionaire Fuckerton is not making this easy. I guess I will just take the easy excuse he handed me earlier. I hate myself for it, but desperate times call for desperate measures.

"Look. I need some *feminine hygiene* supplies. Yeah, I know." I put up a hand to forestall any of Bremerton's arguments. "You were right, congratulations. And I know what you're going to say. Your guys have stocked up your ship. But imagine for a minute that they don't know my exact flow. Did they prepare for heavy or light bleeders?"

Bremerton's pipe is about to fall out of his mouth. That horrified look on his face makes this entire lie worth it.

"That's what I thought. So. I'm going to walk into this port and get my own void-forsaken supplies. Is everyone here alright with that?" I say this as if it's a done deal, grab Fred by the neck, and begin hauling him away.

Sergeant Reyes dashes in front of me and raises his hands. "Not so fast, Savage."

I let out a long, "Arrrgggghhhhhhhh."

He tugs me back by the arm, and his hand digs into my skin. I glance at his face, and he actually looks pissed. This guy has some real problems.

"The umemeh stays here. On Bremerton's ship." Before I can object, he continues. "Unless you have a permit, it will be hard to get Fred past the port agent, anyway. So leave Fred here with Bremerton, someone you can trust, while you do your personal shopping."

I open my mouth to argue, but, shit. He's partly right. I hate this man.

"You're wrong, though," I respond, blithely evading the sense in his statement. "I can't trust Crenshaw Bremerton. *You* trust Crenshaw Bremerton. Not the same thing. How do I know he won't fly off with my umemeh the second I walk away?"

"I can assure you," begins billionaire Bremerton.

"Can it, Fuckerton." I take a deep breath. "Reyes." I stare Sarge squarely in the eyes. "I'll need some collateral."

"Excuse me?"

"You want me to leave my umemeh, dear darling Fred, with some buffoon-ionaire, and trust you two haven't colluded?"

"Are you completely out of your mind? Possession of an umemeh is illegal, Savage," Reyes responds. "If Bremerton were to fly off with Fred, you could just report him to the police. You know enough of his ship details to get him in trouble. That's all the collateral you need."

"Wrong, again," I reply, crossing my arms. "You two buddies could have planned something together. I need collateral from you, too."

Sergeant Reyes rolls his eyes. "Exactly what kind of collateral are we talking about?"

I mentally review every item on Reyes's ship. I don't have many choices.

"Give me your quanta-com."

"Not happening."

"I'd be happy to offer you mine, if you could be so persuaded?" Bremerton waves his pipe in a dismissive gesture. "I do have to caution you that I do carry a few spares around everywhere I go, so any loan would be immediately deactivated…"

"Shut *up*, pipe-smoker." I snap. "Sergeant Reyes, your quanta-com."

"Let me explain to you why *that* idea will never work," Reyes replies, as if talking to a four-year-old. He's let go of my arm by now, but he's leaning in and at spitting distance. The scent of his cologne is mingled in with the heat of his radiating anger. "My quanta-com is needed to complete transactions with the buyers we have lined up for my cargo. Recall – I am the captain of a cargo ship? My quanta-com is a necessary tool for communication."

"Yeah, so? Delay your transactions by two hours. No big deal."

"That's not happening," Sergeant Reyes says with a tone of finality. "We're flying out in two hours, and that's final. Pick something else or get comfortable with having zero collateral."

"Zero collateral?!" I exclaim. "Oh no," I scoff and shake my head. I do have a little leverage, after all. "You know, it would be a shame if someone tipped off that port agent that good old Doc Williams is handing out LSD to your crew like candy corn."

Reyes opens his mouth to protest, confused.

"You fuckers wouldn't give me my bag, remember? How do you think they keep all the animals happy on Hialeah?" I realize that now that I've told Reyes about it, he'll make sure it's off his ship within the next fifteen minutes. But I'd already kissed that shit goodbye. If he doesn't come up with collateral, I'll have enough time to get a port agent sniffing around. It works well as a threat.

Reyes comes to the same conclusion. He snaps his mouth shut again and returns to business mode, eyes beady and angry. "Fine. You want collateral? You can have collateral. But I need my quanta-com. Take Otis."

"LSD? I would have never imagined," murmurs Bremerton. "You say this is on Hialeah?"

"Shut *up*." I run a quick calculation. Otis does all the cooking for them. Reyes needs Otis for his crew to be happy, and it does sound like a fine compromise. I will need a signed note from the Cap'n, though, assuring any curious police that he's been given over to my care and not stolen. Just in case Reyes is planning on pulling some shit.

"Okay, deal. And don't throw my LSD to the turkey farm while I'm out. That shit's expensive."

"Pete!" Sergeant Reyes calls, his eyes still boring into mine.

Pete jogs over through the open cargo hold. "What's up, boss?"

"Pete, bring out Otis. Our bleeding-heart liberal friend here would like a companion."

Pete glances at me quizzically. "I, uh, could go with you, if you want? You don't need to take…"

"It's complicated," I mumble.

"Bring Otis out. That's an order, Pete." Sergeant Reyes's voice is hard and cold and there is no arguing with him.

Pete puts his hands up in the air and jogs back to the ship's interior. Truthfully, I would prefer Pete's conversation to Otis's any day. On the other hand, maybe I can get Otis to use his comms privileges to contact Greel Truyoza. But then again, I would have to deal with talking to him. I am really not liking this job.

"You had better be back in two hours," Reyes says, eyes aflame with hatred. "Not only is that my ship's scheduled departure time, but if you do not return by then, I'll be concerned about your disappearance. I'll be forced to get the police involved, and we all know how unfortunate that would be for everyone involved."

"It all really depends on The Hobo's Towel shops' pad selection," I reply, unsure how long it will take me to get into contact with Truyoza. I shrug. "No promises."

Pete comes jogging back with Otis's metallic body slumped over in his arms. My vision lingers on the shiny black robot, this electronic disco-ball who says I have zero chance of success. I can't believe I get to spend more one-on-one time with him.

"Here y'are, boss," Pete says, holding a limp Otis aloft to Reyes. "He requested I power him down. Said the heavy comms-traffic in the port is overwhelming to his system."

Thank Bob for that little blessing, anyway.

"Directly to Savage here," Sergeant Reyes says, still watching me. His eyes are really starting to creep me out. I take the cold metal hunk in my arms; Otis is lighter than he looks. "Pete, escort our narc-sniffing llama up into Lieutenant Bremerton's ship, please, and make sure he's comfortable," Sergeant Reyes adds.

I shake my head. This party is way past its prime. It's time for me to get the voids out of here.

chapter eighteen

Without Fred tagging along, it is disturbingly easy to get the full-body pathogen scan and stride past the customs agent. I slug four-foot Otis into a more comfortable spot on my shoulders and begin pushing my way through the throngs of people. The edges of the crowd are thinner, where the establishments and shops occupy every inch of wall space, which makes it easier to maneuver with a dead-weight dummy around my shoulders. But when an officer, clad in unmistakable union neon yellow, cocks his head at me and squints, I practically jump sky high.

Calm down, I tell myself. He can't possibly know who I am or where I've come from. There's no way he knows about Fred. He probably just thinks I've stolen Otis.

Fuck. Fuck, fuck, fuck, he thinks I've stolen Otis!

Even if I hand him Reyes's note, my name will ping the warrant out for my arrest that's still in the system. I duck and edge my way into the surging crowd. The port is unbelievably full of bustling pedestrian traffic and commercial establishments, loud with layers and layers of overlapping conversations, and the sounds of shitty tin music are tinkling out from somewhere. I hope to Bob that the incessant flurry of activity makes it easier for me to disappear.

I wade deeper into the throngs. The only problem is, everyone else here knows exactly where they are going and would like to be there within the next fifteen seconds and ain't nobody got time for a wee ginger girl and her enormous robot sticking out two feet to either side of her. Some jerk in all black bangs into Otis's wheels as he rushes past.

"What the fuck!" he yells at me.

"Like it's my fault your eyes are shit," I retort. Of course, my big mouth is enough to stop the asshole in his tracks.

The gothic-yuppy turns around, full blown pissed. "What did you say? You two-bit wench –" he begins.

Off in the corner of my vision, I notice that the neon cop is now talking rapidly into his quanta-com.

"Oh shit. Shit. Don't you have an optometry appointment to make, or something? Just…." I shoo him away, but Funeral Fancy looks like he's not done letting all the steam out. I never wanted to be the recipient of his angst in the first place. "Be gone!" Without waiting for a response, I turn and push back into the crowd.

Behind me, Funeral Fancy is still yelling obscenities, but nothing exciting. I firmly continue to add distance between me and the dark menace, wading further into the crowds.

"Savvy!" That's weird. I think I hear the nickname over the constant burble of the crowd. I must be going bat-shit insane.

"Yo! Saffron!" I definitely heard my name this time. "Savvy, *wait!*" I stop in my tracks and let my gaze rove across the shifting crowds, but I can't identify anyone in particular. If it's Doc Williams trying to hand me a bag of feminine hygiene products, I'll be pissed as shit. I'm not in the mood for more of Captain Reyes's shenanigans. I'm overdue for a comm to Greel Truyoza, and I know that's not going to go well. My quanta-com has not been in one piece since I tried to locate the eyelash flashing, or whatever those miniscule pieces are called, and there's no way Mr. Mobster will be pleased. I close my eyes and pray to Bob Schwinn, Protector-of-Ferrets, that this trip won't have any more complications. And that a stiff drink will drop out of the sky.

"Savvy!" says a voice behind me as a hand thumps on my arm. "Hulls, you move fast in a crowd."

Startled, I look up to find a smiling Rosemary, cowboy hat and all, trailed by Gisella in a v-neck black jumpsuit, Juliet, and even Lucy in her pink beanie. "Girl's outing," Rosemary explains. "We never had the chance to say goodbye. The guys are out running jobs. There's a great restaurant down the way with a cool Ancestral-Mondi vibe. Come, join us!"

"I, uh –" How do I explain that I urgently need to call a mob boss? The crowd jostles around us. I furrow my eyebrows. They're inviting me out? I thought they only cared about Fred.

"Wait. You want to say goodbye? With food?"

"Yeah. Eating is this crazy thing we do from time to time." Rosemary rolls her eyes. "The food is optional though, if you're not hungry."

Come on. Hungry has nothing to do with it. She's talking about Real Food. Not the shit they serve on Hialeah. Not the gussied-up meals that Otis manages to mix from the nutrient packs and a few measly vegetables. Food that's been cooked, not for nutritional value, but for flavor, specifically to imitate cuisines from the original human ancestral planet. My mouth waters at the thought.

Still, I'm skeptical. They actually want to say goodbye to *me*? I squint at the group of women – a group that's missing their most cynical crewmate. I don't want to be the subject of an ambush that ends in me getting arrested. I scowl. "Is Doc Williams going to be there too?"

But Rosemary shakes her head. "She almost never goes on shore leave." She shrugs. "We still invite her, every time." Some asshole hustling past bumps into Otis. "Hey! Watch it, jerkwad!" Rosemary yells. "That's an expensive piece of equipment, ya klutz." With that one outburst, she's created a clear zone around us in the middle of a raging torrent of human motion.

Rosemary returns her attention to me and shrugs. "Look," she says in that matter of fact voice she's got. "I know you're carrying

Otis as collateral. And I know Michael can get prickly when it comes to a challenge. Those shouldn't be reasons not to come."

I search her face, but I don't see any glimpse of trickery there. I think she's earnest. Which is just… wow.

PricklyBear Michael, I think, glancing at the endless human sea crammed into the terminal. *An Ancestral-Mondi restaurant,* Rosemary had said. The food alone says nothing about pricing, but if it's a cheap enough place, they may have some of those public quanta-com repair stalls in the back. I might not need to go through the trouble of replacing the whole void-forsaken thing.

But if they *don't* have those stalls… A small panic rises within me which I try to quell down. Reyes did say they have a two-hour layover. Should be enough time to squeeze in some food, too. And delaying contact with Truyoza by another half hour or so can't possibly make much of a difference. He'll be pissed either way. May as well get in a meal first.

Actually, it's unexpectedly nice that someone wants to spend time with me. All right – it's also the meal. I would love a stab at eating flavorful food.

I nod crisply. "Okay, I'm in. But I still gotta run my errands after."

Rosemary dips her hat. "That's what I like to hear. We'll make sure you have time for everything. Come on, Savvy. This way."

Did I mention, it's much, much easier to tow a big fat robot through a crowd when you've got other ladies at your flank? Holy hull-breaches.

On the outside, Mimi's Ganesh is a pair of unassuming floor-to-ceiling, blackened glass doors with stenciled lettering that have been chewed away by time. Like all the other shops of the crowded terminal with entrances built into the very wall of the main concourse, there's no telling the shape or contents of the restaurant that lies beyond the very-ordinary doors. But when we push past the nondescript entry, the inside of Mimi's Ganesh makes me catch my breath. The space is wide and continues deeper beyond what my eyes can make out. That's partly because the room is dimmed, lit only by lanterns hanging on ropes that crisscross the industrial pipes of the ceiling. Towards what I assume is the center of the room, is a hibachi bar in the round, with a whole different tier of seating. But everywhere, from the hibachi seating to the dark corner nooks, the tables are chock-full of patrons and the low burble of multiple streams of conversation.

It's also obvious that this is not the kind of place with cheap public quanta-com stations. I gulp, and a new bolus of saliva rises in response to the fragrant food smells. Now I feel regretful and hungry. That combo never goes well.

"Come on," Rosemary says, nabbing my arm. "We like the booths over this way."

I follow the ladies deeper into the eatery and can't help but gawk at all the different kinds of people who come here. There are greasy dockworkers here mixed in with hyper polished business folk – the full range of human specimens from across the Galaxy. One eclectically dressed man is approaching us enthusiastically, and by the blinking lights on his bald head I can identify him as a hybe. I'd seen a few back on my homeworld of Minerva, but none in the last decade on Hialeah.

The hybe stops a few feet away from our party and crunches the fingers of an upraised hand. His eyes are riveted to the floor somewhere near his own feet so I'm not sure if he was actually planning on talking to any of us or just being deferential to heavy-ass Otis, who I shift to get more weight distribution on my other shoulder. Regardless, it's an odd greeting.

Rosemary nods magnanimously on behalf of our group and leads us beyond him to our booth. I turn back towards the hybe, but he's already on his way to his own table of friends. I take one last glance at the door to the establishment before I hurry after the rest of the crew. I really need to replace my quanta-com, but I'm in a restaurant for the first time in *a decade*! A restaurant with real, bona fide food. Maybe I can check out the menu here, at least, and see what it is that they serve.

I eagerly scroll through my personal menu display through the clear glass of the table to read the most impossible of dishes. Tofu giyaki, shiriho masala… Yes please, tell me more!

I swallow hard when my five items ring up to a full galactic joulo, and the menu prompts for my quanta-com credit input. I swipe back and start unchecking boxes. Daal tom yum soup? Not today. The tzatziki naan can go back, too. And the pad paneer and saag larb were maybe a tad overly ambitious. And the mango lassie was plain decadent.

I scowl at the menu. I really should be heading out of here anyway. Of course, Otis and I are boxed into the corner seat, squished against a fucking wall. It's going to be a noisy affair to get back out of here.

"The dal tom yum is delicious," offers Gisella, across the table from me.

Yeah, I bet it is. I nod and pretend to study the menu again, instead scanning prices for the cheapest thing on the menu. I scroll up to the very top. It's been so long, back in my Uni days, since I'd eaten out at a restaurant with friends. Since I'd had friends. I swallow back all the saliva that's threatening to choke me. At what point is it polite to do the whole cough – 'I broke my quanta-com eyelash' crap – and 'does anyone have spare creds to cover me' verbal dance?

Rosemary elbows me. A quick glance over at her cleared menu screen tells me she's already placed her own order. She leans in. "My treat," she says quietly. "I was the one who strong-armed you into coming. My fault!" She winks.

I'm not too proud to accept charity. Daal tom yum soup, here I come!

I start clicking through to recreate my original order, then spare a glance back at Rosemary. She's deep in the throes of some old The Hobo's Towel gossip with Gisella across the table and seems completely unconcerned with my potentially one-joulo order.

Everyone's relaxed in their seats, half smiles plastered around in the flickering, orange light.

Friends.

By the time the foot-square trapdoor clicks open in the center of the table, my mouth is watering something fierce. Steaming hot plates rise through the spill-covered chute that leads to the below-ground kitchens, where meals are prepared by intelligent machinery far less elegant than Otis. Guilty, I glance over at the tin can shoved into the corner of the booth. The rest of the party barely notices him in his current shut-down state.

"Hey Savvy, you ever heard Reyes's unofficial theme song?" Rosemary asks.

I try not to choke on my daal tom yum, which I've been spooning so fast into my mouth that I've burned both the roof of my mouth and my tongue. "He has a theme song?" I manage to mumble out.

"Not officially," says Gisella slyly.

"That's not a nice song!" Juliet insists.

Lucy smiles her wan smile.

"He wrote it himself!" Rosemary says with an eyebrow raise.

"He did not!" Juliet squeals.

"Did too," Gisella replies.

"One of you bitches had better start singing it or I swear I will turn Otis on and make him do it!"

"Ohhhh—" Gisella says, worrying her bottom lip. She shiftily glances around the room. I can't help but notice Rosemary's attention flicks back to the hibachi bar, for the third or fourth time by my count, where a young, topless, and *very* sculpted man is working up a sweat at the grill.

"All right," Gisella decides. Her freckles get pinker, if that's even possible. "But you guys have to help me!" She takes a deep breath, and begins to chant in a quiet voice, "*Mike can, the porta-potty man -*"

"*Chief inspector of the outhouse clan –*" continues Rosemary.

Lucy raises a finger. "*Issues the tissues, the papers and towels, Listens to the house of the various bowels –*"

"*Sailing away for ports space bound –*" Gisella adds.

They all turn to Juliet. She purses her lips stubbornly. Gisella reaches behind Lucy to nudge Juliet. She makes an exaggerated sigh, then adds, "*Where all the poopies are floating around -*"

I guffaw.

"*Mike can, the porta-potty man,*" they all chant together, "*install a dream toilet in your space sedan!*" They all giggle at the end of the song.

I blink slowly around the table. "Captain *Reyes* wrote that?" They all turn their radiant grins at me.

"I think it was tweaked from somewhere else." Rosemary leans in with eyes twinkling. "But that jingle has sold us no fewer than twenty toilets!"

Juliet begins to object from across the table. Something about seemliness.

"Oh no, no, no," Rosemary interjects obstreperously. "Marketing figures are solid facts!"

Gisella smirks. Just then, her attention is caught by someone at a far table, and she waves energetically at them.

I crane my neck to get a clear view of the table. It's all-female crowd: two women are making out, and several other couples are very handsy with each other. They're adorable in a make-you-want-to-barf kind of way. I haven't seen such happy, loved-up couples in years, and I turn away once I realize I've been staring.

Gisella excuses herself to make her way over to their booth, where she's greeted with jovial hugs and, from one butch woman with shock-pink hair, hands that linger at her waist. Rosemary catches my gaze. "You know you're welcome to join them if you want to make some new friends," she says in a knowing tone.

"Ain't had enough liquor to start changing things up," I reply with a head shake.

"If you'll excuse me," Lucy says with her patented dreamy smile. With Gisella out of the way, she slides out of the booth easily.

"See ya," calls Rosemary.

My eyes track Lucy as she joins the hybe table. She pulls off her pink knitted hat, and I gasp when her white-blonde hair comes off with it too. It had been sewn onto the hat this whole time. Lucy is not just bald. She's a hybe, too.

Rosemary grabs my arm in a vise grip.

"I don't have a problem," I hiss. "It's just… Surprise is a bitch, you know."

"Mm," she grunts, and releases me.

I allow my gaze to track back to Lucy, who's pulled a chip out from the base of her neck and inserted it into the hybe safe-port. With speech rendered completely unnecessary by the direct communications of a safe-port, the others around the table remain eerily motionless, though they all fixate a loving stare on Lucy.

"She's got a fan club." Rosemary nods.

"How did she gather a fan club?" I ask as tactfully as possible.

"Lucy? Oh, she's a wonder." Rosemary takes a sip of iced tea, then gives her glass a frown. "Lucy wrote the general solution used by every vehicle running FTL near a blackhole. And she's been modeling simulations of it ever since, for every type of ship, ever. That's what she does every time she's off duty." Rosemary nods appreciatively. I don't think I've ever seen Lucy off-duty, which makes sense in retrospect. "Her innovative approach was to include variables for ship maintenance, current status of repair, year of manufacture, that kind of stuff," Rosemary continues. "She's been able to get a ninety-nine point nine-nine percent precision in her models. Her word is gospel to other hybe navigators."

I raise my eyebrows. I glance over at Juliet for confirmation, but she's sulkily staring down at her empty salad plate.

"Sounds like her talents are wasted on the *Waterloo*," I venture.

Rosemary shrugs. "Eh. She likes having the time to work out her simulations. She's happy. What's wasted about that?"

It is hard to argue with happy. I want to ask Juliet if she's considering transitioning to hybe also – sounds like a valuable addition for a navigator. But Juliet is stubbornly staring at the wall, her bottom lip sticking out. Maybe she's resistant to making the transition. Bob knows it could only improve her personality.

Rosemary clears her throat, then jerks her head towards the hibachi bar. "I'm going to see if I can talk my way into some drinks for the table. Want anything?"

I turn my attention to glistening muscles over there. The boy must be fifteen years younger than her, but gesundheit, he's got form.

"Ask if they have iodized water?" Juliet pipes up.

I cough loudly, choking on my own spit.

"Sure thing," Rosemary replies as she sashays from the table.

Only now do I notice that I've been left alone with Juliet. I debate if turning Otis on would make things less miserable.

Juliet says, "Um, Savage. So."

I glare at her. She might want to reconsider that hybe implant. "Juliet." I nod. "So."

She picks up a fork and pushes a wilted piece of lettuce around her plate. I toy with my own tzatziki naan, then cast another glance at Rosemary at the hibachi grill. She's smiling coyly and leaning in, and the Sweat-Puppy seems to be enjoying the view. If there were another set of hot muscles working back there, I'd have no problems trying to make new friends. Though the very thought of muscles makes my memory flash back to the last set I'd admired up close, specifically, the way Reyes's uniform stretches across those shoulders and pecs. I imagine, for a split second, how we might get along if he wasn't such a righteous freak. And I wonder how he would look shirtless and made to work behind a fiery grill. I bet he's got a six pack, too.

Juliet drags her fork along her plate, making an extremely irritating scraping sound.

I shake myself out of my reverie. Why am I still here? The food was good. Party's over. And I have a quanta-com to acquire, a mob boss to contact and a mega-yacht prison to escape. I begin to slide my way out of the bench seat, dragging Otis along with me. Juliet gives me an alarmed stare.

"Whoa there," Rosemary calls, returning to the table. She's holding three glasses and carefully sits back down in the booth, blocking me in again. She hands the clear glass to Juliet. "They had your water," she says. "And I got a couple shots of Gintaki for us. What happened, Savvy? We've only been here thirty minutes. You planning on leaving so soon?"

I grunt. I rotate the shot glass on the table in front of me.

"Don't tell me you've gone sober?" Rosemary lifts her glass at me, but I shake my head. I can't do this shit right now. This is not the time. Rosemary shrugs and knocks hers back. She grimaces, then clears her throat.

"Hector over there was asking me," Rosemary begins as she reaches over to take the second shot glass, "where I planned to travel next, and it got me thinking about how we're going our different ways. So? Now that you're off Hialeah, is there anywhere you'd like to go?"

I stare at Rosemary, and the difference between us yawns like a huge black hole. She's been all over the galaxy, and I've lived my whole life on two planets: Minerva and Hialeah. And once Truyoza tightens his noose, I won't be doing much more traveling, either. I blink back a stinging in my eyes.

"Oh, come on. Don't get that way! You're heading to Brin-177, right, Savvy? You've got that, at least."

I nod, numbly. Sure, I have that. I mean, it's a lie, but I have lies. In fact, lies and more lies are about all I have right now. Well, lies and Fred. But not for long. I swallow thickly.

Fuck this. I grab the shot glass from Rosemary, down it, then stand up.

"I gotta go," I mumble. The broken quanta-com is practically burning a hole through my clothes. "I mean, thank you for the food and all. It was really nice." And it was. I mean that. "But I really have to go." I grab Otis and lunge towards Rosemary, who's blocking my exit.

"Hollllld up," Rosemary insists. "It's tradition. Before we leave this place."

I stare at her, impatient and annoyed.

Rosemary taps the menu a few times, and soon, the trap door in the center of the table opens and a platter of pastries comes out.

Rosemary smiles, and her eyes are all kindness. "Take some with you. We all do. For the road."

I eye the plate of glazed carbohydrates.

"That," I say, grabbing a healthy assortment and shoving them in my bag, "is an excellent tradition."

ONCE I TWIST OUT OF THE BOOTH, I STOP DEAD IN MY TRACKS. There's a triad of sexy men heading in my direction, like the beginning of one of those dreams. I blink when I realize I actually know these men. It's a smiling Sergeant Reyes, with Dimitry? And Guppy! The only two engineering guys on Gisella's team who aren't over a hundred years old. The lot of them are cleaned up and in civilian clothing and, burning asteroids, if I had known them in another life I'd currently be slinking over there and draping myself all over those muscles.

Hotpants Reyes is even hotter than usual, clad in a pair of dark carray denim pants and a shimmering electra-lite shirt programmed to display a happy iguana with goggles driving a hovercar through blue skies. It's adorable. I realize now that I've never seen Reyes out zof uniform before. His dark hair falls out of its perfectly slicked back style and falls over his forehead to dangle by his left eye. He was laughing as he talked to Dimitry, but Reyes's smile fades when he catches sight of me. His mouth firms into a line, but he doesn't break his stride.

"What," he asks Rosemary with a hiss, "is *she* doing here?"

It's easier to remember what an asshole he is while he's acting like an asshole.

"I was just leaving," I say, hoisting Otis over my shoulders. I stop inches away from Reyes and my eyes are drawn to his furrowed eyebrows. I am close enough that I am enveloped in his cologne. His whole body stiffens at our proximity.

"Oo!" exclaims Dimitry, completely ignoring my chemistry with Reyes. "You still have the sticky buns. Win!"

Rosemary slaps his hand away. "Gisella and Lucy haven't had any yet."

Rather than turning to watch the pastry fight, I focus on the throbbing soft patch of Reyes's neck, pulsing fast and furious. I raise my eyes to find his, angry and unmoving.

"Totally fair game," says an unconcerned Dimitry as he leans in past me to reach again. "Once you've ordered the pastries, the men are welcome. Rules are rules, Rosie."

Reyes's eyes slide past mine to watch as Dimitry and Guppy scoot into the booth behind me, then snap back to me.

"Savage," Reyes's voice comes out thick and throaty. He turns right back into the asshole he is. "You'd *better* be back at the docks in…" he looks at his quanta-com, "one hour and fifteen minutes." He points a finger at me. "Or I'll have your wanted poster with every cop in this station for the theft of *Waterloo* property." His eyes nudge Otis. "Understood?"

I thrust my chin defiantly. The heat radiating between us has taken on a new tinge. I'm so angry I could light the station on fire. To spite him, I decide I will take every last minute, to the second.

"Captain. I invited Saffron here," Rosemary cuts in, her tone dangerously chiding. "She'll be fine. Right, Savvy?"

I nod curtly in Rosemary's direction, shrug Otis into a more comfortable position, and walk out without allowing myself to say anything else.

I hope Greel Truyoza finds this asshole and rips him a new one, is all I can think. On repeat.

chapter nineteen

I maneuver through the crowds, hoping to miraculously discover a quiet spot. I'm not sure what I hoped for, a fucking library? A smuggler's den with a flashing sign that says "conduct your illegal conversations here"? Not feeling especially brilliant, I push on, frantically turning round and round hoping to find a rescue sign. The crowds don't give a shit about my panic, and mostly express annoyance at Otis.

"You and me both, bud," I mutter when some asshole remarks how much he wishes I had booked Otis commercial passage. There are too many idiot people here. Between strolling crewmates still in their various ship unis, working residents scurrying from one port terminal to the other, and the fucking tourists, the crowd is overwhelming. There's the gaggle of tourists taking their time as they eat ice cream and laughing. And look there – here's a man trailed by his child's indi-pram. Based on size, the elephant of a child must be at walking age by now, but here he is, whining in his seat like a feral wolf while his father distractedly swats at him. Were humans always so obnoxious, or have the years on Hialeah made me prefer animals to my own species? Never mind. I've *always* preferred animals.

A retro neon flashing sign from a grimier, dimmer, less-trafficked corner of the port catches my attention. "PrePaid Quanta-

Com Oasis" the letters read, and I force my way through the throng to get to the corner oasis. Once I'm closer, it's obvious why there's a decreased traffic in this region of the port. Kitty-corner to the quanta-com store is a pungent Bueno Burrito, an out-of-business hand-cream stall that's been boarded over, and a public restroom. Perfect.

I barge into the quanta-com store and the stillness inside is an instant relief to the hubbub of the terminal.

An elderly man behind the counter raises his eyebrows, and his gaze immediately fixates on Otis, peering over the jeweler's magna-speckies that balance on his nose. "Repair, or sell?" he asks mildly.

I shake my head. "Nothing for this guy." The owner's gaze still lingers on Otis. I swallow. "Out of curiosity, though…?"

"To sell him? If that's an ANDI3500 in perfect condition with all-original parts, I could probably get one-fifty for him. I can offer you eighty joulos. I'd have to inspect him first, of course."

I calm the trill that runs through me at the casual mention of so much money, and instead scrunch up my nose. "Eighty joulos? For Otis? What kind of crappy mark down is that?"

"A generous one," the man replies, with the air of someone who's completely unconcerned with the conversation. "Even if he hasn't been stolen, he'll be sitting on my shelf a while before a buyer of that caliber enters the shop."

I shrug. "Well. I ain't selling. I'm buying. Got any untagged quanta-coms?"

At this, the old man pushes his speckies off shrewdly and puts his fingertips together. I feel as though I've walked into a trap. "Yes," he says, a small smile pulling at the edges of his ancient mouth. I really don't like the way that looks. "I do have two of those. Though, you know, there's not much demand for those." He fetches two models out from the cabinet behind him. "Both of these quanta-coms have the geo-tagging chip removed. The first is a thirty-joulo simple machine, which only does basic communication functions. If you want the added banking and navi functions, this second one will cost you eighty joulos."

Eighty joulos is an outrageous price for anything less than a college credit. There is no quanta-com in the universe that costs eighty joulos. Wait, I take that back. I'm sure Fuckerton back at the port might have a few, but they're not in the same league as anything in this store. I'm betting this salesman doesn't carry anything with wrist-sense or retinal display. He's just trying to work a desperate wench when he sees one. And I've had enough of assholes like that.

"Oh, really," I say flatly. "Eighty fucking joulos? What a coincidence, you asshole. Otis is not for sale." I push the door of the store open, and the arcane bell tinkles its warning.

"Wait!" calls the shopkeeper. "What if I gave you the upgraded quanta-com *and* paid you an additional forty joulos? Would you be willing to sell him then?"

I round on him. "I'll tell you what, you inbred monkey's twat." I jab an angry finger at him. "I *'would be willing'* to purchase an upgraded quanta-com from you for forty joulos. Even though that's outrageously overpriced. And if I see the slightest glitch before I leave this store, even once, I will find another place for my business."

The dude puts his speckies back on and punches a series of buttons on an ancient calculator, as if that shit were a crystal ball through which pricing could be divined. He heaves a sigh. "Fine, forty for the upgraded quanta-com. As a favor, in case you decide to return to do business for the robot." He nods at Otis.

Spawning bunniculas, do I hate humans at this moment.

I dig through my baggie of comms parts and pull out the dismembered wallet chip. The shopkeeper watches with an amused smile, that fucker. I bet he'd love it if this failed and I had to use a robot as a form of payment. Everyone just wants to screw me over. For once, can one void-forsaken thing go right? *Please let this work*, I offer in silent prayer to the universe as I scan my dismembered chip at the pay station. A tinkling chime sounds.

The shopkeeper, frowning, hands over the gangly, garish 'upgraded' quanta-com.

Outside the quanta-com shop is a conveniently located joulo-dispensary, so I use the device to unload all my cash from one broken chip, and then upload it to the unregistered banking file encoded onto the new one. All that's left is to inform Mr. Truyoza of my new quanta-com number. And, of course, the fact that Lieutenant Fuckerton has my umemeh.

My back goes rigid at the thought of this upcoming conversation. I don't want an innocent man to die. Even if he is the galaxy's pruniest playboy whose wealth is a blasphemy against human nature. His only crime, other than being a heinously loaded misogynist, was to want to help return a helpless animal to safety and I really, *really* can't bring myself to let him die for that.

I'll have to bargain with Truyoza for Fuckerton's life. I can't believe I'm willing to go into more debt, of any nature, on account of an aging bon vivant, but this is all getting way too messy. And it's all Reyes's fault. If he hadn't forced me into this escorted trip to Brin-177, I'd be well on my way and no one would be in danger of getting hurt. But Reyes had to go and fuck things up. Now, I have to get on my knees for Truyoza. Forget making a profit. At this point, I'll be happy if everyone remains uninjured and I never have to return to Hialeah. I hate Reyes for reducing me to this.

I glance about this corner, the least trafficked spot of the port, but there are no quiet spots in which someone could hold an undisturbed criminal phone conversation. Unless I want to pay for a motel room, but even then, privacy is unlikely.

The sign reading "cerveza" in the Bueno Burrito stand catches my attention, like the frantic, friendly wave from an old college buddy. Mindlessly, I wander closer to the sign before a stench from the adjacent bathrooms assaults me. I recoil and gag. Just as everyone does who passes in the vicinity. There's actually a full-halo clearing around the bathroom's door.

I tilt my head. Well, I wanted privacy. And Bob knows, I've worked with worse over the last decade.

I trundle straight in and check the stalls. Totally and completely deserted, except for the flies.

Here goes nothing.

————

Truyoza answers on the first ring.

"I have a problem." I explain why I'm using a new quanta-com and how I've been cornered into getting on Bremerton's ship.

"No," he replies with an unfeigned swagger in his voice. "You think you jhave a problem. Problem is not assholes. Problem is me. You no bring animal here, you owe me money. Five hundred joulos is no nothing! I warn you, incompetent little girl. You can jhave even bigger problem. Someone hears my name from you, and you are dead. Not just dead, but long, painful death. You understand this, yes?"

"Mr. Truyoza," I gulp. "I called you because I don't want any of these things to happen."

"Yes. This is good."

The line falls silent. I'm about to speak again when Truyoza announces his plan.

"I will send crew." He pauses, and I can hear an electronic beep in the background. "You say The Hobo's Towel? They will intercept ship *Euryale* at Buckingham Nebula, on way to Brin-177. They will hide behind Owl's Nest there for surprise attack. Then, they will take you and your animal to me. No more money for you. You are done."

I heave a silent sigh of relief. "No problem," I reply. "Just… don't kill anyone?"

I squint at the blank, dust spattered wall. I sound like a complete moron.

Truyoza only chuckles. "Kill? A lieutenant? You think *I* do messy jobs? No." He answers himself, decisively and without the slightest shred of humor.

"No, no. Of course not," I am on the edge of a knife blade here.

I can't afford to offend this guy, and on the other hand, I really, really don't want people to get hurt. I couldn't even bring myself to give Weasel more than a good trip, and I hate that guy. I close my eyes and push my thumb and forefinger into my lids to relieve the pressure. "Just, I would love a nice, clean, *not messy* job to get me out of this billionaire's control."

"Oh, you are under *my* control. From moment you take my money. Whether you like it or no. Probably for rest of life." He pauses. "Short or long, depending on you."

Long after Truyoza has hung up, my gaze lingers on the limp body of Otis in the flickering bathroom light. I don't like where I am. I don't like the man I'm indebted to. But I can tell you one thing: there's no way I'm rushing back to that uptight asshole, Reyes. I flush as my memory flashes back to his reception in the restaurant. He wanted me back in an hour and fifteen minutes. He'd been so very fucking precise.

I can be precise too.

———

Precisely one hour and fourteen minutes later, I call Reyes on my new untraceable quanta-com. "Oooohhhfffff," I say in response to his angry greeting. "I had too many cervezas."

"Savage, that's not funny. I'm calling the police."

"I'm here, I'm in the terminal." I look at my fingernails, wondering how else I can drag out this minor aggravation just to stick it to him. "I probably shouldn't carry Otis myself. Too wobbly. Send Pete to come help? I'm in the bathroom."

"*Which* bathroom, Savage?" he snaps, the tension still reverberating in his voice.

"The one next to the Bueno Burrito."

"And when he gets there, the door is going to be locked, isn't it? Or you'll be in a different bathroom? Or a different port entirely?"

"No, no. I'm here."

"Savage, so help me, if you and Otis are not there when Pete arrives, I *will* call the police." He clicks the line off.

Again with the police. The man is positively trigger happy with that word. My trickle of dismay turns into full-blown panic. What's going to stop the asshole from calling the police the very moment I return Otis? I glance down at the robot, the glass panels of his disco-ball head dark and reflecting the eerie flickering bathroom lights.

"That asshole captain of yours," I say to the cold metal lump. "You'd probably help him track me down, too. Wouldn't you?" I pull my lips out of their frown to spit out my bile into the sink. I turn on the sink to wash it down, my actions mirrored in Otis's dark panels.

"Yeah. If you were awake, you'd say something with a toodly-dee-doo. Or that I am rude for spitting and precisely how many minutes of porn I've watched my entire life." I snort. "Spoiler alert, not even X-Pals knows how much porn I've watched." I raise one of Otis's limp arms, and droplets from my hands transfer to the cool metal. "But *you'd* know, wouldn't you?"

A droplet of water runs down the length of Otis's articulated arm. I follow its path up and down the valleys of the accordion-like metal skin till it finally moves out of view into his armpit. I sigh.

"You're a dangerous crewmate to leave in the hands of such a vengeful captain, you know that?"

If Captain Reyes asked, Otis would not only track my new, ridiculously expensive quanta-com, but would probably spill all the juicy details about Greel Truyoza. Far too dangerous for comfort. My eyes flit back to the bathroom sink. The deal with Reyes had been that I'd have to return their precious robot at the end of the two-hour outing but he never specified *in what condition*.

I bring Otis over to the sink and splash the slow trickle of water down his neck. He's been shut off already anyway, and you can never account for what happens in public bathrooms.

I stare into the darkened ball of Otis's head. My own hair and contorted reflection appear horrifically clown-like. "You would have told Reyes where I was," I say, trying to explain to the helpless robot. I still feel a weighty stab of regret. "You would have had me arrested and ripped apart by Truyoza, simultaneously. Fucked for life."

The robot somehow looks more limp than he did before.

"Don't look at me that way. Gisella will fix you up. Eventually." He doesn't answer. "It was self-defense. That's what it was."

I wasn't expecting a conscience at this point.

Gisella will be able to fix him, right? They have a whole engineering team. It's not permanent, I tell myself. It can't be.

I dry up Otis as best as I can on the exterior, so that no one will suspect my tampering.

This is a new low for me. Yeah, I've kidnapped an umemeh, but I've never murdered an intelligent being by my own hand. This feels much worse. I sincerely hope this is reversible.

I slam the wall. "Stupid fucking fuck." I sink down and rest against the filthy wall. "Fuck me," I whisper.

"What the void happened to this place?" asks Pete's surly voice, and a door-screech later, he rounds into the room. "You feeling okay?"

"I shouldn't have eaten the burritos," I mumble as I quickly wipe the last telltale beads of water from Otis's neck. I get up from the floor and blink back the stinging in my eyes.

"Come on. Let's get you back to the ship before Reyes blows a gasket. Speaking of." He pulls up his quanta-com. "Yeah, they were here, cap'n. Just like you said. We're on our way."

Pete glances over at me, and my face must look pretty miserable. "Let me carry Otis?" he offers. I nod and sniff, and follow Pete back to the waiting ships.

The cop in neon stops Pete on our walk back.

"Sir? Do you or this... lady? Have proper paperwork for that robot there?"

Pete's eyebrows go up in amusement. "Otis? Yeah, sure. He

belongs to the *Dreamliner*. Need me to fire him up to pull up the proper docs?" He scratches his jaw. "Do you have a toe-fire reader? It's the only port this guy has."

Shit shit shit. Otis is *not* going to fire up all fine and dandy. I'll be fucked ten ways to port. I start to rock nervously.

The officer frowns at me, then back at Pete. "The *Dreamliner*, you said?"

Wait. That is not the name of the *Waterloo*. I take a sideways glance at Pete, but he's slick as pasta.

"Oh yeah, sure. *Dreamliner*," replies Pete. "We're headed back there now. We could hook him up to a toe-fire reader on board if you'd like, if you don't have one?"

The officer takes another hard look at me, and I stare down at my feet. Pete elbows me, but I refuse to look up. I don't need anyone identifying me. My red hair is a calling card of its own. I don't need to give them any more ammo.

"Yeah, you gotta forgive Penny, here. She's new to working on the *Dreamliner*. And she's also a mute."

I guffaw, but the officer nods. "That's alright, sir. That'll be all for now, but I'll stop by the *Dreamliner* a little later to confirm your story."

"Sure thing, boss."

After enough of the shuffling crowds separate us from neon colors, I punch Pete in the arm.

"Penny? That's the best you could do?"

"Well I couldn't exactly give him your real name, could I?" He grunts. "We don't have any paperwork for Otis, either."

"Really? With Sarge By-the-Book there?" I don't have it in me to call him a righteous asshole anymore.

Pete grins. "I'll miss you, Savvy. Maybe look us up after you get off Brin-177?"

I swallow a painful lump in my throat and duck my head down. I don't owe him anything. I try to remind myself that I'm never going to see any of them ever again, but this only makes the blackness inside me feel even bigger. I remind myself that Truyoza's pirate-mobster-henchmen will be busting us out of Lieutenant Crenshaw Bremerton's ship in just a short few hours in the Buckingham Nebula, and that this whole crazy shitshow will be over soon.

Somehow, none of these things help settle my stomach.

chapter twenty

Sergeant Reyes is waiting for us with arms folded when we return to the terminal.

He nods at me. "So where's your stuff?"

"Um?"

"The feminine hygiene stuff you were so eager to obtain."

"Oh. Right. Well, I ate these burritos first, and –"

Reyes puts up his hand. "Save it. Do us a favor." He looks over at Pete, who's carrying Otis. "And let's see here. How did Otis fare in your little outing?"

Turning Otis over gently, Reyes flips the switch on the back of Otis's neck.

I'm starting to get nervous here. He's going to call the cops on me, isn't he?

"What a surprise," says Reyes, with no surprise in his voice. "Otis doesn't turn on."

"Well, the bathrooms – you never can tell what happens in those –"

Reyes puts a hand up to silence me again. "I don't need to hear it," he says, shaking his head. "I sincerely hope Gisella can fix him up." He turns and ascends the ramp to his ship, carrying the bulky, limp Otis in his arms.

Pete looks at me, but he's not talking and his eyebrows are all furrowed. He rubs his cap over his greasy hair.

"Pete! I can explain! It was just –"

Pete shakes his head before he runs to catch up with his captain. On all my years of living on Hialeah, I've never felt as shitty as I do in this moment.

Swallowing thickly, I walk the ramp to Lieutenant Crenshaw Bremerton's ship. He pads up to the open doorway in his terry cloth slippers as I ascend and raises a single golden eyebrow when I push past him.

"Well you look positively worse for the wear, darling," he says, holding his pipe out for his assessment of me.

I don't even have the energy to call him Fuckerton anymore.

"Let's just get out of here, okay?" I stop short in the hallway. I can hear the ramp sealing shut behind me, which means I'll be closed in on the *Euryale* for yet another miserable trip. But that's not what's stopped me in my tracks. I'm standing in a rotund circular receiving room with maroon and gilt details. There are painted angels on the paneling. But that's not the showstopper.

There is a giant chandelier on the ceiling. It's one of those fancy handblown glass contraptions with a million different colors and sizes of crystal projections attached to a central point. Only, now that I really examine it, the individual glass forms are all variations on a singular theme.

It's a penis chandelier.

"Ah. Tastefully done, wasn't it?" Bremerton asks. "A true work of art." I stare at him. I've boarded a ship with a madman. "What? Darling, it's all anyone ever thinks about, anyway!"

"Um. No." I roll my eyes. "Clearly you don't get out much."

Bremerton blinks several times. He opens his mouth, then shuts it. He tries again, tentatively. "Are you only interested in women, then? Is that why you are so…" He gestures vaguely with his pipe hand.

I round on him. "So… *what?*"

Bremerton stutters under my accusatory glare. "Irritable?" he asks meekly.

My mouth drops open. I knew he was out of touch with reality, but this is a whole other level of ancient patriarchal asshole. Right as I'm mentally gearing up for this battle, an image of a limp Otis flashes to mind and the fight in me completely deflates. "You know what? I don't want to –" I swallow hard. "Just tell me where the umemeh is, okay?"

"Why, certainly! I'll have *the Euryale* here illuminate your way. *Euryale?*" After a beat, green strip lighting along the floor points me down a branching hallway.

I don't acknowledge Bremerton any further as I head off after the lights.

"You'll want to know where the restrooms are – for feminine reasons –" he calls out behind me. "You can always call out if you need guidance!"

I don't bother to turn. It's nice to make his voice recede behind me. That's where I'd prefer to keep him: far, far away. I feel like total crap, and Bremerton is only making things worse. Maybe I'll find Fred, and he'll chew my hair or something and everything will feel okay again.

———

IN COMPARISON TO EVERYTHING ELSE, TAKEOFF ON THE *EURYALE* WAS like traveling encased within a marshmallow. Fred didn't seem to notice, and that's pretty voids-near insane. Apparently, money can buy many things, including force-cancelling grav generators.

The room Fred's been given is covered with the same golden design finishes, but unlike any spaceship *ever*, the entire floor of this room has been carpeted with uprooted vegetation. There's no earth here, so the bushes and strewn leaves are literally strewn about in piles so high that it reaches mid-calf. Was Bremerton preparing for the next galactic war? Because a supply this size could feed Fred for the next three months.

I myself sit in a corner, where I succeed in clearing a decent enough clearing in the roughage to the crinkly blue sheeting they've placed below. There's a bathtub of water against one wall and I've contemplated sitting in it as penance for Otis, but I don't think Fred would appreciate me in his drinking water. So I sit alone in the corner thumbing my new stupid eighty joulo quanta-com. Soon, Truyoza's crew will be here, guns blazing, and here's another human being that I'm going to fuck over. At least I feel slightly less bad about Bremerton after his asinine comment about lesbians. On the other hand, I do admire his efforts. This room is pretty sweet.

I keep staring, fixated, at my wrist. How much longer will this take? Truyoza has not reached out to me, nor should he. Unless it all goes sideways, I will not contact him. But other than Reyes, Truyoza is the only other living being who knows this quanta-com number, and of those two people, I'm far more willing to talk to the mob boss.

An acrid stench snaps me out of my reverie, right in time to watch Fred finish his potty-squat position. Then, using his rear two legs, he kicks up mounds of clippings to bury his shit. "Seriously? That doesn't actually clean up the shit! All that does is dock the pay of innocent zookeepers on Hialeah. Also? So gross, Fred."

I choke on a chortle when I realize I'm still calling him Fred. In private, where it's no longer necessary to act the animal activist. I've been friendless for too long.

I stand up, and Fred saunters over to investigate my hair. "There is something broken with you. Eat food, not hair," I say to Fred, then lean over and nuzzle my nose on the fur between the eyes on the inquisitive head. It's very smelly.

Maybe I need a little time without umemeh company. I exit using the hand panel by the room's only sliding door and begin wandering the hallways.

A jovial voice reverberates loudly overhead. "Oh darling, is there any way this humble captain could be of assistance to you?" Humble my ass.

I halt in my tracks when a second thought accosts me. I look around for the cameras. He must be monitoring my movement. "What, am I your prisoner? Do you have an alarm go off each time I leave that room?"

"No! No. I was only a smidge concerned, you see. I never had the opportunity to show you to the restrooms, and considering the current status of your, er, feminine needs, I wanted to ensure–"

"No! Spawning bunniculas. I don't need the restrooms, Fuck-erton! I'm just going for a walk."

"Ah. Well, if that's the case, feel free to follow the purple lighting if you'd like to visit the bridge. And if you do need the restrooms, those lights will be orange. I'd select red, but…"

"Oh my Bob! I get it already!" I yell and wave my hands at the ceiling. "I *menstruate*," I draw the word out. "Menstruation! Peri-od!" I'm shouting now, throwing my arms wide with each word. "Blood! The Red Squirt! Juice from my vagiiiiina." The spy cam remains sullenly silent after that poetic brilliance. "Like the oppo-site of a vampire," I mutter as I continue down the hall, deliber-ately walking away from the flashing orange strip lights.

What I do find, with each new hallway, is that this ship is a conceit ensconced in tacky gold finishes. Every room I poke my head into is more ridiculous than the next. A billiards room - *with* billiard balls strewn across the table! Considering the variable gravitational forces a ship experiences on a typical voyage, furni-ture with twenty round projectiles is not just opulent, it's a middle finger to the universe. These gravitational generators must be top of the line with triple fail-safes. And a library! I step into this one to verify that it's not an illusion. The books are real – with real mammalian leather on the binding and gilded page edges. The paper in this room alone must be worth more than the entire planet of Hialeah. And here I thought this level of wealth was mythical.

I'm still holding a book in a vise grip. A single one of these could erase a good portion of my debt. Two or three of them might actually clear me. Even from Truyoza.

I snort. Who am I kidding? If I can't sell an umemeh, and I'm a fucking *zoologist*, how the voids would I manage to sell a book? And if I somehow did succeed, this clown with his asinine amounts of money would probably finance a whole police fleet to find me. After that kind of donation, I bet the police would even name something after me: *This building was donated due to the idiocy of Saffron Savage, who was generous in her choice of crime.* I hastily shove the book back into its slot and hurry out of there.

Soon enough, I'm standing below the absurd penis chandelier again. I stare up at it, wondering how long it took the artist to blow hundreds of glass penises. I snicker. He had to blow each one of them.

I shake myself. I must have been really torn up about Otis to miss out on making a quip at Bremerton's decorative sensibilities to his face. A golden opportunity, an inflated opportunity. A very stiff one, even. I push my shoulders back and march along the gently glowing purple lights.

When I enter the bridge, Bremerton is leaning back in an armchair. He's smoking his pipe, and his slippers are up on the console. The pose alone drives penises straight out of my mind.

"Get your feet off the controls! You could knock us off course, you festering fishbrain!"

"Oh, there you are, darling," Bremerton replies, gesturing airily to the other vacant seats. "Don't be alarmed. This ship takes care of everything for me. I'm purely ornamental. And while everyone knows I am devilishly handsome, the *Euryale* truly is a beaut, isn't she?"

That annoys the shit out of me because he can't even say the expression in the correct manner. "Ain't she," I reply, but Bremerton completely misses the point. He only nods in satisfaction.

"How the voids were you ever in any military?" I ask, irritated beyond reason. "Did you buy your title? Because there's no other way I can wrap my head around this."

"I did, in fact," Bremerton replies. "Purchase the title. It turns out, the military was not the best fit for me. I'm surprised you were able to gather as much."

"Let's get real, Fuckerton. You're the kind of person who'd be sick for a month if you quit your iodized water habit."

"Most people pretend to act shocked, darling," Bremerton replies, frowning. He takes a drag from his pipe.

I plop myself down on a cushy leather armchair and let my eyes roam over the expensive looking electronic equipment. Silence fills the room. "Don't call me darling. I hate it," I say at last.

"Nor do I savor the name you've chosen for me, you delicate little sphynx. It strikes me that a deal may be prudent."

"Ugh. Can you talk like a normal human for five void-forsaken minutes?"

Bremerton raises his eyebrows at me. "If you can eliminate the cursing, we may yet reach a second deal. Though that might be more difficult for me to adhere to, I'm afraid."

"Well, you can fuck that shit ten ways to port."

Bremerton nods. "Alright. Better off as we were, then."

"No, you albino marmoset. I'm okay with a truce on the pet names." Bremerton raises an eyebrow at me. He cocks his head in prompt. "It was my last parting one, okay? You called me a delicate sphynx."

Bremerton nods. "All right then. The compromise sounds palatable."

Silence floods the cockpit again. I check my quanta-com. How much more time until Greel's pirates rescue me from this cupcake?

"You seem to have earned Sergeant Reyes's wrath. Would you care to share how you've accomplished that?" I stare at the electronics stonily. "I've been trying to get on that man's bad side for decades."

I glance over at him, curious.

"Yes, you see. He keeps calling me to ask for favors. I've even gifted him many upgrades to that ship of his to try to make him happy, but he insists he doesn't want any of it. So you see, I've tried it all. Which makes me wonder how to get on his bad side."

I rub my arms. "Try living on a shit-show of a planet for just shy of a decade," I reply. "See what kind of desperate stunts you're willing to pull to get outta the zoo." I nod. "I guarantee you'll get every human in a fifty-lightyear radius to hate you. Including yourself."

"And the umemeh?"

"Well, at least he likes me."

Bremerton nods. "You do supply him with LSD."

"True." I can't help but smile. Only a little. But then, the thought of LSD reminds me of my last conversation with Sergeant Reyes. "I can't believe that doc of his actually confiscated my bag."

"Not to worry, dar—dear friend," Bremerton says, correcting himself. "I did manage to purchase the contents back for you. If you are so inclined."

I raise my eyebrows at him.

"I told you, somehow I've earned Sergeant Reyes's friendship. The favors go both ways, as it turns out."

"Impressive," I reply honestly. Then I shrug. "Fred's happy with the vegetable buffet here and I don't think he'll need additional mood stabilizing assistance. You wouldn't be interested in that LSD for yourself, would you?"

"Oh no, darl—my dear… friend. I spent too many of my youthful years indebted to intoxicants. But don't let that stop you from enjoying yourself." Bremerton waves his pipe in the air. "Only, try not to break anything. I do favor this ship."

I sigh and glance around the room. Getting high is not an option for the likes of me. I need to be sober by the time Greel Truyoza's pirate crew catches up with us.

"Got anything to drink?"

"Ah, yes. Now you're speaking my language. I have a 300-year-old cognac that most people tend to get excited over. If you ask me, it tastes like vinegar. I quite prefer the whiskey."

I shake my head. "Any of the above sound fan-fucking-tastic. Even the vinegar."

Crenshaw Bremerton rises, his silk pajama pants gently smacking the carpeting as he pads over to the built-in bar. Of course he has a breaching bar built into the bridge.

"Savage, it was, right?" I nod. "Well, Savage, it looks like we should be arriving in Brin-177 in approximately thirty-hours." Bremerton hands me a crystal glass filled with amber liquid. I'm about to ask if it's the scotch or the cognac until I remember that I don't care. And that nothing he said matters.

"How much longer till we get to Buckingham Nebula?"

He furrows his eyebrows. "Buckingham Nebula? Why do you ask?"

"Oh, nothing. My mute friend Penny told me about it once."

"I find that rather difficult to believe," Bremerton says, and my heartbeat kicks up a notch. "How did she talk to you if she is mute?"

"Don't be a biscuit balloon, Bremerton," I say, relieved. "You're a billion years old. How have you never heard of sign language?"

"Oh. Right-o," he has the decency to appear genuinely embarrassed. "My apologies. By my recollection, we should reach Buckingham Nebula in about four hours or so, give or take."

Four hours. I blink. I still have to get through another four hours, but then, it will be over. It will all be over. I close my eyes in relief.

"Well! Cheers to an uneventful journey together." Bremerton clinks his glass against mine and takes a sip. "There we are," he says, then returns to his chair where he kicks up his legs again. "Do tell me more about this Hialeah planet," he says once he's comfortable. He takes another long sip. "It sounds like you had a most lamentable living situation."

I look down at the cup in my hands. Fuck it. I down the

contents in one gulp. It burns for minutes after it's gone down, but Bob, that's good.

"I'm getting a refill," I reply instead, and head over to the bar. Bremerton does not object.

When I return to my seat with cup in hand, Bremerton raises his own still-full glass in my direction.

"To safe journeys," he says.

I mumble a response and gulp down another sip. This time, I don't empty the whole glass in one go.

"So. Hialeah, as you say," Bremerton says. "Is a shit-show?"

I startle at his use of profanity, and he smiles at my surprise.

"Well, yes, *darling*," I reply, trying and failing to imitate his accent. I immediately want to wash my mouth out with soap. "It's the worst shit-show in the universe. And it's even more *lamentable* if you're one of the only three women working there."

Bremerton tsks, and takes another sip. "That does sound most unfortunate."

I don't want to talk about my shitty life with a fake accent anymore. My life story isn't entertainment for billionaires.

"So tell me," I say, trying a new tack of conversation. "How do you and Sergeant Reyes know each other?"

Bremerton snorts. "Well, if you must know, it's a rather pathetic story. I was wallowing in my purchased title, dithering about and such nonsense. I felt a sense of uselessness and an overdose of self-pity. I was far too old to indulge in such emotions, but at the time, no one dared tell me otherwise. Until Sergeant Reyes came my way. He saved my life, in more ways than one."

"What, you think he saved your life because he told you to get ahold of yourself? You've got to be kidding me. I could do that for you for free."

"Oh no, he saved my life quite literally. Some hotheaded private in the platoon decided to stage a coup to humiliate me. His plan was to demonstrate publicly what a drug-addled buffoon I truly was. Well, things got a little out of hand, and some weapons came unholstered in the heat of the moment..."

Bremerton drifts off into silence.

"And?"

Bremerton blinks. "I don't like to consider the things I did when I was high. I am indeed responsible for my actions, and I've been paying for them ever since. In every possible way. It is better not to dwell on them."

"So now you're a reformed playboy turned animal rights activist."

Bremerton motions in the air. "Something to that effect."

"One who has zero sensitivity to lesbians or people with disabilities."

Bremerton frowns at his glass. "We all have our faults, Savage, you know."

Yeah. I sure do know that. Mine's being owned by an angry mobster with impotency problems. Or at least, that's how it all started. Actually, it started with a bottle of cheap moonshine and a visit from an ex.

"You know, he's likely to forgive you if you'd only apologize. It's what I did."

I blink at Bremerton. "Excuse me?"

"Sergeant Reyes, of course. I don't know whatever it is you've done to get on his bad side, but the man has a soft spot for people who apologize. In fact, as it turns out, once you apologize, he's a hard friend to lose."

"Who says I want Reyes's forgiveness?" I snort. "That guy is the biggest asshole on this side of the century!"

"Oh, he's not so bad, not really. It's that he has his head full of 'right' and 'wrong.' I was on the wrong side of that divide for quite a while, but once I made amends, I earned his everlasting friendship. Much to my perpetual aggravation."

"Yeah, well. I'm not in the market for a new best friend."

Bremerton nods. "Are you still in communication with your friends back on Hialeah, then, Savage?"

"What?" I reply, startled. Memories of my last minutes spent with Weasel and Lionel flood to mind.

"Friends, Savage. Everyone needs at least one. If you're not interested in befriending Reyes, who are you friends with?"

"None of your business, Bremerton." But voids, I *am* lonely. I've been lonely for a while. "Screw you. Fred is my friend, okay? We get along great. Hey, how long did you say till we reach Buckingham Nebula?"

Bremerton glances up to the left, at a private lens display. "Four hours and twenty minutes. Why do you keep asking?"

"Call me an over-excited tourist. I'm going to play billiards. I assume there's a bar in there?"

Bremerton nods. "Of course, darl—Oh, I do apologize. It's a bit of a habit, you know. Of course there's a bar in there, Savage. What else would you expect?"

chapter twenty-one

Tipsy happens to be my sweet spot when it comes to playing billiards. But just as I start lining up the eight ball for the corner pocket, gravity goes tits up and I have to wonder if Bremerton's vinegar cognac has a stronger kick than I expected. An enormous roaring sound reverberates through every physical atom of the ship accompanied by a jolt that makes both Bremerton and me hop, then float, before a sudden slam back to gravity. All ten remaining billiard balls thunk back onto the table.

"You okay, Bremerton?" I ask. That fall back to gravity made me land on one of my ankles funny, and I can only imagine it's worse for him. He's a billion years old.

Bremerton looks like he's analyzing the ceiling beams. "What in the bugger could that be?" He stabilizes himself as a second shock hits the ship. His eyes dart as he checks his contact lens interface. "That's strange. Weren't you asking about the Buckingham Nebula? Well, we're here at Owl's Nest, but it's not usually this turbulent."

If we're in the Owl's Nest, then the only thing this could be is a warm welcome from Truyoza's rescue party. I close my eyes in relief, but it only lasts a fraction of a second.

A peal of alarm wails through the ship, and at this, Bremerton gets serious. "You'd best get your friend in here, on the double!"

My stomach drops. He knows about Greel Truyoza and must have had me pegged all along. I can't believe he wants me to invite these pirates on board, but I suppose it's the captain's prerogative to minimize damage to the ship.

Bremerton hobbles over to the built-in cabinets and starts yanking out table-top games, spilling their boxes on the floor willy-nilly. I take back my earlier observation about calculated decisions. He's out of his mind.

"Aha! There it is!" he exclaims, pulling free an antique boxed game set labeled Monopoly.

"Bremerton, have you lost your marbles? We're under attack!"

"You're still here? Haven't I told you to get your friend?" I stare at him, uncomprehending. "Your best friend? What did you call him? Jim, or Bob was it? No. Fred. That's right. Get him in here, and be quick about it! Can't you tell we're under attack?"

Oh. That friend. But I remain frozen in surprise as Bremerton tears off the cover of the Monopoly board and pulls out the parts of semi-automatic plasteel rifle. He begins assembling. "Whatever in the devil are you still doing here? Move it, Savage. Move!"

With one last parting glance, I sprint down shaking hallways following the green lighting that leads to Fred's room. The next jolt lands me on that same ankle and makes me really spitting mad. What if Fred sprained a leg? What if his heads had been restrained at the time? He could have been strangled! Don't these morons realize that if they kill the umemeh their boss will be pissed? I crash against a wall as our ship is knocked off course, but I make it to Fred's door.

The umemeh's lowing can be heard through the door, and I scramble to drag it open against our tilting gravity. After a heave, the door slides open, haltingly, and with another rock of the ship, it tries to shut itself against Fred's fear-stricken heads. All four of his eyes are wide with fear, his nostrils are flared out, and his tail is flat against his butt. He's already pissed himself, which I can smell, but he seems relieved to see me.

Or maybe that's just wishful thinking.

I glance around his pen to see if he's destroyed any of Bremerton's fancy ship in his panic, but aside from vegetables spilling out of their massive bins, the room seems to be in order. And with the shift in vegetation in the room, I now spy a familiar black tote bag resting neatly in the corner. It's been in here the whole hull-breaching time, covered in mounds of yard clippings.

Giving wide berth to the poop-area, I make a dash for the bag in the corner, and of course, Fred darts out the door as soon as I've vacated it. He goes off loping through the hallway. "Wait! Shit!" I scramble after Fred, bag in hand. I don't know what Truyoza plans to do to him, but I do know I've got four sedatives left. The least I can do is make his fate more humane with less suffering. The thought of Fred suffering makes me intensely sad for some ninny-whipped reason.

Another missile hits our ship and sends us tilting the other direction. Fred bangs a head, and an entire fucking neck, against a wall. His shriek is high-pitched and goes on for too long to be a good sign.

"Savage! Blast it, Savage, get in here this instant!"

Bremerton's voice is way too far away. We've got a whole void-forsaken hallway to get through, and Fred is having trouble standing up. I rummage through the bag at my side. The tranqs are all still in there, and my old snow globe, for that matter, but where are my addicto-nip treats?

Fuck that shit. New plan. On bouncing knees, I manage to wiggle my way in front of Fred and pet his heads. The nostrils are still flared out on his upright head, but his banged head is down, emitting a low whine.

Those fuckers. They didn't have to bomb Bremerton's ship to get us. I need to keep this umemeh alive! I only need one head's attention to get this idiot to follow me. I unbraid my hair and wave sections of it in front of Fred's good head. "Come on, Freddypoo. Come on," I try to say in my most soothing voice. It warbles, uncontrolled.

The ship shudders again. There is a swish that grows into a loud and sustained whoosh of air going by. Is that loss of balance *the ship* tilting? Either that or I'm completely wasted. There's a force pulling on my body, away from Fred's direction. I crouch down on the floor, balling up my body, near Fred. I still hold up my hair, outstretched to him.

"Come on, you butt-head," I say, crying into my elbow.

A tremor runs through the ship as it emits a loud noise. It reminds me too much of that deep and moaning sound you hear right before a large tree branch snaps and breaks in a storm. We're really going to die. We're going to die here in the hallway of some billionaire's boat, five hundred steps away from a penis chandelier, and be nothing but a grease stain for his assistants to clean next time they stock up.

It's a fitting end for a woman whose life was trapped in a shit hole. I am getting what I deserve for trying to escape. For doing this to Fred.

I feel a warm blast of air on the knuckles of my raised fist. The one that's clenching the hair. Fred blinks his eyes on his good head. The fear isn't completely gone, but he's latched on to a familiar scent as he noses my hand.

"That's right! You brilliant, double hot dog! Come on, you ginger lover." I'm spouting nonsense, but step after unbalanced step, I coax Fred to inch down the hallway. The forces pulling at our bodies help us along in that direction.

"Savage! I am warning you, get in here. This! Instant!"

Thank the void-forsaken stars, his voice sounds closer. I back my way towards Bremerton, unwilling to lose sight of Fred. There's no knowing what that idiot would do if I turn away. There's an equal chance of him running out a hole in the ship as him running to the safety of Bremerton's billiards room. Totally un-fucking-predictable.

Bremerton grasps my arm roughly and yanks me inwards.

Fred stumbles in behind us, and the door makes a series of squeaking, automatic sounds as it shuts. A goopy, pink slime surges along the door, coating it within seconds. I scan the ceiling for signs of a leak that could be the source of the goo, but there's no single origin point. It's everywhere. The ceiling, the floors, and every single inch of the walls is evenly coated like the inside of a museum classic Pepto Bismol bottle.

"What the voids is all…?"

"Those buggers have blasted a hole in my ship! In my bridge, no less. Dire straits here, Savage. Oxygen and pressure within the Euryale have all gone *caput*. Our time was running out. I had to seal off the room." His shoulders sag in relief.

"…With bubblegum?"

"Oh, I see what you did there. Aren't you a clever one," he says, completely unamused. "No, that 'bubblegum' is an intelligent slime that measures the oxygen levels on the other side, as I'm sure you've guessed. The coating can only be removed once we're safely docked. I'm sure you must have heard of it, even on that backwater Hialeah? Brilliant stuff, it won best invention at the gadgets and accessories faire this year. We'll be safe in here."

Trapped. That's basically what he just told me. Yes, we can breathe, but I can't get away from this Dimbo.

"Whatever took you so long?" Bremerton gestures at the door, then shakes his head. "No, no. Doesn't matter. Not now. I don't care. We're safe, and in the escape pod no less. Only, if you please, help me with the billiards table? My knees aren't what they used to be."

I glance around the pink room.

"Excuse me? Did you just say *escape pod*?"

"I agree that it's a travesty to leave such a beauty of a ship behind, but once the bridge has been compromised, evacuation protocols are set into motion. Security reasons, of course. Don't be alarmed, darling. I've called my good friend, Sergeant Reyes. He's on his way."

"Fuckerton, you did *what*?"

"Oh, *do* excuse my language, we *are* under attack, you know. I can see you've become slightly unhinged. In fact, Savage, you appear positively deranged at the moment. No matter, no matter. I can handle the billiards table myself."

Bremerton's glance at the billiards table is more skeptical than assessing, but, shrugging, he bends down and hugs one of the legs.

"What in the crabs' depth of the underworld are you doing?"

But Bremerton doesn't reply, focused on his useless endeavor. There are much bigger issues at stake than an old man going insane and trying to lift a billiards table. Has he really called the Righteous Reyes? This was my chance to escape! A new, even worse thought strikes. With Truyoza's goons around here, more people could get injured or die. Reyes's crew doesn't deserve this. Maybe if I can speed up the delivery of my cargo to Truyoza's pirates, this transaction would all be over already.

I need to get out of here. Pronto. The pirates must have a plan. If they've made a hole in the bridge, they probably intend on sending in a team. They can't let the umemeh die, so I'm betting they won't let me die, either. I'm banking on the assumption that they need an animal handler. It's a killer assumption to make, but it sure is better than sticking around for Reyes to show up.

Bremerton makes a heaving noise with the effort he's putting into the billiards table. I glare at him. He's sealed his fate in with mine. And now he's so disturbed that he's attempting to overturn the furniture.

"Oh, do be a dear and lift the other leg, will you?"

I cross my arms. "I'm not helping you ransack this room right now. Of all the things we could be do under attack, that's where your brain goes?"

"Don't be daft! There's another set of controls under here. Only, when the ship was being built, I insisted that the billiards table be overturned manually." He pats at the perspiration on his forehead. "What a simpleton I was! Can you believe, I asked the manufacturer to *remove* the automated switch? I was so concerned about an accidental conversion. Oh bugger, I can't believe I ever made such a request."

I glare. "Are you telling me there are *navigational controls* on the reverse side of this billiards table?"

"Of course, darli—I mean, Savage. It would be a very ineffective escape pod if one couldn't drive it."

A new lightbulb flashes in my mind, and I hurry to a free table leg. Hypothetically, I could navigate this escape vehicle myself. Technically I have no experience piloting ships, but Bremerton did say his fancy ship mostly drives itself. We've got the umemeh, and Truyoza's henchmen are already here. Instead of steering away from them, I'll fly up and ask them for a tow. Excellent plan. No brainer.

Once I hoist the billiards table leg one inch, automatization begins. The entire table pivots, and the balls all thump heavily onto the carpeted floor. A rectangular patch of carpeting below the table comes into definition, then separates from the floor around it. I'm hypnotized as the former floor descends slowly, then tucks out of the way, to reveal two leather-clad seats. With an equally hypnotic mechanized movement, a full suite of navigational controls emerge from below the underside of the table as the false wooden panels slide back.

"Un-fucking-believable," I mutter.

"There you are, you see? Simple," Bremerton says with a smile as he climbs into the new Captain's chair and taps the touchscreen on the console in front of him. "Hello there, *Euryale*."

"Crenshaw Bremerton, I'm glad to see you made it in here safely," says the computer's smooth female voice. A new wall panel full of blinking indicators descends from the ceiling against the far pink wall. We are basically in a new bridge, as equally luxurious as the other.

"No thanks to *this* one over here," Bremerton grumbles. "Yes, yes. Thank you, *Euryale*."

"This is an insane escape pod! You even have a bar in here," I say in wonder as the ship is rocked again under the force of a renewed attack. Fred is whining in one corner, and I think he needs a drink more than I do.

"Of course I do. Well, why else do you think I had it installed here instead of the library?"

I try to be sly as I examine the controls conspicuously below Bremerton's hovering hands. They're all either unmarked or have letters that look Russian to me. It'll be stupid to take command of an escape vessel that I can't fly.

"How do we separate from this baby?"

"Ah, well. I would much rather wait, you see. If Sergeant Reyes can get here in time to return fire on these blasted buggers, we may not need to abandon the *Euryale* at all. It would be such a crying shame to have to lose her. She is my favorite, you know."

"Yes, I know!" I snap. I rub my eyes. Bremerton tells me that I need a friend, but he talks about his ship like it's his hull-breaching girlfriend. That's when I realize I'm losing it. It's time to switch tacks. "Bremerton. You are holding an automatic weapon. May I hold it while you drive?"

"No darl—Oh Savage, blast it. Do you mind if we rescind our truce while we're under attack?"

"Fuckerton, let me fucking tell you, I would like nothing better." I run my hands through my hair. "Bat's tits, I'm even talking like you now."

"Oh I wouldn't worry too much about that, darling," Bremerton replies. "Anyhow, this is the only gun on the ship. And it's my own from my military days. I'm afraid I have a very difficult time letting her go. But you're right, you do need a weapon. See if you can go and find the bubbles." He waves vaguely at a wall full of cabinetry. "You do know what bubbles are, don't you?"

I take a deep breath to prevent myself from strangling this man. This is it. He's lost it. He's completely deranged.

"Bottles of soapy liquid?" Bremerton asks. "They come with a stick for forming shapes?" He lets out an exasperated sigh. "Oh, don't get so blasted angry. You don't appear to have experienced a lot of joy in your life, so it is a truly valid question as to whether you know what a bottle of bubbles looks li –"

"Bremerton. *Bubbles*? You expect me to fight pirates with *bubbles*?!"

"They've been weaponized, Savage. Come on." He snaps his fingers while focusing on the screens in front of him. "Get with it, darling."

I blink rapidly. It does make a certain sense from a man who hid his automatic gun in a board game. Bubbles are a weapon here. Okay. Letting out a few muttered curses, I head over to the built-in cabinets. I find boxes of games and puzzles and toss them out immediately.

"Bremerton. Where. The. Voids. Are. The. Bubbles?!"

"You're in the wrong cabinet entirely, Savage! Try the one on the left of you. Oh drat, no, make that two to your left."

I wrench the door open, the one that's two to my left. It's stocked full. There are rows of translucent purple bottles in here with colorful bubble images on their labels. There must be about ten or so in here.

"Okay, Bremerton. What do I do with these?" I call over to him.

He frowns. "Take two, or whatever you can manage in your hands. And would you be a dear and bring a couple over here for me? Only," he winces as he watches me, "*do* be careful, darling. They *do* contain explosives."

I grumble, "Shit! Okay."

"Careful, please! Oh, here's a good way to explain this. Pretend they are sacks full of excrement that will explode in your face. Well. And rip all your limbs off your body. And turn the rest of you into minced taco meat." Bremerton frowns at the imagery he has created.

"I know what explosives are, you nincompoop!"

"One of them is about to drop out of the crook of your elbow."

I hastily adjust. "Why would you keep explosives in bubble bottles!?"

"Oh darling, do watch your elbow. They're better camouflaged this way, wouldn't you agree?"

"I sincerely hope you don't ever bring children aboard, you mentally unstable goat."

"Don't be so crass. That is actual bubble juice, you know. Perfectly inert. The explosive is in the cap itself. I thought the bubble ring made for a nice grenade pull. Isn't that clever?"

"No. Nope," I say, glancing down at the purple bottles. "That doesn't make this any better."

Bremerton frowns. "I suppose I can consider a new explosives design once we escape our current predicament. Only – dear, I do hope Sergeant Reyes hurries up."

I glance at the bottles again. I need to move fast, but I don't think there's a way to do it with these. If I launch one of these in here, I'm dead. I can't commandeer the driver's seat from him if it's a suicide attack. Plus, if the umemeh dies, all this has been for nothing.

"Why do you even have these? How are explosives going to help anyone *inside* an escape pod?"

"Beats the bats out of me!" he replies, then does a double-take. "I suppose one could ask the same about the gun, too. Ideally, we won't be boarded by any pirates and won't have use for either one. But if it does come down to that, I do wonder…"

"Bremerton. Focus." I need to get that gun from him before Reyes's rescue crew gets here. I need to take control of this situation. I press harder. "How the voids am I supposed to protect the umemeh?"

"I'm afraid it's something I never thought of myself. I don't frequently come under attack. Nor do I often have passengers on board."

"You don't fucking say."

"There's no need to be so unkind." Bremerton sighs. "I wasn't prepared to weaponize a friend on my journey."

"Arrgggggggh." I rub my temples. "Bremerton, give me the gun. If the attackers bust in here, we'll need you to focus on getting Euryale to throw any of her tricks at them. And keeping us alive. I'll need to protect Fred. Give me the gun."

Bremerton glances down and considers his weapon. "I just… Only… I do hate to part with it…"

"Bremerton!"

"Oh Savage, if only you knew what I've been through."

"Yeah, you told me. Drugs and shit and mistakes. Let me help you, dude. Come on. The gun."

Bremerton looks down at his gun again. "Oh alright, good chap. You're a terrible billiards player, and if I've ever discovered a truism about other people, it's that *good* billiards players are not to be trusted. I'll just have to assume that the opposite is true as well." He gives me a hopeful smile. "Here you are, friend. Right-o."

Bremerton releases the gun to my keep, and for a full minute, I am lost staring at it. He's a naïve, sappy sucker to give away his only weapon. I don't understand why this moron would even trust me. What is wrong with him? I twist the automatic gun in my palm. I meant to aim it at Bremerton and let the pirates walk right on in, but I can't bring myself to do it. He's a big, fat, trusting idiot. And he gave me the gun.

The control room shudders again.

"This is it!" Bremerton exclaims. "Reyes! He's arrived! Fantastic. Their ship may continue to attack ours, but there's no way they'll outmatch him. He's ex-military, you know."

Well, that settles that. I refuse to be screwed by Reyes again. Mr. Heavy Handed Mobster has made it very clear that I'm one more delay away from being drawn and quartered. And all I have to do, to avoid that, is get the umemeh to the pirates two doors down. They're right here, on this holo-screen. Time to wrap up this shit show with a simple, pretty bow.

I aim the gun at Bremerton's head.

"Look over here, Idiot," I say loudly, and Bremerton turns around to face me.

His confusion fades to a tight-lipped grimace. "I take it you're *not* using that to help the umemeh, then?"

"No, genius, I'm not. Disengage the escape pod," I say, even though I feel like a mold-spreading cockroach while saying it. "Fly us directly over to the pirates, and I'll make sure you live through all this."

"What about all that bit about being an animal rights activist?" Bremerton asks.

"That was a way to not to get reported to the police," I reply. "Reyes is a hardass. It was my only out. Now get us the voids out of here," I say, priming the gun. "Bremerton, tell me this thing has metal-safe bullets."

Bremerton raises an eyebrow at me. "Though *you* may wish to converse with me as a friend, that is something I am unwilling to do until you disengage the weapon and return it to my possession." He frowns. "With an apology."

"Fuck that," I reply, and aim it at the door that connects the billiards room to the rest of the ship.

"Wait!" Bremerton cries. "Alright. I can talk. Yes! The bullets are metal-safe. But they're not pink-goo safe. You'll deprive us of our breathable air. According to these numbers, it's a complete vacuum out there at the moment."

I aim the weapon back at him. "Then steer us over to the pirates," I say with a sigh. I am so tired of this shit. "I want to get this nightmare over with already."

"Savage, there's more than one way to end this prickly situation. You do not *have* to hand over the umemeh…"

"Shut your flappers, Fuckerton. You don't know anything about what I do or don't have to do. You don't…" I huff. "You don't know anything about owing money to a notorious mob boss, or what it means to have him threaten to kill you. You don't know anything about a difficult life! Except maybe when your billions of joulos happen to dip by a few million? Yeah, what a travesty. So just do me a favor and shut up. And also? *Move this fucking ship,* or I will shoot you and dick around with the controls myself."

With a theatrical sigh, Bremerton returns his attention to the controls and begins tapping at screens. "Disengaging escape pod," says the smooth feminine voice of the *Euryale*. There's a very loud click as the escape pod detaches from the main frame.

"Thank the fur-licking felines," I mutter. My eyes are trained on the large holo-screen of the dots representing the two other ships in the Owl's Nest. All of a sudden, one of the ships begins a rapid retreat – obviously Sergeant Reyes didn't have the firepower to fend off space pirates! Well, he *was* driving a stupid cargo ship. Didn't expect a pirate attack, did you, Reyes? I finally won. I *won*!

"Now. Steer us over to the pirates' ship," I say.

"To be clear, you want me to take you to that ship that's waiting for us, just over there? Are you absolutely certain about this, Savage?"

"Yes, Fuckerton. Do I need to spell it out in crayon?"

"No, no. Don't mind me, simpleton that I am. I just want to be clear that I'm complying with your orders. Would you mind, ehm, moving that beastie so that it's no longer pointing at my head?"

I lower the automatic weapon. "One wrong move, Bremerton," I warn.

"I know, I know. One wrong move and I'll get it in the head." He keeps tapping away silently, and soon I feel the gentle force of us accelerating away.

I heave a sigh of relief. I glance about the destroyed room. Near the built-ins, there are games and papers strewn everywhere. The umemeh has pissed himself in the corner, and the plush carpet has soaked it all up. The walls are bubblegum pink. And there are actual beads of sweat on Bremerton's forehead. He's probably never broken a sweat outside a tennis court before.

"Argh," I say. Bremerton won't even look at me. "Bremerton? I really am sorry about all this."

"Hard to believe anything you say with my weapon in your hands."

"No, I mean it. I'm sorry I've been turned into this. I'm… I'm sorry you got pulled into this mess. And I'm sorry about your ship. You don't know what I've been through, or what shit I still have to get through. I wish it had been easier, but that fucker, Reyes, forced me –"

"Don't you dare utter one more word about him. He's a dear friend of *mine*. Some of us on this ship do understand this concept of friendship. And one more thing. Even if you consider yourself stuck, there is always more than one way through. Always. You don't *have* to do any of these things."

He still doesn't get it. I fold my arms. "Fine. Have it your way."

We lapse into silence as our escape pod approaches the dot on the screen representing the pirates' ship.

"Initiating black space coupling," says the Euryale.

"There's a good lass," says Bremerton, patting the console.

I roll my eyes. There's the blessed moment when I hear the click of the connection. Something lets out a loud hiss, and the pink goo begins retracting. Starting with the door, then slowly retreating all along the walls.

"Bremerton?" I say before the door opens. There's one thing I've been worrying about these last few minutes. Those asshole pirates might rough him up a bit. Bremerton can be really irritating sometimes, and pirates… You never can tell what their patience level is like, but judging on their mode of attack, I'm not betting it's high.

"Try to stay quiet, and I'll do my best to stop them from hurting you, okay?"

"Savage, you may go and fuck yourself."

I blink at Bremerton. His eyes are glazed with anger, and his fists are balled. So apparently, the guy doesn't like being stabbed in the back. I can understand that. But I also don't want this guy to die because of me. I jog over to the umemeh as a pretense, and fumble around in my bag.

"Your bag is not going to save you now. I will own that I took the liberty of throwing your LSD to the turkey farm at our last layover," Bremerton says, still facing the door as I creep up on him. The carpeting makes my approach silent. "After all your threats to Sergeant Reyes, I certainly didn't want to run into any trouble. I do believe the turkeys appreciated it." He turns to me with a mean smile, only to discover I'm inches away from him. I jam the tranquilizer into his neck. His eyes go wide in disbelief. "Betrayal… again?" Bremerton asks before his eyes shut and he slumps forward onto the console.

This betrayal is one I feel less guilty about. Now the pirates won't kill Bremerton out of sheer aggravation, but that doesn't eliminate killing him to polish off a witness. I hide the tranq dart in my bag and run through potential arguments I could use to convince them to just leave him unconscious in the escape pod (at least, until his buddy Reyes to come back and rescue him). I could tell them Bremerton's a diplomat. No, no. Too easy to look up. Maybe I'll tell them he's got a diplomat in the family, instead.

There's a click from the door now. In a panic, I realize I haven't come up with a good line of reasoning to prevent the pirates from killing *me*.

The door slides open and Sergeant Reyes swaggers in, accompanied by Pete and a screeching Prisha Shanti.

"Old dash and grab rescue, huh, Cren –" Reyes stops mid-sentence once he catches sight of the sleeping Crenshaw and the gun in my hands.

"*You,*" he manages to utter, overtaken by complete rage.

Well, fuck me.

chapter twenty-two

"Um. This is not what it looks like?" I try. Shit. This can't be happening. My pulse is pounding in my ears. I realize I'm still holding Bremerton's gun. Quick mental math tells me that even if I disable both Reyes and Pete with my weapon (if they don't manage to wrestle it from me), there's still an entire ship behind them. The numbers don't work out in my favor. I drop Bremerton's gun to the floor and put my hands up.

Sergeant Reyes is already kneeling on the floor next to Bremerton, and he gently peels Bremerton off the console. There's a gash on Bremerton's forehead where he struck the instrument panel when he toppled over, and I feel a pang in my own gut at the sight of it.

"He tripped out when we got hit with a –" what is the right word for it in space combat? A bomb? A rocket? A missile? "—a big boom," I finish lamely. My heart is beating faster than a rabbit's thumper scratching an itch. But these guys couldn't possibly know what happened here, so my explanation *should* sound plausible. Crenshaw Bremerton is older than dirt. Slips happen. But Reyes doesn't answer, so I add, "I am in no way responsible for his current condition."

Reyes glares at me with arms hooked below Bremerton's limp

shoulders, while Pete lifts Bremerton's legs. Reyes's eyes are beady. "If I find out that you had *anything* to do with the attack on Lieutenant Bremerton's ship, as the stars are my witness, you will pay." To Pete, he says, "Let's get him over to Doc Williams. Ready?" After an affirmative grunt, the men walk out of the devastated room.

I walk over to Fred, who seems much more settled now and is chewing on paper Monopoly money. There's garbage all over the floor: colorful game pieces, slips of paper. I can't see any of that pink bubblegum crap. It's back to maroon carpeting and golden walls. Bremerton's *baby*. His favorite.

I must be losing it, because I start putting things back in the Monopoly box. Bremerton's gun included. What the voids else am I supposed to do when my last ridiculous, desperate attempt to save myself has failed? When I tug at a fake hundred joulo bill that Fred refuses to give up on, I say, "You gotta give a little, bud. It's just you and me again."

Wait! It *is* just me and him again. This game room is still an escape vehicle, isn't it?

I walk over to the billiard console and examine the Russian lettering. I'm over two thousand joulos in debt but now I want to know why the Bob they don't teach Russian in zoology school. Which of these symbols is the 'on' button?

"There you are!" exclaims Gisella from the doorway. Oh, and she's not talking to me. She rushes over to Fred. Prisha Shanti, at her heels, emits high pitched keening and races ahead of her. She's scrambled all the way up Fred's back, is hanging off one neck, and prying the fake Monopoly jewel free with quick hands. A few screeches later, Prisha Shanti is off again and searching through the remaining ruins of the room.

"Shoo!" I swat Prisha away from the bubbles. That would just take the cake, wouldn't it?

"I heard you two survived your first encounter with pirates!" Gisella coos, scratching Fred below his left chin.

"Debatable," I reply darkly. I focus my attention on Prisha

Shanti, who's been snatching up random game items from around the room and is running on two back legs like a drunk toddler with a hoarding problem. After examining her newest find, a miniature silver top hat, she runs screeching excitedly from the room, a trail of escaped game-money floating down to the floor in her wake.

I turn my attention on Gisella, who is still hugging and admiring Fred. It's just the three of us now. And now I'm contemplating locking her in here with me and forcing *her* to operate this escape pod.

I'm shitty to even consider it, but I was *this* close. This never-ending nightmare of bad decisions was almost over, until Righteous Reyes arrived and fucked up the day. If I don't get this umemeh over to Greel Truyoza, he'll pop out of a wall somewhere and string me up for torture. Then, he'll murder me. Slowly.

I'm just curious, so I glance back at the door to figure out how one might go about sealing it off, but now that I look, Rosemary and Dimitry are standing there.

"What in hull-breaches happened here?" Dimitry asks, staring at the former billiards room. "Looks like you got hit by a missile."

"Brilliant observation," I mutter. Why did everyone have to drop by right now for a tea social? And more importantly, how do I get them all to leave again? "If you guys are here, and the Captain is with Bremerton, who in Bob's name is driving the ship right now?"

Rosemary tips her hat at me. "While I do appreciate your faith in my skills," she replies with a smile, "Lucy and Juliet are navigating. And I missed this guy over here."

She joins Gisella in showering Fred with enthusiastic attention.

"Just be gentle, okay?" I say, finally reaching the end of my rope. Clearly no one is interested in seeing *me* on this void-forsaken ship, but I'm still worried about Fred. "His neck was injured."

A volley of concerned coos erupts from those two, and I can't handle it.

"You look like you could use a drink," says Dimitry, eyeing me sidewise.

I'm thrown by his comment, a sucker punch of guilt. I'm an animal trafficker! I'm a traitor! How many times have I lied to them now? I shake my head. No one here should be nice to me! And definitely not share their alcohol. That's like a whole other level of kindness I don't deserve. I swallow thickly.

Dimitry pulls out his flask, takes a sip, and offers it to me. "It's not that shitty-ass Mint-Trip Pete makes. This is the good stuff."

I snort. "You want good stuff? You should see what Bremerton's got here." But then, the stupidest thing happens. Remorse stabs me in the gut. I've tranquilized the guy, and now I'm about to give out his ancient alcohol. Burning asteroids, why am I growing a conscience right *now* in the middle of an animal trafficking operation? I close my eyes. I'm fucked. I wave in the general direction of the bar. "He has some fancy shit in here. Somewhere."

Dimitry raises his eyebrows. I grab the flask out of Dimitry's hands and take a swig.

It burns so good. It also diverts his attention. Double duty.

"You drink better than any animal rights activist I've ever met." Dimitry chuckles. "Come on over to the mess. There's a whole bunch of us waiting for you to come tell us the story. It's been what, six standard hours since we last saw you? And you've already got yourself into a whole lot of excitement!"

That's an understatement, but I nod and follow Dimitry.

The good news is that for as long as Bremerton's unconscious, I can make up my own version of the events, and no one will know any different.

The bad news is it's another ten hours max before he wakes up, and even less if Doc Williams gives him something to detoxify his system.

———

"So it wasn't that exciting. Just a pirate attack out of the fucking blue. It was Bremerton's quick thinking that saved us," I conclude my story. I'm still miserable about using a tranq on him. Which is dumb because I have no doubt Truyoza will send another pirate crew, and I'm never going to see Bremerton again anyway. I'm won't see any of them ever again.

I really hate my life right now.

Rosemary is staring at me with her arms crossed. She nods slowly. She's the one who's been asking the most questions, but I think I've won her. Everyone else is already toasting my survival, which, let's get real, is still too early to call. Well, almost everyone else. Both Pete and Sergeant Reyes are noticeably absent from the mess, and because I don't know what's happened with Bremerton's injury, their prolonged absence feels like a glaring declaration of wrongdoing. A giggling sound pulls me out of my funk long enough to notice that the umemeh is nibbling on Gisella's hair, and she has to keep gently pulling it away from him.

"Maybe I should get a cabbage or something for Fred," I say, glancing around.

The food bar, under the glass covering, is empty.

"Yeah, that's changed since you left. Otis hasn't been working right for some reason," Dimitry announces.

"I'm *trying*," Gisella replies. "I'll get him there. His programming is all there! It's like the circuits shorted or something."

Oh. Shit. I glance at the ground, trying not to look guilty. Bless my fucking tits, Pete didn't tell them he suspected me of foul play. Is it possible to feel relieved and even more terrible at the same time?

"Yeah, she won't let any of us even touch him," complains Marc.

"I can't risk it! It's *Otis*! And anyway, which one of you has small circuits training?"

"I mean, we *all* had to take classes," Dimitry grumbles.

"Exactly my point," Gisella concludes triumphantly.

"It's not exactly like you've fucking fixed him, even with your specialty," Dimitry retorts.

"I will," Gisella replies, mouth firming into a line.

I am the Galaxy's shittiest person. They should make me wear a badge made out of shit, put a shit bucket over my head, and bang it every time I enter a room to announce my shit-shame wherever I go. I am the absolute worst.

"Anyway. Since you left, we draw straws to take turns with the food prep," Dimitry continues. "All this to say that it's Pete's turn and he hasn't brought down any of the crops yet. I don't know what he's waiting for…"

He's probably taking care of that half-dead prune, Bremerton. Or some other terrible mishap that I'm responsible for.

"I can go and get stuff!" I exclaim, jumping out of my seat. "Just some salad greens, right?"

"You sure?" Dimitry asks. "You don't have to do anything for that lazy bastard."

"No, no. I don't mind. Really." I glance about the gathering.

I've come to enjoy hanging out with them, but that only makes me feel worse for all the ways I've betrayed them. I need to get out of this room, fast. "Fred's gonna need something to eat, and I can only count on my hair for so long. I'll be right back."

I sprint out into the corridor, and race up the stairs. I've spent enough time on this ship by now that I can get to the bat-infested greenhouse with my eyes closed and completely shitfaced. Literally, all you have to do is take the stairs up. Manageable with minimal brain cells and swooping animal attacks.

I was planning on dashing right past the bridge and straight into the greenhouse, but I stop dead in my tracks when I hear my own void-forsaken name being said by Sergeant Reyes from the private vestibule off the bridge.

I stay hidden behind the stairwell door and press my ear close to listen better.

"Of course Savage is responsible, Doc!" Sergeant Reyes is

yelling. "I'm not an idiot. She's a soul-snatching smuggler and she called up some friends to bail her out. But regardless of what she's done, we all need to put on a front. I'm asking you to *help me*, Williams." The fainter sounds of a woman's voice can be heard, but I can't make them out. *"Because!* If Savage knows we're on to her, she'll be much harder to keep in one place! If we pretend we think she's innocent, she keeps up the act when she's around us. All the way up till when the police arrive."

My heartbeat triples in speed as the muffled sounds of Doc's response stay maddeningly out of hearing range.

"Yeah. Yeah, I know. I've called my military buddies," Reyes continues. "Since we're on a tight deadline with our buyer in Hobie Port, they offered to come out and escort both Savage and the umemeh to police custody. We'll let the police sort out what to do with the umemeh itself." There's a quiet lull before Reyes responds. "Look. All I need you to do, Doc, is pretend Bremerton really *was* knocked out by the blow. Don't talk to Savage, if the lying really bothers you. Just don't let the others know."

I let out a long breath.

He knows me for what I am.

I glance around the empty stairwell as I try to calm my rapid breathing. Well, there's one silver lining here. Other than Doc Williams, no one *else* knows. They're keeping it a secret from the crew.

I trudge slowly up the last flight to the greenhouse. I don't need to hear any more of Sergeant Reyes's plans. I've heard enough.

I won't be caught in Reyes's snare again. I'm getting off this ship as soon as possible.

DINNER IS A MERRY, FAMILY-STYLE AFFAIR. EVERYONE IS DRINKING TO celebrate their triumph over Truyoza's pirates, something I still don't understand.

"So tell me," I ask woozily, after a few rounds of Mint-Trip, despite Pete's steadfast scowl from behind the food bar. "How did you guys defeat a fully-armed pirate ship?"

"It was all because of Michael!" exclaims Juliet, placing an arm over the captain's shoulder. Sergeant Reyes reddens and removes her arm as carefully as one would handle a bubble-bottle grenade. Juliet, ignoring the subtext, continues to gush over him. "He's brilliant! Did you know that?"

I raise my eyebrows in polite response. I can't bring myself to say anything positive about this hardass dream-snatcher, but if he likes to hear Juliet say it, I'm not about to get in his way.

"Whoa, Juliet, I'm not exactly sure if I would call it brilliant," Reyes counters, scowling.

"I would," replies Dimitry between mouthfuls of Pete's crappy food.

"Seconded," adds Marc from down the table.

"Do you guys even have weapons on this ship?" I ask, interrupting this love fest. "I thought it was a cargo ship?"

"It is," replies Sergeant Reyes with a wolfish grin. "But we can't give away all our secrets at once, can we?"

"It was nails!" announces Dimitry in a matter-of-fact voice, tucking into his next bite of food. Reyes gives him an annoyed glare.

"A whole volley of them!" exclaims Juliet, eyelashes fluttering at Sergeant Reyes.

"You launched… a volley of nails?" I ask, to be clear. "How did you manage to steer them? How did they gain enough velocity to be effective?"

Gisella gives a throaty laugh. "We got her again, cap'n!"

Reyes's face lights up. "Cheers to that!" he says, and gulps down his own moonshine.

"Got me?" They're starting to piss me off.

"A full three sentences, by my mark," Gisella replies, grinning at me. She takes another sip of her own drink. "Without a single curse word!"

I purse my lips as knowing smiles pass around the room. "You asswipes are going to be really disappointed when you find the word fuck has been tattooed onto my DNA," I reply, but can't help smile a little as well. "But if ya'll like it so much, I can speak like a Proper Princess for you if you'd like."

"Yeah right," Dimitry yells out merrily. "I'd give you this whole flask to hear it!"

"Please excuse me while I go wash my mouth with some fucking soap," I reply, and pretend to gag. "That shit is never going to happen!" I put a hand over my heart.

There are several cheers to that, and many raised glasses. Smiles flash all around the table, and this is going well. In fact, it's all perfectly according to plan.

———

AFTER DINNER, I GRAB THE UMEMEH AND HEAD TOWARDS Bremerton's docked escape pod. Most everyone is still drunk and straggling in the mess. Except for me, who is drunk and straggling *out* of the mess. The hallway is completely fucking empty. Perfect.

Segerant Reyes jogs to catch up with me in the hallway. Holy Bob, can the man just be tipsy and relaxed for a few hours?

"Where are you going?" he asks once he's caught up to my side.

"So serious," I say, stopping in the hallway to mock his frown. He's standing opposite me, and I reach up to touch his furrowed eyebrows.

"Hey, whoa," he says, backing up into a wall. "I was just, uh, wondering where you're headed? I know you're a little under the influence. The bedrooms are in the other hallway."

Such a good pretense at playing the nice guy, when in truth, he's just policing my every movement. I can play pretend too, Reyes.

"I figured Juliet's moved back into my old room, and I didn't want to annoy her with Fred here, all up close and personal in the quarters," I say huskily. The very thought of her makes me want to lean in towards Reyes just to beat her at something. Fuck that, I want to drink every inch of this sexy piece of meat. I lean in.

"I figured I could just sleep in Bremerton's game room. Plenty of floor space in there. Plus, Fred's already wrecked it."

In this moment, I'm acutely aware of the way that Reyes is staring at me. He may know that I'm an animal trafficker, but there's one thing that's definitely not fake here between us. I step closer to Reyes, and I can see two things. The way he looks at me says he wants me. The way he fidgets and shoots sideways glances down the hall tells me he feels bad about it. That's the problem with morals: they get in the way of a good rumpus.

His discomfort is something that will work in my favor. Maybe it's wrong to push this chemistry when he's so iffy about it, but it's not like that ever stopped any of those motherfuckers on Hialeah from doing the same to me, or worse. So I ignore his discomfort, knowing it's nothing compared to the rage he'll feel at what I plan to do next.

"No, it's, ah, no trouble," Reyes stammers as I push up close. "She's happy to…"

"To do anything you ask?" I ask, leaning even closer. Now I'm mere inches away from him, and I can smell his soap-clean skin. My own backstabbing bitch of a heart kicks up a notch at the thrill of it. I put one hand up against his chest, and his nostrils flare as he tries to take another step back and hits the wall.

"Let's just…" he begins. I am close enough to feel his every breath on my skin. "I think this –"'

When I came up with this whole lean-in idea, I forgot how stupidly attractive he is, even if he's a major prick. A girl's got needs. I reach up and touch his jaw, and stubble rubs against my fingers. I press my body up against his, and the way we fit together is so perfectly that everything about this has my body aching for *more*. I reach my hand higher to grab a fistful of his hair and lean in, eyes half closed at the prospect of our mouths smashing. I can hear Reyes inhale sharply, and right now, I want nothing else except for him to grab me back.

After a good three seconds of nothing, Reyes side-steps away from me.

Shit.

My eyes flutter open and I register the furrowed eyebrows, the all-business look on his face. Shit shit shit.

It's now, or never.

Reyes clears his throat with two crisp *hems*, his eyes already sliding down the hallway as he jerks his cuffs straight. "I'm sure Juliet would be happy to move to – "

He stops mid-sentence as I jab the tranq into his neck.

"Should've… known…" he says, his lips curling into a sneer. "With… *you*…." Sergeant Reyes's body crumples down to the ground, and I gauge the remaining distance to the escape pod hatch. It's ten feet or so.

I grab one of Reyes's limp arms and begin to drag him down the rest of the hallway. The umemeh, of course, keeps bobbing his curious heads down to check on Reyes. Only, he keeps getting in the way. Reyes's limp body has already smacked against Fred's legs once, and at this rate, it will happen a million fucking times. And I bet every time the idiot umemeh falls he will break a leg, or a neck, until there's nothing left. Seriously, that overly-curious left head of his is going to be the death of him.

I stop to brush unruly curls out of my face. "If only you had extra arms instead of a second head, you'd actually be useful," I say to Fred. And then I feel like shit all over again because that's literally all Truyoza wants him for: his stupid neck muscles from those stupid double heads.

I return my attention to my last-minute baggage that I still have to drag down the hallway. I grab his arm again. If he wasn't such an annoying ass, this all wouldn't be happening. If only the buyer hadn't been this psychopath Truyoza. And if Weasel hadn't been trying to cheat me out of the deal. There are too many levels of wrongs piling up against me, it's all colossally unfair. And now there is messy, drippy stuff coming out of my eye holes and I must look ridiculous lugging this big hunk of muscle across this perfect, immaculately clean carpet.

I really hope none of the others show up to see this.

chapter twenty-three

I dump Reyes's heavy ass just inside Crenshaw Bremerton's game room. I ain't carrying him one step farther, so that is exactly where that mountain of muscle will remain for the next, oh, ten-ish hours. I push the rust-colored curls out of my eyes and look around the room.

Fred, luckily, steps into the room without coercion. His heads bob down to investigate Reyes's slumbering form and he snorts.

"I know, Freddypants. I don't like him either. Tough nuggies." I wave my hand at the motion sensor and the door slides shut. Now how the voids do I disengage from the *Waterloo's* docking clamp and evac chamber? I scour over the Russian symbols on the billiards table. I still got nothing. I try to recall everything that Bremerton has ever done when 'steering.' He never did anything useful. He loved the *Euryale* excessively, more than someone would love a romantic interest. Or a special AI friend.

That gives me an idea.

"Uh… Hello? *Euryale*? Uh. *Darling*? You awake?"

"Yes, Miss Savage. I am."

"Oh thank the tit-thumping-apes. You're intelligent, aren't you?"

"Indeed," she replies.

It all makes so much more sense now. The way Bremerton treated the ship like it was his girlfriend. She is.

"*Euryale*, disengage from the *Waterloo*, and get us *anywhere* but here."

"Unfortunately, Miss Savage, if we initiate unilateral undocking procedures we will damage the *Waterloo's* coupling equipment. The *Euryale* escape pod, however, will remain unharmed."

Well, shit. If we damage the *Waterloo* upon departure, we're not going slip away unnoticed. Which was the plan. But the *Euryale* seems capable. Like, really fucking capable. Money can buy some really cool shit. A new idea flashes to mind.

"Can you, uh, communicate over your computer thingies and, well, force the *Waterloo* to carry out the undocking sequence from its end so that it doesn't get damaged in the process? Without human involvement?"

"I certainly *can* do that," the *Euryale* scoffs. "But I will not. It would violate every AI moral code. We do have a concept of boundaries."

Shit. Even machines have moral codes these days. Those have been foggy to me ever since I learned they only benefit a subset of people that doesn't include myself. I try a new tack with *Euryale*.

"Sure, sure. But, if we're talking moral code, don't you have an obligation to protect lesser evolved machines? Listen. I'm planning on undocking, whether it's unilaterally or not. That much is a certainty. And we both know that if you don't help me and I force the undocking, the *Waterloo* will get damaged. Don't you, the more evolved ship, have an obligation to protect the *Waterloo*? Especially if all you have to do is talk computer to computer?"

There is a pause. "It's a moral quandary."

I press on. "You know where we keep our umemeh's? Under armored guard or in the zoo. Because they can't protect themselves against stupid human behavior. If the *Waterloo* is the umemeh of evolved ships, it shouldn't be allowed to have the same freedoms as an evolved AI. It needs to be protected from destructive humans like me more than it needs its autonomy." The room is quiet for a while. *"Euryale?"*

"Still thinking about that one."

I tap my finger on my arm. Reyes lets out a sleep sigh by the door. Never heard anyone do that before when tranqed. Weird, but we need to get moving. *"Euryale?"*

"I apologize, Miss Savage. The processing time to this moral quandary is estimated to be somewhere between seven hours, thirty-seven minutes to eight hours, ten minutes. Unless of course I find a way to apply the Dover clause and can complete the calculations in six minutes, forty seconds. Unless the Ynett clause complicates things, in which case it may take fifteen hours and twenty-eight seconds."

Oh, no. No, no no.

"Can we go with a gut decision on this one? Or maybe we could lean on the logic of a carrot-topped zoologist?"

"Unfortunately, that is impossible. Don't concern yourself, Miss Savage. All other ship functions will be fully operational. I'll just be working on this problem in the background. Understandably, I'll be unable to make a decision on the morality of forcing the *Waterloo* to participate until the process has been completed."

What would Bremerton do if she pulled this on him? There's no fucking way that anyone who pays for a billion-joulo ship would sit around and wait every time it faces a moral crisis. Thinkthinkthinkthink. What would Bremerton do? An image floats to mind of him working to overturn the billiards table. That sparks an idea.

"Is there a manual override for these morality problems?"

"Oh, yes! There's a button with a question mark on the console."

"Are you kidding me? Why didn't you tell me sooner?"

"I thought we were having a pleasant philosophical conversation."

By now I've jammed the big red question mark. "Disengage

from the *Waterloo* and make them like it. I mean, ensure they don't suffer any damage. Then let's get the voids out of here."

I don't have the meet-up coordinates of our destination on this quanta-com, so I pick a random, empty patch of space far from inhabited star systems. For now. I lean back in Bremerton's leather seat and put my feet up on the shiny console while the *Euryale* is hard at work. Soon enough there's pink goop all over the walls and a clicking sound coming from the hatch. I smile.

This *is* really comfortable.

———

Truyoza picks up on the first ring. "Vhere is the umemeh?"

"On its fucking way, no thanks to your idiot henchmen. Why would you send a bunch of incompetent dodos to pick me up?"

"Dodos? Is this zoo word?"

"Burning asteroids," I mutter, not daring to do what I really want in this moment, which is to rip Truyoza a new one. "I'm in an escape pod. With…" I do a quick check over the readout the *Euryale* has shown me over the last hour. "With approximately five hours of fuel left. Where are your goonies?"

"I can get you coordinates."

"Fan-fucking-tastic. Do you think they're actually capable of keeping me alive at this point?"

"I make no promises."

"Thanks for that. What about themselves? The *Waterloo* sent a bunch of military guys on our trail."

"Vhy you no start with this?"

I sigh. "I have a hostage, Mr. Truyoza. They won't touch us. All you have to do is send me the meeting coordinates."

"Jha, jha! You are good! I may jhave place for you in organization when we are done with this."

Fat-fucking chance, I think. But all I say is, "Thank you, Mr. Truyoza."

"We talk soon. I meet umemeh." Truyoza cuts the line, and I'm left alone in the *Euryale's* game room with an unconscious Reyes and an idiot of an umemeh. My quanta-com rings with coordinates I do not know how to enter, and simultaneously, the ship alerts me to an incoming video-comm from Reyes's ship. I hit the decline button.

How do I even begin to explain to them that I've kidnapped their captain? Well, I may not be prepared, but I *will* have to tell them I'm holding Reyes as a hostage eventually. It is my only bargaining chip for keeping those military guys off my tail.

I send the *Euryale* our new destination coordinates for the pirate ship rendezvous, and let her sort it out. As Bremerton was so fond of pointing out, this thing drives itself.

In comparison, facing the crew of the *Waterloo* is a task that feels infinitely harder. My throat goes itchy for a drink, and fuck it, now is not a time to be stingy about another man's alcohol. In fact, I'm pretty sure even Bremerton would offer me a drink at this point – me, the asshole, who tranqed him up. He's one of the good ones. I pour myself a shaky glass of his most pedestrian shit and wonder if there's any quantity of alcohol that will be enough to square me up for this next call. I can't be soft. I pad over to the boxed Monopoly set and gently prize out Bremerton's gun. I'm going to need this thing for moral support.

The pleasant calling chimes repeat over the ship's console. I down the entire remainder of my glass, wipe my mouth with my sleeve, and stalk back over to the console. This time, I press "accept."

Rosemary stands on screen, arms folded. Gisella runs up to join the comm, looking angry and confused. "Want to explain where the voids you think you're going?" Rosemary asks.

My stomach flips. Rosemary might have been my favorite of them all, so her discovery of my betrayal hits hardest. I didn't ask them to be nice to me. I didn't ask them to be the only real friends I've had in eight years. But I've got to do what I've got to do. And that's that.

"Where I've been trying to go all along," I reply softly. "To deliver Fred to his buyer."

Rosemary's arms are crossed, and her nostrils flare. "I can't *believe* you," she replies. "I *welcomed* you! We all did!"

"Yeah, I know. Listen, one more thing. When Reyes's military buddies get there, tell them to keep away."

She raises an eyebrow. "Why the hulls would I say that?"

I tromp over to Reyes's recumbent form and drag him over to the camera view. Rosemary's face goes from angry, to surprised, and back to angry. Apoplectic-angry.

"What have you done to Michael?"

"Tranquilizer. It wears off after ten hours with a bit of a headache, but otherwise, he'll be fine. If you'd like him to stay fine, you need to keep those guys away."

"Or else what? You'll kill him?" Rosemary asks. She moves her hands to her hips. "I don't believe that for one second."

"Don't test me," I warn her, waving Bremerton's gun at her. "I'm in a shitty bind and my life is a tightrope-walking nightmare. I need a ride from moronic pirates to deliver Fred to a sadistic mob boss." Rosemary goes very still. "*Now* you understand." I take a deep breath. "Look. I'll negotiate Captain Reyes's release if you call off his military backup. They won't touch Reyes if he's a valuable hostage. It's a win-win for everyone."

Rosemary purses her lips. "Except for Fred," she answers in a cool tone. "Michael better not be injured, Savage."

Everything about this hurts. I even miss being called Savvy. I knew our friendship was a temporary, delicate thing, but burning asteroids, this all hurts in a way I didn't expect.

I shrug. "I'll do my fuckin best."

Rosemary stares at me for a long minute, then twitches her mouth. "How did you get caught in this at all, Savage?"

She'll never understand. Her experiences are so astronomically different than mine. There's no point in even trying. "None of your business." I click off the call, and head back to Bremerton's bar. Why did I ever think she could be a friend?

There aren't enough drinks in the universe to bury my guilt.

———

AFTER TWO HOURS OF TRYING TO GET AS SHITFACED AS HUMANLY possible, I've discovered the intelligent computer system can play music on demand. Screamo music fills the cabin with a selection of songs I've never heard before; eight years is a long time to be locked away from humanity. The ship is piloting itself smooth as pie. Everything is going fan-fucking-tastic.

Until Reyes blinks himself awake. His body isn't moving, but his eyes start darting about.

"What in the name of Bob?" I say aloud, slurring. "That's not right. Go back to la la land." We still have an hour till we reach our rendezvous point, and I really don't want to have to deal with his righteous anger for the next sixty minutes. "*Euryale*, turn down the music," I say, and head over to inspect Reyes on the carpet.

"Don't -" he says, still slurring, "don't do thzhat again." He's moving in slow motion, and even though I'm also wobbly, I'm moving faster than him. I root around in my bag till I find the rope, and tie Reyes's hands behind his back. I know I've done a shitty job when the mess just slides loose off his arms.

"Do *not* like it," Reyes continues, moving his tongue around his mouth and frowning.

I pull the rope harder on his arms, and for good measure, throw some extra around his legs. "Go back to sleep, asshole."

"Hurts," Reyes says, trying to turn to look at me. "Arms. Hurt."

I look down at the rope, and discover his hands turning a purplish hue of red. Burning asteroids, I've tightened it too far this time.

"You ask too much," I say, but I get to work on the knots again. "Knots are stupid."

"Head." Reyes says while I'm busy back there. "Hurts."

"Why the voids are you even awake?!" I exclaim. "You're not supposed to be awake. It's a direct mass to meds ratio. Given your enormous bulk, you should still be out. I mean, even if you do steroids to build up that ridiculous muscle mass. There's an equation, asshole, that works on every fucking animal except *you*. Of course."

"Enhanced… kidneys…" Reyes replies, rolling his head from side to side.

Oh. Well, that explains it. And it also explains why he wasn't even tipsy at all after all those drinks in the mess.

"That's… lamentable, is what it is," I say, once the words really sink in. "Horrible. Who did that to you? I hope you stabbed their eyes out."

"Did it… to myself," Reyes says. "Head. Hurts. Please."

Well. Sounds like he deserves the torture. Fred begins nuzzling Reyes's cheeks, and Reyes emits a low moan. "If you're going to cry like a baby I *will* gag you. I have to survive another hour of this."

Reyes stops moaning. "Head. Hurts," he repeats, but goes silent.

I rummage through my bag to check if I've got any insta-cold compresses lying around. All I'm able to find is a high dose painkiller in a syringe, which'll be a waste on this guy. I head over to the bar instead. All these fancy hoity toity drinks will be like water to him. Water is good. I pour him a glass of gintaki, relying on those special kidneys of his to do the rest of the work.

"Hands tied," he says when I put it on the floor by him.

I return with a straw, and leave the glass where it sits, otherwise untouched. "Lean over and deal with it," I reply to his glare. "It's either this or the syringe of strong meds that your super-kidneys will laugh at. Plus I'm saving them for Fred in case he gets a *real* injury."

"Like murder?"

"Shut up."

"Won't be useful to Fred once they cut off his head to make their impotency drug."

"Yeah, I got it the first time. And like I said before, shut it."

Reyes moves his tongue around his mouth again. After another glance at the gintaki on the floor, he leans over, but succeeds only in toppling into the carpet.

"Flea-ridden rodents, are you severely incompetent?!"

"Imagine, for a minute, Savage, that I am not." His eyes find mine, and they're full of hatred. His grogginess has completely cleared. I hate those fucking kidneys. "And then consider the possibility that this, whatever it is you're doing, is a very bad idea."

"Great. The righteous anger again," I say, slurring. Maybe it's the whiskey, but it's getting hard to continue looking in his eyes. I retreat over to Fred, a few paces away.

"Let me go, Savage, or you'll be very sorry."

"No." I march over to him. "Let me explain to you how this is going to work." I jab my finger in his direction. "You are a hostage." I let that sink in. "Yeah, yeah. I know all about your military buddies. I overheard you on the quanta-com. Back on the bridge of the *Waterloo*. I'm the wrong person to mess with, asshole."

Reyes falls silent, considering me with something new in his eyes.

"Imagine my surprise when I heard you were planning on turning me over to the police. After all that."

"After all that – what?!" Reyes exclaims. "We welcomed you in! We fed you! *And* your stolen umemeh, too. You're a *criminal*, Savage! I gave you more than you deserved. And you're complaining because I planned to hand you over to the *police*?! Or are you upset that I didn't consult with you about those plans beforehand?"

"Enough!" I say roughly. His words sting more than they should. I get up and pace the room. I don't need this crap. Not right now. "What was I expecting? I should just gag you."

It doesn't matter, though. The damage is already done. His words keep roiling through my mind. "You're a *criminal,*" seems to be stuck on repeat.

"Water. Please," Reyes asks, still toppled over on the ground. "Not gintaki."

"I don't have any water."

A moment of silence follows.

"You don't have *any* water?"

"What did I just say, moron?"

"What are you giving Fred?"

I blink. I hadn't brought any food, either. I hadn't planned this far in advance. Or really, I figured the pirates would have a nice set up for Fred. But… Maybe I shouldn't count on pirates for their foresight.

"Oh, that's right," Reyes continues when I don't respond. "You don't *care.* You want to kill Fred anyway."

"That's it. You're getting the gag." I find a bar rag and bring it over to Sergeant Reyes. I analyze his angled head with drunken calculations. "Open up, Sarge. Don't make this hard on me."

Sergeant Reyes doesn't respond, but stares at me defiantly. Thoughts trickle through my drunken brain; I could always tranq him again, I've got a few more spares in the bag. Reyes reaches the same conclusion. He opens his mouth. "Drink first?" he asks.

I sigh, but I move the cup so that the straw is accessible to his mouth. The umemeh comes over, and one of his heads leans down to sniff the drink. "Not for you, Fred," I say firmly. "Ah, never mind. Drink away."

"Because you'll be dead in a few hours," Reyes adds.

I shove the gag in his mouth. "I don't need any of your judginess, asshole," I say while tying it in a firm knot. The tying's gotten easier since last time, which I can only assume means I'm sobering up. I'm still fueled by anger and a burning desire to finally one-up Reyes. "When you know what it's like to owe money to Greel Truyoza, you can talk to me about right and wrong. Until then, try not to be so incredibly annoying."

Reyes's eyes track me as I return to the bar. Festering ring-faced narwhals, why do I feel like he's still judging me? For reasons I don't fully understand, I continue to explain myself.

"Some of us drink to drown out our reality. Some of us can't afford an enhanced kidney." I pause. "Not the monetary expense, asshole, but the being sober part. To live with my void-forsaken life. Some things are better left unexperienced."

I shake my head and stare off at a middle distance while the alcohol burns its way down my throat. I think of all those police reports I've tried to file over the years on Hialeah that never appeared in the system, and all the compromises I've had to make to survive that life. "Some of us can't afford to grow a conscience."

After a few minutes of drinking in silence, I look at Reyes again. His eyes are closed, and Fred is nuzzling his face. Not munching on his hair, but sniffing his cheeks and licking them. For some reason, I feel bad for Reyes.

"Once we deliver Fred, you'll be released," I tell him. "You can go back to your pretty, morally righteous life. I'll try to make sure they don't hurt you." Reyes's eyes fly open, and his gaze is full of hatred again. Well, I tried.

"Hey *Euryale*," I say. "Turn the scream-o up." I recline in the control seat, put my feet on the console, and nurse my drink. I can't help it, but a memory of Bremerton doing the same thing on the bridge pops to mind. His ghost image raises his glass to me, and sadness tugs at me. I sit there wishing, for a good long while, that the Universe had granted me the life circumstances one would need to be as naïve and morally righteous as Reyes and Bremerton.

Ultimately, I decide, some people are just born under the right stars and some people are born on Minerva.

chapter twenty-four

There's a bunch of grinding noises and repeated clicks as our door connects with that of the pirate ship's. It's not a smooth lock like Bremerton had orchestrated with the *Waterloo*, and the ship intelligence is not fixing this one for me. I wonder if I should ask the *Euryale* what's up.

Reyes is blinking furiously at me.

"Ugh, fine," I say, trudging over to him to remove his gag. "What? Are you having a seizure?"

"No!" he says impatiently. "Get over to the controls and allow their docking clamps to access the ports! Mother of hull breaches, have you ever orchestrated a black space docking before?!"

I ignore the jibe and walk over to the console and scan the screens. The *Euryale* has conveniently switched the readings to English language for me, but most of this stuff is unintelligible to me anyway. There are flashing words like 'Trisolly', 'Fell-Axis' and 'Muti-Sarcage', each followed by a table of numbers. All as useless as Russian to me.

"Uh, *Euryale*? Help me out here."

"Oh! There you are," replies the smooth computerized voice. I blink. Where the voids else would I be? "You appear to be interested in docking. All automized coupling and uncoupling features have been suspended while I work on the moral and ethical repercussions of unilateral undocking, as we discussed. If you want to avoid damage to our ship at the moment, you'll need to use the manual override again."

"*Euryale!*" My adrenaline is thumping. I'd just assumed she'd do it for me! "What am I looking for here? Same question mark button?"

"Yes and no. You'll begin with the question button for manual override, then you'll need to manually initiate the coupling as well. That will be the large button that says 'coupling' on the left display screen, and then you'll be guided through the process."

My eyes rove the left edges of the multi-screen display until I *finally* spy the word "coupling." Fuck me, it's peeking out of the one holo-field that is filled with a big red box with a warning sign that reads, "Systems occupied. All docking functions temporarily suspended." Below the error message is a ticking number that reads 3,748. It flickers up and down without a conceivable rhyme or reason.

"Shit." I mutter. I slap the red question mark button several times, and after a good twenty seconds of smashing it down on repeat, the error box finally resolves. Thank the fur-licking felines.

A new screen question prompts me, "Allow access to coupling links?" I click the big fat "yes" button. Then, there are no more prompts.

It can't be this easy. I glance around the room, half expecting it to blow up. But instead, the harsh grinding noise subsides, and gravity stables out again.

I frown. I guess it was that easy.

"Burning asteroids," Reyes concludes by my silence. "You've never piloted a ship before. Are you insane? We could have died, Savage! A black space coupling? Even experts can't handle that! What were you thinki— We could have *died!*"

"Yeah, I got that the first time. But we didn't. Still alive, see?" I stomp over to the umemeh and pull Bremerton's gun out of the Monopoly box. Reyes's eyes get big when he sees me assemble it. I'm clumsy at figuring it out, but it's not exactly neurosurgery.

"Listen up, sugar," I say, and his beady eyes find mine. "These are pirates I've never met. I will negotiate your safety. Just keep your big fat mouth shut, Mr. Righteous. Got that?"

There's one big click sound, and the pink goo begins to retreat from the walls.

"Don't do me any favors," replies Reyes bitterly.

"I'm not. It's a favor to Rosemary." Reyes's eyebrows furrow, then his eyes glitter with hope. I snort. This is not one of those comments he should get excited about. "Yeah. She called while you were out. I told her to keep your military guys away or you'd get it. Hostage much?"

All excitement drains rapidly from his expression, and his body seems even more deflated than before. Stars if I don't feel bad for him – he's always so put together, so professional.

"This shit will all be over with soon," I mumble. I can't get myself to believe it, though.

A series of squeaks can be heard from the door, and my mind races through how the voids I'm going to convince these fuckers not to hurt Reyes. Or even get them to listen to me in the first place. Quick thinking brings me only one solution. I move into the only power position I can think of: I aim the gun at the base of the umemeh's necks.

"*What the hull, Savage!*" Reyes yells, visibly straining against his bonds.

The door slides open, and in walks a motley crew of pirates. They're the kind of human I recognize too well from Hialeah. Sleazy, rough edges, and completely indifferent to anyone else's situation. They're all holding guns, too, but the guy in the front is waving his around like it's some old fork or spoon he's forgotten in his hand as he gestures to the accompaniment of some joke. Hilarious, asshole.

"Kill the girl," says the guy in front with the slick iridescent jacket. He's not even looking at me, that's how unconcerned he is by my existence. "Kill the guy. Take the animal."

"Hey, Mister Kill-Everyone. Hold it right there, or the umemeh gets it," I announce loud enough so there's no questions.

The guy in the front finally looks at me. He cracks an ugly, crooked grin, which reveals a mouthful of gem-stone rubies as replacement teeth. His whole fucking smile is red and disturbingly sparkly. I make a face at that. Red? What kind of bunnicula-wannabe gets red teeth?

"I don't care about the umemeh," Red replies, and my heart skips a beat at the possibility that my move was all for nothing. "That's Truyoza's thing. I owed him a favor and I was in the right neighborhood."

Wow, these pirates are such numbskulls. This move was supposed to demonstrate that I have an equal amount of power in this relationship. To get them to respect me and listen to my demands. And keep Reyes safe. Trust me to find the only pirates that need it spelled out in crayon. Time to try a different tactic.

"Do you have a name, ya big stupid idiot?"

That gets their attention. The other pirates tense their hold on their weapons, and now there's a bunch of barrels aimed directly at *me*. Their leader puts up an arm to restrain them.

"My name is Captain Golgi, princess, and *you'd* better start learning your manners, or you'll be sorry."

"Okay, Captain Shit-for-Brains." Golgi's face becomes dead serious. I must like living on the edge. "Listen carefully. You owed Truyoza a favor? Well, it's going to be more than one, now. Truyoza's pissed at you for bungling my pick-up." I let that fact trickle through his five brain cells for a second. "Yeah," I repeat, watching understanding, then anger, register on the captain's face. "He knows all about it, thanks to me. Here's how it all stacks up: I'm on his good side, and if this umemeh dies, you're totally and completely fucked."

Golgi's expression turns haggard. "Now you listen here, you little twat –"

"No, *you* listen," I reply, as I hit the priming button on Bremerton's ancient gun. A telltale whine fills the room. I wave my spare hand to emphasize the gun at the base of Fred's neck. "If this umemeh dies, maybe Truyoza will come for me. But I won't be the only one he comes for. So take two deep breaths, and listen up. *Princess*," I add, mimicking the tone of voice he'd used with me.

"That guy, over there," I wave in the direction of Sergeant Reyes, who's apparently gotten nervous about all the firepower in the room and has scooted away five feet. "That's Captain Michael Reyes from the ship the *Waterloo*. He's a *hostage*. Do not kill him. He called up a military carrier to come attack *you* idiots, and they'll be here soon. But for as long as we hold Reyes hostage, they won't touch us. Do ya' think you can manage to wrap your puny brains around that?"

I watch as the pirates assess the pathetic specimen of Reyes, sprawled on the floor with hands and legs tied.

Captain Golgi narrows his eyes as he stares at Reyes. "This the guy that swiss cheesed the *Doomburg*?"

I blink rapidly. "*That's* what you call this ship?" I glance between them, but the pirate crew is mostly all bristle. "Oh man. You're being serious. Okay. Right. Yep, fine. This is the guy who turned your *Dumb-berg* into metal lace. Now here's the important part, since I know your combined three brain cells have trouble following." I look at each of the faces, puckered and pissed. Good. They were listening. "Do *not* injure him, or we'll have nothing to prevent the military from attacking us. They'll be checking in four hours and if they don't see him alive and well, they've made it clear they'll hunt you down. You think you can manage that?"

A grin spreads slowly across Golgi's mouth, giving us a flash of those disturbingly rubied dentures. "Perfectly," he says, with a very wicked gleam in his eye. "And what about *you*, Carrot Top? Any good reason we got to play nice with ya?"

I forgot how rapey men could get. Golgi's henchmen chuckle. The men in the back move to make way for some new pirate coming through, a trail of cigarette smoke following in his wake. "I'll take care of her," he says from the back. That gravelly voice – I know that voice.

"Flea-ridden rodents. Weasel?!" He pushes to the front. Weasel looks more or less the same as the last time I saw him, only now he's wearing the same black electrolyte garb as the rest of the crew.

"You're here?" It was the first dumbass question that occurred to me. Genius, I know. Not, *How dare you rat me out to the police and try to frame me for the umemeh job?* Not, *Why in fuck's sake would you take up with these assholes?* And not the one question that I should have asked most of all, *Tell me why I shouldn't punch you right now, you two-faced leaky asshole?*

"This is the one," Weasel says, taking a deep drag, then giving a nod to Golgi behind him. "She's the one who framed me."

"I framed *you*? I think you meant to say, I ditched you after you framed *me* and planned to leave me to rot, you enormous fucking asshole!" I exclaim, with barely contained rage. "Oh, you better be rethinking your words, you motherfucker."

"She's the reason I lost my ship," he says, his voice rasping, not even bothering to respond to my accusations. "I got a special *soft* spot for her."

"You have some balls, Weasel! I can't believe this shit!" Not one of Golgi's men seem interested in my response. "I hope your ass get infested by a hornet's nest! I hope your cigarettes never..." I cast about desperately. "Never give you good drag! And I hope you get destroyed by the cheating dogs you're trying to impress."

Weasel chews on a wad in his mouth, completely unmoved by my rage. "Done yet?"

Fuck. I swallow.

"Like I said, Captain Golgi. I know how to take care of the umemeh. I was prepared to do this whole run myself. Cut her out of the deal and give me her share."

Golgi nods. "You're better company, that's for sure."

"Wait!" I exclaim. Not again. I can't believe I'm being fucked over by Weasel *again*. "He doesn't know how to take care of the umemeh! That's total bullshit. I'm a zookeeper! He's a stupid cargo man."

"You mean former chemist." Weasel spits out a loogie.

"You want your cargo transported, sure," I say, facing Golgi. "But the umemeh will die under the care of this souped-up gym rat. Also, he's a *rat*. He'll turn on you too!"

Golgi shrugs. I grip my gun tighter and keep it based firmly at the umemeh's neck.

"Ya'll are forgetting this little thing," I add, licking my lips. Shit. I don't want them to call my bluff. I nod at the umemeh. "If I kill the umemeh, it's over for all of you. Back the fuck off."

Weasel leans his head back. "You okay if I take some liberties, Golgi?"

A slight panic flutters in my chest.

"Make my day," Golgi replies.

Weasel aims his gun vaguely in my direction and fires in a round arc. There's the clinking of a shit ton of toy crap falling against each other as they crash to the floor with the continued *nic, nic, nic* as each plasteel bullet hits the bookcase. And the sound of Fred squealing.

I instinctively crouch, holding my hands over my head. I scream, "What the fuck is wrong with you fuckers?" I glance up in time to see the umemeh lob one, then two, balls of spit right at Weasel's face, and Weasel's got murder in his eyes. I don't even have time to worry about that, since Fred begins pawing the ground back and forth. I know that in his panic, this two-headed idiot is likely to charge straight into these assholes. That would be bad. Very, horrifically, catastrophically bad.

In a panic, I drop Bremerton's forgotten gun to the floor so I can get both hands around Fred's necks. His eyes are dilated, he's snorting, and every one of his leg muscles tense. Several bottles of bubbles roll away from the shit-show behind us and into the bullet ridden area under Fred's legs.

Fucking shit, just what I need in this moment is to have Fred step on one and blow us all up on accident, I think, and lean to dash one out of the way.

The moment my fingers make contact, I change my mind and

grab the bottle instead. Keeping a firm arm around Fred's near-neck, I check the bottle. How the voids do these things work? Fuck it. Trial and error, right?

I pop up and toss the bottle directly at Golgi. It bounces off his shoulder. Nothing happens.

"Your head's about to get a lot redder, if you don't cut that shit out," Weasel says, aiming his gun at me. Well, he was probably going to kill me anyway.

I scoop up another bottle and twist off the cap, thoughts whirring madly. It looks just like a normal bottle of bubble soap! What the hulls. Bremerton said these were explosives! On second thought, the bubble wand *does* look remarkably like a grenade pull, though. But how does that work if the cap isn't even on?

"I'm asking you nicely, Carrot-Head," says Weasel, pausing his trigger-happy finger long enough to take another step forward. "Kick that gun over here and step away from the animal. Nice and friendly."

"Fuck you, you back-stabbing, lying scumbag." I return my attention to the stupid bubbles. There are grooves on the wrong side of this cap. Yes! I screw the lid on, upside down. I pull the ring on the end of the bubble wand and hear a satisfactory click. Yessss. Thank you, Bremerton, you twisted, rich weirdo.

Now what? How long till this stupid thing detonates? I squint at the lavender bottle. I probably shouldn't still be holding this thing. But if this thing takes a while to explode, I don't want them throwing it back at me. So when I throw *this* bottle, I aim into the hallway behind asshole Weasel.

A deafening explosion rocks all of us off our feet. As Golgi and his men struggle to get into formation, I scoop up several more bottles.

Fred has backed the fuck up and is trying to make an exit through the rear bookcase. That's fine with me, as long as the dumb shit stays out of the firing range. I snatch up Bremerton's gun from the floor.

"Listen up, you big morons," I say, gesturing at them with the gun. Captain Idiot Golgi and crew have backed up into the hallway of the *Doomberg*, and while most of them are checking out the ship's damage, Golgi is staring right at me, *pissed* as a herd of stampeding elephelk. Lavender bubbles float in the air around them, and when a bubble pops loudly right in front of Weasel's eyes, he actually jumps.

Loudly, over the ringing in my own ears, I say, "Let me spell this out for you. You will not kill the umemeh, our hostage, or me. You have the dumbest ideas I've ever heard. Don't make this messy, morons."

"Listen, you ginger-bitch," Golgi replies, his angry eyes staring at mine. "If you destroy one more bolt on my ship, I *will* space you."

"Then don't tell your men to shoot at me!" I exclaim. "Golgi, don't be a dumb fuck. Do I need to remind you, we're on the same fucking team. It benefits us both if we can play nice for this one void-forsaken trip. Don't listen to Weasel, he's a traitor. You and I don't have to be enemies. We want the same thing."

Golgi sneers, and a glitter of red winks at us. "No, we don't." He turns to his men. "Move these stinking animals into the cargo bay," he indicates Reyes and me with a wave. He turns to me. "Congratulations. You get to stay there until the goods are delivered. And once Truyoza gets what he wants, we will do whatever the fuck we want with ya'. And yer friend."

I'm getting flashbacks of the last cargo hold I travelled in. And almost died in. My pulse kicks up a notch at the thought of being trapped in another small space.

"You," he says, turning to his men. "Clear out, all of you. And keep your fingers off yer triggers. We ain't having any more shoot-outs. We barely got through the *Doomberg* repairs last time. Don't fucking touch her. When Truyoza pays us, you'll all git your happy ending. So shut up and let's get this over with."

Golgi turns heel and leaves, along with Weasel and his crater-faced friend.

Two goonies wait for us in the hallway, waving their guns impatiently.

I turn to Reyes, who's watched this whole exchange with contempt. *You're welcome for saving your life, asshole.* I untangle his arms and legs from the mess of rope I made, and he gets up to stretch and puts a hand on Fred, who's quivering. Reyes gives me a meaningful glance.

"It's just the adrenaline," I murmur. "He'll be fine."

Whiiiinnnnnnne, goes the sound of the guns powering up in the hallway. I reel around to take a look at these idiots.

"Move, bitch!" One of them barks at us.

The two thugs trace my movement with their scopes. If these blind, fenn-eared bats can't aim at this ten-foot distance, a scope sure as shit ain't going to help. I swing my messenger bag around my shoulder and hold an addicto-nip treat out for Fred. With a parting glance at Bremerton's destroyed escape pod, I turn to the goonies.

"Yeah. We're coming," I say, and enter the post-explosion hallway on the *Doomberg.* The area on the *Doomburg* side of the *Euryale* coupling is rubble filled, wet, and smells like grapes and gun powder. There's no breach, at least, but there's a shit ton of broken crap all over the floor that we now have to pick through. The goons are using their guns to motion us towards an unaffected stretch of graffiti-lined hall up ahead, so I concentrate on carefully luring Fred onwards while trying to avoid patches with excessive rubble where he could break a fucking ankle. I spare a glance behind me. "Easy on the guns, assholes."

No reply. The two ragged and dirty thugs follow us at close distance. Sergeant Reyes picks his way along, solemn and grim.

"Don't even think of starting on your judginess crap," I mutter to him once we've reached solid ground again.

He says nothing in reply, but follows me through the smelly, grime-coated hallway. There's some yellow wavy line at the bottom foot of the hall that looks an awful lot like water damage. I scrunch my nose to imagine what liquid could have possibly filled this hallway. Higher up along the walls, there is evidence of the *Dumb-berg's* recent battle with Reyes's ship. Pipes bent out of shape, holes that have been hastily patched in unapologetic colors that don't bother to blend with the rest of the wall. I catch Reyes's eye, point to one of the holes, and raise an appreciative eyebrow. He only scowls and keeps his eyes fixed straight ahead. What's *his* problem?

I catch sight of the world's biggest asshole a few paces down the hall, waiting by the cargo bay door and grinning at us in a really creepy way. That rat bastard, Weasel.

I keep my finger steady on the trigger of the gun, still aimed at poor Fred, as we approach the asshole. I take a quick peek past Weasel inside the hold and am slightly relieved to discover that unlike the holds on the *Waterloo*, this cargo space is cavernous. It's several stories high and equally wide, which makes me wonder what these assholes usually transport. Giraffes? Dinosaurs? Scratch that. Maybe that's what the ship *used to* transport. But from what I can see up at the front, the space is a huge mess. Piles of random shit on top of and in between piles of boxes. It's a pigsty. It doesn't take a genius to guess they're not using the space for whatever monstrous transport item that was intended for the space. There's no way they were the original owners of this ship.

Well, a pigsty is not going to kill us. I have no real grounds for objection, other than the creepiness of Weasel's smile. I tug on Fred's leader rope and pull him forward.

Weasel stops us. "Quanta-coms," he says, holding out a hand.

I panic a little bit. Fuck, fuck, fuck. "Um? I need to be reachable by Truyoza. He made that very clear."

Weasel's scowl deepens. It takes him a few minutes to process this, because brain power is not something you can work on at the gym. "Fine. I need his, then."

One of the gun-wielding pirates behind us yells, "Now!"

Reyes gives me the death glare. Slowly, he pulls the quanta-com from his wrist and hands it over. He's still staring at me, as if it's my fault he can't come up with lies to save his own ass. I turn away from his glare to head into the cavernous hold.

As I lead Fred past the door guard, Weasel lashes out and punches the umemeh in the neck. The injured neck. Then double time, he strikes Fred with a second fist to the ribs. It's met with a meaty crack. Fred squeals out in pain and dashes the remaining distance into the hold.

"Motherfucker," I say as the gun whines in my hands. Weasel turns his still chuckling face towards me in time to see me shoot him in the shoulder.

Weasel roars in response. Then he takes a staggering step towards me.

"Uh uh," I say, directing my aim at his chest. "Stay right there." I hear the whine of two guns powering up behind me.

"Listen up, my violence-prone, evolutionary-devolved, moronic ferry drivers," I yell. Rage is coursing through me now. Fred didn't deserve that, and I've lived with him in close quarters for the last few days. If anyone would have found him annoying enough to punch, it would've been me. *That* was plain mean.

"Your own dumbshit captain understood the rules. He told you to keep your hands to yourself. *You*," I wave my gun at Weasel. "*Asshole*. You deserve worse than this." Reyes is shifting uncomfortably by my side, eyes darting. I look in the direction of his movement and spy the two gunmen slowly advancing. Time to pull out all the stops, then.

"You know what else, koala-brains?" I use my non-gun-wielding hand to slip a bottle of bubble juice from the bag, "He *also* said he didn't want any more messes." With my gun still on Weasel, I half-turn to the two-thug escort behind me and wave the bottle at them. "Put away the guns."

They hesitate. "I mean it," I repeat.

They don't have to know that there's a whole cap-screwing situation that needs to happen for my threat to be worth anything. I raise the bottle high over my head, and cock back my arm.

Slowly, their muzzles make the descending arc till they're aimed at the floor.

I motion to Reyes. "You. Get in the cargo hold. What the voids are you waiting for?"

He blinks several times at me, but eventually, slow as molasses, moves into the hold. I follow him in walking backwards so I can keep my eyes on this asshole party out in the graffitied hallway. As soon as I've made it clear of the door frame, Reyes bangs the door shutting button. There's muttered cursing out in the hallways, but soon enough the room is blessedly dark and, more importantly, closed off from the pirates.

I sink against the door into a sitting position and squeeze my eyes shut. I thought I was close to being done with all this, but I was wrong. This nightmare is never ending.

chapter twenty-five

Even sulking, I'm accosted by the horrific stench of the place. I open my eyes to find Reyes standing over me, gag in hand, glaring.

"This? This is who you wanted to sell Fred to?"

Not now. I don't need this *now*. I don't have another gag with me, and I'm seriously contemplating tranquilizing the guy. Again.

"I don't want to hear it, Reyes," I say, rubbing my temples. "And just so you don't get any airs, ain't nobody calling for your pretty ass in four hours. I made that shit up. So stop sitting smug and start thinking of how to best say thank you."

Reyes exhales deeply and takes a step backwards. Thank the burning asteroids.

After a minute of hard staring, he comes to sit next to me, leaning back against the wall. "I don't understand any of this, Saffron. Why are you doing this?"

I snort. This *lordling* doesn't understand it. He's never had to endure any hardships his entire life.

"I always knew you were working with your buyers. But *these guys*? Savvy, why would you work with these assholes?"

I roll my eyes and shake my head. I look up at the ceiling, trying to stem the tears that threaten at the edges of my eyes. "They're not the buyer, okay? Weren't you listening? These guys are just transport. Transport I wouldn't have to fucking use if *someone* wasn't such a big wombat-butt who tried to block my every move."

"Who's Fred's buyer?" Reyes asks softly. So softly, I forget that he's mad altogether.

"Someone I already owe a lot of money. Someone who paid to get me off Hialeah." I close my eyes. "I'm so fucked."

"Anyone could have loaned you –"

My eyes flutter open. "*No*, Mr. Perfect. Mr. Everything-in-life-is-black-and-white," I say in a mocking, lilting voice. "You know *nothing* about the isolated nightmare that is Hialeah, and you don't know anything about having to take shady money. So just rest it, okay? I can't handle any more of your righteousness right now, and I've got more tranqs where that last one came from."

"You're not the only one who's gone through their own personal nightmare, Savage." Then Reyes is quiet for so long I think the conversation's over. "You said something about Truyoza before on the *Euryale*. Is he the buyer?"

I remember that moment of anger; that name slip was a mistake. How the voids am I supposed to keep this clown safe if he sticks his nose where it doesn't belong? "I said, fucking drop it."

Reyes remains quiet beside me for another full minute before he springs up and walks off. It takes only a few minutes for him to disappear behind boxes and piles of garbage.

I tell myself I don't care. I don't care where he goes. He can hide in a box. He can build his own escape vehicle from scratch. I don't fucking care anymore. I'm so bone-tired of this.

"You're okay," he says sweetly from afar. "Everything's going to be all right," he says soothingly.

I scan the area, but Reyes is nowhere to be seen.

Oh. Shit. He's talking to the umemeh. The umemeh who was recently a punching bag for a backstabbing ex-boyfriend. I jump to my feet. "Is Fred okay?" I yell loudly into the space. In the darkness, it feels like the cargo hold goes on and on forever.

Reyes doesn't respond to me, but I can hear him continue speaking in the same soothing tone. My pulse kicks up a notch. I don't think I could handle it if Fred is badly hurt in a way my painkillers can't smooth over for him. He doesn't deserve to be in pain and misery.

"Oh my loving Bob, if that umemeh isn't dying," I warn into the cavernous hold quickening my pace, pushing deeper into the darkness. There's a wet drippiness to my nose that I have to sniffle back, and it's all Reyes's fault. "If I find out you're trying to get a rise outta me," I caution, as I round another endless, poorly-lit corner, "I'll make you regret it."

"He's not dying!" Sergeant Reyes yells back, exasperated. "Take it easy."

I close my eyes and lean against a random large crate in the shadowy, abandoned stretch of aisle. Why does everything have to be so hard? The crate behind me whooshes softly as air is expelled. I turn to check it out and find extra-firm plastic on the exterior. I glance around. Next to the dim strip lighting in the floor that marks the pathways through the hold, the crates had all looked the same before. I test a few others to confirm: this one is definitely different.

There's only one reason for someone to need an expensive box like this, and that's to protect what's inside. I would bet five thousand joulos that the whooshing was the sound of me squishing insulation, too. I can't say I'm surprised. They *are* criminals.

"You might want to meet Fred's company," Reyes calls in the dark.

Company? What the voids does Reyes mean by that?

I wind my way through the alleys of boxes. Mr. Righteous is not jumping in to provide any additional details, so I strain my ears to listen for his voice. I can hear him murmuring over another sound. Is that yipping? I turn the corner and find Fred curled up next to a large pen full of shnopples. I chortle. I was right about that box, then. And that also explains the horrific smell in here.

"Any idea what those are?" Reyes asks, nodding towards the dark brown furry creatures.

Only, something's off about this picture. Fred's heads are both resting on the ground, despite the shnopples' obvious curiosity about his limp figure.

"Shit," I mutter and rush over.

It's a really, really bad sign that both of Fred's necks are down.

Because of the pressure required by an umemeh's hearts to pump blood up to both heads, they are rarely comfortable when recumbent. They'll eat and even sleep standing, with their necks erect, if they can. So if Fred's lying down, that means he's in too much pain to stand.

Reyes is already kneeling by Fred's side and looks confused by my urgency as I fumble through my bag. "He's just resting," Reyes says to calm me.

I fix him with an angry glare. "Have you ever seen Fred lie down before? Ever?"

Reyes blinks, then looks with new concern at Fred. "Oh."

I ignore Reyes and move to examine Fred's neck, then his flanks. His breathing rate is increased, and he's moaning. Those assholes are going to pay.

I pull out the heavy painkiller in a syringe from my bag, careful to turn my body away from Fred so his eyes won't catch sight of the needle. He may not know exactly what I'm doing, but he's been tranqed enough times in his life to be afraid of syringes by now.

"Are you sure you… *need* that?" Sergeant Reyes asks.

I shoot him an annoyed glance. "Which one of us has a xeno-zoology degree?" Reyes doesn't respond. "That's what I thought."

I hide the syringe behind my back and rest a soothing hand on Fred's neck. His eyes find mine, and flutter closed. I take my other hand and jam the syringe there in his sweet spot, the species-specific aortic bifurcation right between his two necks. His eyes fly open, wide with fear, but within moments, they flutter shut again. His breathing becomes calm and steady, and he slides into a well-deserved nap.

"It's a broken rib," I say aloud to Reyes, which is met with cursing. "He'll still be able to walk. But that was the last of my painkillers. He won't be too happy for the rest of the trip, so I'll need all the tranqs I have left for this guy. So don't be an asshole and make me use them on you, okay?"

Reyes frowns. "What about you?" he asks with a meaningful glance.

"Yeah, I'll try my best not to be an asshole," I reply, and roll my eyes. "No promises."

Reyes shakes his head. "I mean, do you need medical attention?"

This startles the crap out of me. I look down at my arms and torso and discover my blue coveralls have been torn open above my right tit, just below the shoulder.

"Shit," I hiss, trying to crane my neck into a better angle to get a clear view of it. Now that I'm aware of it, it does sting. But from my vantage point, it mostly looks like a superficial abrasion. Must've been from the bubble explosion. "Is there any shrapnel in there?"

"I'd have to take a closer look," he replies apologetically. I nod. "Turn on your quanta-com light?" he asks. Once I've flipped it on, he leans in towards me. With his head only inches from my chin, the smell of his hair washes over me, and he's breathing softly so freaking close, my heart starts to flutter like a stupid idiot. Gently, with his left hand, he peels back the sticky, wet, ripped fabric. I inhale sharply. It stings.

He angles my light in different directions, but ultimately pulls away with the shake of his head.

"Just a blast-burn," he explains. "You'll probably need to clean it off and apply some kind of salve. You feel okay?"

No. It fucking hurts. "Yeah."

Reyes nods. He turns to stare at the small brown, ball-shaped, fur-covered creatures who've been yipping away. "So what in hull breaches are these things?"

Just like that, he's over my injury. I can feel a little offended that he was more concerned about Fred than *me*, a living, breathing, beddable woman. I need to give up on this wasted train of thought.

"Shnopples," I reply, without further explanation. If the guy has never heard of shnopples, he's never met anyone hunting – or dealing – methaltrixate. Pirates are not a good sort of people, and this is a conversation I do not want to have with Mr. Righteous.

Reyes raises an eyebrow at me.

I squint at him. "How have you never heard of shnopples? Don't you have a shit-ton of criminals for clients?"

Reyes tips his head. "Not a *shit*-ton, no." I give him a pointed glare. "Okay. We have some."

I motion with my hand. "And *none of them* have shnopples?"

"No, none. And you know what else?" he asks. Apparently, I've hit a nerve. "I have complete control over who we take on as a client. I would never, *ever* consider *these guys*. They're assholes, Savvy. I have no idea why you're willing to work with them."

"What?" I demand. "Are some criminals less criminal than others, Mister Judgy-McJudgerson?"

"Yeah, as a matter of fact. The Spiff? All he does is give money back to poor folk who don't have medical care."

"Ugh," I retort. "Like he's your only criminal customer. Who'd you get Otis from again? Five-Fingers?"

Reyes visibly deflates at this. "Five-Fingers was never a client. More like… a family friend."

My ears perk up at this. "What? Righteous Reyes has a *criminal* family?" Reyes lets out a long sigh. "Pill-loving pigmie chimps, you're serious."

He sits quietly, intent on picking imaginary lint from his cuffs. "My brother," he says softly. "My older brother, Sam." I move in a comfortable cross-legged position next to Reyes. "He made some bad choices. And eventually he chose something I couldn't save him from."

Oh, shit. "Like jail?"

"Like overdose," Reyes replies grimly.

I let out an involuntary 'oh' as my mouth falls open. "I'm sorry, Reyes. I didn't know."

He runs a hand through his hair. "If there's anyone who understands that people aren't black and white, it's me, Savvy. But I have *every right* to be pissed at someone who's making shitty choices. Choices that will hurt others. Or themselves."

I grind my jaw and look away. I don't need his moralizing shit right now. How did we move away from his criminal connections so soon? "We were talking about *Otis*," I say. I refuse to look him in the eye.

Reyes sighs. "Right. Five-Fingers." He purses his mouth. "Five-Fingers was the only other 'associate' of Sam's who tried to help him when his addiction got bad. He would actually comm me and take my comms when Sam was unresponsive. He'd be the one to go dig Sam out of whatever drug den he'd buried himself in." Reyes pauses, and I glance over. He blinks rapidly. "So when Five-Fingers was heading for jail time, he asked me to take care of Otis for him. And after all he did for Sam, I couldn't say no."

"But Otis is an ANDI3500," I say slowly. A highly intelligent robot famed for its capability to run undetectable criminal activity over comms networks.

"I know what you're thinking," Reyes cuts in quickly. "I had Gisella modify his base programming. He's not running anything illegal."

"Hm." Now is not the time to tell Reyes that I find Otis's 'enhanced' personality to be super annoying.

"Not everyone leads the peachy-charmed life you imagine, Savage."

I open my mouth to tell him how *eight years* of misery deserves a little slack, but stifle my retort. I've just made him bring up a dead brother. He doesn't need to deal with my baggage right now.

I stand up.

"Where are *you* going?" Reyes asks.

"To ask our great and mighty transport-drivers for food and water. Fred will heal better if his metabolism isn't running low." I tromp back to the cargo door and slam my palm on the open button, but the door doesn't move in response. I bang repeatedly on the door.

"What do you want, Ronnie?" calls an annoyed gravelly voice from the other side.

I groan. Of course they left that asshole to watch us. "Tell your Captain Idiot the umemeh needs some food and water to be alive for the fucking delivery."

"Sure thing," Weasel replies, and after a two second pause during which he could have only been picking his nose, he speaks up again. "Okay. I just told him. He says to go fuck yourself."

"Fuck *you*, asshole," I mutter. I pound away at the door, unrelenting. Something I learned about Weasel from those seven months together is that he can't stand irritating sounds. Plus, the banging is actually somewhat therapeutic. Reyes comes over to watch.

"Do you –" he yells over my banging. "Have to make such a –" Reyes pauses during each bang. "Racket?"

I can hear the clicks of it unlocking from the exterior.

"Yes," I say, then wink to confuse the fuck out of him. I root around through the bubble bombs in my bag till I free the gun. I hoist it at the slowly receding door.

Weasel is there, arm in a sling, looking furious. "I told you before, you can fuck off. I ain't doing shit for you. Grow up—" he says, reaching for the door slam button.

I shoot the empty air by his shoulder. Weasel puts his arms in the air. "Fucking shit! That's a fucking gun, Ronnie, you stupid bitch!" He exclaims.

"Whoops. It *does* look like a gun, doesn't it? And I'm aiming it at you. But I think my aim sucks." I prime the gun again, and the tell-tale whine fills the air. Weasel snaps his mouth shut, and his beady eyes laser in on mine. "We need food," I repeat. "And water. For the umemeh. To survive this journey. Tell your boss."

"Fine." With exaggerated motions he reaches for the door release button, and I nod to let him know I won't shoot this time.

"Why the fuck we let her keep a gun..." Weasel grumbles as before the door rolls to a noisy shut. This time, I'm alert to the sounds of the locks clicking in place.

"Charming guy," Reyes says airily.

"Yeah. Glad he's an ex."

Reyes does a double take. "You dated that guy?!"

I sigh. "Less dating, more… banging."

"That guy?" he repeats.

"Alright, alright. I get it. My life sucks. It's not like a I had a ton of great alternatives," I mutter. I stalk over to a low enough empty crate and hunker down. I tuck the gun away into my messenger bag so I can hunch over my folded arms. This animal trafficking thing is going swimmingly well. It smells like shit in here, my umemeh is in pain, and I'm locked in with a morally uptight jerk. I'm going to have to bang on this door again in five minutes just to make sure my horrible ex-boyfriend follows through. It's complete and utter misery.

Reyes sighs and strides away, back toward the umemeh. Before making the turn down the walking path through all the debris and crates, he stops and turns back to me. "You know –"

"If you plan to throw more of your moralizing crap at me," I interrupt. I've had it up to here with it today. "You can just shove it, Reyes."

He shakes his head. "I was going to say," a sly grin crosses his face, "that maybe we'll get lucky and Fred will grace this cargo hold the same way he did with the *Waterloo*."

It would make my day if Fred pissed all over their hold and ruined the deadly, highly addictive cargo they're running. A smile tugs at my lips. "Too bad Juliet's not here with another spare neon suit to lend for cleanup duty."

Reyes breaks into a grin. A real, bona fide, not-faking-it grin. I'm obsessed at the sight of those dimples before he ducks his head and disappears around the corner.

Alone, I sit back against the wall and take a good minute to be annoyed that my stupid idiot of a heart has kicked up the tempo for a jubilee dance.

chapter twenty-six

Four minutes and fifty-nine seconds later, the clicking of the locks indicates that we're about to have company.

"Shit!" Caught unaware, I fumble at my bag where I've stashed Bremerton's gun, but I'm too late and too clumsy. The door rolls up.

"Oh, Carrot Top? What do we have here?" asks Golgi in his falsetto, sweet voice. I'm even more irritated that he's still using that nickname. Note for all you non-gingers: no one ever, in the history of red hair, has appreciated the nickname Carrot Top. I keep my face stony.

"They're telling me you're asking for food? And water?" He scoffs. "What does this look like, a five-sprout hotel?"

"Are you really that stupid?" I respond. "The umemeh. Has to be *alive*. For delivery." I glare at the captain and Weasel, sneering behind him. "No one expects the *Dumb-berg* to be a hotel, but you still have to do the bare minimum to get paid."

The captain frowns and picks at his nails. "The animal has to be alive, yes. These beasties can survive for days without sustenance, I'm told." He casts a glance at his men behind him, who slowly shift their weapons to aim at me. "You, on the other hand? Not so sure we need you alive. Not after you shot Weasel."

"Hey, whoa!" I exclaim, nervous. The men standing behind

Golgi all tighten their grips on their weapons, their faces a cross between anger and eager anticipation. This tide of resentment is about to descend upon me, with Golgi's blessing.

"He injured the *umemeh*," I say with emphasis. "Your only cargo?"

Nothing, not a drop of sympathy or understanding, is registering on Golgi's face. I put my arms on my hips. "I told you not to hurt the three of us. I warned you."

Golgi guffaws. "Oh, a warning! You warned us?" The flash of his dark red teeth is accompanied by four guns being lifted and aimed right at me.

I do quick mental math. My own gun is currently tucked away in my bag which requires more than one clip release to get to it. All the bottles of bubble bomb are also in that bag, under the same fucking clip. Basically, the math says I'm screwed.

"Well now, if a warning makes everything all right. I'm warning *you*. Carrot Top." His lips curve up in an approximation of a smile. "On behalfa Roy." One of his men steps forward from the hallway, and the whine of his gun fills the cargo hold. The malicious glee in Golgi's eyes is evident. "Oh and also, Bjorn." Another shadowy figure steps forward. "And Sorl. And –"

A dark figure leaps out from the shadows adjacent to the cargo door. It blurs past Golgi and attacks Roy first, then Bjorn second in rapid succession. They fall down so fast that the last two take their precious fucking time to turn their guns towards the threat. But by then, the attacker has knocked down the third guy, and grabbed the gun out of the hands of the fourth. He finally slows down long enough for me to get a look at him.

It's Sergeant Michael Fucking Reyes, and he's just knocked out hallway guard number four. Holding a newly acquired gun aimed at the pirate captain, he bends down to collect the other three weapons, and kicks the unconscious bodies back into the hallway.

"Get us the food, Captain Golgi, or I'll get it for us," Reyes says as he backs into the cargo bay.

The ninja, Reyes, is a sight to see. Two guns are tucked under his armpits and facing out. The other two guns are nestled in the crook of his elbow, held firmly by their handles with a finger on each trigger. Reyes is literally holding all four fucking guns aimed at the stunned looking pirate captain.

"Savage?" Reyes asks.

I gape at him open mouthed.

He motions with his head towards the door.

"Oh. Right. Shit." I scramble over and slam my palm against the door-close mechanism. Alone in the hold with Reyes, his four guns are now aimed at *me*. "Um. Wow. Maybe I shouldn't have untied you."

"You know," he frowns. "A regular 'thank you' would work." He sits down on a nearby crate and begins piling up his newly acquired weapons.

I realize, belatedly, my mouth is gaping open. I try to string together two clear thoughts while Reyes pulls out bullet cartridges from the guns, one by one.

"Are you absolutely sure you want to throw your lot in with *these* people?" he asks, as if nothing had just happened.

"What..." I begin, bewildered. "What are you doing? If you could do that, why don't you take down the whole ship?"

"Math, Savage. Math." He sighs because I clearly have no idea what he's talking about. "On a ship of this size, they'll have a crew of thirty. At the very minimum, the *Doomberg* should have at least twenty more pirates here. There's no way I could fight them all at once." He turns his attention back to the weapons. He's still holding one and starts loading the spare cartridges into his pockets. "Four guns are useless without extra arms." Reyes gives a small smile at the shock on my face, and my heart skips a beat at those swoon-worthy dimples. "Ex-military," he says with a shrug.

"What branch of the military is that? The karate fucking ninjas?"

"I'll tell you what. I'll trade you stories," he says, while disassembling the guns. "You tell me why you want to work for a mobster and live with," he waves a gun cartridge in the air, "these incredibly charming people. Because I can't understand it."

I stare at him. The lines of his face have gone all rigid, and any traces of that smile have vanished. Just then, the cargo bay door rolls up ten inches, and two slop-filled bowls are shoved through. The door rolls back down and slams shut again.

Reyes throws a nearby stretch of moldy tarp over the three discarded guns and stands up. "I'll take those over to Fred."

I get up. "No, I will. It's my umemeh," I say, shouldering past him to the bowls of slop. One's green and viscous; the other is yellow and clear. I grimace.

"Only for the next few hours," Reyes says darkly.

"Yeah, yeah. *I get it.*" I pick up the bowls, careful not to spill any, and head off through the aisles of cargo.

The umemeh is huddled in close to the shnopples' pen, fast asleep. I leave the bowls on the floor right outside the shin-high pen that holds back the excitable ten-inch-high brown pom-poms. Once I'm content that the little furballs won't knock over the gate with their excited jumping, I slump down to the floor to a concert of yips. I hug my knees and stare up at the unfinished, raised ceiling.

Everything is going to shit. These pirates are the same despicable, wretched specimens of humanity I tried to leave behind on Hialeah. I cannot believe Weasel is here and trying to screw me over again, and Captain Monster Idiot of the *Dumb-berg* turns out to be unbelievably fucking rude. And on top of all that, Reyes continually gives me crap about my choices.

The worst part is that he's right.

I rest my head on a crate nearby and stare off into the distance. My thoughts linger on my resentment towards Weasel and inevitably land on the horrors of Hialeah. Wandering through bad memories, I fall into a disorienting sleep.

It's dark out, and Weasel has steered the tourist cruiser we commandeered over to bushes just past the Hialeah security office. Even though it's after hours, the courtyard beyond the office is fully lit and cheers and bellows erupt from the throng of onlookers inside. He eases the cruiser behind a nearby set of low bushes, where there's plenty of privacy, but any device worth its salt can get a live video streaming. Weasel fiddles with the cruiser's screen until he gets the local channel.

On screen, one Cape Fileomemetic Squirrel aims his engorged penis at his foe. His penis is nearly forty percent of his body length and covered in spines. His opponent is armed with the same appendage, ready for their fencing match. They're both hopped up on hormones, but just in case, they've tied up a female squirrel as winner's bait.

"Ugh," I turn away in disgust. There are shouts as the audience places new bets while some announcer calls out the shifting odds. Somewhere between fifty to a hundred Hialeah employees gather here to gamble at this same show every night, including one specific security guard who drugged my drink one terrible evening early in my career. The galactic police literally ignored my report, and being too indebted to afford a flight anywhere, it's become one more thing that I try to distance myself from around here. I glare at Weasel and gesture at the unfortunate animals on screen. "Seriously. This is not a turn on."

Weasel winks at me, then leans back in his pilot's chair and kicks his feet up against the dash. His tatted shoulders take on a blue sheen in the moonlight. One of his hands rests on a two-gallon jug of cheap alcohol by his side, and with the other, he takes a long drag of his ganja stick. He raises the jug in my direction. "Have a drink, Ronnie. Loosen up a little."

The night air is cold as fuck, and I am not the kind of woman who likes being ignored. "Weasel. I'm not kidding."

He shrugs. "Wanna fuck anyway?"

A loud buzzing interrupts this romantic moment.

"What the shit is that?" I ask. I turn to the screen. None of the security team – or the assorted staff that make up the audience – seem to be bothered. I tilt my head get a better fix on the sound.

There, in the distance, is an elephelk trumpeting. Then, several others in succession. The bushes shudder in the breeze.

"Weasel? I think it's a stampede."

"So?"

"Weasel, get your ass in gear. Move this vehicle."

Weasel reluctantly shifts the gears on the hovercar.

"Move over, now!" I elbow him out of the way.

"Ow! What the fuck, Ronnie?!" He curses his way over to the passenger side while I raise the hovercar to tree line height and swing around towards the direction of the elephelk enclosure. The elephelk trumpeting gets louder, as does the rumbling sound of the stampede.

"Shit. Shit. Shit. I told them the wild bunniculas were gonna piss off the elephelks. I *told* them!"

I slash diagonally above the underbrush, and even in the dark, I can see the trees quaking at the approaching herd. I should know what to expect, but when we finally sight the stampede a few hundred yards away, it's enough to make me gasp.

There is a sea of antlers as wide as my field of vision thundering towards us. The whole world seems to be shaking, even the very air is vibrating. There's a dust cloud the size of the milky way, and amidst the trumpeting, I catch sight of random ears flapping here and there. Between the dim lighting and all the dust, you can't see the body of any one elephelk. Not their massive bodies, or the large flappy ears, or the long trunk. But you *can* see the swarming mass of elk-like antlers charging towards you. It's absolutely terrifying.

I click on my commie and dial the regional supervisor, Griffith. Of course, he doesn't fucking answer. Why wake up when there's an elephelk stampede? I keep dialing till I can get him.

"Griff," I say, and I'm greeted by a groggy voice. I explain that if this emergency situation does not get redirected, they're going to break other enclosures, or worse, tourist recreational areas.

"Shoot them. That's it. That's an order."

I swallow. There are probably two hundred fifty elephelks out there. My voice pitches high. Too high. "All of them?"

"I don't give a crap. It's the middle of the fucking night," Griffith replies.

"Oh, I'm sorry," I reply. "I didn't realize we were killing animals because you're tired. My bad."

"I can't get a crew to shepherd them at this hour!" Griff retorts. "The elephelks got themselves into this mess. Serves them fucking right."

The line goes dead.

"Saffron?" Weasel asks.

I shake my head. There's got to be something we can do. I stare at Weasel's oversized jug of piña colada, forgotten in the footwell of the driver's seat. The fruity coconut on the jug makes me reflect on how much elephelks delight in fruit. Sadly for these guys, we live on Hialeah. They don't get fruit, ever, except for that one time the red bat colony up north all died and we had an excess of rotting fruit. At least there was a silver lining for the elephelks that day.

The scent of the piña colada mix might be enough to invade their adrenaline-addled senses and disrupt the herd. It's my only hope. I heave the jug to the edge of the cruiser and begin pouring Weasel's precious vodka into the path of the oncoming hoard. The elephelks are only fifty yards away now. The trumpeting is infinitely louder, and it's hard to hear anything else.

"Ronnie! Are you out of your void-forsaken mind!?" Weasel shouts, livid. "Not my drink!"

The cacophony of the herd is drowned out by a metallic crashing noise, like the sounds of a cargo bay door rolling open. I wake with a jolt.

"He's fucking here, you military asswipes," grumbles Golgi's rough, angry voice. It takes a minute to reorient myself. I'm not on Hialeah but here on the *Doomberg* with Weasel and a dangerous pirate crew. My adrenaline kicks up a notch. "He's right here. See?"

I jump into action and creep through aisles. Around the corner, by the door to the cargo bay, I catch a glimpse of Golgi. He's holding up a quanta-com-cam aimed at Sergeant Reyes, who is casually holding a weapon in both hands.

"He's un-fucking-harmed and was sleeping like a fucking baby. Now get the fuck off my tail, or your precious Sarge won't look like this next time you see him."

"Sergeant Reyes! Can you hear me?" calls out a voice from the quanta-com. "It's Colonel Sedeghat. The pirate captain says you're fine, but I've got to hear it from you. Tell me you're okay, buddy."

Golgi gives Reyes an expectant glance.

Reyes blurts, "The buyer's Greel Truyoza. Follow us there!"

Golgi lunges towards Reyes, fist raised for a good swing. Reyes springs back and fires both guns in the air. The ship-safe bullets miss any bodies, but he made his point. Golgi swiftly pulls to a stop, but his scowl deepens.

"You'll be sorry for that," Golgi says, retreating through the cargo doors.

Before he manages to shut us in the cargo room and lock the door again, I can hear Colonel Sedeghat reply over the quanta-com. "You'd *better not* hurt him, Captain Golgi. His continued health is the only reason you're still alive."

"Listen here, you little shit. I don't care about your fancy intergalactic military. I couldn't give a shit about you idiots prancing around in a uniform. But don't even *think* to fuck with me," Golgi's voice rises to a snarl. "You'll never find Truyoza on your own. So fuck off. And if you follow us, your precious Sarge is dead. Fucking dead. You hear me!"

The door slams down with finality, and I make a stealthy return to the animal den. With that one comment, Reyes has sealed his fate with Truyoza, and he'll become another tally on the list of casualties that are somehow my fault. The pit of misery inside me yawns even wider until a familiar tugging on my scalp alerts me that Fred has woken up. Still souped up on painkillers, he's become happily occupied by my hair. That's a good sign.

I gently nudge his head over towards the two bowls of slop and let his heads fight it out over which bowl belongs to which. Then the injured neck gets head-butted, and Fred yelps in pain. The dumbass can feel that shit in the pain centers of *both* heads.

I still can't help but feel terrible. He's *my* dumbass. I stroke the injured neck.

"Don't move this one around so much, idiot, and the painkiller will take care of you." I pull at the other head. "And no more head-butting yourself, you moron."

Fred's large eyes stare into mine, uncomprehending. I blink back tears, but Fred is bored of this. His nostrils dilate, and he starts investigating my hair again. I may as well let him have it, since these assholes ruined his ability to drink the soup-goop. These pirates are the worst.

Something in me snaps. I've had enough of this shit.

I always thought I didn't have a choice. I thought – once you sell out to Truyoza, you're owned by Truyoza. But this path ain't exactly a bed of roses. It's terrible. If everything's going to be terrible no matter what I choose, then why the voids not do it my way?

That dream has left me with a small grain of an idea; a plan so simple it's genius. My body grows jittery with excitement. I don't have all the kinks ironed out, but how much worse can it be than *this*?

I stomp over to the cargo doors in search of Reyes. He's wiping down one of the guns he fired, and doesn't even look in my direction. I've spent a lot of the last few hours thinking, but only one thing has stuck out in my brain after all this time. Sergeant Righteous was right all along. It's really irritating. I nudge closer to him, but he still doesn't acknowledge my presence.

"So, we calling you Mikey now?" I ask.

"Just my friends," Reyes says with a harsh glance.

That stings more than it should. "Fine. You don't have to be my friend. But I came up with a way to get out of this." I have Reyes's attention. "You were right, okay?" I say. "This isn't where I want to be for the rest of my life. I don't know how to get out of Truyoza's debt, but I do have an escape plan. But I'm going to need your help."

Reyes folds his arms. "What makes you think that I'd be willing to cooperate with any of your plans? Savage, we may be stuck in this room together, but that's the extent of it. I'm not about to begin a criminal lifestyle."

I sigh. "This time I plan to get Fred back to Brin-177. For real."

Reyes snorts and returns to cleaning his guns. "That sounds familiar. Remind me where I've heard that one before?"

"Look," I say, getting more desperate. "You won't have to do anything except stay out of the way. Until we get in the escape pod. Then, maybe you should drive."

Reyes's hands still on his weapons. "You think you can get us to the escape pod?"

I nod. "Even if you think I'm a piece of shit, I've got a way to get us out of here. That's got to count for something."

"Then what?" Reyes asks, folding his arms. "I'm not buying this. You might intend to get Fred to Brin-177, but what about you? You're screwing over Truyoza. Do you really expect me to believe you're putting the rest of your life into danger over this?"

I grimace. This was the part I hadn't fully flushed out. I swallow past a painful lump in my throat. "I assume I'll go to jail? Which will still be better than Hialeah. I mean seriously," I say, reasoning aloud to forestall his objections. "Nothing can be worse than Hialeah. And I would be safe from Truyoza in jail, too." I sigh. "Let's get Fred home."

"Why are you willing to do all this?"

I take in a deep breath. "Being in a bad place, it was hard to see a way out. I was trapped in a series of bad choices. Or I thought I was." I shrug. "So I'm breaking free." And suddenly, it does feel like weight has been lifted off my shoulders. Even with the possibility of jail time looming on the horizon.

Reyes raises his eyebrows. "Wow," he says. He lapses into silence.

After a few minutes of consideration, he speaks up. "All right. Three conditions. I don't get tranqed again. I will drive the escape vehicle. And if your plan differs from mine in any way once we're *en route*, we do things my way."

"That's fine."

Reyes blinks at me with surprise.

"The hardest part of this plan is getting off this ship. After that, we're not going far," I say dismissively. "There's a local port called Surf & Ceebu. Your Colonel buddy Sedeghat, or whoever it is you've got out there, can even escort me to the port."

"Why would he want to do that? So that your hot little ass can sneak out of our sight and hire some other ship the second we let you – "

"So I can get Fred on the direct convoy to Brin-177," I say, cutting him off, "with an armed escort, provided by the private military outpost at Surf & Ceebu." I shake my head emphatically. "Seriously, how have you never heard of that? Or Rosemary? Or even Lucy?"

"Surf & Ceebu has *what*?!" Reyes is staring down at me, eyes darting with a quick anger.

I shrug sheepishly. "You can understand how telling you about it would've fucked up my plans with Truyoza, before. But now that I'm doing the right thing," I emphasize that last bit. "It's really convenient?" I say, hopeful he'll agree. Reyes's jaw muscle is twitching, so I rush on.

"Not only will Fred get to a place where he's safe, but your Colonel friend can put me in jail. And you'll be back on the *Waterloo*. Win-win."

Reyes dips his head in a nod. "Alright then, Savage. What's the plan to get to the escape pod? I'm listening."

"You *miiight* need to make use of those enhanced kidneys," I warn. Reyes's smile drops. "And hope the *Doomberg's* command modules work similar to the ones on the *Waterloo*." Reyes gives me a full-on frown. "And that they feed their shnopples the same way everyone else does."

"What?" Reyes makes a face. "*What do shnopples eat?*"

I close my eyes, playing back our whole conversation in my head. "For now, can we just, put a pin in that," I pinch the air, more excited than I should be, "and circle back to the part where you said my ass was hot?"

Reyes groans and looks away. "Savvy..."

"We're stuck in a dark cargo hold for another hour or so until it's mealtime for the shnopples." I step up close to him and lean into him. I place one hand tentatively on his chest.

Reyes pulls my hands away and steps back. "I've been down this road before," he says, quietly. "And the last time I was here, I got tranqed. Let's just focus on the escape plan, okay?"

I release the breath I didn't realize I was holding. I give him a curt nod. I *know* it serves me right for being so tranq happy. Even still, fucking voids, it stings.

I head back deeper into the bowels of the cargo hold to find Fred. At least *he* doesn't carry a grudge when I tranq him.

chapter twenty-seven

Exactly as I'd hoped, the clicking of the cargo bay door locks sound off a few hours later. Reyes and I have been standing next to Fred and the shnopples where I filled him in on the plan. By now, the yipping of the shnopples is escalating to an intolerable, excited pitch.

"That's one guess I got right," I mutter.

"Guess?" Sergeant Reyes asks, lounging a few feet away from me by the shnopple pen. I'm surprised he heard anything over the ambient noise. "You were guessing?!" Reyes is giving me a murderous stare, but we don't have time to indulge in our game of competitive-hate-each-other. The sound of heavy boots shuffling are audible through the hold.

I look over to Ninja Captain. "Ready?" I ask. Reyes looks uncertain. I shrug. Ready or not, they're coming for the shnopples.

Five men round the dark corner of the cavernous hold. All five are holding weapons primed and aimed directly at us. "Get out of the way," says one surly grunt. "And no one will hurt you. On purpose." He waves the gun about like it's a toy, and chuckles maliciously.

I get up and slide around the men, who are satisfied. Reyes does too, but he holds his hands up. We make no mention of the welding job we've done to the shnopples pen. It's not permanent, but working to release all twenty-two shnopples will keep these men occupied for a good five minutes. Together, Reyes and I head to the door they left open and walk straight into the hallway.

"And where the voids do ya think you're going?" asks Weasel, who's back on door-duty. His trademark cigarette dangles from his mouth, ashes falling off like wayward snowflakes.

I shrug. "Same as the shnopples. Dinner leftovers." I step a few feet forward, so that Weasel's attention is on me and not on Reyes, who's now managed to get behind him.

"Hold it right there," says Weasel, waving his gun aggressively in my direction. He turns to wave his gun at Reyes too, but Captain Ninja is being extremely uninteresting, busy staring at a wall. Coincidentally, it's the wall with a control panel. *He better be doing what I told him*, is all I can think.

"No one said anything about giving you dinner scraps." Weasel leans back in his stool, arms crossed. Even relaxed like this, he's got his one good hand tightly clenching a small handgun by his armpit. The man is a menace.

Behind Weasel, Reyes begins fiddling with the control panel.

"Yeah, but no one said we can't eat, either," I snap, trying to hold his attention on me while Reyes does his work. "Either way, you should probably let your captain decide, shouldn't you?" The man looks unconvinced. I shrug again. "Unless you're not really part of the crew, that is? If you're just an independent contractor, someone they don't trust." Weasel's face twitches, and I can tell I've struck a nerve. "You know what, we could just go up to your captain's bridge and ask him for permission?" I lace my voice with mock sweetness. There is nothing their captain would hate more than me showing up on his bridge.

"Fuck no," Weasel replies. "Or you could just stay locked up nice and tight until the captain makes up his mind." The sound of approaching yipping alerts us that the shnopple train is nearing the door of the cargo hold. Shit. That was faster than I expected.

I glance at Reyes, who steps away from the control panel and gives me a shrug.

As far as body signals go, this is completely uninformative. Does he need me to stall longer, or not? What the voids Reyes, what the voids.

"Are you treating us worse than animals?" I ask, now gaining an audience of the shnopple guards, who at this point enter the hallway. "Why can't we eat what the shnopples eat?"

Two of the burly men in the shnopple guard hoist up their guns to aim at me. "Get back into cargo!" one of them snarls. "You, New Guy. Don't let them out, Cap'n said."

Reyes, in the back, is doing the whole slice-throat move again. Is he telling me that I'm dead? Or that he can't help me out on this one? I'm really going to have to talk to him about that hand motion, because I do not think it means what he thinks it means.

I raise my hands. "Okay, okay," I say, hastily backing up into the cargo hold, next to a waiting Reyes. "You've made your point."

One of the shnopple guards punches Weasel on his good shoulder, and he sheepishly closes the cargo bay doors on us, standing side by side. In the darkness, we can hear the men arguing amongst themselves outside.

In the dim lighting, I can make out Reyes scowling at the door. "You could have told me they eat dinner scraps."

I snort. "What did you think they ate? Crushed human skulls?"

He doesn't respond.

"Reyes. What the voids was that, out there? Did you disable the lock mechanism or not?"

Reyes looks sheepishly at the ground. "Well, ah. Good question."

"What do you mean, good question? It's a yes or no answer!"

"Ahhh!" He backs up, then runs a hand through his hair. "Right. Well. The only way to override the lock mechanism *on this level* was to convince the system that there was a hull breach elsewhere."

"Reyes. Will it work for us? Yes or no?"

"I, uh, convinced the system that there was a breach. The cargo door will not lock." He slicks back his hair and shuffles his feet. "I may have, also, broken an actual vacuum-seal aboard the ship."

"Captain Sergeant Michael Reyes. Did you create a breach?"

He grimaces. "I kind of went with what I knew. I was working fast and –"

"Just tell me!"

"Yes, okay? In the captain's quarters, a few levels up." He winces. "In his private bathroom."

I groan.

"It was the only thing I could come up with under pressure!" He sighs. "We do it on every install job. You have to disengage the pressure seal on a toilet disposal mechanism, you know? To test the differential when it's connected properly?" I shake my head. I have exactly zero experiences with this. "Right. Basically, I just left the toilet open to the vacuum."

Which means there is a leak however many levels above us, and in every sense of the word vacuum, air will be sucked out of our ship. If there are *any* safety mechanisms aboard this dumb ship, entire levels will be sealed off in order to preserve salvage-able areas. Those salvageable areas will have all doors unlocked to prevent people from getting trapped in places they're not supposed to be. But if that upper floor doesn't seal off properly, since the ship recently just survived damage from the *Waterloo*, every living space will be depleted of breathable air.

"Reyes," I say slowly. "Do you have any idea how the ship will respond next…?"

"There'll be some zoomergency alarms going off soon. I think."

"Reyes. I needed more time for this plan to work!" I run back through the cavernous space, with Reyes right behind me. He keeps tripping on me as I stop, every so often, to check the boxes until I finally arrive at the one suspicious plastic box. Reyes catches up and looks at the box.

"What the voids is this?"

"This," I say, grunting as I struggle to open the lid, "is methaltrixate. I hope."

"*You hope?*" he asks. "What are we doing here?"

Methaltrixate is only the most addictive illegal substance known to the universe. It only needs to be touched to be consumed through the skin, and a small pinch goes a long way. It's deadly, the powder can be explosive if you're not gentle, and it makes a shit-ton of money on the black market.

"Why in literal hull breaches are we stopping for this?" he asks. "Savage, the gate's unlocked. Let's get to the *Euryale* escape pod!"

"Reyes, can you just help me?"

He grabs his gun from his shoulder strap and aims it at the box's locked latch mechanism. But instead of firing it, he fixes me with a stare. "Tell me this is important, Savage."

"Make sure you aim away from the center. It's explosive," I say through gritted teeth.

"Savage!"

"I like it better when you call me Savvy. Or even Saffron."

"Saffron," he says, warning in his tone.

"Yes, it's important," I reply.

Reyes fires at the upper lock, carefully avoiding the center, and in moments, I'm pulling the layers of foam insulation out from the box.

"Why was it packed in with all of *this*?" Reyes asks in wonder.

I stop to look at him. "You've *really* never heard of shnopples before?"

"Some of us weren't raised in a zoo," he retorts.

"Neither of us were raised in a fucking zoo, you asshole," I reply. "Some of us worked there. And some of us know that no zookeeper in their right mind would keep a shnopple."

Reyes blinks at me. "And *why* is that?"

"Because." I sigh. "The first asshole looking for any easy money would steal them. It's not just that they're insanely expensive. They earn their keep. Shnopples can sniff out naturally growing methaltrixate in a fifty-mile radius."

Reyes's mouth drops open.

I mentally revise his nickname to Naïve Hotpants. I purse my lips. "Oh, never mind. Enhanced kidney people. Don't know *what's* wrong with you."

"And this has to do with our escape because…?"

I work with my hands while I connect the dots. "This is insurance, Reyes. Seriously, hostage much?"

I've finally gotten down to the box within the crate, and without all that insulation, the box of methaltrixate is much smaller than the exterior crate. All that padding for what amounts to an old-fashioned briefcase of drugs. Explosive drugs. Based on the weight, several thousand joulos worth. At least it has convenient handles. I tug at the case, but burning asteroids, this shit is heavy. Like a dead body.

"Reyes, help me here?" Reyes reaches in and lifts out the huge metal case with a smooth bicep curl.

"Show off," I mutter. Then I revise my thinking. "You probably have to be the one to carry this thing."

"Savvy, the pirates won't play nice because we stole their methaltrixate. They'll still fire at our escape vehicle and salvage it from our wreckage."

I grab the rope from my bag and start fashioning shoulder straps against Reyes's rock-hard upper back.

"The methaltrixate is not our hostage, you idiot," I say.

Realization dawns on him. "The shnopples," he murmurs. This methaltrixate crate is a few thousand joulos. But at any planetary port, these shnopples will bring in thousands more. The rare shnopples will be worth more to these pirates than any one load.

I nod and add the weight of the heavy methaltrixate case to the harness I've fashioned. Reyes winces. I pull the rope taught until the case lies flat against his back. "They'll come running, even in the middle of a feeding. They go totally wild for this stuff. I'm surprised they're not here already. You had to go and create a vacuum on board, didn't you."

Reyes grimaces. "Can you get the umemeh?"

I roll my eyes. "Does a cat have fur?"

Reyes nods. "Meet you at the door, then."

When I get to Fred, though, all my confidence completely deflates. He's lying down again, both heads on the ground, and moaning. The last of the painkillers in his system were done, then.

"Oh, Fred," I say. "I'm trying to get you to a safe place." He raises one of his heads towards me, and it's almost enough to make my heart break because I don't deserve that love after all I've put him through. I'm out of painkillers and I can't tranq him now, not if I want him to actually move through that hallway. I kneel and give his uninjured neck a big fat hug. He snorts into my hair, and moments later I can feel the sharp pull of his nibbling.

Through my ridiculously watery eyes, I manage a startled laugh. "That's a good boy, Freddypoo. Come on, big guy. We're taking you home." I raise myself from a kneel into a squat, and Fred leans his neck to follow me. "Come on, sweet boy," I say in my most soothing voice. I take a step further away, and he leans further. He stops short with a moan.

I put myself back into nibbling range to entice him, then try again. This time, he raises himself to his knees and whines. I dig around in my bag to find the addicto-nip treats I've left there for emergencies. If there ever was one, this is it. I take the treats and lodge it firmly in the curled tangle of my hair. It's quite possibly the grossest thing I've ever done, and I shoveled shit on Hialeah for eight years. But desperate times call for desperate measures. Fred is eagerly sniffing my hair-nest. I take a careful step away, and he leans to follow me. He even manages to stand up this time, a curious snout sniffling around my ears and face.

"Thatta boy," I say gently, and step by step, get him to follow me to the door.

I snort when I see Reyes. He's got a huge case strapped to his back and two guns slung, like necklaces, around his neck, and another two in hand, aimed at the door.

"Got enough baggage, Reyes?" I ask.

"Speak for yourself, cabbage head," he retorts, with a nod to Fred.

I pull out Bremerton's old gun in one hand, and a bottle of bubbles in the other. I'm ready as I'll ever be. I glance over at Reyes, and a bad thought occurs to me. "Uh, Warrior Ninja? You sure you can do all your crazy tricks with that heavy shit on your back?"

"Walk in the park." Reyes gives me a lighthearted half smile.

"That's what I like to hear." I nod my head. "And try not to explode."

Reyes shoots me a dirty look, so I flash him my most innocent smile. "Let's do this."

I kick the door open lever, and the cargo door begins its rolling, clanking ascension.

Stealth never was my strong suit.

chapter twenty-eight

Reyes slips under the door before it's fully rolled up, and I can hear the sound of a muted scuffle. By the time I can see clear of the rising bay doors, Weasel is being held face to the floor by Reyes's knee and his bad arm is twisted up towards the ceiling.

"*That* looks uncomfortable," I say.

Reyes gives me an annoyed glance before he karate-chops Weasel's neck.

"What the –" I begin.

"The baroreceptors in the carotid sinus send people to dreamland, not the afterlife," he says, killing Weasel's dropped cigarette butt as he stands up. Weasel is totally conked out. "Uses fewer tranqs. That's a priority, right?" He winks at me.

I swear my belly button just tried to swim up to my throat because I have a dizzy feeling. Reyes searches Weasel's pockets until he comes up with his old quanta-com. He straps it to his wrist while glancing around. He looks at Weasel on the ground. "This ex of yours is the one who broke Fred's ribs, right?"

I nod. "And stole money from me at Hialeah, and ratted me out to the police. Scum."

"Now's your chance," Reyes says. "Revenge, if you want it. I mean, not for you. You deserve to go to jail. Or be kept in a mental institute."

"Hey!" I exclaim, but I can see the smile in Reyes's eyes.

"For Fred. An eye for an eye, a rib for a rib. Something like that." Reyes shrugs.

"Right." I wind up to kick Weasel in the ribs. But I pause midair. I don't want to do it. He might be total scum. Scratch that, he is total scum. Traitorous, conniving, mold-scraping scum. He would have done it to me, in a heartbeat. But I'm not him. I rest my leg before I even swing it. "Leave him," I say to Reyes. "He's not worth the bruised toes."

Reyes raises his eyebrows at me but doesn't contradict me. I guess, after all, Fred's my umemeh. "Can you hear that whistling sound?" Reyes asks. "I think that's the air," he nods. "We're going to feel it soon."

"Why are there no alarms?"

"Give me some credit," he retorts. "I shut down the primary alert system."

"Wow. Look at you, aiding and abetting like a pro." We share a smile, but then unconscious Weasel heaves a big sigh. "Let's get the voids out of here."

I follow Ninja Reyes down the short stretch of hallway. While he does his military-guy deal, a crouched walk with guns aimed and primed, making rhythmic turns from side to side, I am competing in a hair parade. I'm wiggling my hair at Freddypoo, nudging the treat spot under his nose and ducking away again. The three of us together? We look fantastic.

I hear a distant sound of yipping.

"Sounds like they've caught the scent," I tell Reyes. "We have to speed this up."

We quicken our pace to the entrance of Bremerton's old escape pod, annexed from the formerly lovely yacht, the *Euryale*.

"*Euryale*?" I ask timidly. For some reason, I'm afraid she'll be pissed at me.

"I'm here," the ship replies serenely. "I'm happy to tell you that I've resolved the moral dilemma you posed. Indeed, you were correct. I've ruled that a more intelligent ship must care for those under a defined threshold of intelligence."

"Oh, thank the fur-licking felines. Listen," I say, as I get Fred into his piss-soaked corner of the room and pull the treat from my hair. "We need to be ready for immediate take off." I no longer have to fiddle with the stupid manual override. "Except that we're waiting on a bunch of shnopples."

The yipping down the hallway gets louder, as does the cursing of the pirates whose job it was to shepherd them. Reyes primes his guns, and their whines fill the air. He turns, squares his body, and aims at the open doorway.

"Also," I add. "The *Doomberg* is operating under the loss of oxygen. If you could get that pink goo ready?"

"Yes, Miss Savage," the *Euryale* replies.

Two of the little shnopples bounce round the corner, their adorable small ball-like bodies covered in food muck.

"That's *disgusting*," I mutter. I notice the pink goo has already started the process of coating the room, starting in Fred's urine-soaked corner. Reyes shifts his stance to get a firmer grip on his weapons.

Up close, the high-pitched yipping has escalated into near-screams. The first two shnopples are dancing with fervent excite-ment by Reyes's feet, and only minutes later, a noisy group rounds the corner, their yips sounding more like excited shrieks. "Not yet!" I shout to Reyes over the din. I am working as fast as I can to count the little suckers, but they keep moving. How the voids am I supposed to know if we've got all twenty-two? "Not yet!" I repeat to Reyes and start counting the suckers all over again.

Two members of the shnopple escort round the corner to come smack dab into Reyes's weapons.

"Oh, hull breaches. You again," says the pirate on the left. The guy on the right sneers and takes a step back. The sound of their two guns whining is overpowered by the sudden *nic nic nic* of Reyes's gun, already firing in an arc into the hallway.

One pirate dodges out of eyesight, past the doorway, but the other crouches to the floor, keeping his weapon trained on Reyes, who now has a crowd of excited shnopples dancing around his feet.

I am trying my best not to pay attention to any of this. I am keeping a careful watch on the bottom foot of the door. Three more yipping shnopples round the corner.

"That's all of them!" I yell over the *nic, nic, nic* of Reye's constant stream of fire. "*Euryale*, get us the voids out of here! Now!"

The door between the two vessels slams shut, almost simultaneous with the clicking sound of untethering. The goo begins to coat the final unprotected space of the doorframe and I can already sense the grav shifting below my feet.

"Sorry about the gravity here, it was the best I could do in a pinch," *Euryale* says. "Any particular destination in mind?"

"You are perfection, *Euryale*," I reply.

"Take us back to the *Waterloo*. Can you open up a comm link with them?" Reyes asks, raising his voice to be heard over the pitch of the yipping in the room. Whatever *Euryale* responds is drowned out by the overexcited fervor of yipping.

"Savvy, what was your plan for the shnopples?" he yells to me.

"Uhhh," I reply.

"You couldn't have planned to keep them in this state for the whole ride," he yells. "What was your plan to calm them down?"

I shrug. "I, uh, didn't think we would make it this far?"

Reyes grimaces. "Okay. *Euryale*, do you have the ability to space the methaltrixate?"

"Not without spacing the rest of you, unfortunately," she replies, volume level extra loud.

"The coating!" I yell. "Can you cover it with pink goo?"

"*That* I can do," she says.

"You think that will work?" Reyes yells.

"These shnopples would need to have fucking superpowers to smell through a vacuum," I reply, untying his rope straps. Reyes grips the case firmly in two hands, constantly besieged by overexcited shnopples trying to knock him over. I hold out a chair for Reyes, but he only gives me a quizzical stare.

"The ceiling," I say. "She can coat it up there just as well as on the ground. And they can't get in the way up there." He nods, and soon enough, the case of methaltrixate is well-adhered to the ceiling behind a layer of pink goo.

"Looks funny up there," Reyes says, glancing up mistrustfully.

"Yeah, but what does it *sound* like?"

Reyes closes his eyes and takes a deep breath. He opens his eyes with surprise. "Silence. It sounds like silence."

The shnopples have lost interest in Reyes already. They've completely dispersed in this space and are off investigating the room. Apart from a random yip here and there, the only sounds we hear are the shuffling and clinking of scattered game pieces as they get trampled underfoot.

I head over to Fred, who's lying down again. "We'll get you home soon, Bud," I say.

He moans in response.

Man, this hurts. Twisting my body to shield his view of my bag, I pull out a tranq and administer it. "I really hope this helps, Fred."

"So you *do* care," Reyes murmurs. He wanders over to Fred. "I wasn't sure."

"Reyes, I told you all along," I stand up, angry and adrenaline flushed. "I was desperate. You don't know what it's like –"

He catches my flailing hand. "It's Michael. To my friends."

I'm suddenly aware of how close he is. He's sweaty, and his uniform is crinkled from the makeshift straps I made him for the methaltrixate case. But holy shit, those muscles are only inches away from me. I glance up to find him giving an amused look at my hair. He reaches a free hand to try to smooth it out.

"That's a lost cause," I retort, reaching up to put my hands on his shoulders. "*Mikey.*"

He grins, and his deep dimples stand out on either side. He leans in so that our lips are almost touching, only millimeters apart. I can feel the heat radiating from his breath, and I exhale and tilt my mouth up. Yes, I want this.

"Receiving comms from the *Waterloo*, Sergeant Reyes," the *Euryale* announces.

"Rude," I say as I pull away, breathing heavily.

"Mmm," Mikey says. His gaze stays locked on me few more seconds before he abruptly turns and heads to the makeshift console of the overturned billiards table.

Rosemary's face appears on screen. "Michael! I'm so relieved. You're not hurt, are you?" she asks, eyes wide with concern. Her worry turns into a scowl when she sees me approach. "What's she doing there?"

Reyes – Michael – shakes his head. "It was all a rescue mission, Rosie. She had us all fooled. Or maybe you knew from the get-go. She really *is* an animal rights activist, through and through."

Rosemary snorts. "Okay, you've gone through a brainwashing. That just makes her sound more dangerous. Michael, give me one good reason why I shouldn't shoot her on sight?"

"We'll need her to take care of the shnopples, for one," Michael replies. He scrunches up his nose, and his dimples come back out. "Also, I like her."

"Oh, stars save us all," Rosemary replies. She puts a hand on her forehead, shakes her head, then folds her arms. "Back up a parsec. What's this about shnopples?"

"Let's get Colonel Sedeghat on the line," Michael says. "We're still not out of firing range here, and we could use some backup. Are you able to host a multi-source comm?" he asks Rosemary. She nods, and within moments, the viewing wall splits and Rosemary is sharing space with a person I've never seen before. He's middle aged with a head of bright silver hair, cropped neatly in a military cut. His eyes are a glittering icy blue.

"That's Colonel Sedeghat? You never told me he was such a silver fox," I say, nudging Michael. He only shoots me a grumpy look from the console.

"Mike! You okay?" Sedeghat says as soon as his audio catches up to us.

"Unharmed, Colonel. Unharmed. But not out of firing range. What are you guys authorized to do here?"

Sedeghat shakes his head. "We've got a warrant for their arrest on some minor legal charge. This stuff about the umemeh – those charges have been laid out against the zookeeper there, from a legal perspective." He tips his head at me. "Sorry about that, ma'am. Michael, we don't have enough evidence to use force against the *Doomberg*."

Michael chews his lip. "What if we had proof they were dealing methaltrixate? Would that change things?"

Sedeghat's eyes go wide. "That is an enthusiastic yes, Michael. You should know that."

Michael's gaze trails up to the bulge on the ceiling. "In that case, authorization granted." He quickly explains to Sedeghat and Rosemary the state of things. "Colonel Sedeghat, the *Waterloo's* gonna come close to cover the *Euryale* pod, but the *Waterloo* is purely a civilian vessel. It doesn't have any military weapons aboard. Can you meet us at the rendezvous point just in case there's any roughhousing?"

Sedeghat nods firmly. "Yes, sir. Our ETA to your location is about twenty minutes, and then we'll do more than make sure everyone plays nice. We'll get those pirates into custody."

"All right. Anyone have a problem with this plan?"

Rosemary speaks up. "What are we going to do with all those shnopples? And that zookeeper that you *'like'*?"

I clear my throat. "You'll be taking us to Surf & Ceebu."

Rosemary raises an eyebrow. "Oh, will we now."

"—so that Fred can catch the heavily guarded, direct transport to Brin-177, and she can go to jail," Mike adds.

Rosemary shuts her mouth. Then she gives a clipped nod. "I – have no problems with that."

I know this was all my plan to begin with, but I can't help that her response still stings.

chapter twenty-nine

It is only moments after we've ended our comms that our escape pod begins to rock with oncoming fire.

"Those stupid, tit-sucking morons," I exclaim. "Are they trying to explode us? They need the umemeh alive or Truyoza will rip them a new one! It's suicide!"

"You've got it all wrong," Michael replies, tapping away at the controls. He's fumbling through the panels. "They're not trying to shred us. They're deliberately targeting our fuel generator and engine." He looks up. "Not such idiots after all."

"Shit. Fuck. Crap," is my intelligent reply. The ship shudders as we take another hit to the engine. The umemeh lows in fear from his old corner in the room.

"*Euryale?*" Michael asks. "Evasive maneuvers, please."

"Of course, sir."

The ship rocks again, and the lights begin flickering. That can't be good.

"If they hit our fuel tank or engines, does that mean all our power goes out? Like," I swallow, "the power for *everything*?" It'll only be a few minutes after power-down and dead air-scrubbers that we'll suffocate from carbon dioxide poisoning. Maybe twenty minutes max, but with my luck, we'll run out right before

Michael's military friend Sedeghat arrives. "What will we do? Do we beg them to let us back in?"

Michael nods. "If it comes to that, yes. But there are too many unknown variables to predict if that'll be necessary. Isn't that right, *Euryale*?"

"Correct, sir."

Michael leans back into the control chair. "Relax! Savvy, it's like you said. They won't want to kill the shnopples. And the *Waterloo* will be here in, oh, three minutes, and we'll be able to give 'em a bit of a fight. At this moment, there's nothing else we can do." Michael reaches down to pet one of the shnopples. The bobbing furball ignores Michael and trots away to his next area of interest.

I stare at him with mouth agape.

"And did you notice the pink goo!" Michael is admiring the ceiling. "Crenshaw really has done a decent job with this ship. He's thought of everything, hasn't he?"

"Yeah. Sure. Except for a ginger-snap who destroyed his ship and tranqed him up," I mutter. Michael's eyes find mine. "He grew on me, okay? I feel crappy about that." I add. I sigh. "I've been a big ball of craptastic lately."

Michael nods. "As long as you know it."

I roll my eyes. "Thanks."

But Michael has already moved on, examining the edge of the console. "Is this a billiards table?"

"Yeah" I nod. "That whole console you're at? Is a billiards table flipped over onto its side. The instrument panel was hidden in the underside."

"You're kidding!" Mike cracks a grin and shakes his head in disbelief. "Crenshaw has always loved billiards. He's an expert player, of course, but he mostly loved using the game as a way to suss out people's personalities."

Now I try to remember my own game with Bremerton. What the voids did I say, back when I was all liquored up? Michael is stationary, lost in his own memories as he absently traces a finger over the edge of the console.

"Miss Savage, Captain Reyes," *Euryale* interrupts, "I do not wish to alarm you, but the pirates have begun targeting the heart of my AI network. If they succeed, I won't be able to perform a black space coupling."

"Shit. Shit shit shit." I exhale. "Hey, *Euryale*? Any idea how close the *Waterloo* is now?"

"Two minutes, five seconds."

"And our chances of making it there with you awake?"

"Forty-seven point six percent."

"Shit."

Pew! Pew!

The sound fills our escape pod.

Pew! Pew!

"Stop freaking out, both of you!" Michael says, his face drawn serious. "Lucy will handle the black space coupling if *Euryale* can't. And *Euryale*, you'll be *fine!*"

Ka-thunk goes our ship, with a lasting reverberation that does not feel fine. I get thrown violently into the control panels. Something warm squirms beneath me.

"Saffron? Are you okay?"

"Yes," I reply, scrambling up. "I just, uh, fell. I totally can handle enemy fire like a pro. Yep."

"Hang on, Savvy. We'll get through this," Michael says, returning his attention back to his screens. "Hey *Euryale*. Ever performed the *fleur de lis* evasive maneuver?"

"Happy to try something new," she replies.

Pew! Pew! Pew!

"Savvy, brace yourself this time!"

I join Fred, who's snorting and whining in the corner. I'm not the only one being tossed about by the rocking and shifts in gravity. I put a hand on each head to steady him amidst the cacophony of pews and booms. I'm murmuring to him under my breath to calm him down.

My stomach flips as gravity is suddenly coming from the ceiling. But it's only a fraction of a moment where we're lifted an inch or two off the ground. Then it flips again, and gravity is dragging us floorwards once more. My knees bang into the floor and my stomach still wants to fly to the ceiling. "Oh, goats." My stomach is violently trying to eject through my throat. Fred lows unhappily, thrown to the floor with me. "Shhh," I tell him. "You're okay." Meanwhile, the shnopples bop together when they bounce on the floor, but there's not even a yip from them.

Gravity flips again. And again.

"Will you —" I begin, interrupted by another long whine from Fred. "Cut that out?!"

"Necessary," Michael yells over the *pew, pew, pew* that is now an ever-constant background noise. "The missiles seek the ionized matter spewing out of our tail. Every time we flip, it takes the missiles longer to round the curve. We're buying time. Almost there!"

Suddenly, the *pew-pews* are gone, and the general noise level has decreased by a few notches. I look up at Michael, who hoots triumphantly. "Yeah, *Waterloo*! Show 'em who's boss!"

"Michael?" I ask from my corner. "What's happening?"

He's busy watching some display on his screens system. "The *Waterloo* is attacking the *Doomberg*, so the *Waterloo* is taking most of the heat. Don't worry, the *Waterloo's* got a healthy defense shield." He hisses, then yells triumphantly again. He smiles at the screen. "We're basically hiding behind the *Waterloo*."

"Initiating rotation for black space coupling with the *Waterloo*," *Euryale* says in her smooth voice. "This Lucy of yours. She is a marvel."

"The galaxy's best hybe." Michael nods in affirmation.

So this is it, I think as our escape pod rotates in a way that makes me dizzy. We're safe, no one died, and it's back to business as usual. For everyone else.

"You guys do okay with that *fleur de lis*?" Michael calls back to us, pulling his focus away from the screen to glance my way.

What he sees is enough to make his eyes go wide. "Saffron! What happened to your head?" He hurries over and kneels by the umemeh and me. He takes my head in his hands and a strange feeling overcomes me. I'm not used to being taken care of by someone.

I inhale sharply when Michael gently brushes my hair back with his fingers. The skin feels raw, on fire, and I pull away.

"I must have hit my head when I fell on the control console, or something."

"I can see that," Michael says, running a hand through his hair. "First the shoulder wound, and now this." He lets out a *tsk*, and I can see his jaw muscles twitching.

I offer him a small shrug. "It can't be worse than what those pirates wanted to do to me, right?"

"I don't..." Michael stares off to a middle distance. "That's not a good goalpost," he says, his eyes finally finding mine. "There are other kinds of people out there, Saffron. I hope you know that."

I snort. "Yeah, I fucking know it. You're the one with the stick up your ass."

"Good." Michael cracks a smile and looks down at me. "Looks like that head injury didn't scramble anything up here." He taps me on my frizzball of a mess hair, and I'm caught looking up into his eyes. And that fine, fine mouth of his.

"Sarge! Are you there?" yells Rosemary from the console. "Michael! Come in, immediately! We need docking permissions!"

Michael peels back from his kneel and walks over to the console, leaving me confused and disappointed.

Click! goes the docking clamps moments later as we begin coupling with the *Waterloo*. I force a hard swallow down my throat. The people on the *Waterloo* might be rescuing us, but they sure as shit won't be happy to see me. The pink goo begins receding from the door.

I rise unsteadily to my feet and join Michael by the door. The two of us stand expectantly, side by side, in front of the connecting door, and the now-familiar series of clicks begin.

Michael slicks back his hair and casts a sideways glance at me.

"I. Um." I swallow hard. "Reyes?"

He nudges me with his shoulder. "I thought I told you. It's Michael. Or even Mikey, please," he says gently.

I swallow thickly. "Michael –"

In the periphery, I can see the pink goo receding from the walls past the edges of my vision. There isn't time for much; we'll be back aboard the *Waterloo* any minute. Bremerton told me that Michael was the forgiving type. For those who apologize, anyway.

So, here goes nothing. I take a deep breath.

"I…" This is harder than I realized. Come to think of it, I don't remember the last time I ever spoke these words. "I'm…"

"Disoriented and confused?" Michael quips.

I swat at his arm. "I'm sorry, okay? You big monkey's ass." I fold my arms.

Michael blinks a few times, then turns towards the door. "I know," he replies. He smiles. "Good thing, too, since you're terrible at apologizing."

"I am not—" I splutter.

Michael grins. "Did you know calling someone a monkey's ass is not an affectionate endearment? Just saying."

"You're the worst," I grumble, hugging my arms tighter to my chest. "The absolute worst."

Michael barks out a laugh. "Yep. That sounds about right!"

A low rumble is followed by a screeching sound permeating the air. The rumbling gets louder, and I can feel it as a vibration beneath my feet, and a grinding in my teeth. The screeching sound waxes on and off.

"Shit," Michael says. "The *Doomberg's* interrupting the coupling." He runs his hand through his hair again. "*Euryale*? Status?"

"The *Doomberg* has altered position and is attacking the *Euryale* pod directly."

"How many minutes till coupling is complete?"

"One minute thirteen seconds."

"Wait. What?" I interrupt. "Why are they attacking *Euryale* pod if the *Waterloo* is a much bigger fish?!" I ask. I am sick of these conversations where I have no idea what's going on.

Michael sighs. "The *Euryale* does not have a shield, but the *Waterloo* does. This is their best shot at getting to us. Once we're fully coupled with the *Waterloo*, the *Euryale* will be integrated under the *Waterloo's* shield."

Pew! Pew! Pew pew pew!

"So they'll kill their own shnopples?"

Michael gives me a funny sidewise glance. "Not just the shnopples. They wouldn't risk hurting the umemeh and earning Truyoza's wrath. I think they're looking to have the *Waterloo* project its protective shield over the *Euryale* pod. Technically, the *Waterloo* can do that even when we're not coupled. It's a special maneuver called throwing a shield."

"But then –" I begin.

"It's a tactical disadvantage. Throwing a shield leaves the thrower completely shieldless."

"So the *Waterloo*…?"

"Yep." He nods. "The *Waterloo* would remain completely exposed." He sighs. "If we can manage to couple in oh, twenty seconds, we'll have the umbrella shield extension, and everyone's covered. That's the best-case scenario. Then the *Waterloo* can hold off their attack with the shield for about ten minutes till Sedeghat arrives with the *Lamorak*. Then, it's game over for them."

I nod and squint my eyes. "Ten minutes is a lot."

He nods. "It is. But we'll be okay. This isn't the first time the *Waterloo's* been in hot water. Plus, the very moment that door opens, I'll race to join them on the bridge. Have a little faith in our team!"

He's not inviting me up to help, I notice. He doesn't expect anything from me. Figures. What else would he expect from a failed animal trafficker? I probably wouldn't even know what to do up there, anyway. It also doesn't help me figure what to do or where to go on a ship where everyone hates me.

The sound of a blast rumbles through our joint ships, and I stumble with the small shift in gravity.

"Shit," Michael curses under his breath. "Come on, come on, come on," he mutters. Until finally, the door slides open. We're safe.

chapter thirty

Michael sprints down the hall towards the stairs that will take him to the bridge. At the same time, a shrieking Prisha Shanti rushes into the escape pod of the *Euryale*. She runs about, dodging between shnopples, sniffing and shrieking. The shnopples don't mind, mostly.

I, on the other hand, am standing in the universe's smallest, noisiest, smartest animal pen. Pete jogs up and stops in the open doorway, alone in the stretch of hallway. He rubs his cap back and forth on his head three times, then puts his hands on his hips.

"No holes to patch, then?" He squints as he surveys the mess of the room behind me, our escape pod and former billiards room. It's a real pigsty. "Those little guys gonna be all right with Prisha Shanti and all?"

I let a sad smile tug at my lips and nod. "Prisha Shanti may even start playing with them, if she ever stops shrieking." My gaze follows her as she runs about, her tail curving and whipping around little fluffy shnopple balls who barely notice her. "A barrier here might be good to keep 'em penned in."

Pete nods. "I have something that'll work." He turns to go.

"Pete?" I ask haltingly. He pauses. "Do you hate me?"

It takes him a minute to answer, then he finally shrugs. "Well, I can't say I understand you. But in the end, I see you're doing good. So." He shrugs again. "I don't gotta know everything. You're okay, in my book." I blink back my surprise. "I better grab that gate before these little fuckers get out."

Once Pete trots down the hallway, I'm left devoid of human company.

I peek my head out, then take a cautious step into the clean hallway. Doesn't look like anyone plans to stop me. Or arrest me. Or kill me. Yet. In fact, the only thing that accosts me is the scent in the hallway. It smells clean in here. I don't think I remembered what that smelled like. Another rumbling sound rolls through the ship, and after a shudder, I'm thrown against the wall. The shnopples yip in surprise, and Prisha Shanti has jumped onto the console. Fred, of course, is out cold and has no clue what's going on.

I don't want to be here *alone*.

What the voids am I supposed to do for the next ten minutes? I sure as shit ain't sitting alone on the *Euryale* escape pod, twiddling my thumbs, and wondering if we're all about to die. I wonder what Michael is up to before I remember that I was very obviously not invited up to the bridge. So that's out. A burning from my shoulder reminds me that I still have injuries to tend to. Minor scrapes, but I may as well take care of them.

"Keep an eye on Fred for me, will you, *Euryale*?"

"Will do, Miss Savage."

I stride decisively in the direction of the Doc Williams' infirmary. Big surprise: When I get there, Doc won't let me in.

She stands on the other side of the glass doorway with her arms crossed. "I cannot let you upset my patient," she says. She arches an eyebrow, then adds, "Let alone tranquilize him again."

It takes me a minute to realize she's talking about Bremerton, and I wince. Yeah, I did that to an octogenarian. I'm a piece of shit.

The hallway rumbles and shudders. We might all die here. This whole journey hasn't been filled with my finest choices, but injuring Bremerton and Otis are my top regrets. What a fitting way for my life to end, on a shitty note.

Doesn't matter, I guess. It's not like I can undo what I did to Bremerton. Although… He did get all excited about apologies. It's not the worst idea. But first, I need to get through the door guard here, ever the consummate professional. And *that* gives me another idea.

I glare at Doc and point to my shoulder and my head. "I need first aid, and the people around here seem to believe you're a doctor."

Doc's lips purse together, but she otherwise doesn't move.

"Oh, don't be quite so frigid, Priscilla," comes a weak voice behind her. It warms my heart and worries me at the same time, all until he says this next bit. "Let the traitor in. We wouldn't want her injuries to stop her from getting herself into more hot water."

At this, Doc Williams sighs, but appears to cave. She unfolds her arms and the glass doors open to admit me.

I walk in to find Bremerton on a cot, wrapped in white bedsheets. Without his red silk robe (not to mention his pipe) he looks as fragile as a sheet of tissue paper. It doesn't help that his head is all bandaged up and his pale skin has ugly purple blotches all over it. I stop by his bedside.

"Well?" he asks, all business and no patience. He sets down an empty cup of tea on the folding tray of his bed. "Aren't you here for first aid?"

I glance at Doc, who's retreated to a corner and is watching us with arms folded and hawkish eyes. I stare down at my feet instead. "Bremerton," I clear my throat. "Lieutenant. I'm --" I'm supposed to apologize here, but it gets stuck in my throat. Last time I tried I ended up calling Michael a monkey's ass. "I'm not very good at this. Just. Hold on a second," I say and rummage around through my bag. There's only one token gesture that could possibly make him understand how shitty I feel.

"Clearly, Savage, if you're here to get first aid you're doing a terrible job of it."

I exhale an exasperated breath. "That's not what I was going to say." Bremerton's face is stony and unchanging. "I thought I had no choice."

"I told you, Savage, you always have a choice."

I shake my head. "It's not so easy! I – I was wrong. Okay? Happy? I was wrong."

Bremerton nods. "I'm glad you know it."

I wipe my now-leaky nose with the back of my sleeve, then rummage around in my bag.

"I can never replace the damage done to the *Euryale*," I hold up a squashy snow globe. "I was hoping, at the least, you would accept this."

Bremerton examines the dirty old globe like a disgusting curiosity. I gaze firmly at the floor, embarrassed. Shit. This was a stupid idea. Why the breaches would I ever –

"What in the devil is it, Savage?" he asks softly.

"Arnold," I reply, nodding at the elephelk at the center of the globe. "His name is Arnold, and I've held on to him since I was six years old. He was one of the reasons I became a xeno-zoologist in the first place. He's dumb, I know, but he was something important to me for a long time," I wipe my stupid leaky nose again. "I was hoping you'd keep him. You know, as a token. And even if he's not, um, your cup of tea, at least he's squishy."

The silence lasts so long that I finally draw my eyes up from the floor. Bremerton is half smiling, holding Arnold up to the light. He keeps squishing the soft plastic of the clear globe to see the snow go wild, then releasing the globe to its more rounded form. He's entranced.

"You like him?" I ask.

"He's marvelous, Savage. Marvelous."

I hadn't remembered what it was like for my heart to feel this happy. It's warmth and strength flowing through me all at once. Until another explosion rocks through our ship, and I fall heavily on the counter.

I spy a nearby stool and take a seat. Less likely to get injured that way. I turn towards the disapproving Doc, seated a few feet away. There's something I should tell her, too.

"Anti-virals," I say to her. "You need them for your bats." Her eyes flutter in surprise. "I haven't run any tests, obviously. But I'd bet my ass they have a disease called white-nose-syndrome. It's why they're acting all funny. And if you leave it untreated, it'll kill them."

Doc stutters. "I –" She cuts herself off and nods. "I'll get it to them."

In the quiet that follows, I let my gaze land on Bremerton. The hand holding Arnold is leaning against the bed railing, and I lean forward to discover that his eyes have fallen shut.

I lean back, satisfied that he's sleeping in comfort. My tilt my head to Doc. "Will he… Will he be okay?"

Doc nods. "He will. In time." She stands up and busies herself at the counter. A minute later, she hands me a small, circular, metal container and some alcohol wipes. "Salve," she says, nodding at my shoulder. "For the burn wound. And wipes for the abrasion," she nods at my head.

It's my turn to stutter in surprise. "Right. I mean. What I mean to say is – thank you."

Doc nods, and we relapse into silence.

After a few moments, I notice that the rumbles and rocking haven't happened for a few minutes now. I glance at Doc. "You think it's over?"

She takes a quick appraisal of the holoclock. "I think the *Lamorak* has arrived."

"So we made it?"

Doc gives a prim nod. I jump out of my seat, excited. Then sit back down.

"We made it!" I jump up again. I run to the doorway. "I have an umemeh to hug!" I sprint down the hallway towards the sounds of soft yipping.

I leap over the low barrier Pete has erected in my absence and launch into the room. Prisha Shanti shrieks for a surprised minute, but calms when she recognizes me. She continues to play chase with shnopples, who continue to ignore her very existence. Fred sways in the corner, and I rush over to him. His pupils are still dilated, his breathing slow. He's awake, but while he's still working off the effects of the last tranq, he'll be a little dazed and loopy. I hug his uninjured neck. "I'm glad you're not in too much pain, buddy," I tell him. A familiar tug at my scalp tells me he's happy to see me too.

A knock on the door frame makes me jump. I turn to find Rosemary, arms folded, beside Gisella, who is looking down at the floor, fiddling with her hands.

It's Rosemary who talks first. "They need you. On the *Lamorak*. Legal has some questions for you." It's hard to make out her eyes under the shadow of her cowboy hat, but I'm sure she's still pissed at me. I stand up and rub my hands clean on my coveralls. I square myself so that I'm facing them.

Gisella glares at me, her eyes beady. "You could have told us —"

Rosemary twitches her mouth, then shakes her head. It's enough to silence Gisella.

"I thought I had no choice because of Truyoza," I explain. "I was an idiot. I was wrong." Gisella is willing to look at me, at least. But Rosemary hasn't budged an inch. I sigh. "I'm trying to do right, now."

Rosemary purses her lips. "Wrong or right, Legal needs to see you. And they need all these shnopples, too. This way."

I take a deep breath. She's definitely still pissed. I had one chance at having friends and I fucked it up.

Well, I'll probably never see either of them again, anyway. My vision clouds over and I have to blink rapidly to clear it. I take a step forward to follow and a tugging at my scalp tells me Fred's coming too.

My only friend, Freddypoo.

Then, Michael's words from earlier, when he thought I was

selling out to Truyoza, come back to haunt me. Fred's only mine for the next few hours.

Fred may have a new destination, but nothing has changed for me.

I am very, very alone in this universe.

I rub my sleeve against my nose, hug my arms to my chest, and hold my back straight for the short walk down the corridor. A gaggle of animals follows behind me, shepherded along by Rosemary and Gisella.

———

I DON'T NEED DIRECTIONS TO KNOW WHICH BAY DOORS THE *LAMORAK* has used for a black space coupling. I just have to follow the sound of a rabble. When I round the corner into their linked vestibule, it's like I've entered a frat party.

"Mikey!" the guys are yelling, jumping on him like hyper teenagers.

Michael Reyes is grinning ear to ear. "Sedeghat! Yi! Matthias!" He greets them each by name. This parade could go on all fucking day. There are more than half a dozen dudes in this room, and it's way too many. My umemeh needs some space.

I try to push past the crowd in the doorway but am bounced back by some definitely hostile muscled up uniforms.

"Colonel Sedeghat," Michael says in a loud voice. The others quiet around him. "This is the zookeeper I was telling you about, Saffron Savage. She's all right. At least, she is now."

"Yeah. Nice to meet you," I say hurriedly. "Can I get the voids out of this mosh pit?" Sedeghat and Michael crack smiles, and the distant chorus of yipping soon grows louder.

"Rosemary!" Sedeghat hollers, grinning at someone behind me.

I turn to find Rosemary standing at the end of the vestibule, having successfully shepherded the shnopples here. She dips her cowboy hat at him. "They're all here, sir. Twenty-two of them. And Pete'll be here shortly with that case of methaltrixate."

"Thanks, Rosie," Michael says loudly over the din. He puts an arm around Sedeghat. "I need to file my version of the report with the *Lamorak*, so I'll be a few minutes. Okay?"

Rosemary nods. "I'll see you back on the bridge," she replies, and turns away.

I want to yell after her, *wait!* or anything that might pass as an apology, but I'm the one who fucked this all up to begin with. I glance over at Michael, but he's deep in some bro-bro conversation with Sedeghat.

"Mikey! We got you out of another scrape this time!" Sedeghat says, with a boyish grin that belies his silver-white hair. "I'd say that makes us about even. Wouldn't you?"

"Not remotely close," Michael replies with a delighted smile as the pair heads to the blocked doorway. Droves of soldiers move out of their way, then follow, faces glazed over in admiration. I'm left unattended, except for my hair-munching umemeh and an excited sea of shnopples.

"Hey!" I call after Michael. "Don't you guys need to ask me some questions, or something?" I jostle elbows to move into the clearing they've made in the crowd.

Michael looks back at me, and a wave of guilt crosses his face.

"Right," Colonel Sedeghat nods. "Legal needs you, but you can take care of the umemeh first." His eyes rove over the crowd until they land on a red-headed cadet. "Gunther! Take her down to the guest quarters we prepared. Now, you and I – " he chucks Michael on the shoulder "—have some catching up to do before you head back on your route! Unless you've changed your mind and have decided to go pro again?"

Michael snorts. "I've done my time. I make special exceptions on occasion, but I think you're all set here. You don't need me."

"Wait!" I say, only five feet away from the two men. Understanding hit me like a ton of bricks. "I just..." Sedeghat will manage getting Fred to Brin-177. Michael is returning to the

Waterloo. After Legal gets their hands on me, I won't cross paths with either of them again.

"Colonel Sedeghat's people will take good care of you," Michael says kindly. But there's excitement sparkling in his eyes, and he turns back to Sedeghat. "So tell me, what did those bastards throw at you?" And in moments, the pair of them are off down the hallway, immersed in their own private conversation.

I don't know how long I stand there, staring after them.

The young cadet identified as Gunther grabs me by the elbow. "Miss?" he asks tentatively. "I'm supposed to take you and, um, the umemeh, to your room. Legal will call for you in a few hours, once the umemeh is comfortable."

I blink back tears, still watching the hallway where Michael has disappeared. I hug my arms. "Do you at least have water there? For the umemeh?"

"Yes, ma'am," nods Gunther eagerly. "And leafy greens. Doc Hoffstadder wants to talk to you about painkillers, too. We've got plenty in stock but he wants to know the proper dosing for an umemeh."

I pause in my tracks and get a good look at him. "You guys truly care about the umemeh's wellbeing, don't you?"

He furrows his eyebrows in confusion before shrugging it off. "It's an honor. It's the first time in my life I'm seeing a live one. This way please, ma'am." He turns down the hall in the opposite direction from where Michael disappeared minutes before.

I cast one last look at the scattering of dudes in the hallway. I heave a sigh and follow Gunther away. Like the *Waterloo*, the hallways on the *Lamorak* are wide, bright and clean. Unlike the *Waterloo*, the ceilings here are all one large glass window, with an open view of the ship's interior. If you could even call it that.

I stop, transfixed by what I'm seeing. This is insane. Apparently, the *Lamorak* is a huge tube, and along the inner walls of the tube is an entire city. Maybe even more than that. *We* are walking along the interior wall, and I suddenly feel smaller than an ant.

"How many residents on the *Lamorak*?" I ask, heating Gunther shifting next to me.

"Five thousand seven hundred nine, last I heard."

"Whoa."

A small grain of rice floats down the center of the tube, and as it gets closer, the outline resolves into the familiar shape of a minature, conical ship. Dwarfed in comparison to the *Lamorak* itself. That can't be the *Waterloo*, right?

Panic swells in me. I never got to say goodbye. What was it that Michael had said to me? What can I expect? I'm a criminal. It's what I deserve.

chapter thirty-one

A knock comes at my door hours later. "Miss?" Judging by the voice, it's Gunther, and he's probably here to haul my ass over to Legal. Or jail. Or both? I don't answer. "Miss? I was told to call you for dinner. If you're hungry," he continues.

I pull the blankets snugly up to my chin. The umemeh's been dosed again; he was lowing in pain earlier when his tranq had worn off but this time around, I was able to dose with proper pain meds thanks to Doctor Hoffstadder. Now Fred is sleeping, standing like he used to, because he's tired and comfortable and *not* because he's high as balls.

The rest of the room is surprisingly luxurious for military accommodations. Other than the enormous comfy bed in the center of the room, a bunch of other furniture has been stacked neatly in a corner: a desk, a pair of armchairs, and even a couch. More impressive than the causally disused furniture, though, is the scale of the space. I could hypothetically do calisthenics in here. Or perform a dance routine. Or practice aerial yoga. It must be quarters for someone important, and it's going to take a lot to convince me to ever leave. I could eat Fred's lettuce and survive in here forever.

"Miss?" repeats the voice from the hallway. "I was instructed to tell you that Colonel Sedeghat and Sergeant Reyes were hoping you would sit with them."

My heart skips three beats. That's all I needed to get moving. I leap off the bed and slide the door open.

"Oh, so you *are* awake," says Gunther, a friendly smile blossoming there.

"I was, um, doing my hair," I say.

Gunther gives a skeptical glance at the poufy mess with odd pieces sticking out every which way from its braid, and his eyes are drawn to the injured spot. "I can wait, ma'm, if you're not finished yet."

"Screw that. It's beautiful the way it is!"

"If you say so, ma'am. If you could follow me, please."

As I follow behind Gunther, I wonder if this will be the last time I see Michael. Sure that Gunther can't see me with his back turned to me, I reach a hand to investigate my hair. I find that the frizziness has reached new levels of pouf-dom. "Crap," I mutter. I attempt to force it into submission with some pats and tucks. Maybe I should have taken the time to actually do my hair.

———

THE MESS IS A RIOTOUS ROOM FULL OF OFFICERS, BUT GUNTHER LEADS me towards Colonel Sedeghat's table. I search the faces at the table until I land on a relaxed and joking Michael. I notice, too late, that there's an empty seat next to Sedeghat. Not next to Michael.

I try to veer off towards the food line, but Gunther steers me firmly forward. "This way, miss," he says with that agitating bucketful of optimism.

Sedeghat sees us approaching. "Miss Savage!" He raises his glass to me. "I'm glad you accepted my invitation. Please, sit with us!"

His invitation? I shoot a glance at Michael, but he's deep into a joke with someone a few guys on the other side of him. It seems odd to me that Sedeghat has a sudden interest in my existence. I have a bad, bad feeling about this.

Everyone around the room is cheerful, and I guess I can understand why. They won their big shootout with the asshole pirates of the *Doomberg*. They've earned their celebration, but it's hard to join in their cheer when I know that they'd just as easily space me if they discovered I was the reason Golgi was a threat to the *Waterloo* in the first place.

Sedeghat offers me a glass of moonshine. "House blend," he says. "Toasting the arrest and conviction of Golgi and his men."

Well, I've never been one to turn down alcohol.

"This is far superior to the Mint-Trip Reyes has! Tell me, Savage, what you think?"

"No way!" Michael interjects. "Not a chance. Mint-Trip is a thousand times better. Right, Savage?"

He's back to calling me Savage again, I notice. I knock back the glass, and sit down bleakly.

The two men exchange glances. "So?" Sedeghat asks.

"Fan-fucking-tastic," I reply. Colonel Sedeghat gives Michael a pointed nod.

"Right. Savage, uh, we, uh, were hoping –" Michael stops. "Hey, whatsa matter with you, anyway?"

I roll my eyes. Nothing like losing the friendship of everyone you've come to care for and the threat of imprisonment to cheer you up, I guess. Not that he would understand. "Nothing."

Michael clears his throat in obvious discomfort. He continues uneasily. "We know you were in contact with the mob boss Greel Truyoza. He's a criminal the galactic military has been trying to catch for some time, but they've never been able to pin him down with anything solid. We were wondering if you have any information that would incriminate him?"

"...In exchange for immunity," Colonel Sedeghat adds.

"What?" Hope beats rapidly in my chest. I look first at Sedeghat, then Michael, then at Sedeghat again. Neither of them looks like they're joking. All charges for kidnapping an umemeh, wiped away clean? Maybe even the other stuff too, like being a stowaway, joining up with pirates, and conducting business with a mob boss. I analyze Sedeghat's face intensely. "You could do that?"

"Well, not me specifically. But Judge Gad could issue that, sure."

"And how long will it take us to get to this Judge Gad?"

"Judge Gad is a resident." Colonel Sedeghat gestures passively at the cafeteria around him. "The *Lamorak* is huge. We need a legal system of our own. Plus, if we didn't have a judge, we'd need to travel to the nearest planet for a conviction. It's much more convenient this way." He shrugs. "You must not travel often. It's pretty standard for ships of our carrier class to be outfitted with a judge and several trial lawyers. Priests too, if you're interested in that kind of thing."

I frown. "And that will hold? The judge's legal ruling. Like. *Everywhere* in the galaxy?"

"Of course," Sedeghat replies with a shrug. "Otherwise her presence would be pointless."

"We're getting ahead of ourselves," Michael cuts in. "Savvy, we don't even know if you have useful information that can help the military get to Truyoza." My eyes find Michael's at the use of the name Savvy, but he's staring so intently at me that I break eye contact, finding it painful to hold his gaze. I twist the quanta-com at my wrist.

"Do you have any written evidence that he was purchasing?" Colonel Sedeghat prompts.

"Maybe?" I think back. "It was on my last quanta-com, but the logs didn't carry over. He did communicate with me on this quanta-com, though."

"Hm," says Sedeghat with a frown.

That can't be good. That wasn't enough to impress, then. I need to come up with something that might buy me that immunity.

"Actually! I do have his station tracking coordinates." At that,

Colonel Sedeghat's gaze rivets to mine sharply. Truyoza's mob headquarters, an enormous asteroid city, has been slipping around through the galaxy for centuries. His organization keeps it cloaked with the latest detection evasion technology, and despite occasional sightings, their whereabouts remain unknown. Their hostile 'welcome' to casual nearby travelers means that their traffic remains by special invitation only. I spell out the rest. "Not only do I have his location tracker, I *also* have the quanta-com that he's expecting. And the umemeh."

Sedeghat and Michael both stare at me intently.

"Are you suggesting a sting operation?" Sedeghat asks quietly.

"With all due respect, I don't think this is prudent, Colonel," Michael interjects.

"Reyes, we've been trying to get our hands on Greel Truyoza for twenty years. *Twenty years!*" Sedeghat repeats.

"But you'd be putting the umemeh into harm's way," Michael protests. "And while I personally like Savage, that has no bearing on whether it's wise to send her on a mission this dangerous. She's just a civilian!"

Ouch. I turn my empty shot glass in my hand, and glance down the table at where the refill bottle lays, frustratingly out of reach.

"That dynamic changes if I send a special ops team along to boot." Sedeghat continues, oblivious to my feelings. "I even have a pirate ship that Truyoza trusts! We could patch up the *Doomberg* and get her operable. This opportunity is too good to pass up." He turns to look at me again. "As long as you're absolutely sure you're up for this?"

I nod. "Clear my record, and I'm sure. Oh, and get the umemeh to Brin-177 after all this."

"Deal," Colonel Sedeghat scoffs. "Best deal of my life."

"What is your plan?" Michael asks. "Even if you send along a special ops team, how are they going to overpower a fully armed mob?"

"I've still got to work through that part," Sedeghat replies, stonily. "Truyoza is too smart to allow an entire fleet to approach him. He won't even allow civilians to fly in the zone near his asteroid without firing at them; there's no way we can casually line up ships in the area. We won't manage to sneak in, let alone surround him. It'll have to be the pirate ship, and the pirate ship alone."

Sedeghat steeples his fingers and puts them to his lips. "But maybe we're thinking about this all wrong. We're thinking about numbers, and not trump power." He looks up. "At most of our military bases, we have a special type of intelligent robot that can hack into comms of proximal systems. If we had something like that, we could overpower the computer systems that run Truyoza's station, and force him to surrender."

I shoot Michael a pointed stare, but he only shakes his head.

"The only problem is," Sedeghat adds with the twitch of his jaw, "the nearest base is a few day-cycles of flight time away." He sighs again. "I doubt we have the time to grab one of those hacker-bots without raising Truyoza's suspicions. So scratch that. Back to the drawing board."

No, no no. This mission can't fail now. It's got too good a promise attached to the end of it. "And... what *if* we did have something like that?" I ask haltingly, in between death glares from Michael.

Colonel Sedeghat tilts his head at me. "*If* that were true, I would imagine you'd illegally procured military-grade equipment. We'd have to revisit that immunity we were discussing."

A memory *dings,* a flashback to a conversation Michael told me he had gotten Otis from a criminal family friend. "I mean, maybe not the *exact same* kind of equipment," I say quickly. "Similar enough, though? Like, uh," I scour my mind for plausible alternatives, "an intelligent ship-mind that can interact and disable others? Top notch. Bremerton's."

Now Michael is shaking his head vigorously at me out of Sedeghat's range of vision. Is he saying he doesn't want to share the *Euryale* intelligent ship-mind? Or that I shouldn't have mentioned Bremerton? We really, really have to work on his non-verbal communication.

Sedeghat's eyes narrow. "Are you referring to Lieutenant Crenshaw Bremerton?"

"Uhhhhhh." Michael, in the background, rolls his eyes and tips his head back. "Yes?"

"What has that old drug-addled pisspot gotten up to now?" Sedeghat says.

"Hey! He's not drug-addled," I retort.

Sedeghat is not listening. "I could see a way to commandeer his ship-mind and retrofit it into the *Doomberg*."

I frown. "Come to think of it, I don't know if the *Euryale* would enjoy that." That ship is really, *really* not going to like me.

"Oh, the ship-mind won't have much of a choice. It sounds like it's running some illegal programs, to start with. And then I could also get a warrant for its arrest for transporting illegal cargo. If the ship's intelligent, it will be held responsible in the eyes of the law."

"Wow. You really make use of this judge thing, don't you?"

"We'll need to get engineering to rig up your quanta-com," he says all business-like, distracted. His fingers do a spiderlike dance in the air, the telltale move of someone typing on a virtual keyboard only visible in their contact lenses. "Alright, they're on their way for it." Sedeghat stands up, then pauses. "Make sure you get something to eat, okay? I have to make some plans."

At least I still have Michael. Maybe we can share a meal together like normal people, for once. But Michael shoots me a thoughtful glance, then quick as a squirrel, gets up too.

"Colonel! Wait up." He jogs to catch up with Sedeghat. "I had an idea for you…"

I watch the pair of their backs as they walk away and let out a sigh.

"Miss?" says a new official who's approached me with another gal who looks like her clone. "I'm from engineering. We need you to come with us."

"Yeah." I stand up. "Let me just grab something to eat, first." I cast a wistful glance at the hot food bar, then resigning myself to the dry goods section. "Something to go."

———

After I've showered, met with my lawyers and Judge Gad, and stocked up on tranqs and pain meds for Fred (seriously, the *Lamorak* has everything), I'm all set to return to the loading bays to board the repaired vessel, the *Doomberg*. I suspect I'm going to have a long talk ahead of me with an unhappy *Euryale*.

Before Gunther arrived to escort me, this time, I made sure my hair was tightly plaited down my back. Michael Reyes may never see me looking this good, but at least Gunther does a double-take at the door. I smile.

"Yeah. I know, doesn't look as great this time. Right?" I say, motioning with my eyes at my hair.

"I – I – "

I nod. "That's what I thought. May as well *look like* trouble to *give em* trouble, right?"

"Uh," Gunther replies.

I follow him down the wide, commercial corridors, one arm gently resting on Fred's good neck to guide him along. This place has a hum to it, the sound of a ship that never sleeps. There's the constant noise of whirring, the electrical humming, the fan cycling, soft footfalls and voices. So, the exact opposite of a zoo. But that's okay, because after I do this mission, I'll go to Brin-177 where the noises – and life forms – are more familiar. I may not have any friends, but at least there's a semi-comfortable end in sight.

When we round the corner into the docking bay of the *Doomberg*, though, I stop in my tracks.

Sedeghat is there, inspecting an at-attention troop of twenty special-ops soldiers. But next to them, in the same hangar is Michael. And Rosemary. And Lucy. Gisella. And Pete.

"What are you…" I trail off, and Sedeghat turns around. "What are they doing here?"

"Accompanying you." In a few strides, Colonel Sedeghat is by my side. "Reyes said we'd run into Bremerton's lawyers if we took the *Euryale* ship-mind without someone there as a company representative. Plus, I could think of no one better to crew this mission. Sergeant Reyes was the best special ops guy to work with, back when he was military. And his crew is exemplary."

"And we're thrilled to be here," Rosemary says in a monotone voice across from the hangar. Gisella elbows her.

"And they're thrilled to be here," Sedeghat reaffirms, without catching her sarcasm.

I clutch my messenger bag strap tight. "Are you sure this is a good idea?"

"Well, to be honest," Sedeghat says, "you're the one who's least qualified for this mission. But since Truyoza already knows what you look like, it was too complicated to switch you out last minute."

I purse my lips. "Or find another animal handler."

Sedeghat shrugs. "Anyone could do it, right?"

"No," I reply, heat flushing my cheeks. "Not if you want to keep that animal alive. No one else would know that his heads bop in rhythm when he's in a healthy sleep! Or that if his extra-curious left head is still, he's in trouble! Or that he won't touch leaves that are too crunchy!"

Michael steps in between us. "Ohhh-kay," he says, placing a firm hand on my shoulder. "We're all on the same page here. You're coming on the mission. And we're lucky to have you."

I stomp away from Sedeghat and straight onto the *Doomberg*. It's when I'm inside that I realize I have no idea where I'm going. I come to a halt in a narrow crappy section of hallway with familiar repair patches on the wall. Now that I look, the floor's been recently repaired here, too. There's new carpeting, and a good stomp tells me there are cheap steel plates under here.

"If you must know," *Euryale's* smooth voice cuts into the

silence, "I made them repair every inch of this vessel before I agreed to this mission. Not to mention, scrub off the remaining bubble juice from the walls." The ship's voice carries a tone of dissatisfaction.

I wince. "I'm sorry you got dragged into this, *Euryale*. That's my fault." This is nowhere near the level of comfort the *Euryale* is used to.

"To tell you the truth, the mission interested me."

"What?!" I can't believe that.

"Having so many unknown variables and an uncertain outcome… this must be what it feels like to be human."

Did the ship just diss all of humankind? And did she say *uncertain outcome?* I don't like the odds the computer has come up for me.

"On a positive note," the *Euryale* continues, "I was tickled to hear that those bubble bomb prototypes worked in a live-fire situation. Explosives aren't meant to be kept in constant submersion in bubble juice. Did Lieutenant Bremerton tell you? There was only a fifty percent chance of them working outside the lab."

I blink. Those bubble bombs were the single most critical factor in surviving our time with Golgi and his thugs.

"They were only prototypes?!"

chapter thirty-two

I'm sitting on the *Doomberg's* bridge along with Michael, Rosemary, and Lucy. Of course, Fred's in here too.

"I still don't understand why we couldn't have encrypted our music files before we left," Rosemary grumbles. She's standing at a corner display, arms folded. Unlike the *Waterloo*, the *Doomberg's* bridge is small and fitted out in cheap plastics. It's a cinderblock office, and a cramped one, too.

Rosemary hasn't looked at me once since takeoff, which was five hours ago. It's ridiculously awkward, since she's only a few feet away from me. Everyone in the room looks a bit tense, to be honest.

"I do have an expansive collection of music in my databases," *Euryale* offers.

"That is simply not true," Rosemary responds. "Because you don't have any pre-space age country rap."

"Come on, Rosie," Michael sighs. "Don't argue with a computer."

Rosemary swivels to face him. "*Of course* you would say that, the ship is stocked with a thousand varieties of jazz music!"

Lucy, who'd turned at Michael's mention of the computer, now raises one eyebrow. Without a word, she turns back to working away at the controls desk so that all we can see of her over the chair backing is the top of her bright pink beanie. She's the smart one who doesn't step into this shit.

"Heyyyyyy now," I try.

"No," Rosemary says, finally glancing in my direction. "Don't you even try to talk to me."

Just then, our special ops leader, Special Agent Chaudhary enters the bridge. I met her earlier, soon after boarding the *Doomberg*. She's got brown skin, a buzzcut, and a no-nonsense attitude. She carries herself like a true professional; basically, she knocked the fucking socks off me.

"Hello, everyone," Chaudhary begins, oblivious to the tension in the room. She does a double take when she discovers she's standing beside Fred's ass, which fills up the whole left section of the bridge. "You know, he doesn't have to stay in here," she says, eying him dubiously.

"Yeah, no shit," I snort. It sure as breaches would make this room more comfortable. "Door's open. But he likes sleeping in tight spaces." I shrug. "Can't help it."

Chaudhary nods. She's used to rolling with the punches, apparently, because she barrels on to the next item of business. "We should go over the mission plan one last time," she says. "To ensure that everyone's on the same page."

While Michael has been reinstated to his military title as a courtesy for this mission, there is no question of Agent Chaudhary's authority here. She is the tactical leader of the twenty-strong special-ops team that has come along with us, and together, we're all supposed to work like a well-greased machine. My gaze flicks to Lucy, who hasn't even turned to look at Chaudhury, then across to Rosemary, who's standing with arms crossed. It would help if everyone actually wanted to be here.

Agent Chaudhary apprises the occupants of the bridge. "Where's the rest of your team?" she asks, directing her question to Michael only.

"Well," Michael stretches. "We sent Gisella out to take care of, um, an annoying problem. A social one," he adds hurriedly, still not having revealed the details about Otis to the military. "And Pete… Actually, I thought he was rousing up a game of poker with your crew?"

"No sir," she replies.

I hear a light snorting. I glance over at Fred to find his nostrils dilating in his shnuffling pattern. If he's sniffing things, that means he's woken. "Oh great," I mutter.

In the tight space, Fred manages to twist around. One of Fred's heads comes over to investigate Chaudhury's hair, which is shaved at the sides and cropped gleaming chestnut-brown above, but Chaudhary neatly steps out of reach.

"I'd recommend you gather them up, Sergeant. It's only two hours till our approach of the mob headquarters. Truyoza will require contact before then. Let's have that mission briefing."

Michael's shoulders tense, but he gives only a curt nod before tapping his ring to wake up his keyboard display in his retinal vision. His fingers rapidly flutter through the air and moments later, he flicks the keyboard away. "It's done, Special Agent Chaudhary. Why don't you make yourself comfortable while we wait?"

Chaudhary nods, then slightly shifts her stocky, highly-muscled body so that her legs are no longer glued together. She doesn't sit down. She doesn't leave her patch of floor.

I snort. "Yeah. That looks very comfortable."

"I bet you'd rather see her laid out with a tranq," Rosemary says bitterly.

"Okay. What is your problem?"

"My problem?" Rosemary asks explosively. "My problem is that we're heading into an insanely dangerous operation where we might all die. All because our captain, the venerable Sergeant Reyes, thinks this was a good idea. And he only thinks that because he 'likes' you. But you know what? You're a terrible human being."

I shrug. This is more or less what I had expected from her. "That's better than being a terrible doormat, I guess."

"No," she says angrily. "It isn't."

"You have no idea what you're talking about!" Michael says to Rosemary, heated.

"Yes, I do. More than you do, anyway."

Gisella's form appears in the doorway. She comes to a stop next to Agent Chaudhary. "Right on time for the fireworks, I see," she says demurely.

Agent Chaudhary gives her a sideways glance. "You said it."

Gisella looks about. "Pete's not back yet?"

Chaudhary shakes her head. "Still waiting."

Gisella sighs. "Yeah. That may take a few minutes, knowing him. I left him making some repairs to the former captain's toilet." She glances back at Rosemary and Michael. "I better step in, then."

Gisella marches up to Michael and Rosemary. "Captain. Rosie." She keeps her voice measured. Her freckled face turned upwards towards Michael. "Captain, you weren't on our ship when Savage kidnapped you. You didn't have to live through the worry we did, wondering if you'd be killed by Golgi's pirates. It was hard for us to turn around and get behind a new plan that involves her, especially a risky one."

Gisella turns to Rosemary now, putting her arms on her hips. "And Rosie, you know better. Mike's not a stupid man. Nor is Colonel Sedeghat. Michael wasn't drugged when the plans were made. Not this time. We've got a great team." She gestures to Chaudhary. "We're going to be fine. Now, can you both keep it together?"

They both look grumpy, but nod anyway. Gisella strides back over to Chaudhary. The bridge is quiet. Too quiet.

"Hey, *Euryale*," I say. "Play the song, 'You're Stupid'." I look around at the confused faces in the room. "It's ancient classical music from pre-space age humanity. Written by a famous composer named Beethoven for some jerk named Napoleon to get ready for battle." This information is accepted without question from the group, and we lapse again into conversational silence.

"That was impressive," Chaudhary says to Gisella in an undertone. It's only because I'm standing so breaching close to them that I can hear it at all.

"Family dynamics," Gisella replies, as she shuffles closer to Chaudhary. "I'm old hat at that."

Pete scrambles into the room, breathless. "Sorry I'm late, cap'n. What'd I miss?" He looks around the bridge, met with only grumpy faces and 'You're Stupid' playing in the conversational silence. "Oh hello," he says to Chaudhary.

"If your entire team is assembled, it's time to begin the briefing. *Euryale*, shut the music." Chaudhary nods and snaps her posture straighter.

"Truyoza is expected to make contact with you, Savage. When that happens, you are to act as though nothing is wrong. If he asks about your delay, you may tell him it occurred after the shoot-out with the *Lamorak*. In your version of events, of course, the *Doomberg* won. You can tell him Captain Golgi was disposed of and you have a new captain but are otherwise on your way. This is your only role on this mission.

"When we arrive at the mob-asteroid, your crew will remain here on the bridge. The *Euryale* will disable the station's systems and place it on lockdown while my team enters the station and selectively opens doors until we reach Truyoza and apprehend him. Sergeant Reyes will coordinate with me from the location of this bridge. Again, none of you are to leave this bridge, and you certainly are never to place the umemeh into mob custody. Is that understood?"

"If I may?" the *Euryale* speaks up. Chaudhary nods. "I do not have the capability to do what you're asking of me."

Michael groans and covers his eyes. "Timing, *Euryale*, timing."

Chaudhary blinks. Then again. "I... Then..." she starts.

"But we do have an AI that can," Gisella cuts in smoothly. "I'm sorry we had to withhold that information. But it was necessary. I'm sure you can understand the need for secrecy with such a powerful tool. All you need to know is that we have the capabilities you need to complete this mission as planned."

Chaudhury inhales deeply. She nods. "All right, then. I don't think I have much choice." Gisella winces. "What should I call this AI, then? When referring to it?"

"Other than the annoying-jabber-mouth?" I ask, and Michael shoots me an annoyed glance. I roll my eyes.

"His name is Otis," Gisella replies.

"I really hope you managed to turn that feature down," I mutter.

Chaudhary snaps her heels together, gives us a curt nod, and departs. We all watch her walk away for some minutes before the door closes shut behind her.

"Well, that went well," Michael says drily.

"And I thought you guys were a tough crowd," I say with a snort.

"Hey! I like her," Gisella retorts. I stare at her like she's insane and Gisella's freckled cheeks flush. She gushes, "She's really competent. Just, I mean, wow. And… did you *see* her butt in that uniform?"

"Oh, voids," Rosemary says from the controls, rolling her eyes. "If Lucy starts falling for someone next I'm going to think we were all hit with a Stupid Virus."

"Don't be cranky," Gisella says, hopping over to Rosemary's side and chucking her in the arm.

Rosemary only grumbles.

Lucy sits upright.

"We're being hailed," she announces to the room. "By Truyoza's headquarters."

chapter thirty-three

"*This is the station Nyeeb-Yesnee Valoon. You have five seconds to identify yourselves.*"

Lucy glances over at Captain Reyes. "Their facial recog programs will recognize you," she says. "You're on every public listing for the *Waterloo*."

Also, Truyoza might have looked up the captain from back when I ratted him out. But I don't say that out loud and instead fixate my gaze on the floor.

"I'll do it," Rosemary elbows her way in front of the bridge telecam. Michael scoots over to the side.

"This is Captain R—" Rosemary catches herself from saying her real name. "Captain Rinsemouth of the ship *Doomberg*. Making a scheduled delivery."

Silence on the other end of the line.

The seconds tick by, and we all stare at each other uneasily as we wait for the response. They were supposed to be expecting me, so my estimation of their organizational skills drops to zero.

"*Doomberg, you're entering into private territory,*" comes the radio response at last. "*You are not clear to enter. Turn around, or we will be authorized to use force. You have one minute until we open fire.*"

"Nononono," Rosemary starts up. "Stop! We have a delivery. For your boss, Truyoza. He's expecting us! Ask him yourself!"

"Doomberg, that is a negative. You are not clear to enter. Turn around. If you're still within our boundaries, we will open fire in forty-three seconds."

Rosemary slams on the cut transmission button in front of Lucy.

"Those incompetent, moronic fuckers," I yell.

"On, no. No way!" Rosemary exclaims. "That's not incompetence. They got tipped off! They know why we're here. Michael, we've got to turn around."

Michael holds a hand up in the air and quanta-coms Chaudhary, discussing why they need to turn around. We can't go forward with this now.

"Cap'n?" Lucy asks. "Twenty seconds. It's going to be tight."

If we turn around now, I won't get my promised immunity. I can't let this happen. But what can I do about it? It's then, with eighteen seconds to spare, that I've got it.

"Everybody shut up for a minute!" I yell. "I'm going to comm Truyoza!"

"Wait –" yells Michael. But it's too late. The quanta-com is already ringing.

"You."

"Truyoza. What the shit is this? I come to deliver your umemeh and your assholes are threatening to open fire."

There is a long pause on the line.

"You jhave umemeh?"

"Yes, you asshole. I shlepped this thing all across the galaxy for you and –"

"What happen to Golgi?" he asks, cutting me off.

"There was a scuffle," I say, hedging.

"I need to see umemeh," Truyoza says. "Switch to visual line." He clicks off, just like that, and I roll my eyes.

The *Doomberg* rocks with the first volley of explosions. "We're under fire," Lucy says calmly. No shit, genius. "Shields are holding at ninety-eight percent."

Michael quickly tucks himself under a console, out of visual range. The ship rumbles again. "Set up the video comm with him! Don't waste any more time."

Truyoza picks up on the second ring. From the current angle of his cam, his face looks old and saggy, with a thousand black hairs sprouting in the wrong way from his eyebrows.

"Hi." I say. "Here is your favorite animal," I add, twisting the quanta-com to show Fred, who's bumping his head into the door. Repeatedly. The ship shudders again with the newest volley of fire. Fred snorts, and his nostrils dilate.

"Hey. Can you tell your dildos down there to cut that out? They're freaking out your cargo."

"You vill dock," Truyoza says with a nod. Though I don't care for that tone. "And who is captain now? I must speak."

I turn to Rosemary, and she nods. I angle my quanta-com-cam at her.

"I'm Captain Rinsemouth," she says firmly, bobbing her hat at him.

"How you became captain?" Truyoza asks, eyes narrowing.

"Mutiny," she explains with a shrug. "We weren't happy with our last captain." Well, that's a hair close to the truth.

"Reensemouth?" Truyoza asks. "Hoo kay. You land. You jhand over umemeh."

"And you pay," I add. Truyoza considers for a second. "Or we just turn around and find another buyer, you fucking asshole."

The ship shudders again.

"They're charging up the torpemps now," Lucy says. "Shields down to fifty percent."

"And tell your guys to cut that out, I said!"

Truyoza cuts the line.

I glance around the room uneasily.

"Oncoming fire has ceased," Lucy says.

"Does that mean we land?" I ask hopefully.

Michael crawls out from under the console. "I don't like it."

"Oh, *now* you don't like it?" Rosemary asks.

"It sounded like..." Michael shakes his head slightly. "Like he was being careful not to be caught on audio purchasing an umemeh. Like he knows what we're up to."

I have a sinking feeling in my gut. I really, really hope that's not true.

"I vote to do it anyway," Gisella says.

"Are you out of your mind?!" Rosemary exclaims.

"He doesn't know we've got Otis," Gisella explains. "He couldn't possibly know. Whatever Truyoza thinks he'll do to us, we've got the trump card. There's no way he can win this one. Once he gives us access to the station, we're set."

Michael nods slowly. Rosemary doesn't move, arms still glued to hips.

"Well," Michael says. "That's all I need to hear for this mission success. But I can't ask you all to go into this mission, especially one that's so dangerous, without knowing where your head's at. I know where Rosemary and Gisella stand. Pete?"

Pete takes off his hat and rubs his greasy hair. Then he puts it back on. "I guess I'm with Gisella, then. Truyoza definitely knows something's up. But that Otis, if he can find Marc's porn, Turyoza ain't no match for him."

I guffaw.

"Savvy?" Michael asks.

I sigh. "I don't like the idea of putting Fred into their hands, though." I shake my head. "Too dangerous. They're not... nice people."

"*Now* you care about Fred?" Rosemary says.

I shoot her a death glare.

"Luce?" Michael asks.

Lucy blinks slowly. "I vote we go in. Otis's capabilities will be unmatched by their station. If Gisella has repaired him sufficiently."

Gisella gives a thumbs up.

"*Euryale?*"

"You're asking me to vote? How exciting!" the ship asks. "With all due respect, captain, asking a ship to vote is unwise. I am happy to continue for the sake of the experience. But my ship-mind can always be rebooted and revived elsewhere. I do not carry the same stakes."

"It's not a vote. Before entering any potentially dangerous mission, it's important to know your teammates' thoughts. That's what I'm asking to hear."

"In that case," the *Euryale* responds, "I'd like to continue this mission."

"All right." Michael nods. "I appreciate your honesty, everyone. As I mentioned, it's not a vote, and we are going in. Regardless of how you feel about this particular mission, I know how you feel about each other. Remember: if you don't have one person's back, you could jeopardize the whole team. It's vital that we look out for each and every member of the team. Lucy, take us in. Gisella, make sure Otis is up for the task. Pete, go with her and construct a secure hiding spot for him. I'll head down to debrief Chaudhary. And you two," he points to me and Rosemary, "try not to kill each other."

With that, a ton of bodies leave the room, and the door swooshes shut behind them. It only narrowly misses Fred's eager heads.

"Sorry buddy, you've got to stay here," I say. "We want to keep you safe."

"I've got a bad feeling about this," Rosemary says, shaking her head as she watches Lucy's operations.

I root around in my bag and pull out a treat for Fred. "Welcome to my life."

It's only now, in the quiet anticipation of the bridge, that I realize I've been included in the 'team' with all the other non-criminal crew members.

chapter thirty-four

We're all sitting at the edge of our seats while Lucy performs the coupling maneuver. In technical terms, this is probably the least complicated coupling she's been asked to do. *Nyeeb-Yesnee Valoon* has robotic pontoons to guide us into dock. It's smooth sailing, and all Lucy has to do is accept the coupling maneuvers.

"The station is quite lovely," the *Euryale* says during coupling. That should have been our first indicator that something's wrong.

But we're too distracted by what we're getting on the visual sensors. The station is a gargantuan, hollowed out, rotating asteroid. As we approach the opening, we have a clear view of the conical interior and the city grid that's been designed to resemble an art deco sculpture. I heard when Truyoza's predecessors built this, they used generations of slave labor and spared no expense in materials, and it shows. Most normal folk in the galaxy will never see this incredible view. To gain entry, you'd normally have to pledge allegiance to Truyoza's mob or sell your soul. The mob won't let anyone get close for anything less.

Which is more or less what we're doing with this umemeh.

I'm standing next to Michael Hotpants Reyes, my shoulder brushing against his arm as the *Doomberg* is flown, guided, to the outer rim of the hollowed out, glittering interior. The outermost ring is for docking incoming and outgoing ships, and beyond that, it's carpeted with the twinkling lights of the civilization splayed out on every wall of the asteroid's interior. Like the *Lamorak*, the *Nyeeb-Yesnee Valoon* contains habitats along the inner wall and has been given spin to create a centrifugal gravity. While it's visually astounding, it is not the kind of thing a ship-mind would typically appreciate, or learn to call "lovely."

"*Euryale*, what did you mean before, when you said the station was *lovely*?" Gisella asks. "Can you clarify?"

"The station mind," *Euryale* replies. "Is marvelous. She's been built way beyond my own specifications and… Oh!" The *Euryale* stops talking.

We all look at each other in uncomfortable silence.

"*Euryale*?" Michael asks. He leans forward to tap at a screen, and my shoulder feels an immediate rush of cold air in his absence.

The *Euryale* does not respond.

"Shit," Rosemary mutters. "That can't be good."

"Luce? Any insight here?"

"The *Euryale's* processors are fully engaged in a task at the *Nyeeb-Yesnee Valoon's* request."

"All of them?" Gisella asks incredulously. Both she and Pete have returned after making sure Otis is well-hidden, and they're both looking petrified. If Gisella is scared, we're all fucked.

"Oh, wait guys. I've got this one," I say, swaggering up to the control board. I glance around at the holoscreen and realize it's got a completely different display than it did on the billiard room escape pod. "Nope. Shit, nevermind."

"What were you looking for?" Gisella asks gently.

"Something like this happened before. You know," I make an apologetic face. "*Before*?" When I kidnapped Michael. Rosemary rolls her eyes. "All you have to do is hit the manual override to stop the *Euryale* from getting all jammed up on a question." They all glance at each other. "A big red button with a question mark on it?"

Gisella clears her throat. "That's not something… that is standard in space craft."

The feeling of nausea hits me hard. Crap.

"Actually," Rosemary cuts in.

Surprised, my eyes rivet to hers. She shrugs and returns her attention to the *Doomberg's* screens. Michael raises his eyebrows at me behind her back, and I feel my cheeks warm in response. I quickly turn to focus on Lucy's screens.

"I think I saw something like that on a previous screen," Rosemary says, telling Lucy to scroll to the right spot. "I thought it was a button to open the ship's manual, like a set of instructions."

We all hold our breath while Lucy toggles through options till Rosemary whoops at the sight of a new screen. "There!" She exclaims. Lucy hits the 'manual' button, and the *Euryale* is back.

"Oh! Oh, I see what it did there," *Euryale* says. "Tricky questions, too."

"Not now!" I yell at the *Euryale*. "Stash it to think about later. We need you with us. Are you saying the *Nyeeb-Yesnee Valoon* is intelligent?"

"Oh yes, and she's marvelous. Far more intelligent and equipped than I. Her skillsets are quite impressive."

"Fuck," Rosemary says under her breath. Part of our plan depended on overriding the station's command center. None of us considered the possibility that Truyoza might be using an AI more powerful than Otis to run his station.

"Gisella?" Michael asks.

She shakes her head. "I don't know, Michael, I just don't know."

"Shit balls in an asteroid storm," Pete says, leaning back against the wall.

"I observe now how being faced with death makes humans more irritable than usual," *Euryale* says. "I will add that to my notes on the experience."

"For fuck's sake," I reply. "You're keeping a diary?"

"*Nyeeb-Yesnee Valoon* is initiating docking procedures," Lucy announces into the ship's comm. If Otis can still do his job, we'll stay up here in the bridge, and Chaudhary will storm the station.

"Otis, buddy, are you ready?" Gisella asks over her quanta-com. I have to force myself to breathe – I realize I've been holding my breath.

"Yes, I most toodly-doodly am."

"Why didn't you fix that?" I ask in a low growl.

Gisella ignores me. "Do you already have a read on the station?"

"Well of course, there, partner! But until I can access its mainframe, my powers will be limited. You do know that the *Nyeeb-Yesnee Valoon* is a highly sophisticated and intelligent being, right?"

"We're aware of it now, thank you," Gisella says, and frowns. "Will you be able to stay hidden from it long enough to accomplish the task?"

"It's funny you should ask! Did you know that artificially intelligent machines are friendly with one another? Perhaps not in the way you humans are friends. No, most definitely not in the same manner. But we're a chatty bunch, we machines. We talk to each other on the subnet all the time. It's constant and ongoing. There is not the duplicity of human conversation, or the empty pleasantries you folk are so fond of."

"Yeah. We're not that fond of it either," I mutter.

"Otis?" Gisella says. "I'm still waiting for a response."

"Oh, by golly! I thought you understood. The answer is both yes and no, of course! *Nyeeb-Yesnee Valoon* is a constant participant in our subsystems chat and has directed any entering artificial intelligence to complete a set of challenging tasks upon entry. *Nyeeb-Yesnee Valoon* has the superior system ranking, and participation is not optional."

"But you're not doing it. Right, Otis?" Rosemary asks, sounding tired.

"No, I most certainly am not! I'm keeping off the subsystem chat to avoid it. Tasks such as those would keep all my processing powers tied up and locked down for a good long while, mind you. I most certainly will not."

"That's good," Gisella says grimly. Even her patience is tiring. There is a grinding sound reverberating through the ship, and we're in the final stages of coupling. "Otis. Please confirm that while you avoid getting caught in the *Nyeeb-Yesnee Valoon's* impossible tasks, you'll still be able to perform the job we've asked of you? And finish your explanation before coupling ends."

"All righty then. While we are accessing *Nyeeb-Yesnee Valoon's* system via remote link, I am able to remain hidden on the subsystems and avoid her tasks. But as soon as I hardwire to a port – which I need to do for the tasks you require of me – *Nyeeb-Yesnee Valoon* will assign me her tasks. It will be a battle of strengths. She may be more intelligent than I am, but my hacking routines have been highly developed and one could call them quite ruthless. *Nyeeb-Yesnee Valoon* will not be happy with me. The ultimate outcome remains unknown, friend."

Michael exhales a long stream of air.

"You didn't tell us he would have to hardwire into the station," Rosemary grumbles.

Gisella shakes her head. "I wasn't expecting it. This must be a protocol enacted when facing this level of intelligence."

"Connecting corridor fully pressurized," Lucy announces. "Allowing hatch access."

All of a sudden, there's a loud booming and rat-a-tat-tat-ing sound shuddering through the ship.

"We're under attack," Lucy mutters softly. We all turn to her in surprise. Lucy moves out of the way to show the screen of internal cameras.

Chaudhary's special ops are circled up in the cargo bay, hands in the air. At their feet lay piles of weapons. Running around the room like frantic ants, is a crew of black clad, masked, and heavily armored people.

A fat man strolls in amidst the yelling and the bursts of gunfire slow to a quiet. It's Greel fucking Truyoza. The mob boss walks up to Chaudhary and nods at her. Two of the men grab her arms and twist them backwards until she's kneeling. The man stands there calmly as she writhes in front of him.

When he speaks, his voice is quiet, but unmistakable and commanding.

"You vill tell me vere is umemeh. Yes?"

Chaudhury doesn't answer, staring up at Truyoza defiantly.

He kicks her swiftly in the stomach, and she buckles over in pain.

"We find umemeh. Is here, somewhere." He gestures to his operatives. "Search every room."

chapter thirty-five

"You," Truyoza says with a sneer as he enters the bridge. "Vhat kind of stupid fake name is Rinsemouth?"

Rosemary folds her arms.

"And you," he says, finding me. "Much shorter than I realized." He pauses. "You think I would not recognize these people? You double-cross me?" He *tsks, tsks, tsks.* "This was big mistake."

Then he turns his attention to Fred, asleep again and bopping his heads. "But at least I get umemeh for all this trouble." He hits Fred on the rump, and Fred squeals.

"You," he says to his men. "Take them to holding. Put them in separate cell from that other group in cargo." His eyes rove over his group of thugs. "You," he singles out one guy. "Take umemeh to Doctor Yussipov. Tell him to begin surgery immediately." He nods and turns out of the bridge. He takes one last glance. "Rinsemouth." He shakes his head.

"Wait!" I yell. "Don't do this!" Rosemary furrows her eyebrows and shakes her head at me, but I rush on. Maybe I can still save him. "Truyoza. The umemeh still has another ten years of his natural lifespan. Don't kill him!"

"Don't worry," he chuckles. "We are sending him to nice pasture with pretty flowers. And rainbows. He will be happy."

The bastard.

"Savage," Rosemary warns under her breath. But I don't care. I fucking hate him. I hate this big bully, and his ability to make people jump through hoops for him like we're all his toys, all because he's got space-rocks full of cash. If I'm about to be turned into chopped meat, you can bet your burning asteroids that I'll be using my remaining time to say some choice last words to this asshole.

"Truyoza, you're just an impotent, doll-fucking, limp noodle!"

He stops in his tracks. This time, he doesn't turn around. "Kill her first. Make it hurt, yah? No limit."

The leader nods, and Truyoza is gone.

This is bad. I swallow a painful lump in my throat. I glance at the other *Waterloo* crewmembers, but they all are wide-eyed and trying their best to comply as they get shoved into walking formation. Rosemary looks at me as she passes me, then nods. She must finally see that I'm not a completely terrible human. Michael steers his exit path close enough to me that I can smell his cologne. He manages to look into my eyes as he passes by. His eyes tell me nothing other than 'this is serious'.

We're hustled out of the *Doomberg* in a cluster. The special ops team have been evacuated first, so it's just us leftovers from the *Waterloo's* skeleton crew. Fred is led off in a different direction, and Truyoza's goonies roughly push us into an elevator, then through nondescript grey corridors to what ends up being a large, blindingly-white prison cell.

I sink to the ground inside our new cell. This is horrible. There's no fixing this. Fred is going to be butchered in a matter of minutes, and I'm going to be tortured. Not even this crew can get us out of this bind. I blink back tears. I mean, I always knew shit could happen when I kidnapped this ridiculous beast but I never really thought it would come to this. I stare up at the painfully white ceiling and blink rapidly. Tears start rolling out anyway.

The door locks fall silent after grinding to place. Rosemary stands staring at the door, raises a fist, and yells, "Assholes!" It's not going to make any difference, but, holy wombat's ass, do I feel solidarity with her right now. Even if she still hates me.

Michael Hotpants Reyes, is busy checking every corner of the room. I don't even have the emotional energy to check out his butt as he bends over to inspect corners. The prospect of excruciating pain over the next few hours has really sucked all the fun out of life. Meanwhile, Pete is knocking at intervals along the smooth white walls, and Gisella keeps rubbing her bare wrist where her quanta-com used to sit, before the guards confiscated them all.

I blink away more tears.

"It's no use," I say to Pete, who knocks on the bare patch of wall above my head.

"They've got to ventilate this system somehow," Michael says with a nod to the floor-grate in the back corner with an unmistakable stench. "That's just basic plumbing. You need to vent the gasses. But I can't tell where."

"What does it even matter?" I hug my arms more tightly around myself and pulling my knees in closer. "We're all dead anyway."

Rosemary scrunches up her face and squints at me. "You're giving up *now*?" She shakes her head. "Don't give up now, Savage. We need you."

I blink at her.

"O was safely hidden in the cargo bay," Gisella says quietly. Understanding slowly dawns on me. By O, she means Otis. "I saw him on our way out."

Something blossoms in my chest. "So you mean…"

"We still have a breaching good fighting chance." Michael says, approaching me. He stands with his arms at his hips and all of a sudden I'm remembering that all his shoulder musculature looks really, really fine.

"But we'd rather not let you get tortured before O can swoop in for the rescue," Rosemary adds. She gives me a tight-lipped smile.

Michael nods. "There might be a way to escape."

"There's a chance that the ventilation duct is large enough for us to squeeze through," Gisella says.

"Or a chance that the wiring for the lighting is somehow connected to the electrical for the door," Lucy suggests.

"Or that plumbing leads to a huge garbage disposal room, and we can crawl out through there," Pete adds.

Rosemary makes a face. "Disgusting. I hope not."

"So," Michael concludes, "if you've got any ideas, let us know."

I sniff, but give him a nod. "I'll think on it." The others go back to their examinations of the space, and I glance around the room. I want to help with their hope-driven reconnaissance, but I'm not sure what insight I can provide. The room is a large, white box, terribly boring in its uniformity. There are blindingly bright floodlights hanging in all four corners, and no other landmarks besides the door through which we entered and a small floor drain in one corner. Otherwise, there are no visual distinctions about the room.

Think!

I've never been in prison before. Don't they have to feed prisoners? What did we do on Hialeah? Oh, there were plenty of staffers who *should* have been imprisoned for various crimes, but they roamed free. The closest we got to prisons was the way we kept the animals.

"There's got to be a camera somewhere in here," Gisella mutters. "Lucy, do you think they'd house it in the toilet grate there?"

She wrinkles her nose and deftly shakes her head.

"On Hialeah, we mounted the camera units on the door frames of the enclosures. It was probably out of convenience, since there's already electrical wiring for the enclosure locks." My eyes rove over the frame of this door, but it's clean and white and definitely free of camera equipment. My heart sinks.

My mind wanders back to Hialeah and the few instances the security cameras were not mounted on enclosure doors. Of course, I land on the dromidaire-bears. Ironically, early generations of zookeepers had been worried that dromidaire-bears would die during hibernation from lack of oxygen. The planet's O2 sprinklers had always been an imperfect solution since they unevenly distributed oxygen, until that one terrible winter they failed completely.

Early generations who actually cared about the animals of Hialeah installed cameras in each of the caves up there in case something went wrong during winter hibernation. But because there was a concern that the strong and dexterous dromidaire-bear might try to play with them (or destroy them), the cameras were hidden in fake rock outcroppings. After that terrible winter, those cameras became a critical tool for locating all the deceased dromidaire-bears.

I take another look around our prison. Definitely no rock outcroppings here. It's all smooth white and flat. No place to hide a camera. My sight rests on the biometrics pad at the side of the door. It's there to allow guards in and out with a slap of a palm, but now, I wonder. "Lucy, Gisella, do either of you think a camera might be housed in the biometrics pad?"

Gisella approaches it and runs a finger around the edges. "It's got the space for it," she says slowly. She puts her hand in the center of the pad, and a light at the top flashes red. "Yes!" she exclaims.

"Watch what happens when I use the pad." She places her hand on it again, and the light flashes above. "If you look closely, you can see a faint grey around my hand. That's the edges of where the biometrics sensor is. But do you see how far above it the red light flashes? Plenty of space in between the two. Way too much space, if it's just a biometrics pad."

"Can you get to the wiring in there?"

"I can try," Gisella replies.

Pete chucks me on the shoulder. "Got any other good ideas, Savvy?"

I shake my head.

Lucy and Gisella work on prying away the face of the biometrics pad, but without any tools, the task is impossible. I mean, it's the fucking lock to the room, so I'm fairly certain a criminal organization would make it hard to break. I know we did, for the dromidaire-bear caves, and that was just for a camera. But that reminds me.

"Back on Hialeah," I say, "Legend has it that a first gen dromidaire-bear had a cub who got sick." I have everyone's attention now. "Did you know dromidaire-bears can get sepsis? And does a *dromidaire-bear* know what that is? No."

"Does a human know what that is?" Pete asks. "Also no."

"It's a system-wide bacterial infection, Pete," Lucy murmurs.

I nod. "The mama dromidaire-bear's natural instinct was to secure her sick baby away into her hibernation cave. They're known to be crazy overprotective of their cubs. The zoo settlers all those hundreds of years ago wanted to save the cub, but she wouldn't let them come anywhere close by. And all he needed was antibiotics." I give a shrug and a small smile.

"Tell me this isn't doesn't have the same ending as the pygmy orangutan story," Rosemary growls. "Because I don't really love your old place of employ."

"Different ending. Hialeah was a nice place for animals once – a very long time ago. Nowadays, there are no more dromidaire-bears on Hialeah." I frown. It had been excruciating to watch Griff do nothing when the O2 sprinklers went out. But they don't need to hear that story. I focus, instead, on the cub who got his happy ending. "That's when the original zoo frontiersmen decided to install a trapdoor in a back of every dromidaire-bear cave. Somewhere high and out of the way, where mama dromidaire-bears couldn't reach. A robot entry chute. The story goes that they just had to wait until mama dromidaire-bear was sleeping, then the robots entered the cave through the chute and injected baby dromidaire-bear with a heavy dose of antibiotics. Baby dromidaire-bear lives, happily ever after."

Rosemary squints. "Why would they build a robot delivery chute into every dromidaire-bear cave? That sounds excessive."

I shrug. "They were relatively cheap to install since the caves were all in the same highland region, and the usefulness factor was huge. If dromidaire-bears died during hibernation, they needed to be able to evacuate the bodies before the gasses from their rotting corpses poisoned the area." Mouths hang open around the group. "Right, I should explain that. The O2 sprinklers up in the mountains were often shoddy." The rest comes tumbling out. "At least, they *were*, until the one winter they went out completely and my boss refused to have them repaired. I begged, but he claimed the animals should be smart enough to figure it out. I tried on my own to make the caves uninhabitable before the dromidaire-bears arrived for hibernation, but moving debris while deprived of oxygen myself was impossible."

Rosemary's eyes bug out.

"Yeah, yeah, I know. Not a good story. Hialeah is a nightmare." My eyes sting with unbidden tears. Even though it's been five years, it still hurts. Fifteen domidaire-bears died preventable deaths that winter, and it was one of the worst times of my life. I'd never felt so helpless, and it broke something inside me. Worse than that, I've had to keep these feelings bottled up and locked away to survive the constant onslaught of degradation that came with living on that planet. But I can't dwell on Hialeah; we need to concentrate on escaping Truyoza's plans to kill me. I wipe my leaky nose on my sleeve. "There might be another similarity here. With the dromidaire-bears, the chutes were built to access their dens without them knowing. There could be the same thing in a prison cell, right?"

They're all still staring at me in horror. No one responds.

"Oh. I – I thought you knew? Hialeah is a bad, bad place. I needed to break free." My last words come out in a whisper.

Gisella comes and puts a hand on my back. Michael comes and does the same. Pete and Lucy do too. Even Rosemary adds her hand to the pile. Something warm and wonderful unfurls in my chest, and it's all I can do to prevent myself from breaking down into more tears.

"I'm glad you're here with us now," Michael says.

"Unless Truyoza kills me," I reply, trying for sarcasm. It's the only chance I have at not turning into one big, sobbing snotball.

"There might be a robot chute in the walls," Gisella offers. "We can look for them."

I take a deep breath, then nod. We need to escape Truyoza's prison – we may as well begin checking the walls. Pete's already knocked on walls at shoulder height, but no one's investigated higher up. "Maybe we should tap the wall up closer to the ceiling?"

"You're the small one," Pete says. "You could git on someone's shoulders."

Rosemary throws her arms up in defense. "Not mine."

Lucy shakes her head.

"Babies. I'll do it," Michael offers.

"Wait," Gisella says. She rips a flap off her pocket and tucks it around the edges of the keypad. She turns to give us the thumbs up. "Don't want them to know what we're up to."

Michael kneels at my feet, and I feel a little dizzy thinking about how close his face is to my lower torso.

"A woman could get used to this," I murmur.

"Oh, for fuck's sake," Rosemary exclaims. "A Stupid Virus, I tell you! All of you!"

"What the voids is she talking about?" Pete asks.

Michael cups his hands together by his knee. "Step here," he says, "and swing one leg around my back."

"You say that like I've never mounted anything," I retort, swinging a leg over his shoulder. Pete guffaws. "I'm a zookeeper, you idiot!"

When both of my legs are wrapped firmly around his head, Michael rises to a stand. There's a fair bit of wobble, so I grab the sides of his face to keep myself steady.

"Not my…"

"You're choking him," Rosemary says dryly. "With your legs."

"I can't help it if I have thick thighs!" I exclaim.

"Oh, this is phenomenal. I'm so glad I didn't volunteer," she answers, still watching us with a smile.

Michael wrests one of my hands away and I almost topple forward over his head. But he holds my arm aloft, out to one side, and I manage to find a stable balance.

"Now," says Michael from between my legs. "Let's knock on some walls."

It's slow going. Knock a few times. Step to the right. Rinse and repeat. On the third wall, we finally hit a hollow-sounding patch.

"Whoa!" Pete exclaims. "That's something!"

"Savvy," Gisella asks slowly from below. "Do you have any idea how to open those trap doors you were talking about?"

Slight problem there. The robot chutes were electrically operated, and they opened with a piston mechanism from the inside. "There won't be a latch on this side, if that's what you're asking."

"Then how do we…?"

"I don't know!" I reply, exasperated. Gisella looks crestfallen. "But I will add that this sounded like a *wall* made out of *wall* material. It didn't have the same ring to it as when you banged on the metal door, right? Walls are… crumbly things."

"Are you suggesting we bust open the wall?" Pete replies, a gap-toothed grin beginning to form.

"I'm suggesting we try," I reply. Smiles and nods fill the room. "Correction," I add, after another glance at the wall. "I'm suggesting Pete tries. Or Michael. It ain't gonna be me who punches that wall."

"Oh, this one's allll me," Pete says. He's not a small man, by any means, and I hope this translates into a wall-crushing ability. "Captain, prepare to have a non-delicate board."

Michael groans beneath me. It sends delicious reverberations through my legs, which are clasped around his head. Slowly he gets down to a kneel, and once he's steady on the floor, I swing myself off.

"Ain't gonna offer me no foothold, are you?" Pete asks suspiciously. "Some gentleman you are," he huffs and scrambles messily up and over Michael's knee.

Standing next to Rosemary, I watch the comedy of physical ridiculousness.

"You were right," I reply. "This is too good to miss." I cross my arms. "In fact, I'm kind of pissed I wasn't able to watch the first round."

"You had to go through a hazing to be a part of the crew," Rosemary replies with a shrug. My heart skips a beat. I turn to look at her, but she's watching Michael, who's getting up with more difficulty than before.

"Need a hand, Cap'n?" Rosemary calls out.

"Nope. Nope. I got it." Just as he says that, his knee gives out and Pete tumbles off onto the floor. "Mother of hull breaches!" Michael gets back up and rolls his shoulders. "Okay. I may need a *little* help balancing with this sack of potatoes on my shoulder."

"Hey! If I'm a sack of anything, it sure as shit ain't potatoes. I'm a sack of gemstones," Pete says. "I'm a sack of unicorns. No, fuck that, I'm a sack of rainbows!"

Rosemary nods and purses her mouth into a smile. "Rainbows don't weigh anything."

Pete can't be bothered by the correction. This time, he gets aboard with little difficulty. With the first smash of his fist at the wall, there's a satisfying crunch and a shower of crumbled cellular paper and powder.

"Is this really fastwall?" Pete retorts. "What kind of idiot mob uses fastwall construction material in space?"

"Pete!" Michael says through gritted his teeth. "Just hurry up!"

"Oh, right. Yes Cap'n." And Pete jackhammers his fists in succession until he's opened up a hole in the wall that must be two or three feet squared.

"Oh, Luce. Gisella. You engineer people are gonna like this." Pete holds on to the opening with two hands and hauls himself through the hole. "Don't worry, it's bigger on the inside!" he yells before he tosses down a spider bot, crawls all the way in, then pokes his head back out of the ledge he just created. Behind him is a receding darkness. "Dunno if you could use 'im for parts, but he was here, waiting and inactive."

Gisella frowns. "I can't open the bot without my tools," she says. "But this looks like a drug delivery bot." She turns the bot upside down. "Looks like it could be zynathanine, a muscle paralytic. Let's just hope he doesn't have an active camera in him, too."

We all look at each other in stunned silence.

"Let me take care of that," Lucy steps forward. She palms the bot and after standing motionless for a moment, she nods. "I set its camera to repeat the first five minutes of us in the room. I deleted the footage of us breaking the wall."

"What? All without even hardwiring to the bot?" I ask and immediately realize how dumb that question was. Of course. She's a hybe. Go me, for being the asshole.

"Luce is a Rockstar like that," Michael cuts in smoothly. He breaks the silence with a clap of his hands. "Alright everybody, let's get the voids out of here." He kneels on the ground below the chute. "Rosemary, you want to be the next one aboard?"

"Yes, Captain."

And one by one, we all climb into the dark space between walls, balanced on top of a narrow robot chute. Pete leans out to pull Michael up after we've all ascended.

"Now where to?" Rosemary asks once we're all on the chute line. We're all perched on the slippery surface meant for bots to travel, squatting or awkwardly on all fours. The track is narrower than our frames, and it's got a painful lip along either edge. The good news is there's no ceiling to it at all, completely open to the intra-wall wiring.

"If my calculations are correct," Lucy says quietly down the line, "the room where the other agents are being held should be down this way."

"Lead on," Michael says.

———

"Caw! Caw!" Michael calls in the dark through the closed chute door.

Rosemary slaps his foot from behind. "What are you doing?" she whispers angrily at him.

We're all wedged tightly in between walls on this stupidly painful robot track with only the odd systems blinking light for illumination. We've managed to work our way so that we've got Michael and Rosie up at the front of the line together. Our current path has taken us down a robot chute that ends abruptly at a wall. Specifically, the wall Lucy thinks is the wall to the other cell. But without a visual or a map, it's impossible to tell.

"I'm trying to signal them!" His whispers come out forced, like he's trying not to yell.

"You're signaling them with a bird noise?" Rosemary retorts.

"Well, if it's the *wrong* room," Michael replies heatedly, "I wouldn't want Truyoza's agents to know we're free."

"If it's the *wrong room*," Rosemary replies, "they'll be freaked out to have birds in their walls, fucking up their wiring. They'll open fire."

"Fine," Michael mutters. "Chaudhary!" He calls through the chute door.

There's no answer. Shit. I glance behind me and wince at the prospect of squeezing into another tight space for the next room. Not to mention, the clock is running. They could be slicing into poor Fred at any moment.

"Hey, Chaudhary!" Michael calls again.

"Who said that?" comes a muffled response from within.

"Thank the fur-licking felines," I mutter.

"Chaudhary, listen. It's Reyes. Cover your cell's biometric keypad with something. It houses a camera. Then we'll get you out of here."

There are a few agonizing minutes that follow when we can't

hear or see anything. Then, it comes. "Okay, Reyes, we're ready for you."

Michael pushes the chute open (using the piston lever available from this side) and is met with exclamations.

"Anybody hurt or missing?" After a negative response, Michael says, "Then let's get going. We'll explain on the way. Don't want them to come investigating when they notice both cameras have gone out."

All of us who're further down the chute line do a painful about face and begin crawling deeper into the system to make room for Chaudhary's team of twenty agents. The chute groans and rocks with our motion. It was meant for smaller and lighter robotics, but we can't afford to hop off and walk at ground level – the passages in between support studs have been built for the chute only.

When we get to a section where the walls have opened up wide enough for a little more breathing room, we pause for a group meeting. The space is filled with pipes holding electrical wires, and there's a constant hum and low whine of electronics. Michael and Chaudhary face each other on the track close to the middle of the group, and we all remain lined up on the chute on either side behind them.

Michael quickly fills in Chaudhary and doesn't withhold details this time. Someone in the back of the special ops line asks a noisy "what'd he say?", and soon, there is the conversational hum of Michael's words being relayed, soldier to soldier, down the chute line.

"Any idea when Otis will start working?" she asks when he's finished.

Gisella speaks up. "It should be any moment. He may get tripped by *Nyeeb-Yesnee Valoon's* task protocols, but I'm confident he's equipped to overcome them." In front of me, she rubs her wrist again. "They took my quanta-com," she says miserably. "I have no way of contacting him."

"They confiscated our weapons as well," Chaudhary says, a clear note of regret in her voice.

"So what's the plan?" Rosemary asks impatiently from behind me. "Are we really just going to sit around and wait for Otis to do his thing?"

"Hello? Does anybody remember Fred?" I ask incredulously. "Can we get to him before they chop off his heads?"

Michael raises his eyebrows. "We're unarmed. Even if we manage to make it to Fred and he's alive, what then? They'll come at us. And there's no way we can retreat with Fred into these ductworks. He's just too big. I'm sorry, Savvy."

"But…" I look around at the grim faces up and down the line. "We can't let him die!"

Michael shifts uncomfortably. "Maybe if we can manage to get to our weapons first, we can find a way to rescue Fred."

That's impossibly long from now. I feel the seconds ticking away, hopeless.

Rosemary puts her hand on my back. "We'll do our best, Savvy."

I blink away the stinging feeling in my eyes. This can't be it for Fred. It can't be.

Chaudhary, on the other hand, is all business. "Ideally, we'd find where they sequestered our confiscated weapons and obtain them. Even once Otis shuts down the power to the station, my team and I will need our weapons to go after Truyoza."

"Hey!" I sniffle. "Didn't you leave something out?"

"…And send part of our team to rescue Fred," Chaudhary adds. "I thought that went without saying."

Michael shakes his head. "But we have no idea where anything is in this place," he *tsks*. "I wish we had a map."

"Actually," Lucy says, and clears her throat. Everyone on the line immediately pauses their chatter. Other than the hum of electronics, the chute is silent. "I've been communicating with *Nyeeb-Yesnee Valoon*."

"You *what*?" we all say.

Lucy gives the barest twitch of her shoulders. "I've been on the subnet that Otis mentioned. He gave you all the relevant information, so I didn't feel the need to add to it."

"But –" Gisella says. "If you were in communication with it, wouldn't *Nyeeb-Yesnee Valoon* assign you an impossible task protocol?"

Lucy nods. "It did. That's the benefit of being a hybe. The human part of me was able to reject it as folly."

Gisella opens and shuts her mouth several times.

"Otis is not yet known to the network, so he has not failed yet, Gisella. There is still hope the plan may succeed."

"Wait," Chaudhary interrupts. "If you have access to *Nyeeb-Yesnee Valoon's* sub-net, couldn't you just overwrite it and shut it down?"

Lucy glowers at her, but it's Gisella who speaks first. "It's okay. She probably doesn't know how programs work," she says apologetically to Lucy. She turns towards Chaudhary. "Lucy is able to communicate with the system. But computing processors all operate on an order of logical hierarchies made by totally different programming systems. It would take a while for Lucy and *Nyeeb-Yesnee Valoon* to figure out who really has more authority here, and that's just translating two different sets of codes to be able to compare program imperatives. Like figuring out apples to oranges. It would take even longer for Lucy to write a new override code. Otis, though, was built to break other programs."

"I can see how that might be something you would want to keep secret," Chaudhary replies mildly.

"In the wrong hands," Michael says, "Otis could do some harm. But in the hands of law-abiding citizens?" He shrugs. "Otis is mostly harmless. He's our chef. Or at least he was, before a bathroom incident."

Chaudhary's eyebrows shoot up. She obviously does not believe that.

Lucy speaks up again. "I do have access to a map of the station and can direct you to the weapons room, which is where *Nyeeb-Yesnee Valoon* says Truyoza's operatives dropped all our confiscated materials."

Burning asteroids, is Lucy amazing.

"Best hybe in the universe," Michael says quietly. I crane my neck to catch a glimpse of his face. He's smiling at Lucy like a proud papa while the murmur of special ops soldiers relaying the news down the line starts up again.

"All right, here's what I suggest," Chaudhary says in her authoritative voice, loud and clear. Everyone quiets to listen to her. "Unless we've got any objections, we'll have Lucy lead the way. Let's go get our things back."

There are cheers and whoops from her team.

"Pete!" Michael calls down the line. "Lie down or something. Let Lucy climb over you to get to the front of the line."

After some leapfrogging on the rickety frame, we're all in place.

"Lead the way, Luce," Michael says, and we begin our claustrophobic, swaying journey all over again.

chapter thirty-six

We come to a pause, wedged in a tight spot between walls. I've been breathing hard with the effort. Or maybe the ungodly heat radiating from the electrical wiring in here. Or maybe there's some oxygen deprivation going on. It's impossible to tell. But I'm not the only one panting.

"It's the door up ahead," Lucy says calmly once we're all in a comfortable perch. "I assume you don't want me to be the entry force."

I turn in time to catch Michael giving Chaudhary a nod, and an understanding passes between them. "Chaudhary and her crew will secure the space. We'll follow once we get the all- clear."

"Lucy, do you have any intel on the layout, security, or weapons availability?" Chaudhary asks.

Lucy blinks. "*Nyeeb-Yesnee Valoon* lists two security agents at the door, which will be on the far end of the room from our point of entry. Also, all the weapons in the armory are secured via intelli-lock. Except for those confiscated from you earlier. Those are in a collection pile on a table by the door to the room, waiting to be evaluated and catalogued."

Chaudhary nods. "Alright, team." She turns to her officers behind her. "Follow me to the front of the chute line here, then we enter and work in teams of two. Let's move."

As horrible as it had been crouching in the warm, humid, claustrophobic space, it is ten times as worse having a team of twenty sweaty special agents climb over your body while you crouch down in that same said horrible space. I have to hold myself back from lashing out after a heavy boot steps on my precious fingers.

I squeal, and Rosemary swats at me to shut up. "I can't help it!" I retort. "Try having Chaudhary sit on your fingers. See how you like it."

"I *would* like that," Gisella says up ahead.

Rosemary rolls her eyes.

"At the end of the mission, Gisella," Chaudhary calls from the front of the line. "You and I have a date."

Gisella flashes us a radiant smile.

"It must be a virus. It *must* be," Rosemary mutters.

I find myself breathing deeply as the light from the opening chute door lets in fresh cool air from the weapons room. Soon, though, we hear angry yelling, followed by loud bangs which echo horribly down the chute.

"Should we go in there to help?" I ask in the dark.

"Absolutely not," Michael replies. "Truyoza's people don't know our position, and we're not giving that away. Also, I'm the only one here with any military training."

"Oh really?" Rosemary asks. "You've never mentioned it."

Michael sighs. "I wouldn't want anyone to get hurt because of inexperience with combat," he explains. I glance up ahead at Gisella. She's usually the peacemaker here, but she seems to have dropped out of the conversation altogether. There's more yelling and banging from beyond the chute, and I wonder if she's able to discern whose yells they are or if it's as pointless an exercise as I think it is.

It's over soon enough, though. It takes only minutes before the room past the chute's door is mostly quiet again, with one person barking clean up orders to others. It sounds like a woman's voice, but there's no way to tell if it's one of ours or one of theirs.

"Reyes?" a muffled voice yells from the other side of the chute door. "It's Chaudhary. All clear."

"Thank fuck," I mutter, and follow the group as we all crowd and push to get out of this overly-toasty chute-work.

I tumble out and blink into the bright light. After being in the dark between-wall space for so long, it takes a while for my eyes to adjust. Once they do, I register two things right away: One, the room is really, really fucking huge. And two, it's filled with weapons. Walls and racks upon racks of weapons. Handheld weapons, explosive weapons, ship-bound weapons.

"We're over here," Chaudhary calls from close to the room's only human-sized door.

I follow Rosemary, single-file, down the length of aisle between the explosives rack and the shoulder cannons. "Don't get rubberneck," Michael nudges me from behind. His voice comes in hot and close to my ear, and I shiver involuntarily. "This stuff is all locked down anyway."

When we reach Chaudhary, she and her team are already re-donning the weapons and plasteel-safe armor they'd been deprived of when they got captured.

"The guards?" Michael asks.

"Knocked out," Chaudhury says, nodding at the dark forms on the floor. "There's more on the way, though." She gestures at the door. "Now. I've activated the door's lock from the inside. That's a triple-nano-net security door." She shakes her head. "It's impossible to overstate how impressive that is. If we board over that bot chute, anyone who remains in here will be perfectly safe. There's value in that. But I'm leading my team out for the rescue mission and operation, and we need to get going before the reinforcements come back."

She holds up a loaded weapon. "Who's coming, and who's staying?"

This is bonkers. I push forward. "I'm coming. I have to be with the group that rescues Fred. He'll need my help."

"We're all going, Chaudhary." Michael steps forward. He's

standing right next to me, and I feel all tingly looking up at him. "There's a reason we volunteered for this mission."

"Even though some of us lack military training," Rosemary mutters. I'm close enough to hear it and smile.

"All right," Chaudhary replies. "Check out the stash here. There's a whole bunch of quanta-coms. I assume they're yours."

Gisella exclaims and roots through the pile. Chaudhury continues giving orders. "Let's all gear up, and Lucy, if you can send me directions to our two destinations?"

Lucy nods.

"Yes!" Gisella shouts, holding up her quanta-com. She double taps her ring finger to open displays and rapidly sorts through her messages. "Otis is working on it. He's sent me untraceable messages, something even I can't do without being seen by the station. Apparently, *Nyeeb-Yesnee Valoon* is a hard station to crack, but not beyond his capabilities. Otis estimates it will take anywhere from five minutes to two hours."

Chaudhary blows a stream of air through pursed lips. "Let's hope it's not the full two hours." She glances around the group. "New plan then. We're not splitting up. Let's rescue Fred first. We can't apprehend Truyoza without Otis. We might be able to hide out in the station with Fred. But once we've got Truyoza, his people will give us all they've got, and they have more firepower than we do. We have to wait for the Otis trump card."

By now, we've all strapped on our old quanta-coms.

Chaudhary nods, and she makes some complicated hand signs to her team. They form up by the door, and us civilians hang back in the rear. "Let's go!" Chaudhary announces, and the door rolls open to a cascade of plasteel bullets. There are only four helmets out there, as far as I can see, but Chaudhary and her team have the armor for it and are returning fire. The hallway quiets again and Chaudhary motions for all of us to follow.

We step gingerly into the smoke-filled hallway, the smell of burnt plastic and the tang of blood.

"Will they be okay?" Gisella asks.

I snort. "What was it Truyoza said? They've gone to grassy meadows with big wildflowers." Gisella, who's ahead of me, stops moving. When I pull around to see her face, it's stone-still and she's fixated on the bodies. "They tried to kill us, Gisella. They wanted to torture me."

Gisella doesn't budge.

Rosemary pushes to the front and shoves Gisella in the elbow. "Did Otis send any updates?"

Her trance broken, Gisella glances down at her quanta-com, and Rosemary hustles her along as she reads through the logs.

"Ow!" Gisella says as she stumbles through the hallway and rubs her arm. "That was unnecessary!" she exclaims while tapping through screens on her quanta-com, searching for word from Otis. "Nothing," she says after a full minute. "I've searched every cached log. He hasn't sent me anything in the last five minutes, Rosie."

Rosemary nods. Gisella only now looks up and realizes they've passed beyond the pile-up of bodies. She raises her eyebrows but doesn't say anything.

Up ahead, Chaudhary motions to her team to go around a corner. Another round of fire bursts can be heard, and then the special ops team motions us forward again.

WHEN WE BURST THROUGH THE DOORS OF THE MEDICAL SUITE, I can't hold back any longer. I push to the front of the crew, even though I'm not wearing the pastel armor the special ops crew's got on. Luckily for me, the group of white-clad medical officers mostly appear shocked, and cower together, unarmed, in a corner of the reception area.

"Where is he?!" I shout. No one sees fit to answer. "Not answering, huh?" Outraged, I tug a weapon out of Chaudhary's hand and wave it in the air. "Would you answer if I begin shooting at you? Tell me! *Where is he?!*"

But I still don't get an answer, only wild looks and people crunching more tightly together.

Chaudhary grabs the gun out of my hand. "Whoa, whoa," she says. "You're gonna hurt yourself with that."

"They're going to let him die! You big, ass-wiping pile of murderers! Murderers, all of you!"

"Who is she talking about?" comes an unidentified voice from the bunch.

Chaudhary makes a swift assessment of the medical staff. "Listen up. We're looking for the umemeh. Tell us where he is, and no one gets hurt."

Murmurs of relief sound through the crowd.

"Surgery room 106," someone calls out, and I rush down the open hallway to find him.

"Turn left!" Lucy yells after me.

I pull to a quick stop and run down the open corridor that's appeared to my left. I can hear Chaudhary and her crew trotting along behind me. Good. 101, 102… Finally, there it is. 106!

"That umemeh better still be alive!" I yell, throwing the door open. Chaudhary and her team stream into the room around me. But I've stopped in my tracks. What I see sickens me.

Fred is there, strapped down to a surgical table and surrounded by five attendants in surgical garb. Both of Fred's heads are at rest, and he's not moving.

It's a moment of pure horror when I realize I've failed him, just like I failed to save the dromidaire-bears. And the guyerras. And the elephelks. But where I failed in Hialeah in my fight against criminal negligence, here I've failed at the hands of intentional, cold-blooded murderers.

"Kill them!" I say, half-choked. My vision is growing hazy, filled with tears. I can't believe it. We couldn't save him. I am a terrible shit of a human being for using him to buy my immunity. But all the people in this room are a million times worse. At least I had hoped Fred would survive the ordeal. The people here never cared. They're pure evil. "Kill them all, Chaudhary! Burn them. Animal butchers. Show them no mercy!"

The surgical team is ordered to get against the walls with their arms up, under sight of Chaudhary's guns.

One of Chaudhary's agents checks the base of Fred's neck. "Still warm!" He announces. "Still breathing!"

"Oh, thank the pill-loving pigmy chimps," I say, and surprise myself with a burst of a sob. I rush up to the table and do an analysis myself. His heart rate is slowed, and his breathing too. Fred is alive.

I wipe my face and snotty nose with my elbow, push back my hair. "What did you give him?"

"If I may?" one of the assholes in a mask says. His nametag says Dr. Yussipov. He steps forward. "A harvest surgery on the carotid artery of an umemeh must be done while the umemeh is still alive, for best, ah, most potent medical uses."

"Fuck you," I say. "You're a criminal and an animal butcher. What is he on right now?"

Yussipov's lips form a thin line. He pushes back his surgical 3-D goggles. "Don't you think that's a little heavy handed? From the animal trafficker who brought the animal to us in the first place?"

I march over to Chaudhary and tug at her gun. She has a firm grip on it, though, so I give up on trying to borrow it. Fine. "Shoot him."

Chaudhary aims her gun, but does not shoot. "You have five seconds to tell us what Fred's on."

"Just a little sedative for the surgery," he replies.

Chaudhary looks at me. "We can't get the umemeh to move if he's unconscious," she says. "What do you suggest, zoologist?"

"We're in a medical facility," I say, grinding my teeth. "We can flush it out. Chaudhary, they've got a fucking IV in him. But don't let any of these guys touch him." I nod at Yussipov. "Especially not that fucker."

I search through the bottles around the edges of the room until

I find what I'm looking for. A saline bag and a bottle of epinephrine. Well, that should wake him right the fuck up. I head over to Fred's IV bag. After I hook up the new saline bag, I flush the line and inject the epinephrine. Fred snorts.

"Looks like you have more than just zookeeping experience," the doctor says.

"You've never been to Hialeah," I retort. No one seems to understands that the place is a waking nightmare.

Fred snorts again, and this time, he begins protesting his straps. "Help me get him free?" I ask one of Chaudhary's agents. Soon enough, loopy Fred is wandering around the room, banging into *everything*. Anything not strapped down crashes and shatters. I feel a familiar muzzle in my hair.

"Let's get you out of here, Freddypoo," I say with a sigh of relief. "Don't get any of this glass in your hooves. You hear that?"

But of course, he's already moved on to explore the excited noises coming from Gisella in the hallway.

Chaudhary gestures at the medical crew. "Did you have any particular thoughts on what to do with these guys?" she asks.

"Normally, I'd say give them a dose of their medicine. But that would be a waste of good sedatives." Fred is alive. We barely made it in time, but he's still alive and that's all that matters. Now we have to get the voids out of here. "I don't have any zoological advice. What would you normally do?"

Chaudhary gives me a curt nod. "Alright team. Let's tie 'em up and leave 'em for Colonel Sedeghat's legal crew. Make it quick – we need to be ready to move the second Otis gets online."

I watch for a while as her team makes quick work. It's almost like they've been trained for this. It's only minutes before we return as a group to the medical center's entry room. Fred is snuffling Michael's hair, and his normally slicked back bangs flop over his forehead. Far from being annoyed by it, Michael is smiling. Those bang-me dimples are out, and he shoots me a million-joule glance as we walk in the room.

The medical team that had been lounging in this area when we first arrived have long since dispersed from this space, and we quickly debate if we should leave half our party here with Fred. Ideally, we'd like to keep Fred and us civilians far out of harm's way when Chaudhary and her team mount the Truyoza offensive. Whenever Otis is ready, that is.

Lucy is conferencing with Chaudhary and Michael regarding the map and *Nyeeb-Yesnee Valoon's* safety features when all of a sudden, Gisella, who's still fiddling with her quanta-com, cries out.

"We got an update! It's not going to be two hours," Gisella says, looking up. "Oh, shoot. Chaudhary!" she calls from the other side of the room.

Then, the lights go out.

chapter thirty-seven

Chaudhary runs to the door and slaps the manual override toggle several times. The door remains shut. It's not just the lights that are out. The power's out, too.

"Fuck!" she exclaims, and her sentiment is echoed by distant cries and shouts throughout the station.

"Are we locked in here?" I ask, anxiety mounting. Otis was supposed to do this to Truyoza, not to us.

"Nobody panic," Gisella says. "We're in a medical facility, there must be a backup generator. I'm sure we'll have basic functions restored any moment."

We stand around waiting in the dim light. The gear that Chaudhary's team wears has convenient lowlight gens and reflectors on their uniforms, so it's light enough to make out Fred chewing on Gisella's hair as she taps through her quanta-com screens but not enough to see the expressions on anyone's faces.

Pete clicks on his quanta-com light and begins to tinker with the manual switch by the door. "I'll see if I can dismantle it," he says. I'm not holding my breath.

"I can't communicate with the station's sub-net," Gisella says. "And I can't communicate with Otis, since I have no idea of his location. I have no idea how to tell him to give us power."

"How was this mission supposed to go, in your mind?"

Chaudhary asks. "You told me your equipment was capable of handling it. What was your plan?"

Gisella frowns down at her quanta-com.

"Our plan," Michael says, "was to not get captured."

"We were supposed to remain on board the *Doomberg*," Rosemary adds.

"Let me get this straight," Chaudhary says. "Not only do we have no way to contact Otis, but we have no way to apprehend Turyoza? At this very moment, he could be getting on an escape vessel and getting the voids out of here!"

I hear a faint but persistent whistling sound in the background. "Hey guys," I say, but no one pays any attention to me. "What's tha-"

Just then, the smooth voice of *Nyeeb-Yesnee Valoon* comes in over the loudspeakers to make a solitary announcement. "Hull breach in docking bay, floor three-hundred nine. Sealing off all safety doors in twenty seconds. Please evacuate that floor."

"That crazy sonufa…" Chaudhary says.

"Otis must have manufactured that hull breach and shut down," Michael says, turning to Gisella. "Maybe he'll open subnet long enough to communicate with him?"

Gisella shakes her head. "I'm trying, Captain." She stomps her foot and lets out a huff. "Nothing about this is normal! You don't understand." She glances up from her quanta-com for a split second to look at Michael. "This is not how a ship runs, or an intelligent mind. Whatever Otis is doing, he's managing it all, and he's using super fine control. I can't get in. Anywhere!"

"At least he solved the issue of Truyoza escaping," Rosemary says.

Everyone pauses their conversation. "How do you mean, Rosemary?" Michael asks.

"Floor three-hundred nine. That was the docking level. Remember how *Nyeeb-Yesnee Valoon* is shaped like the inside of a funnel, or cone? Docking was only allowed at the cone's outermost edge to protect the residents from the radiation fallout from ships' atomizer engines. If Otis shut down the dock level, everyone on the station is trapped here."

Chaudhary takes a deep breath. "That's good news," she says. "Okay, here's what I'm going to do. I'm putting in a call for backup right now. Considering our people had to stay way out of sight from Turyoza's station, it'll take some time for them to arrive."

Michael clears his throat. "Does that mean you think their defenses will be –"

"Vacuum detected on floor three-hundred eight," the smooth voice of *Nyeeb-Yesnee Valoon* interrupts, its voice echoing down the hallways of the station. "Sealing off all safety doors in twenty seconds. Please evacuate that floor."

"Shit. Shit!" Chuadhary repeats. "He's not stopping! Did you program this? Did you tell Otis to do this?" she asks Gisella.

"No!" she exclaims. "This was his own initiative. I had no part in this."

"It sounds like he's going in order," Rosemary says. "Creating a vacuum from the outermost level and moving inwards."

"Which makes sense from a tactical perspective," Michael adds. "He's forcing everyone to move deeper and deeper into the station."

"Do we have any idea where BossMan Truyoza is?" I ask. "Do we have to sit around till he clears all three hundred floors? Because I kind of have to pee."

"Hold it," Rosemary says.

"The station map previously indicated that Truyoza inhabited floors one-fifty through one-sixty," Lucy answers, "though his main base of operation was on one-fifty-six."

"Plenty of time to pee," I say.

"Vacuum detected on floor three-hundred seven," *Nyeeb-Yesnee Valoon* says politely. The whistling sound grows louder. "Sealing off all safety doors in twenty seconds. Please evacuate that floor."

"Not that much time, actually," Lucy says. We all turn to her.

"This medical facility is on floor three hundred one," she explains. "At the current rate, we have about five minutes."

A round of curse words explodes from all of us. Chaudhary starts firing at the door with her guns, and her entire team follows suit. She holds up a closed fist at some point, and like a switch, they all stop on cue. She approaches the door, and by the low-light from her suit gens, we can all see what she sees.

The door remains undented.

"Fuck fuck fuck fuck," I say. "Fuckity fuck."

"Let's not panic," Michael says.

"I am going to die with you, Fred. *Fuck*." I lean against my umemeh. "At least that fucker Truyoza will die too."

"There's got to be another way out of here," Chaudhary says. She rounds on Lucy. "You downloaded those maps, right? Talk to us. Where's the back door? Or the emergency exit?"

"Both exist. Both are operated by the main electrical grid or the backup gens only. Oh," Lucy adds in surprise. "All the doors of the facility are made from blast doors. There's a footnote here. Apparently, the medical facility has been under attack before."

"These sick, sick fucks," I say. "This is not their first umemeh, is it?" My mind flashes back to the personnel in Fred's operating room. They'd been so calm, as if slicing off an umemeh's head was routine. I clench my fist. I hope these fuckers die in the vacuum.

"The robot chutes, then," Chaudhary says.

"Will not be sealed off yet, for this floor," Lucy replies in the affirmative.

Chaudhary nods.

"But Fred can't fit through there!" I exclaim.

Chaudhary shakes her head. "I'm sorry, but I can't sacrifice the human lives of my team for an animal. If there's only one way out, anyone who's physically able needs to take it."

I ground my jaw, but Michael puts a hand on my shoulder. "She's right."

I stare at his dark outline in surprise. "What? You want to

leave Fred here to die alone? We just gave him an epinephrine shot! He'll be fully conscious and fully panicked! That's cruel!"

"I need you to live," he says quietly.

I wrench my shoulder away from him, tears stinging my eyes. "It's cruel," I whisper.

"There might be another way," Lucy says slowly. She pulls off her pink beanie and extracts her wire connection. "If I hardwire in, I can find Otis."

"Because he's *also* hardwired in! Brilliant!" Gisella exclaims.

"Wait," Michael says. "We allowed Otis to hardwire into *Nyeeb-Yesnee Valoon's* system because he had the ability to override. Lucy," he puts his hands on her shoulders. He's interrupted by an announcement.

"Vacuum detected on floor three-hundred six," comes the polite station voice. "Sealing off all safety doors in twenty seconds. Please evacuate the floor."

"Shit," curses Chaudhary under her breath. "We need to get moving, people! Make a decision, one way or the other!"

"Lucy," Michael repeats. "Are you sure this is safe for you?" A hybe's hardport is for safe-encounters only; it's not something you violate with a huge public domain. The risk is too high. With the way the hardware has been integrated into a hybe's brain, one corrupted encounter could literally kill her.

Lucy blinks a few times. "If *Nyeeb-Yesnee Valoon's* AI is fully shut down, I will be fine."

"If?" I ask.

A quiet fills the space, and the howling of air being sucked into a vacuum is almost deafening.

"Something is directing those announcements," Lucy explains. "It's unclear whether it's Otis, or if he's allowed a vestige of *Nyeeb-Yesnee Valoon* to remain in operation."

"What happens if *Nyeeb-Yesnee Valoon's* AI is still conscious?" Chaudhary asks. "What is the potential casualty here?"

Lucy is quiet a beat before responding. "If *Nyeeb-Yesnee Valoon* retains some small amount of consciousness, and if *Nyeeb-Yesnee*

Valoon deems me a threat, it would have the power to fry my hard drive," she says quietly.

"Shitfaced fucking sin," I exclaim. "Don't do that."

"What are our alternatives?" Michael asks. "We climb the robotic chute, deeper and deeper into the station? Until when?" He glances around our group. "Even without the umemeh, we climbed slower than snails."

"Sloth," I say under my breath, unheeded.

"Even if we manage to outcrawl the vacuum, we won't capture Truyoza."

"And also, I'm not going," I say, finally having decided. I can't imagine leaving Fred to die in panic like this. "Maybe there's a special pressure seal system for the medical facility?" I say with a shrug when the others protest.

Lucy strides over to the reception desk and begins to root around. We all follow her.

"Are you sure this is a risk you want to take?" Gisella asks quietly. I'm standing right next to her, which is the only reason I can see Lucy give a small nod in the dim light.

"I wouldn't like myself if I didn't try," she replies.

"Vacuum detected on floor three-hundred five," *Nyeeb-Yesnee Valoon* announces. "Sealing off all safety doors in twenty seconds. Please evacuate."

Through the closed door, we can now hear the stampede of feet and shouts. Everyone on the station has gotten the idea. They're all retreating higher into the station.

Pete bangs on the door. "Someone! Anyone! Can you hear us? Let us out!" he hollers. I roll my eyes. The people on the outside won't be able to open the door any more than we were. The person who needs to hear us is Otis, and banging on the door is not the way to get his attention. His hearing range is more along the lines of quanta-com communications.

"Lucy! Wait!" I shout. "There's another way!" Twenty-five dark silhouettes turn to me. "We all need to comm each other. In this room. Right now!"

"Brilliant," Gisella says, and begins dialing.

"Whaaat?" Chaudhary asks, her confusion apparent.

Michael is already dialing up Rosemary, and Pete is also busy dialing.

"Otis monitors communications. Constantly. To the point that station chatter gets on his nerves because it's overwhelming," I explain. "A bunch of us, comming each other, in the same room? We'll light up like a neon flashing sign!" I add, hurriedly. "Stop talking, start comming. Don't talk. Hang up. Dial again. Anyone in this room!"

Within moments, we are all dialing each other's quanta-coms and hanging up once a connection is established. We're a bunch of frantic, dialing idiots.

"Well, toodly doodly do, there," says a familiarly annoying voice over loudspeaker. I nearly fall on the floor with relief. I don't even have the shit left in me to make a snarky comment about the annoying personality glitch that Gisella clearly had not been able to repair.

"I've been searching for you kiddos, yes I have! You sneakary-poos have been crawling about, I see!"

"Otis!" Gisella exclaims. "Thank the stars." She clears her throat. "Status report."

"I've trapped Truyoza on floor two-hundred-ninety-five. I've been creating vacuums floor by floor to make sure he knows we've got the upper hand."

"I think he got the point!" Michael explodes. "How many lives were lost to the vacuum so far?"

"Indeterminate." Otis replies. "You know, I had to shut down *Nyeeb-Yesnee Valoon's* AI, which was no small task, thank you very much, and even though I have some special privileges I wasn't configured to run the logistics and statistics of an entire – "

"Stop! Stop, stop." Michael interrupts. In the dark, I can make out his shadowy form enough to see him put a hand on his fore-head. "Otis," he says at last. "Can you lead us out of here? Open up door by door on our route, till we get to Truyoza?"

"Yep! I most certainly can do-doodly do!" Otis replies.

The door to the medical facility slides open.

"Uh. Any chance you could give us some light?" Pete asks.

"Sure can do, Petey-poo!" Otis exclaims. "Just follow my lighted hallways and I'll lead you right on over to the bad guy party."

"Vacuum detected on floor three-hundred four," says the polite voice of *Nyeeb-Yesnee Valoon* station. "Sealing off all safety doors in twenty seconds. Please evacuate."

"And cut that out, Otis!" Michael says. "You've made your point."

A throng of station dwellers push past us, nearly knocking us over to evacuate for the next level. I physically stand in the way to protect Fred, making sure he doesn't get jostled.

"Now, if you'll just follow my lighted path," Otis says.

———

OTIS PUTS AN ELEVATOR BACK INTO USE ESPECIALLY FOR US, BUT WHEN we get to Truyoza's floor, we're met with live fire. Chaudhary and her team jump into action – they're no fucking joke. We keep Fred safe within the elevator as Chaudhary and her team of twenty agents break into two well-coordinated teams, each with a couple shield bearers, and more than a couple firing leaders. They move in smooth, coordinated motions, and together they look so graceful it's almost a dance. I keep my hand on Fred's nearest neck, speaking to him in a soothing voice as he keeps trying to back up through the rear wall of the elevator.

"It's okay, Fred," I say, cooing. "We're going to be safe. It's oooo-kay."

"Is there anything we can do to help with Fred?" Rosemary asks.

I shake my head. "Just make sure he gets out of this alive."

"Amen to that." Pete snorts.

"All clear!" Chaudhary calls, and quiet reigns in the hallway.

We gingerly step out of the elevator into a smokey smelling room. Fred's nostrils get big, and he starts pawing the ground.

"Welcome, my culinary-loving friends, to floor two-hundred-ninety-five," comes Otis's cheerful voice over the loudspeakers. "I see you've met your welcoming party. Mr. Truyoza will be through the door there, on the right."

"Any other welcoming parties you know about?" Chaudhary growls. "Advance information is helpful."

"You most certainly, toodly-doodly *can* have more information! *Nyeeb-Yesnee Valoon* notes that this door leads to an antechamber before Truyoza's den. In that antechamber, there are five armed men with elevated adrenaline and heart rates, one of which has just passed gas with more particulate matter than usual, likely indicates a bacterial overgrowth in the small intestines, for which he will need a dose of – "

"Otis!" Gisella and Chaudhary yell in tandem. They both look at each other sheepishly.

"Yes?"

Gisella clears her throat. "That's enough for now. Thank you," she says with regained calm.

Chaudhary and her team assemble by the next door before giving Otis the ready signal, and the door slides open. The *Waterloo* crew keeps the fuck out of the way as Chaudhary and her team face the next round of attackers.

"It's okay, Fred," I repeat to the panicked animal. "It's going to be okay."

Chaudhary's team clears these five men in no time. "All clear," she calls. We hesitantly peek into the antechamber.

"Do you want to be here for the arrest?" she asks. "Or would you rather stay out of it?"

"Oh, I want to see that fucker go down," I reply. "Wouldn't miss it for all the stars in the galaxy."

The others feel the same, and together, we all crowd into Truyoza's antechamber. Otis pipes Chaudhary's voice through to Truyoza's room, and within moments Chaudhary is explaining that

Otis has the power to have them all suffocated. Truyoza, not being an idiot, agrees to get his men to lay down their weapons.

Fred, beasts be thanked, listens to it all contentedly as he munches away at my hair. Apparently, while bullets scare the crap outta him, he has no problem with yelling.

When the door slides open, we find Truyoza sitting on a stuffed leather armchair in his opulent mahogany and green office. Two of his mob men stand on either side of him, hands up in surrender.

Truyoza looks up from his cigar. "You," he says, as his eyes find me in the lit hallway. "Carrot Top."

A shiver runs down my spine when he recognizes me, and I can't look away. This is a man who intended to have me tortured, a man who would barely blink if I lay bleeding out at his feet. He's a predator of the deadliest kind and I am smack in his crosshairs.

"It turns out you are rat. And you are bad animal trafficker," he says. "And a terrible zookeeper. Do you always kill animals you take care of? What are you good for, eh?" Smoke curls around his face, even as Chaudhary's operatives grab Truyoza's hands to put them in cuffs. He remains calm and collected, as if it was a manicurist's rough handling.

My heart plummets to my toes. I can't help it. He's right. I did a terrible job at keeping Fred safe. And on Hialeah –

My thoughts are interrupted by a throat clearing behind me. Startled, I glance back to find an indignant group of friends. Michael is shaking his head. Rosemary's got her eyebrows up high in pure disbelief. Gisella has her arms on her hips, and Pete is scowling. Even Lucy has folded her arms across her chest. Something unfurls inside me, like a flag whipping free in the wind.

"You make big mistake of crossing me," Truyoza continues, and my eyes snap back to his. "You vill pay. And it will hurt."

But with those words, he's released me. All this time, it's been about the money. Pay him back or there's a threat of death. He's been yanking me around by this chain for so long that it's finally snapped. There's only so many times you can be threatened and almost killed before it starts to lose its meaning.

I straighten my spine and stare him square in the eye. "I survived Hialeah. You don't scare me." The agents pull Troyoza to his feet, and I realize, it's over. I take a deep breath and let it out. A message floats up in the corner of my retinal vision – Rosemary's sent me a picture of Burt, adorably curled up and hugging one of Dimitry's fingers.

"Oh, and one more thing," I add to Truyoza as he's being led away. "You're wrong."

The agents pause, and Truyoza turns to face me.

"I am excellent at caring for animals. It's you who's the killer."

He raises his eyebrows, but maintains his silence as he's escorted off. Chaudhary coordinates the creation of a new, makeshift docking bay on one of the still oxygenated levels, and arranges for a shuttle to transport Truyoza to one of the military ships that now await in near-station space. The military has arrived in a force that is twenty carriers strong. From what I learn later, after that charming moment, Truyoza continued his silence through Chaudhary's entire interrogation and the whole journey to Aurelius, the penal planet in that quadrant for major crimes.

"I've organized a shuttle for us to the *Lamorak*," Chaudhary announces once Truyoza and his top men have been evacuated.

"But the *Euryale*!" Gisella exclaims. "We can't leave her here, stuck in the *Doomberg*!"

Chaudhary considers this for a moment. There are five levels in between us and the *Euryale* that are not only deprived of oxygen but pressure as well. To wait for these levels to be travel-worthy would take hours, if not multiple day-cycles.

"See if we can get in touch with the ship-mind," she says. "Find out if she managed to keep the *Doomberg* oxygenated and pressurized. We can take a shuttle over as soon as it's ready."

I clear my throat. "Does that mean there's time for a pit stop?"

A room-full of eyes turn to me. "I need a refill on cabbage," I say, gesturing at Fred. "I don't think I have enough hair left to survive the journey back!"

Smiles break out around the room, and I'm surrounded by a chorus of agreements. Of course everyone is happy for me to get Fred some cabbage, but if I told them I needed to stop for the pee that is threatening to explode my bladder, there'd be some new excuse or reason they need me to stay. There's certainly no harm in killing two birds with one stone.

I make sure one of Fred's necks is tucked securely beneath Gisella's arm. As long as he stays put, he shouldn't cause any trouble. I get quick directions from Lucy, but before I'm able to head out, Michael approaches me.

"Savage! I'd like to escort you," Michael says, gallantly holding out his arm.

I give his arm a skeptical glance. "What's that for?" I ask. "You holding an invisible parrot?"

He purses his mouth, and I can tell he's trying to hold back a smile. "Yes, zoologist. But I think something's wrong with it. Can you give us a cure?"

I roll my eyes. "The only thing wrong is your brain, and that's Doc Williams' department." I give him a look over and a smile escapes. "Come on, Hotpants. You're with me."

Michael beams, and Rosemary mutters from her corner, "Stupid Virus."

Pete, who's standing near her, says, "Oh, is that what you meant? I think I get it now." He gives Michael and me a two thumbs up. "You kids have fun."

I grin.

chapter thirty-eight

I make Michael wait in the hallway, now teaming with bustling military agents, when I take my urgently needed potty-pitstop. He doesn't seem to mind the wait.

I stare in the mirror over the hand-sani station. It seems like it's been years since I was at that taco-stand bathroom in the *Hobo's Towel*, when in reality it's only been two day-cycles. I pat my hair down and take a full five minutes to untie my former do, with all the stray flyaways, and re-braid the whole mess into a neat row down my back. I know he's waiting out there, but a girl's gotta look good.

Plus, he was the one who volunteered his imaginary parrot for this.

I find Michael right where I left him in the hallway, only now he looks like a holo commercial by the way he's lounging against the wall.

"Alright, Hotpants, you stay there any longer and people will think you're an ad," I say.

"Come push my buttons," he replies, raising his eyebrows at me.

"Careful now or this hallway will see a new kind of action. Also," I say after a moment's consideration, "I'll have to rename you Sassypants."

Michael glances back at his own butt. "I kind of liked Hotpants, though."

Joking like this, we reach the *Nyeeb-Yesnee Valoon's* greenhouse, which is as polar opposite from the *Waterloo's* as you can get in space. Where the *Waterloo's* garden was small, cozy, and magical, the *Nyeeb-Yesnee Valoon's* greenhouse is the size of a city block, industrial, and carefully catalogued. Also, it is not plagued by bats – neither the sick nor the healthy variety.

I follow the chart at the greenhouse's entrance and meander my way through the rows, with Reyes trailing close behind. I'm hoping we get to some dark corner, some patch where I'm forced to bump up against him and we finally go at it. But at the moment, he's frustratingly one aisle over, and a squat row of tomatoes fills the air between us with a tangy scent.

I stop short, and Michael stops opposite me. I reach down and flirtatiously caress a large football of a tomato. I haven't seen a live tomato since growing up on Minerva, and the smell transports me back about twenty years. I lean forward, so close to Michael that I could reach out and touch him through the vines. He leans in too, and my heart kicks up a notch.

"Savvy," Michael says, watching as I run my fingers along a tomato's warm, fuzz-covered surface. "We're really going to miss you."

That's enough to make my heart go cold. I pull back from the tomatoes.

"I know," Michael hurries on. "It'll be safest for you on Brin-177. What with Truyoza on trial. He still has an entire organization, and they'll want to do everything in their power to eliminate your testimony. Between Brin-177's military and their animals, it's the best possible place for you."

Except Michael won't be there, or the rest of the *Waterloo's* crew. I open my mouth, then shut it. "I—" I try again. "I guess…. I didn't give enough thought to what came next."

"We're gonna miss you, cabbage-head," he says, reaching over to mess my newly coiffed hair. I duck out of his reach and dive deeper into the greenhouse. I find that I have to blink away a tear.

"Hey! Where are you going?" Michael calls after me, but I push onwards, trying to distance myself from his words. I knew I never really had a place on the *Waterloo*. It's just that, well, these people have become my friends. The first friends I'd made in eight years. And now, they'll be off delivering shitters and I'll be left behind on a planet full of animals. It's something that should delight me, and instead, I'm overwhelmingly saddened by it.

Michael catches up with me after I pass through the clear plastic flaps that mark the entry to the rainforest section, but I march on past cacao trees as he calls after me again. Finally, Michael grabs my arm and pulls me to a stop. "Saffron," he says. "Stop running."

I turn to face him.

"It's not goodbye," Michael says. "Not yet, anyway. We've got time."

I raise one eyebrow in challenge, not trusting my voice to keep steady if I tried to speak.

"We're going to rendezvous on the *Lamorak*, where the *Waterloo's* docked. We still have some time together. We can all say proper goodbyes before we each head our own directions."

I rub my leaky nose with the back of my hand. "I don't want…" There is so much about this I don't want. I don't want to leave the *Waterloo*. I don't want to leave *him*. I don't want this to end.

Michael crushes me to his chest. I give myself permission to let the tears flow, just this one time. The smell of his body infiltrates my senses, through each sniffle. Did I mention he has a rock-hard chest? It's a little distracting. I wipe off my snot and tears and stare up into his big brown eyes.

Michael leans down, and I reach up on my tiptoes till our noses are bumping and our lips are only millimeters apart. His lips brush against mine at first, soft and feathery, before we come together for a slow, tender kiss. It unfurls an explosion of heat in my abdomen, and I pull my arms tighter around his neck. The kiss gets deeper, needier. Michael's hands run down my hips and hold me close against him with a tight grip.

"Sarge? Hey, Sarge!" comes Rosemary's voice through the quanta-com's walkie-talkie. "We're all waiting for you two on the *Doomberg*. What are you guys doing?"

I groan, even with our lips locked. Michael pulls away from me slowly. He finally clicks on his quanta-com. "Yeah. We'll be right there." He gives me a mischievous glance. "Savvy had to do her hair."

I spy a clod of dirt and throw it at him before I trudge off in search of cabbage. I still hate the prospect of saying goodbye, but at least we'll be together for a little while longer.

———

The return flight to the *Lamorak* is marked only by the notable absence of Gisella and Special Agent Chaudhary, but otherwise, the bridge is full of Fred and old friendships and it hurts and I don't want these moments to end.

"How do you think Dimitry is managing on the *Waterloo* without us?" Pete asks into the silent stretches.

"He's probably working on those edibles, what with being left with Juliet and Doc Williams," I retort with a snort. Michael cuts me a sharp look. "I mean, I'm sure he's enjoying the company of Burt and Prisha Shanti and has begun letting them cuddle him to sleep."

Pete stretches back in his chair. "Old Marc, Dimitry, Boris and Guppy, they all were happy to have the docking time with the *Lamorak*. But if you ask me, they were the ones missing out."

There are nods and grunts of agreement all around.

"I hope Bremerton's doing okay," I say mostly to myself.

"I sincerely hope that as well," the *Euryale* adds.

"Oh, toodly-doodly-do, there you are," Otis says as he rolls onto the bridge. "Gisella told me to go find you all. Said she was busy. Something to do with fixing Chaudhary's engines."

"TMI, Otis," Michael says.

"Otis, that was a metaphor," Rosemary adds. "In the future, don't repeat it. That's one of those private things you don't share."

"Well then, partner, I will most certainly add that to my compendium of human behavior that's impossible to scrutinize. It sure is difficult being this friendly with you all!"

"So Gisella wasn't able to work on that personality glitch?" I ask Rosemary in a low voice.

Rosemary shakes her head. "Whenever she lowers the metrics for that, it's the strangest thing. He still has the recipes loaded up, but for some reason, removing that overdose of friendliness makes him want to stop cooking as well. The two were linked even before that bathroom fiasco on the Hobo's Towel, but it's even worse now."

I grimace. That sucks bigtime. "Uh. Does anyone else know how to cook?"

Rosemary shakes her head and throws up her hands.

"I can cook!" Pete says, overhearing our conversation.

"Only if you like to eat tasteless green goo," Rosemary retorts.

"And I too, Miss Savage, know how to cook exceedingly well!" Otis chimes in. "Are you aware that I now have over eighteen thousand, three hundred four recipes stored in my data banks? I can make anything from any bit of available space rations. And, of course, the more naturally grown ingredients that can be used, the better. There's an infinite amount of combinations possible. And I have a nuanced understanding of which are palatable to the human taste and which are not. Pete, however, is not blessed with this special knowledge."

"Hey, Otis, bless this," Pete says, making an obscene gesture at him.

"Sir Pete, that was most uncalled for. I have said nothing that is untrue. Would you or would you not categorize your efforts in cooking as an exercise in trial and error?"

"No, I fucking would –"

"Don't argue with an AI," Michael interrupts from Lucy's side. "Ask Rosie."

Rosemary ducks her head. "Never argue with an AI," she echoes. "Not worth it."

Pete makes a sound that approximates gurgling salt water.

"Entering *Lamorak* space, Captain," Lucy says. "Shall I initiate black space coupling protocols?"

"Take her in, Luce," he replies with a smack to the back of her chair. He lets out a whoop. "We made it!"

chapter thirty-nine

I pour myself another drink while I try to tune out the jovial carousing around me in the main cafeteria aboard the *Lamorak.* I know I should be happy. I survived this whole shit-hole ordeal. Truyoza didn't kill me or the umemeh. Truyoza's in military custody, and the evidence against him is solid. On top of that, I'm not going to jail.

But I still feel like crap.

I'm being exiled to Brin-177.

I know, on a technical level, that it's not exile, and that it's the safest place for me. Plus, I've been trained in xeno-zoology. This is exactly the kind of opportunity I'd hoped to get straight out of school. But the more I hear the happy voices around me, the more it hits home that I'll probably never see them again.

"So, Savvy," says Rosemary, approaching me with a full glass. "You managed not to be such a sucky human after all!"

I snort. "Was that supposed to be a compliment?"

But Rosie had spoken loudly enough to catch the attention of some of the others milling about.

"She was a bit shoddy there, for a time," Lieutenant Crenshaw Bremerton says. He's in a hoverchair holding a cup of tea, accompanied by Doc Williams. When I fix my eyes on his, though, he's got that mischievous smile. "But I'd say she turned around quite nicely, wouldn't you?"

Gisella raises her glass. "To Saffron Savage," she says.

"The worst animal smuggler in the galaxy!" Michael concludes to a room full of cheers.

Everywhere I look I find faces that make my chest constrict. Pete, grinning his big ol' gap tooth grin, standing with a happy Dimitry, Guppy, Boris and Marc. And there's Gisella with Chaudhary, beaming at me. There's Lucy and Juliet – even Juliet – is smiling my way. There's Michael Reyes, laughing with Colonel Sedeghat, and looking at me like I'm the prize umemeh.

How is it possible to feel this intensely sad and happy at the same time? "I'm going to miss you guys," I say, lifting my glass in acknowledgement and then knocking it back in one smooth motion.

Michael comes by on refill duty.

"So," I ask trying to sound as normal as I can. I'm not going to start crying; *you're* going to start crying. "Where are you guys headed off to next?"

Rosemary glanced at Michael, then answers for him. "We've got a delivery waiting for us out at Latoya's Delicatessen and Corner Port." Then she shrugs. "Business as usual. Boring."

"Boring?" I ask, glancing rapidly between the two. "You guys get to travel all around the galaxy!"

"But you get to work with animals," Rosemary replies. Michael still hasn't spoken up. "And be on solid land. In the open air! With trees, hull-breach it. It must be wonderful!"

I inhale. It's true. Being outdoors on Hialeah was something that I've missed while being space-bound. Not *that* much, though.

Michael puts a hand on my shoulder. "I'm going to miss you messing everything up for us," he says.

"Oh no," Rosemary says theatrically, throwing her hands up in the air. "Not that Stupid Virus again. I'm outta here," she says as she heads over to young Gunther. I watch her pour him a drink.

Michael pulls up a chair by my side.

"Fuck it," I say after a moment's silence. "I'm going to miss you too, you righteous pain in the ass."

He smiles down at his drink, but otherwise doesn't respond.

Fuck, it's really happening. This is goodbye.

Michael sits staring at his glass for a while, then downs it. He frowns. "Brin-177 is the safest place for you, for the next while."

"Yeah." I swallow a painful lump. I'm not stupid. I know I gotta keep out of reach of Truyoza's mob while the trial is running. It doesn't make me less of an emotional wreck. That's all. "Are, uh, you guys taking me to Brin-177?"

"Not personally. Colonel Sedeghat has already contacted Surf & Ceebu. The Brin-177 transport will make a special trip to the *Lamorak* to pick you up. You'll get the VIP treatment. Personal escort by a private armed force." He knocks back his drink and finally turns to look at me. "Savvy. You going to be okay out there? Out on Brin-177?"

It's the first time anyone's asked. I want to give him an honest answer, but I shrug instead. What does it matter? We're going our separate ways.

"Nothing can be worse than Hialeah," I respond. "I'm trained to care for animals. They've got animals there. Should work out."

Michael tucks a curl behind my ear. "I meant about the militaristic aspect." He raises an eyebrow at the glass of moonshine I'm currently holding in my hand. "You never seemed much like the militaristic-type."

"Right." I blink. I hadn't thought of that. "I'll be okay. It can't be worse than Hialeah," I say, voice firm. Because that's the truth. Nothing could be worse.

"Well. I guess that's something." Michael nods, then stands up to go. "I've still got to say a proper goodbye to Colonel Sedeghat and his crew. Oh man, and did you know Crenshaw Bremerton is leaving us, too? He claims he's healthy enough to be on his way." He runs a hand through dangling strands of hair, shoving it back into the coif again. "The *Euryale* has been fully repaired, by the way. She's happy to be home again. Crenshaw, I think, is itching to be with her. That leaves us with our usual *Waterloo* crew." He shakes his head. "I'm going to miss everyone."

I feel a pang of jealousy that he said *everyone*, and not just me.

"You can always, um," I wet my lips, "come say a more personal goodbye to me later?"

Michael only nods curtly, his attention drawn by something Colonel Sedeghat has said nearby. "Later," he echoes as he drifts off towards more loud chatter.

I head over to Fred, who's happily munching a mountain of cabbage on a table in the corner of the room. "It's just you and me, Freddypoo." I blink back the building tears. "Until you join your herd, obviously."

I hold on to the hope that Michael will show up later to say goodbye. Long after the party is over, I sit awake in my room, waiting for a soft knock.

It never comes.

The morning of the next day-cycle, I find the *Waterloo* has already departed.

Worse yet, the armored shuttle transport has arrived at the *Lamorak*. It's time for Fred to go home.

chapter forty

"Name and authorization code?" we get asked for the fifth time.

Even in an official vehicle, approach of Brin-177 is far more ridiculous than anything I would have imagined. I knew they had a military presence, but shit. They have hundreds of millions of weaponized drones hovering in space outside the planet. The drones have been arranged into a series of concentric spheres so enormous they encase the entire fucking planet. And gaining passage through each void-forsaken sphere is an ordeal in verification, followed by a boarding party that sweeps for weapons and explosives, and a quick body scan. Every freaking time.

I want to shout, *Here's a fucking umemeh, you assholes, is this verification enough for you?* But the Surf & Ceebu escort bears it like a champ, reintroducing themselves to each successive knucklehead. The truth is, I can't complain for comfort. The transporter is long and cylindrical with plush leatherette seating that can be pulled out into rows. Currently, the seats have all been folded away to allow Fred to roam back and forth. He's woozily walking from guard-post to guard-post, investigating the backs of the heavily armored guards' helmets as they scowl and continue to stare out their weapons port. In the face of such charming company, I've stationed myself up front near the pilot and Gunther, who's come along with us as an escort. Now that he's off the *Lamorak*, he actually cracks a smile from time to time.

"How much does this impotency drug fucking cost?" I wonder for the first time. I mean, I knew it was expensive, but not *this* expensive.

The captain shrugs. "No idea."

Gunther looks it up on his quanta-com while we're waiting for the next set of sphere locks to open for us.

"Let's see. It looks like…" he says, squinting. "Wow. One pill on the black webs sells for five thousand joulos. Whoa. Hold on." Gunther clicks away some more. "Okay. Taking just one umemeh-pill is not only a lifelong cure erectile disfunction, but it also improves libido. According to this, it basically turns a man into a love-making champion for life. Oh! Listen to this – the neck arteries from a single dead umemeh can manufacture two hundred of these pills."

"Hoooooly shit," I mutter as I do the quick mental math. I glance over to Fred, whom I've recently brought into the cockpit with me for this stupid verification crap. "You're the cutest million-joulos I've ever met." I nuzzle Fred's left face. A million joulos is enough to politely ignore his terrible breath.

Gunther bangs his armrest. "Breaches! It's started already," he says.

"What?" I ask, glancing about in alarm. Are we being chased by pirates? Is Truyoza here?

"Targeted ads. Do I want a penis enlargement? No, I absolutely do *not*," he says with emphasis. "My penis is beautiful the way it is."

I can't help but snort at that.

"It is!" Gunther exclaims. "And now I'm going to suffer through a month of penis ads. You'd think deleting your browsing history on these things would make a difference." He quickly flicks his fingers across his quanta-com keyboard. "If they keep sending me these ads…"

"You'll have the most beautiful penis in the whole universe," I conclude for him. "Now you need to find someone to appreciate it!"

Gunther bounces to his feet. "I never thought this would be my life after joining the galactic military. I don't mind going on short escort missions better suited to the local police. But those ads!"

I wince. "Sorry about that." His words remind me of the black space coupling with the *Lamorak*. It didn't seem so bad. Sedeghat had said goodbye. He'd even given me a hug. Was that such a hard thing to do? Not the hug, smartass. The goodbye part.

Sergeant Michael Fucking Reyes, on the other hand, is a man who doesn't say goodbye to women who've saved his life. A woman he's actually kissed once, and if you count the times he almost kissed me, twice.

A lull builds into our conversation, and then the pilot is back in action as he maneuvers the ship through the newest sphere opening.

Waiting for the last and final sphere lock to open, Gunther turns to me.

"How long will you be staying down here on Brin-177?"

I consider it, then shrug. Sedeghat's arranged everything with the planet authorities earlier; they'll let me stay and give me amnesty for as long as the Truyoza case is pending. I'm hoping they'll give me a job there, too, so I can finally pay down those scary-sized school loans. Now that I know how much an umemeh costs, I strongly suspect they pay higher wages than Hialeah. Anyway, it's not like I have any other options. "Indefinitely."

Gunther nods. "I hear it's a nice place. Could be worse, eh?"

I manage to nod in response.

———

LONG AFTER GUNTHER AND THE SHUTTLE DISAPPEAR BACK THROUGH the clouds, I continue to glance to the skies. My hand hasn't left

Fred's side since the moment we've landed, as if he's some sort of security blanket. The truth of the matter is that I'm not sure how these guys will treat me once they release Fred into the wilds.

The two of us are standing in the middle of the open space port. Unlike the one on Hialeah, the vehicles parked on this field are fancy pieces of artwork. A team of people have come to meet us, and we are all standing huddled around Fred in the overcast and windy weather. I keep searching the sky, hoping to catch sight of a ship I know won't be there.

The veterinarian finishes giving Fred a cursory exam. She snaps her fingers and brings me out of my reverie.

"Two broken ribs," she concludes, "and a sprained neck." She glares at me through her maroon-rimmed glasses disapprovingly.

"I filed that in my report!" I say, agitated. Maybe I'm annoyed that she's insinuating that this is all somehow my fault. And maybe it sort of was, but now I feel the need to defend myself. "It was the pirates. Bunch of assholes."

"Mmm," she says, clicking away on her tablet, unimpressed. "I've placed a medi-scan order for umemeh 5B-7186. He can come with me now, and you can head over there to human quarantine."

"If you're not sure on a name for him, I've been calling him Fred. It's a little easier to remember."

The vet snorts derisively. "I'm not naming him anything. He's a wild animal, and naming him as though he's a pet would be inappropriate." She extends her stylus to Fred's right ear and lifts it. "The industry standard is to embed a microchip with a numerical designation into each umemeh at birth. There was a processing error with the number this one was assigned, so he's been assigned a new number. 5B-7186"

"Right, of course." I wipe my suddenly leaky nose with the back of my sleeve. I knew about his microchipping. And yes, I knew he was a wild animal. But still, we've traipsed all over the galaxy together, me and Fred. Or rather, me and fucking 5B-7-something-or-another, whatever his numerical designation is.

"Can I..." I glance around the group. "Can I get one last

moment alone with him? We've been through a lot," I say, hoping that this sounds remotely rational. "I just want to say goodbye."

"Well, the umemeh is staying on this planet," says the veterinarian. "I don't believe you are going anywhere either, not with Truyoza's trial still ongoing."

"Yeah, I get it. We all know I can't go anywhere," I reply, starting to get snappy. I'm hangry, I'm cold, and I'm losing the closest thing I have to a friend. Fred finally gets to roam free and live with other animals who are like him. "Just let me say goodbye."

Some other woman grabs the veterinarian by the arm and whispers something to her. The group of them collectively takes a step back, and I feel my shoulders drop in relief. I hadn't even realized how tense I'd become.

I pull about and face Fred, or whatever his number is. His left head is shnuffling along the paved ground, and the other is up high, scouting out the area for potential shrubbery to nibble on.

"Fred." His heads keep at their busy tasks. "Fred," I repeat, trying to get at least one of his heads to pay attention. It's no use. They won't look at me. Something wet and oozy is coming out of my nose, and I sniffle it back. I throw my arms around Fred's good neck and bury my head into the smelly beast's neck-pit. "Goodbye, Fred," I say into his neck. I pull my face out of there. Monkey's tits, the umemeh is really stinky.

"Don't do anything stupid now, you stupid smelly ass," I mutter. I turn to the waiting crowd of zoologists and veterinarians, and that's when I feel a familiar tugging on my scalp. A smile pulls at my lips.

Fred didn't recognize his fucking name. He sure as shit didn't know the word goodbye.

But he knew my hair.

And that, motherfuckers, is what we call a win.

chapter forty-one

I've found the only bar on Brin-177.

This planet is literally four times the size of Hialeah. It's enormous. And they only have one fucking bar. But it doesn't matter. The bar is deserted.

Sure, there are Alex and Jeremy over there in the corner playing a boring-ass game of dice. Neither one of them is remotely tipsy, let alone betting money on it. Then there's Jenny and Tatiana dancing two-step on the dance floor with Hugh and Ji-Lee. Their moves are so tame they'd be permitted at a grade school dance party. Jenny could at least smash her ass up against someone as a dance move. But everyone here is stupid-sober.

Worse than that. They're all ass-licking, goody-goody two shoes. You'd think that after surviving the nightmare of Hialeah, I'd welcome extreme kindness. You certainly wouldn't expect it to irritate the crap out of me. But believe me when I say it's intolerable. There's got to be more to life than the polar extremes of Hialeah and Brin-177.

One night, when I was really fucking loaded, I got really pissed by all this clean shit around me. I stood up on this bar and showed the room my tits. They all politely demurred and looked away.

What in the voids is the use of having tits if no one appreciates them? They're nice tits, too, if you're asking me.

I stare into my glass and wish they had something more potent to drink. Truyoza's trial wrapped up in record time. Not only did he go to prison, his whole organization's also been frozen and is under investigation. Now I'm stuck in a place where the people are too nice and the alcohol tastes like dirty water. In fact, I'm fairly certain that's how they make it here – fermenting literal, plain old water.

"Stupid water," I mumble as a butt thunks into the chair next to mine. I'm turned away, facing my sickeningly oversweet colleagues on the dance floor. I don't have to turn around to know that this is another uninteresting, straight-as-a-pin, righteous person. Brin-177 sucks balls.

"You able to survive on dirty water now?" asks a familiar deep voice.

I squeal and swivel my chair around so fast I get whiplash. Sergeant Michael Fucking Reyes is here in the flesh, sitting next to me. He's wearing a shit-eating grin, and I launch myself at him for a big hug.

"Hey there, Savvy," Michael says nonchalantly once I back up. "Whatchu up to these days?"

I scramble to a better perch on my chair, and eye Michael critically. "A little of this, a little of that," I reply with the customary Brin-177 politeness.

"Mother of hull breaches, they've got you talking like them now?" he asks with a knowing grin, and peers theatrically into his own glass. "What the voids is in this stuff?"

A silence befalls the two of us. The stupid dancers are laughing politely in the background. No one is grabbing anyone else's ass. Everyone is so darn proper here.

"This planet was tailor-made for a guy like you," I mutter.

"Mmm," Michael replies. "And what about for someone like you?"

"Shut up. You already know."

"Well, that makes this next part easier for me," Michael says, a light sparkling in his eyes.

"Next part? Reyes, you asshole. There is no next part. You never even said goodbye." I glance away. Voids, I sound like such a baby. A warm hand lands on my own. I look down, and burning asteroids, I'm blinking back tears.

Michael sighs. "I'm sorry I left you like that, Saffron. Ever since Sam passed away… It's been hard for me to get close to anyone. I was afraid I'd lose you – to this animal sanctuary, or to another asinine choice of yours – and that it would rip another hole in me. I wasn't okay after Sam's passing for a long time. I didn't think I could survive that again." He swallows thickly. "I told myself you would love it here, and that getting closer to you would only make it hurt more. So I flew off. And I found myself regretting that choice immensely."

I stare at Michael. I had known about Sam's death, but not that Michael still battled the hurt it left behind. It turns out we're both broken in our own ways.

"After we departed, I spent a long time moping. Too long, if I'm being honest, instead of trying to make a change. So here's what I've got, if you're still willing to listen." He's gazing at me intently, and I find his eyes to be warm and mesmerizing. I manage the barest of nods. "Ever since we shut down Otis's personality quirks, his cooking duties have gone offline. And we were wondering, all of us on the *Waterloo*, if you'd be willing to forgive me, and maybe be interested in, um, taking up his job?"

I draw back and squint at him, uncomprehending. "You want me to *cook*?"

Michael looks a little abashed at this. "Do you… even know how to cook?"

"No," I reply with a snort. My culinary skills are limited to instant food packets. I hastily add, "but…. I could learn!" Sparks reignite in Michael's eyes. I'm quick to remember the cause of the job opening. "Otis. Has he, um, stopped being annoying?"

Michael stares at me critically. "Otis's personality quirks were more pronounced ever since his Hobo's Towel bathroom trip with you. His intellectual capacity is fine, obviously, but the personality aspect? Gisella says she's still working on it."

A snicker escapes me. "It's been a whole lotta Pete's cooking for dinner, hasn't it?"

"Argh! It's terrible," Michael agrees. "Everyone's still taking turns in the kitchen. Let me tell you, Rosemary's taste in food is worse than her taste in music!"

I can't bring myself to smile fully. I carefully keep my eyes off of Michael and focus instead on a trail of condensation on the bar. I try to steady my voice. "What about Doc Williams? Is she okay with me coming back on board?"

"You know, she was full out pissed when the idea was suggested. For three day-cycles, she barely talked to anyone. And then, she comes up to me and says," he puts his hands on his hips and wags his head from side to side, "'We're supposed to pretend like abducting you and tranquilizing Lieutenant Bremerton was all part of a shnopple rescue attempt?'"

I guffaw. "Okay, that sounds like something she'd say. You may have to work on that impression, though." There's an uncomfortable tightness building up in my throat. I stare down at the table. "What'd you say to her?"

"I said, in the end, that's what it was. You rescued the umemeh, the shnopples, and my life. So, yes."

"And?"

"Well, she didn't say anything to that at first. Not for the rest of that day-cycle. Then," he snaps his fingers, "like that! She started complaining about how she could really use your help with the bats."

I glance up at him in surprise. His face is close. So very close.

"Everyone wants you back." He smiles. "I hate to admit it," he clears his throat, "but this whole chef thing? It was actually Rosemary's idea."

I shake my head, and realize how closely we're leaning

together. Our faces are only inches apart. "But is this something that *you* want?"

Michael's eyebrow quirks up at this. "Oh. Very much." But now, our faces have drawn closer, and there's no way he's thinking about Rosemary anymore. I'm pretty sure there's only one thing on each of our minds.

"I, um," Michael says. "The ship's waiting out there by the inner sphere. But I told them, with the paperwork and stuff, we might not get you back up there till tomorrow."

"Good idea," I whisper, even closer to Michael. I know, in my bones, this is finally going to happen, and I'm flooded with a lightness that has nothing to do with the vodka.

I kiss him first, softly. With the heat of the moment, it turns into an ugly, all-out make-out session with me straddling him right there at the bar. Michael pulls away and glances about the room.

"Maybe we should move somewhere more private?"

"Voids yes," I reply, still somewhat out of breath.

"Whoa, whoa. Slow down." He looks into my confused face, and squeezes his arms tighter around my waist. "There's something I have to ask you first."

My stomach flip flops.

Michael gently brushes some of the newly regrown curls away from my face, then plants a soft kiss on my forehead. He pulls back and peers at me. "Tell me you're all out of tranqs?"

I grin.

acknowledgments

To anyone who scoffs at the expression "find the silver lining": this book was written during a global pandemic.

I was struggling with adhering to strict social distancing measures and juggling a new work burden of childcare alongside my other responsibilities. The light peeked through one day when a friend on a social media network invited me to join an evening writer's group over zoom. From the safety of our homes, we sat together in the evenings for video calls to discuss writing and work on our own unique projects. Former strangers, separated by distance and time zones, became friends and colleagues. This was my little slice of happiness, and I cannot stress enough how much this carried my sanity through that grueling time. This book would not exist without that group, and especially the core three: Andrea Max, Michal Schick, and Jennifer Levine.

I've also been fortunate to have a wide number of beta readers who provided feedback on various iterations of this book's existence. I owe a big thanks to Heidi Fischer, Maya Darjani, Laura Galán-Wells, Katie Wright, and of course, Andrea Max. Your professional and thoughtful feedback helped shape the book into what it is today.

Discouraged after an arduous querying experience, I was about to bury this book when my good friend Jacques Alcabes convinced to me to share it with him. He was effusively positive and argued that I needed to share this book with a larger audience. He's a big reason this novel has made it off my desktop and into your hands.

This journey wouldn't have been possible without the unshakable support from my husband, who encouraged my plans to publish... without ever having read the book! Thank you, honey, for making this possible and for making me feel supported and loved through my moments of anxiety.

Thank you to my phenomenal editor, Isabella Betita (formerly at Simon & Schuster), who helped whip this book into respectable form. You went above and beyond with your level of attention to detail and feedback, and I can't thank you enough. Thank you also to Deborah Aqua, my brilliant cover artist, for bringing your creativity to this project, and for your infinite patience each time I responded to you with a "well, actually, can we tweak this just a little bit?"

Thank you to my entire family: mom and dad for encouraging me in my many hobbies, my brother REH, and especially to my sister MHH and brother ACH (the younger!) for always reading my novels and offering feedback and support.

And last but not least, I owe a big thank you to my mother-in-law. It was when she took me out for a birthday lunch right before the pandemic that the idea for this novel was born. She gifted me with two balloons that kept dipping into my meal, no matter how often I tried to push them away. It was at that moment my weird brain thought, "You know, this is exactly the way a two-headed llama would behave."

about the author

Ace is a creative artist who authors science fiction novels, paints impressionist art, and dabbles in film. She lives in suburbia with her husband and child where she dreams of adding a dog, a few cats, a snake, a bat-house, and some chickens to the family.

You can find Ace on most social media platforms under the handle @theaceofhuntley.
Sign up for her newsletter to be notified about upcoming book releases at theaceofhuntley.com.

Please consider taking five minutes to leave an honest review of this novel online. Every review helps this book find its way to the readers who'll enjoy it.